Miles Gibson

was born in 1947. He spent his childhood in a wet and draughty seaside town on the edge of the New Forest, and now lives and works in London. The first of his highly-acclaimed novels was published in 1984 and translated into several languages. His other work includes a collection of short stories and a book of poems for children.

This edition published in Great Britain in 1998 by
The Do-Not Press
PO Box 4215
London SE23 2QD

First Published in Great Britain in 1987
by William Heinemann Ltd

ISBN 1 899344 33 0

British Library Cataloguing in Publication Data. A catalogue
record for this book is available from the British Library.

h g f e d c b a

Printed and bound in Great Britain by The Guernsey Press Co Ltd.

Vinegar Soup

MILES GIBSON

THE DO-NOT PRESS

And meanwhile the beautiful, the incredible world in which we live awaits our exploration, and life is short, and time flows staunchlessly, like blood from a mortal wound.

Aldous Huxley, *Jesting Pilate*

PART ONE

Home

1

Hazel Pope was twelve years old when she first bared her buttocks for biscuits. It was a hot and dusty afternoon in the summer of 1958 and she had been swimming with the Butcher brothers in a pond of stale water behind the village church. The Butcher brothers, Victor and Bruno, were fat farm boys with clumsy hands and faces brown as potatoes. Victor was eight and Bruno was not quite ten when they bribed the girl to pull down her pants. They had stolen a crumpled bag of biscuits which they rattled at Hazel while they sat on her frock. For a time the girl scowled and shook her head. She was cold and frightened and angry. She crouched beneath her towel and sulked. But Bruno opened the bag and Victor pulled out a brittle star, dusted with sugar and coconut flakes. She sniffed at the star and her dark eyes shone. Her wet hair steamed in the sunlight. And there, on the bank of the pond, hidden by brambles, shivering in her vest and sandals, Hazel took the biscuit.

The sky was empty. The church was locked. A beard of bubbles broke on the water. The girl closed her eyes and there was nothing in the world but the warmth of the sun and the taste of sugar in her mouth. She crunched the star with her small, white teeth while she felt the sweetness melt on her tongue. And the Butcher brothers squatted in silence, watching her narrow, trembling arse, as if they expected to see her fart crumbs.

She was fifteen when she let loose her breasts for cup cakes, pushed against a pantry wall, hair wild, mouth plugged with fudge, while a boy called Arthur searched her shirt. She tried to scream but found she could only manage a sigh as she chewed on the wages of sin.

A week after her sixteenth birthday she learned the price of brandy snaps. She was a simple, solid slab of a girl with vacant eyes and yellow hair that fell in curls against her neck. He was a small, neat man with a pencil moustache and drove the local baker's van. She was too embarrassed to ask his name. He led her into the back of the van and set her free among the wooden trays, rooting for shortcake and macaroons. He stuffed her with sponge. He poked her with cherries. And when she was properly sugared and spiced, he peeled off her dress with his long, white hands and rolled her out like pastry.

In 1965 she left home to live in London, serving in a flower shop and learning to type at night-school. Renting a room in a draughty attic. A plump girl with bad skin. Once a week she wrote a letter home to her mother: small pages of spidery writing composed on Sunday afternoons. Her mother replied with weekly instructions: choose flat shoes, wear warm pants, sleep for eight hours every night, eat fresh fruit, beware of men. Hazel followed her advice.

The owner of the flower shop was a sad little Turk called Freddie Farouk. He was a fat man with a loose, grey face and ears as curly as walnuts. His shoes creaked. His bones cracked. His clothes had a smell of the coffin. His only pleasure was making funeral wreaths, elaborate hoops of doom. He could not endure the bright splash of summer flowers and the shop was draped through all the seasons in bundles of blue, black leaves that dripped with sorrow and darkness.

Each morning, after Hazel had swept the floor and filled the buckets, stripped stems and trimmed branches, Freddie Farouk would arrive to inspect the display. He liked the poppies and corpse – white lilies, but the sight of roses distressed him, carnations depressed him and violets made him maudlin. He was a glutton for punishment. At the end of his inspection he would wrap his nose in a handkerchief, snort and wag his head. The melancholy seemed to sweat from his skin and make his collar curl.

'You're a good girl, Hazel,' he would gasp, slapping his wrist with the handkerchief. And then he would retreat to the back of the shop and sit behind the curtain.

Hazel worked hard among the funeral flowers. She learned to weave hearts from bunches of holly and make buttonholes for widows' weeds. But the winter was hard and the days were dark. She couldn't keep warm in her attic room. The shop was damp and her shoes began to leak. One afternoon she collapsed among the chrysanthemums. When Freddie Farouk discovered the girl she had drained so pale he thought she was dead. He wrapped her in his overcoat, picked the petals from her hair and squeezed her breasts as he felt for her heart. When she struggled he called a cab and sent her home.

The next morning she had grown too weak to raise her head from the pillow. Her face was burning but her hands were blue. She lay helpless under the blankets and shivered herself to sleep. Rain crackled on the blistered ceiling. The dust in the carpet danced on the draught.

When she woke again it was almost dark and the room was filled with lilies. Candles smoked in the twilight and through the fluttering light she saw Freddie Farouk. He was kneeling at the end of the bed with his face pressed softly against her feet.

'You frightened me,' he complained as he studied her with his watery pall-bearer's eyes. 'You looked so bad. I closed the shop to visit you. The landlady gave me the key.' He stood up and wiped his nose. It seemed to upset him to such an extent that, for a little while, he could do nothing but stare at the floor as he snorted and snuffled and cleared his throat.

'I'm sorry,' croaked Hazel, struggling to speak, but the Turk waved his hand for silence.

He walked across to the chair where Hazel had thrown her clothes, shook out her dress with a crack of his wrist and neatly sorted her underwear, paying particular attention to a little pair of lace pants which he folded in the shape of a handkerchief and absently placed in his jacket pocket.

'This place is cold,' he observed mournfully as he sniffed at the rotting pasteboard furniture. The attic room was a pyramid, the floor laid with scraps of carpet and the walls slung with pipes that boomed like drums. A window cut in one of the walls gave a view of a muddy London sky.

'It's cheap,' she whispered. She was wearing a Fantasy Dreamgirl nightdress that was cut too tight beneath her breasts.

'It's not healthy for a young girl to live alone,' he said as he crept towards the bed, and he licked his lips with a soft, grey tongue.

'I'm not afraid,' she whispered and drew the blanket under her chin.

'You need someone to take an interest in you,' he insisted.

'I'm not lonely,' she whimpered. 'Sometimes the landlady cooks me a chop.' Beneath the blanket she was struggling to pull the nightdress more securely over her knees.

He knelt down and without warning placed a chocolate egg upon the pillow beside her head. Hazel pushed back the blanket and wiped her eyes. It was a beautiful polished egg, dark as treacle and tied with a crimson ribbon. When she pulled the ribbon the egg exploded and showered her face with sugar mice. Tiny, pink mice with silver eyes that scattered into her nightdress.

Freddie Farouk sat on the bed, snapped the eggshell between his fingers and fed Hazel with fragments of chocolate.

'What am I going to do with you?' he murmured sadly as he brushed the mice from the pillow.

Hazel tried not to think about it. She tilted back her head and closed her eyes, drugged by the flood of melting chocolate.

'Poor Hazel,' he sobbed as he slipped his hand beneath the bedclothes and searched for her feet.

Hazel filled her mouth and listened to the old Turk weep. He wept so hard she was frightened he would do himself a mischief. He wept so long that she wanted to reach out and comfort him.

But Freddie Farouk was already buried beneath the blanket and rummaging between her knees.

She tried to struggle from his grasp, rolling in mice, her skin shining with the fragrant sugar. She tried to protest but her mouth had been stuffed with the demon egg. He gave a grunt as he kicked off his shoes, moaned as he fumbled with buttons, and then there was nothing but the sound of the rain, the creaking bed, an occasional trumpet of Turkish delight and Hazel blowing bubbles of chocolate.

When Freddie Farouk had done his work he crawled from the bottom of the bed, found his shoes, collected up the lilies (a shame to waste them) and tiptoed from the room.

'You're a good girl, Hazel,' he grieved as he limped downstairs. She never saw him again.

The fruit of this curious encounter was a boy called Frank. At first he was no more than a question mark, a crumb of life, a tiny shrimp floating in Hazel's vital juices. Hazel felt nothing. When the fever had passed she was too ashamed to return to the flower shop, so she found work in a supermarket filling a freezer with fish: grey blocks of Atlantic cod, hake, haddock and lobsters' claws. She was tired but the work was hard and she hadn't fully recovered her health. She took a tonic for the blood but somehow couldn't stomach the taste and after breakfast sometimes she was sick. She was worried, of course, but she blamed her problem on the smell of the fish.

Frank was the size of a kidney bean before Hazel knew she was pregnant. At first she tried to ignore the signs as if, by some feat of concentration, she could reverse the magic and flush the intruder from her system. She couldn't believe it. She *wouldn't* believe it. But her stomach grew hard and the veins rose in her breasts.

She never forgave the little Turk but she blamed her disgrace on the chocolate egg, sugar mice and all the other sweet and sticky gobstopping trifles that had ever led her into temptation.

The weeks turned to months and Hazel counted them. Her mother continued sending instructions, warnings and recipes for soup. But Hazel stopped writing letters home and soon the recipes were replaced with complaints. What was wrong? What was happening? Was she eating? Was she sleeping? So many questions. Her daughter tied the letters in bundles and pushed them under the bed.

During the summer Hazel inflated until she felt ready to burst her frock. Her legs ached. Her breasts creaked. She was fat and tired and constipated. While, under her skin, Frank yawned and stretched soft bones, a wet and wrinkled goblin. During the day he floated upside down in the warm gravy, deafened by the gurgle of Hazel's intestines. At night he anchored beneath her ribcage, eyes closed, face crumpled in concentration, anxiously trying to grow.

August brought a cruel heat that settled on the city like fog. Hazel stopped work on the fish freezer and then lost the strength to stray from her room. She wallowed naked on the groaning bed, bloated, bewildered and drenched in sweat. Beneath the hump of her belly Frank was already complete: a savoury pudding of heart, lungs, liver, kidneys, stomach, bladder, skin and bone.

Storms in September rattled the attic and cracked the glass in the window. Frank rolled and paddled his feet. He pushed and kicked until his head was wedged into Hazel's pelvis and he found he couldn't escape. Hazel crawled shivering under the blanket and tried to ignore the complaints of her prisoner. Fat, frightened and wrapped in a shrinking bag of water, Frank was fighting for his life. At the end of October he was kicking so hard that Hazel went to the hospital and begged to have him removed.

It was a cold and wretched morning. A day fit only for funerals. She wrapped some soap in her best pyjamas and ventured from the safety of the attic. She was so big that she brushed the walls as she staggered downstairs. The streets were wet, the sky black with a blizzard of leaves. It took her a long time to walk as far as the hospital and when she arrived they tried to send her home. What was the name of her family doctor? Where were her parents? Who was the father? Without her medical history they wouldn't touch her if she dropped down dead. Hazel was too frightened to answer questions. So she threw back her head and howled. She bellowed. She bawled. She rolled off the chair and tried to give birth on the floor.

A doctor came running and nurses stood shouting. They carried her into an empty room and used their scissors to cut off her clothes. They pressed their ears against her belly, cleared out her bowels, bottled her urine and measured her blood.

'You don't deserve this sort of treatment,' muttered a nurse impatiently as she scraped at Hazel with a razor.

'It's a miracle you're both alive,' declared a doctor, searching for Frank with his fingers.

Hazel screamed. The pain spread and burned through to her bones. Is this how it was going to end? Had God planned creation to disembowel women? She screamed again. The ritual slaughter of innocence. She screamed until she fainted and fled back to the Butcher brothers twisting like trout through their pond of green water. Standing naked in the long grass. Bare buttocks. Broken biscuits. Shaking crumbs in her clenched fist.

The pain continued. At midnight, in a glare of light, surrounded by strangers, for the first and last time in her life, a man opened Hazel's legs without closing her mouth on a lump of sugar. Frank's world was collapsing around his ears. He tried to resist the slippery slope but nothing could save him. An hour before dawn he slithered on to the table in a puddle of blood and tripe. He blinked. He steamed. Then someone picked him up by the feet and slapped him around so he screamed.

2

Frank's first memory was the smell of food: fried eggs, bacon, potato, hamburger, hot pies, boiled soup and good, sweet tea stewed to the strength of molasses. The smell was blue and thick as smoke, it billowed beneath the ceiling, clung to the walls and rolled in hot and heavy gusts about the floor. Frank sucked at the smell and laughed. He was sitting in a nest at the bottom of a shopping basket. The nest had been made from Hazel's pyjamas. The basket was hidden under a table. Frank was twelve weeks old.

Hazel had left the hospital as soon as she had found the strength to walk. The doctors had insisted that she take the child. She had called him Frank in memory of a boy she had once known who had fed her slices of marmalade cake and asked for nothing in return. The name appeared on the birth certificate but the father was marked Unknown. Hazel wanted to forget the sad, little Turk with the creaking shoes and funeral eyes. She wanted to forget Frank but Frank wouldn't go away.

For the first few weeks she sat in the attic with Frank held by suction against her breasts. She filled him with milk and watched him render it down to a soft, yellow turd. With his mouth open, gulping food, and the turd always hanging beneath him, Frank resembled a monstrous goldfish. Hazel nursed him but could not love him. She dreaded his tantrums and feared his silence. And sometimes, at night, he roared until he woke the house.

'It doesn't worry me what you do with your life,' declared the landlady one night, standing at the door and peering into the grubby room. She stared in disgust at the piles of soiled linen and the purple-faced creature struggling at its mother's breast. 'It's your life but I've got my reputation to think about.

Mrs Giltrap in the room underneath has been complaining about the noise. She's nearly seventy. She deserves to rest in peace.

'I can't help it,' said Hazel, forcing her thumb into Frank's wet mouth. 'I don't know how to stop him.'

'You should have stopped him before he was born,' sniffed the landlady. 'It doesn't worry me but Mr Archer down the hall says the smell gets into his room and clings to his clothes. He says they've started to talk about him at the office.'

'What can I do?' moaned Hazel.

'I'm sorry but you'll have to make other arrangements. We can't have infants in the house. It's not natural.'

'But I can't sleep in the street,' wailed Hazel.

'Has it got a father?' inquired the landlady, nodding at the bundle of misery that kicked in Hazel's arms.

'Yes.'

'Surprise him,' suggested the landlady and slammed the door.

The next morning Hazel sat down and wrote to her mother. She had no work. She had no money. She wanted to come home. A week after she had posted the letter she wrapped Frank in a shopping basket together with his feeding bottle, birth certificate and a note of introduction. She carried her suitcase to the railway station. She left the shopping basket beneath a table at the Hercules Café.

Frank lay in his nest and peered up at the shadows surrounding him. The smell of food had begun to evaporate. It was growing cold. There was silence. He kicked his feet and started to cry. He was tired and frightened and hungry. And then there was the sound of a woman's voice, the shuffle of feet and a face pushed through the gloom.

Frank stopped crying and blew a bubble of pleasure. She was a young woman with a soft, round face and hair as curly as kale. Her mouth was open and she smelt of polish and soap. For some moments they stared at each other in surprise. And then the woman whistled, snatched the scrap of paper that was pinned to the basket and carried it away to the light.

Her name was Olive Ethel Bean. She owned the Hercules Café. She was thirty years old when she found Frank but already she moved like an old woman. Her knees were stiff and her feet never left the ground, so that when she walked she shuffled and dragged the soles from her shoes. Her father, Jumping Jack Bean, had died of the drink and left her the café for her twenty-third birthday and it was work, they said, that had worn her away. She started at dawn with the soup of the day and finished at night by scrubbing the floors. But some women are never young. Olive had been an old woman fresh from the womb. A pale and serious child who hoped for nothing and feared the worst.

She held the scrap of paper to the light and squinted at the scrawled message. My name is Frank. That was it. My name is Frank.

She shuffled back to the table and squatted down beside the shopping basket.

'Gilbert!' she whispered as Frank laughed and clapped his hands.

'Gilbert!' she shouted as Frank kicked and blew a string of bubbles.

Gilbert came out of the kitchen. He was wearing a rubber apron and carried a butcher's knife in his fist. 'What's wrong?' he grumbled as he sliced impatiently at the air with his knife. He was chopping chickens.

'I've found a baby.'

'What sort of baby?'

'He's called Frank,' said Olive softly as she tickled Frank's chin.

Gilbert hooked the knife into his apron and came crashing among the tables, blowing steam and muttering darkly to himself. But when he reached Olive and saw the shopping basket he was so surprised that he couldn't speak. He stood and scratched his head.

'It's a baby,' explained Olive.

'Is it dead?' he whispered.

'No.'

Gilbert picked up the shopping basket and placed it gently on the table. He peered at Frank and frowned. He sniffed. He closed one eye. He studied Frank like a man weighs a cheese.

'Perhaps we should find him something to eat,' he said at last.

'We can't keep him,' whispered Olive. Her face flushed. Her eyes sparkled with excitement.

'Why? We could turn one of the bedrooms into a nursery. I could build him a little bed and make him comfortable,' argued Gilbert. He looked around the café at the rows of empty tables and chairs. The monotonous rain of a dark, February evening washed the windows. He didn't want the child but he didn't want Olive to think he couldn't manage a family. He was ready for anything.

'But he already belongs to someone,' complained Olive and then, as if she feared he might be snatched away at any moment, she scooped the child from the nest and held him tightly in her arms. Frank rolled his head and bubbled peacefully.

Gilbert's face, pale and full as a moon, grew dark for a moment and shone again. 'They know where to find him if they want him,' he grunted. 'I mean, they left him here.' They were always leaving something behind them. Gloves, overcoats, books, newspapers, bundles of laundry, bunches of keys. He'd once found a dead pigeon wrapped in a woman's head scarf. It was a strange neighbourhood.

'But there are laws against it,' said Olive.

'What laws?' demanded Gilbert scornfully.

'Well, I don't know. There are laws about everything. You know that.'

'But he was a gift. Whoever left him here meant us to look after him. That's obvious. And there's no law that says you can't accept a gift,' declared Gilbert. He found the feeding bottle and birth certificate.

'But we don't know anything about babies,' murmured Olive.

She glanced at Gilbert and blushed. They had worked and lived together since the death of her father and thought of themselves as man and wife. Gilbert Firestone was ten years older than Olive. But the difference in their ages was not important. Olive could not have cared tuppence if Gilbert had been eighty. Perhaps she might have preferred it. Old men have poor eyes and like to sleep in their vests. Olive thought nudity unhygienic and received Gilbert's more intimate gestures of affection with a mixture of ridicule and disgust. She loved children but she hated the thought of having to grow them. She couldn't explain it but she knew they would catch in her pipes and tubes. Frank appearing under the table was her idea of the perfect delivery.

'We can learn,' snorted Gilbert impatiently. 'You see people every day who can hardly manage a knife and fork but they have children. Dozens of them.'

Olive was silent. A woman has instincts. A woman only has to follow her instincts. It couldn't be difficult. You didn't need an education to wash and feed a child. It was all part of the natural order. And he looked so helpless caught up in her arms with his belly puffed out and his little legs swinging.

'Do you think he looks queer?' she said.

'How do you mean?' asked Gilbert, leaning forward and giving Frank another sniff.

'Well, perhaps he's soft in the head and that's why they left him.'

Frank looked at Gilbert and bared his gums in a grin.

'There's nothing wrong with him,' said Gilbert. 'Count his fingers.'

'I suppose we could keep him until they come back for him. We could give him something to eat and make him a bed for the night...'

'There's no harm in it,' said Gilbert. He was hot beneath the rubber apron and there were chickens to be chopped. With so many mouths to feed another mouth would make no difference. And what did babies eat? Milk mostly. Stewed fruit. Slops. Dogs eat more.

'Perhaps they'll come and collect him tomorrow,' said Olive.

'Yes,' said Gilbert. 'We'll wait until tomorrow.' And that was how Frank came to live at the Hercules Café.

Olive found him and Gilbert took a shine to him. On that first night he slept in his basket at the foot of their bed. They never planned to keep him. But the days passed and no one came to take him away.

3

Eggs fried in bacon fat and slapped, dripping, between limp leaves of damp, white bread. Sausages, pink as penises, rolling in frying pans glazed with butter. Meat pies, big as bricks, oozing hot and fragrant slurry. Potatoes, baked in their skins and split, like wizen leather skulls, to let their ghosts escape in steam. Hamburgers. Frankfurters. Canned mushrooms slippery as rabbits' eyes. Blocks of cheese the size of headstones. The smell! And the noise! The clank of toasters, the chatter of plates, soup hissing, buckets banging, forks scratching, spoons spinning, chairs screeching, tables groaning and, above everything, the noise of the grinding, slurping, belching, farting customers of the Hercules Café .

It was an old establishment, a dirty brick building on a narrow street of small Victorian sweatshops. The Imperial Button Company, on the corner of the street, had once made glass beads and shaved elephant tusks into waistcoat trimmings. A good set of tusks made five hundred bags of Imperial buttons, plain or fancy. They were sold, by the thousand, in Piccadilly, while far away on the African coast a bag of buttons was all you paid for another slaughtered elephant. When the elephants were gone the button company collapsed. Now it was a grocery owned by a Greek with gold in his teeth. He sold bread, milk, soap and cheese.

The Sambo Rubber Works on the opposite side of the street had made breathing corsets for nursing mothers. The rubber was spun into soft, pink strands and knitted into the shape of women. But between the wars a machine caught fire and the little business melted down. Now the building contained a peculiar smell and a failing beauty parlour.

Next door, the Excellent Boot Company had changed hands

a dozen times and was at present doing rather badly as a shop
selling second-hand furniture. The Monkey Polish Company
was a barber's shop. The Bluebird Engravers was a hole in the
wall that sold cigarettes and pornographic magazines.
Everything changes. But the Hercules Café had always been the
Hercules Café. The original sign still clung to the brickwork, the
heavy wooden letters bleached by the sun and painted every
year by Gilbert who, dreaming of yards of fizzling neon,
revived the name with vigorous coats of red and green and
gold. Gilbert was hungry for colour. One year he painted the
tables blue and the next year he painted the chairs yellow. But it
made no difference. Behind the sweating windows, a hundred
years of cooking had stained the café relentless shades of gravy
and smoke.

At one end of the long dining room a metal counter guarded
the door to the kitchen. Olive lurked behind the counter. Gilbert
worked in the kitchen. He grilled, fried, baked, boiled, poached,
roasted and toasted with the energy of a demon. He was ready
to cook anything that fell into his hands. He was afraid of nothing. He would have skinned and stewed a crocodile if he had
found one crawling among the potatoes in the larder and,
indeed, had eaten crocodile in his travels and kept the recipe in
his diary. Everything that moved between heaven and hell was
in danger from his knife and his frying pan.

Olive carried the food he cooked without question or
complaint. She might have been serving portions of mud cake.
She ran between the tables with her arms loaded with dishes,
scribbling orders, collecting empties and wiping up spills with
a big, grey cloth. Food had lost its meaning. Some of it was hot
and some of it was cold. But all of it was heavy. And where was
Frank? He was growing under the counter. Gilbert built him a
little chair and he sat there each morning, sucking his thumb
and staring up into Olive's skirt. He liked to be under her feet
despite the food that she spilled on his head. He liked the rustle
of her legs and the hot gusts of smoke that followed her from the
kitchen. In the afternoons she would wash his hair and take him
upstairs to bed. She read him nursery rhymes and sang him

songs. But Gilbert paid him no attention until the boy learned to talk.

'Eat your greens,' said Gilbert one evening as they sat around the kitchen table for a late chicken supper. He tapped Frank on the head with his fork.

'No,' said Frank. He was three years old. A small boy with large ears and eyes the colour of rust flakes.

'They're good for you,' said Olive to encourage him.

'I don't want them,' scowled Frank, who was having trouble with his spoon.

'I'll eat them,' said Gilbert. He flicked his fork into Frank's bowl and carried off a mouthful of cabbage. Frank couldn't believe it. He was horrified. He had no use for the greens but he hadn't expected anyone to steal from his bowl. He stared at Gilbert and his mouth fell open. He leaked potato over his chin.

'You shouldn't steal food from children,' scolded Olive. 'It makes them nervous.'

Gilbert pretended to look ashamed. 'I'm so hungry I could eat a horse,' he whispered at Frank.

Frank waved his spoon and frowned thoughtfully at Gilbert. 'You wouldn't eat a *horse!*' he chuckled. He loaded his spoon with more potato, aimed for his mouth, missed the target and plugged his nose.

'Certainly,' nodded Gilbert.

'Don't tease him,' said Olive, drilling Frank's nostrils with the corner of a handkerchief.

'Horses, goats, monkeys, cats, dogs, I'll eat anything,' declared Gilbert and he bared his teeth in a hungry smile.

A few days later Frank went missing from his chair under the counter. He crawled out among the tables, collecting crumbs and coffee stains, until he reached the far corner of the café. There, sitting against the window he found a big, red man feeding a mongrel scraps of fried egg.

For a few minutes Frank sat and stared in delight at the dog. The man had laid his plate on the floor and the dog was licking at the greasy puddle. It was an old dog with sad eyes and a stiff, white beard. When it saw Frank its tail began to work, brushing crumbs around the floor.

'Is that your dog?' said Frank, pulling at the big man's leg. The man peered between his knees and grinned at Frank. 'Yes,' he said. His breath smelt of fried eggs, tea and tobacco.

'What's his name?' said Frank.

'Betty,' said the man. The dog stopped brushing crumbs, cocked its head and glanced suspiciously at its master.

'Can I have him?' asked Frank.

'You're too small for a dog.'

'I want to give him to Gilbert,' said Frank.

'Why?' said the man.

'He eats them,' explained Frank.

'Did you hear that?' the man roared at his neighbours. 'The kid says that Gilbert eats dogs. He probably puts 'em in the pies!'

No one looked surprised.

'They'll never put you in a pie. There's no meat on you,' laughed the man, staring down at the dwarf in the long vest and big knitted hat. He was a strange kid. Something looked wrong with him. Perhaps he was queer in the head.

Olive dressed Frank from the local street market and he sported an alarming collection of coats, vests and knitted hats. Everything was too big for him, his hats slipped over his ears and his sleeves trailed to his knees, but Olive didn't seem to notice. She chose clothes for their warmth and endurance.

'He'll grow into them,' she explained to Gilbert when he complained that Frank resembled a scarecrow.

When Frank began to walk she bought him a pair of shoes that were so big they fell off his feet when he tried to lift them from the ground. Olive stuffed them with newspapers.

'They'll last him for years,' she announced proudly as they watched Frank stamp across the room. Gilbert wasn't convinced but Olive refused to argue with him. And so Frank wandered about the café with his ears pushed under a knitted hat and his feet as long as funeral barges.

While Frank was growing into clothes Olive was growing out of them. She stitched her skirts and darned her drawers as if she were determined to make them last a lifetime.

'They'll see me out,' she would say when Gilbert grumbled about her threadbare aprons or the holes in her shirts. She hated waste. She wore her clothes until they fell apart.

Once Frank had learned to walk he soon taught himself to climb. Then he refused to stay in his nest at night, climbed over their bed and tried to settle in Olive's arms. Gilbert grew unexpectedly jealous. He watched Frank wriggle into the warmth between Olive's fat, forbidden thighs and it nearly drove him mad with frustration. He knew she loved him less than the child. He felt old and foolish and lonely. One morning he woke to find that Frank had lost his way in the dark and fallen asleep with his head caught under her nightgown.

'It's not healthy,' Gilbert complained.

'He's only a baby,' said Olive, hauling Frank out and pushing his face between her breasts. 'He likes sleeping with me.'

'I like sleeping with you,' grumbled Gilbert, punching his pillow.

'That's different,' snorted Olive.

Gilbert growled but said nothing. He wasn't going to share their bed with this little, bright-eyed cuckoo.

The next day he threw out Frank's shopping basket and set to work turning one of the empty bedrooms into a nursery. It was a small room with a narrow window and corners full of shadow. But when Gilbert had finished it was a marvellous kingdom of pictures and puzzles, jewels, junk and curious treasures. There was a puppet with no head, a robot with rusty clockwork, a rocking horse and a tap-dancing bear. The bear was called Basil. He wore spectacles and black leather shoes. There was a wooden bed and an old armchair, a chest of drawers and a table with a bandaged leg. Mice dressed as sailors tiptoed along the tops of the walls and a cardboard elephant blowing a trombone spun on a string from the ceiling.

Gilbert was so proud of his work that he began to spend as much time in the room as young Frank. He sat for hours in the broken armchair while Frank stood at the table with a box of crayons and drew pictures of his simple universe: blue sky, green earth, yellow sun, red house. Pages of scribble that Gilbert saved and glued in a scrapbook.

Later each day, when Frank had been washed and settled into the wooden bed, Gilbert sat in the armchair and read aloud his favourite stories. He loved sitting with the book on his knees, thumbing through the pages while he waited for Frank to wrap himself up in the sheets. He relished the old fairy tales but could not resist changing them. Little Red Riding Hood survived the wolf but skinned and stewed the unfortunate beast with onions, mushrooms, potatoes and garlic. Wretched animal. Frank expressed so much concern for the wolf that Gilbert felt obliged to set it loose on another occasion to pot-roast three little pigs. When Gilbert read stories the frog prince was in danger of losing his legs, the ugly duckling could only be saved by slow cooking with plenty of herbs, the witch succeeded in roasting Hansel and Gretel and Jack curried the beanstalk. Anything could happen and there was always plenty of gravy. Frank listened carefully, sucked his thumb and frowned.

The world felt secure in those early years at the Hercules Café. The mornings were full of smoke and steam that rolled from the kitchen into the dining room until, at noon, lost in fog, blue ghosts sat and shouted, hunched at tables, waving spoons. The nights were full of familiar whispers, pipes banging, locks snapping, rattle of chains, Olive's shuffle on the creaking floors. Summer brought the scent of salad, canned pineapple, sour meat and warm cheese. Winter had different smells: onions, cloves, wet rubber, friar's balsam. Frank grew and felt safe.

'Do you think they'll come back for him?' Olive said one morning as she helped Gilbert unlock the café. Rain hammered on the window. The dining room smelt brown and damp.

'No, it's been years. Besides, they've probably forgotten all about him,' said Gilbert, staring down the rows of empty tables.

On such mornings he wished himself far away from the Hercules Café. His bones ached with the cold. He longed to be in the tropics with the dust rising from his shoes and the sun drilling the top of his head.

'You couldn't forget Frank,' argued Olive.

'But he was only the size of a gherkin when he arrived. At that age they all look the same. They wouldn't recognise him now, said Gilbert. He wrapped his arm about Olive's shoulders and kissed the side of her head. She was wearing a badly darned frock. Her skin smelt of soap. Two of her fingers were plastered.

'He'll never really belong to us,' she sighed. She turned towards him, her face luminous in the half-light.

'We could make one for ourselves,' whispered Gilbert, pressing his mouth against her ear. 'Someone to keep him company.

'Your nose is cold,' laughed Olive, wiping her face as she pulled away from him.

'A little brother or sister. Before it's too late,' pleaded Gilbert, catching her by the wrists.

'Your hands are frozen,' she complained. 'You feel like the Abdominal Snowman.'

'We could start a proper family,' said Gilbert. 'Wouldn't you like that?'

'I don't know,' she whispered. It's easy for men strutting about with that big hairy sausage trying to stuff you like a turkey whenever it happens to take their fancy but it's the woman who takes the risks with the stretching and straining and all the damage to the pipes and tubes in a tangle and in the end they pull you apart like poor Mrs Papworth surrounded by men in rubber gloves snipping out her stomach with scissors and afterwards she wanted to take it home wrapped in paper like a pound of tripe and the surgeon laughed it must have been the anaesthetic she wanted to give it a decent burial.

'One day we'll be too old,' warned Gilbert, bending forward to kiss her again. But Olive shrank from his embrace and hurried away.

Frank was four years old when he first asked Olive the forbidden question.

'Where did I come from?' he demanded one evening, sitting in the bath, scowling and pulling at the worm between his legs.

Olive blushed as pink as sweetbreads and told him to ask

Gilbert.

When he repeated the question Gilbert said they'd found him under one of the tables. Frank was satisfied with the explanation. He couldn't understand why Olive had tried to keep it a secret. He supposed all babies were found, growing like mushrooms in dark corners of old houses. He began to search beneath the tables each morning, hoping to find a new brother or sister. But he was always disappointed. Perhaps there was a season for the growing of babies, like any fruit or vegetable. If you didn't find them when they first emerged did they wither like fallen apples, turn black and rot back into the floor?

It was about this time that Frank began to invite his friends to the Hercules Café. Mr Artichoke was the first to make himself at home. He slept under the counter and no one could see him but Frank.

'He's talking to himself again,' Olive would complain, listening to Frank's muffled voice as he sat and warbled in the safety of an empty cupboard or the gloomy bottom of a laundry basket.

'Don't worry,' said Gilbert. 'It's only Mr Artichoke.'

Olive nodded but she didn't like it. She saw Frank stand in corners, wagging his finger at nothing at all and muttering to himself. She saw him pull his hat down over his eyes and suddenly shriek with laughter. She watched him sit and whisper secrets at the walls for hours and it gave her the shivers.

'That boy is as daft as a brush,' observed Horace, the barber, when he came around for his morning coffee. He leaned on the counter and stared at Olive through a pair of greasy spectacles. He smelt of whisky and lavender water.

'He's as bright as a button,' she retorted, slapping a cup beneath the machine.

'He talks to himself,' said Horace. 'I've seen him.' He pulled a comb from his jacket pocket and tapped a tune on his knuckles.

'It doesn't mean he's daft,' said Olive. 'We all talk to ourselves sometimes.' The machine whistled and spurted steam.

'I don't,' said the barber.

'I'm not surprised. Even you don't want to hear your nonsense,' said Olive.

'You ought to throw away that hat. His hair can't breathe.'

'What's wrong with his hair?' she demanded, pushing the cup across the counter.

'It can't breathe – strangles the roots – suffocates the brain,' chuckled Horace. 'The boy thinks he's a giant artichoke.' He picked up the coffee and stirred it briskly with his comb.

'You've forgotten your saucer,' she shouted as he staggered away to his favourite table.

'Is that Horace?' Gilbert called from the kitchen.

'Yes,' shouted Olive.

'Leave him alone. I'm trying to teach him to drink from a cup,' shouted Gilbert.

While Mr Artichoke stayed at the café little gifts began appearing on Olive's pillow. A sandwich crust inside a twist of wrapping paper. A doughnut with some of the sugar sucked from the pastry. Within a few weeks she had collected a half-eaten sausage, a boiled egg, three biscuits, a dozen sultanas and a stick of cheese. She found a sardine in one of her slippers and a pickled gherkin in the pocket of her dressing gown.

'Someone loves you,' frowned Gilbert, picking hairs from the pickle.

'Don't worry,' said Olive. 'It's only Mr Artichoke.' She smiled, flattered by these curious love tokens. It was strange how quickly she had grown to expect a scrap of food on her pillow at night. When the pillow was bare she felt disappointed.

But Mr Artichoke made a big mistake with the ice cream. It was a fat brown dollop of Chocolate Sparkle. Frank's favourite. It appeared on the pillow late one morning and all through the afternoon it softened and spread until, by dusk, it resembled a cow pat; and then it slithered under the bedclothes and worked its way through the mattress.

Frank, frightened, half-asleep, was dragged from his dreams at midnight and pushed before the spoiled bed.

'Where did this come from?' roared Gilbert, prodding the

puddle as he glared at Frank. It had been a bad day and Olive, scalded with soup, bullied by customers, had wanted nothing but the simple comfort of a clean bed, head down, lights out, good riddance and good night. The wet pillow had been enough to make her fall on the floor and howl.

'Mr Artichoke,' whispered Frank, rubbing his nose and looking anxiously at Gilbert.

'I'm very angry with Mr Artichoke,' sobbed Olive from the floor. She was propped against the foot of the bed like a disappointed china doll. Her dress was pulled over her stomach revealing a pair of polished pink legs. She had tried to undress but found she didn't have the strength.

Frank was quiet for a long time. He sucked his thumb and stared at the bed. 'It's all right,' he said at last. 'I sent him away.'

'Where?' growled Gilbert as he started to pull the bed apart.

'I sent him back to the factory,' whispered Frank. His chin trembled and he burst into tears. He threw back his head and wailed. His eyes glittered. His mouth shone like an open wound.

'Don't hurt him!' screeched Olive, struggling to her feet.

'I didn't touch him!' protested Gilbert as he tangled with the sheet. He threw a pillow to the floor and trampled on it. Frank screamed. Olive opened her arms to embrace him, her dress fell over her knees and Frank was swept beneath it. He blinked in the warm and crowded dark. He clung to her thighs and wept.

Despite Frank's misery, Gilbert was glad to hear that Artichoke had left the neighbourhood. But then he hadn't met Godfrey.

Godfrey was a monster, a poltergeist and thief. He pilfered from customers' plates, robbed the kitchen and raided the freezer; stuck finger in pies, spat in the soup, cracked cups and curdled milk. He scribbled on the walls and piddled on the floor. He was fast, silent and so cunning that no one could catch him. Olive threatened to skin him alive. Gilbert wanted his guts for garters. Frank scowled and said nothing.

'He's lonely,' declared Gilbert one evening as he worked in the kitchen with Olive. They stood at the stove and stared at an ox tongue curled in a pan of water. The water boiled. The tongue began to wag.

'Who?' said Olive.

'Frank,' said Gilbert. He bent forward and sniffed the steam. You can't lick a Hercules tongue. Salt. Pepper. Dash of mustard. Fit for the crowned heads of Europe.

'I talk to him,' said Olive.

'That's no good. He needs someone his own age. That's why he invented Artichoke and Godfrey. Everybody has a secret friend at his age.'

'I didn't,' argued Olive.

'You must have had someone you could tell your secrets to,' said Gilbert. He pushed a fork into the steam and hooked out the purple tongue. A tangle of pipes dribbled water over his apron.

'I had tadpoles,' said Olive. 'The milkman used to bring them.'

'You can't talk to a damn tadpole,' grunted Gilbert, plunging the tongue into fresh water.

'I kept them in a kettle.'

'And you talked to them?'

'Yes. They understood everything I said.'

'That's more than I can do,' sighed Gilbert.

Olive pouted and fell silent. 'Well, what are you going to do about it?' she demanded.

Gilbert frowned. What can I do about anything? Kick off your shoes. Roll down your stockings. Once around the bedroom carpet. Swift and simple. I'll be gentle. Answer to a matron's prayer. A brother for our small son, Frank. Fat chance. Another baby in the house. Yes, that's the truth of it. Bring me babies, dozens of them, grinning, toothless, crawling around on their hands and knees. Bring me babies, hundreds of them, hot and squirming, shot from the rumps of ripe, rude women.

'What?'

'Godfrey,' snapped Olive impatiently. 'What are you going to do about him?'

'Leave it to me,' said Gilbert, smacking his hands on the wet apron. 'I'll fix him.'

The next morning Gilbert had a few words with Frank under the counter. 'Have you stolen Olive's pencil?' he inquired gently. He didn't sound angry. He might have been talking about the weather. He pulled a speckled egg from his apron pocket and tapped it experimentally against his knee.

'No,' said Frank. 'It must have been Godfrey. Damn Godfrey. I'll skin him when I catch him.' He screwed up his face and clenched his teeth as he'd seen Olive do so many times when *she* was angry with Godfrey.

'That's rum. He told me he was going to start behaving himself,' murmured Gilbert as he cracked the egg. He peeled the shell in a delicate spiral.

Frank stared thoughtfully at Gilbert. He stuck his thumb in his mouth and gave it a suck. He felt suspicious. He knew something was wrong. He pulled out his thumb and dried it carefully on his vest. He wouldn't talk to *you*,' he argued.

'Why?'

'Because he's *my* friend,' Frank said indignantly.

'Well, if he's your friend why do you let him do such mischief?' said Gilbert. He bit softly into the egg. The yolk was the colour of apricots.

'I can't control him,' said Frank. The egg smelt like a warm fart. He rubbed his nose and sneezed.

'It will end in tears,' sighed Gilbert.

'Have you seen Basil today?' asked Frank as he followed Gilbert back to the kitchen.

'The bear with the spectacles?' asked Gilbert, walking on eggshell.

'Yes,' said Frank.

'The tap-dancing bear?'

Frank nodded.

'Godfrey stole him,' said Gilbert.

'Godfrey? But he's my friend!' exploded Frank.

'That's the trouble with Godfrey – you can't trust him,' grunted Gilbert.

And it was true. From that moment, whenever something

went wrong in the café and Frank pointed a finger at Godfrey, the little fiend took revenge. When one of the girls from the beauty parlour complained that someone had stolen the doughnut from her plate, Frank complained that someone had kidnapped Hardy Annual, his favourite penguin. When Olive found that someone had salted the sugar bowls, Frank found that someone had peppered his toothbrush.

'You can't trust Godfrey!' he spat.

A month before Frank's fifth birthday Godfrey vanished. He disappeared as suddenly as he'd arrived and no one knew he had gone. But after a few days, when nothing had been scorched, scratched, smashed or stolen, Olive missed him.

'Where's Godfrey?' she asked, one morning at breakfast.

'He's gone,' said Frank.

'For ever?' asked Gilbert.

'Yes,' said Frank.

'What happened to him?' asked Olive.

'I ate him,' said Frank.

4

Gilbert took charge of Frank's education from the beginning. He wouldn't trust Frank to a school and, anyway, Olive was convinced the authorities would seize the boy as a foundling and refuse to return him. So the nursery grew into a classroom, the walls became a map of the world and Frank was taught to read and write.

Whenever Gilbert could leave the kitchen he would hurry away to sit with the child. They wrestled with arithmetic, sweated with science, dreamed in geography and marvelled in history. Gilbert saw the spread of civilisation as the transport of fruit and vegetables through the ancient world. The planet as a plundered larder. God the giant grocer.

Empires rose and fell on the strength of a vine or the thrust of a foreign cucumber. The Romans made Britain a slave to the grape and robbed the island of oysters. The Arabs took spinach and oranges to conquer Spain. The Portuguese bombed India with pineapples and poisoned the cooking with peppers.

Men were remembered, not for their bravery in battle but for the courage of their stomachs. Sir Walter Raleigh (1552-1618) sailor, gave England the first taste of potatoes. Alexander the Great (356-323 BC) conqueror, marched an army on onions and garlic.

Frank had trouble enough trying to spell his name, write the alphabet and tie his shoes. But Gilbert couldn't wait for him. The Egyptians built pyramids and worshipped the cabbage. The Greeks cast a golden radish for the temple of Delphi. The Hebrews ate giraffes. The Romans ate mice.

While Frank learned to buckle his sandals Gilbert tried to explain the shape of the planet, a dark and dangerous, poisonous parcel of men, vermin and mud. When words failed him he hauled a leather trunk from the attic and spilled the contents over the bedroom floor. The trunk was full of old letters, curling photographs, torn tickets, fetish objects, rubbish from his travels.

'America,' he announced, holding a painted pebble in the palm of his hand, souvenir of the Grand Canyon, Arizona.

'Africa,' he declared, flourishing a hairy nut with ivory studs for eyes and teeth.

'India,' he explained, holding a snowstorm trapped in a bubble. Beneath the snowflakes the Taj Mahal.

Frank sucked his thumb and stared at the world spread out at his feet. Once he had managed to pull Africa's teeth and swallow most of the snow in India, he turned his attention to the photographs. There were hundreds of them. A perpetual fog hung over most of the world, but through the fog there were blurred views of mountains, houses, trees and faces.

'That's Sam Pilchard,' said Gilbert, stabbing at a blurred portrait of two young men standing, grinning, through a curtain of straw and dust. 'And that's me,' he added, pointing at the smaller of the two figures, a thin smudge clutching a chicken in its fists.

'No,' said Frank.

'Yes, when I was young,' explained Gilbert.

'Where's Olive?' demanded Frank.

Gilbert scratched his chin. There were no pictures of Olive. One morning, many years ago, he had armed himself with a camera and tried to take her snapshot while she stood in the street to wash the café windows. It was a hot, dusty, August day; the sun shone in her hair and a summer breeze, lifting the hem of her skirt, revealed a pair of plump white knees. She had posed patiently on the pavement, leather in hand and bucket by feet. But as he pressed the button something caught her attention: a bird, balloon or vapour trail drifting above in the empty sky. When the picture was printed her face had the painted God-help-me look of a grieving plaster Madonna. The finely pencilled eyebrows and scarlet rosebud mouth spoke of earthly delights but her eyes, rolled white, were staring intently at heaven. This little snapshot of the virgin Olive was kept secure in Gilbert's wallet until the day it fell apart.

'Olive?' he murmured, scratching his chin. 'This was a long time ago, before Olive.'

Frank tried to imagine a time without Olive and failed. She had always been there, fretting and complaining, simple and safe. But Gilbert knew of a time so long past that it was even before the Hercules Café.

'Sam and me used to travel a lot in the old days,' said Gilbert. 'We came from the same kitchen. Coronation Hotel. Terrible place. Paddington. Sam was mostly breakfast and I was usually dinner. But you couldn't tell the difference. It was all porridge and horse meat in that place. We slept in a corner of the kitchen with the oven doors open to keep us warm. They wouldn't pay us and we couldn't eat the food so we left and went on the road.

Frank grinned and wriggled deeper into his cushions. He saw the two men walking down an empty road with frying pans strapped to their backs.

'Once we started walking we found we couldn't stop,' continued Gilbert. 'We took work wherever we found it but we never stayed long. As soon as we earned the price of a new pair of shoes we'd leave and go somewhere else. We spent a season boiling crabs in the south of France and another stewing snails in Spain. We spent a summer roasting pigeons in Morocco and a winter cooking black beans in Benin. It took us years to walk around the world.' He paused. And how had he spent so many years at the Hercules Café? Too late. Too long. Stayed too long on the way to somewhere else.

'And where's Sam?' demanded Frank, returning to the photographs.

'I left him in Africa,' said Gilbert. 'Cooking for the cannibals.'

'What does he cook?'

'Little boys – when he can catch 'em,' growled Gilbert and ruffled Frank's hair with his hand.

Frank was seven years old when the classroom moved to the kitchen. He already knew the names of all the spiders to be found in wild pineapples; the mystery of the world's weather system; the dimensions of the pyramids; the length of the perfect hot dog. Now Gilbert was ready to teach him one of the most important facts of life. He was going to explain how grain and water make a kind of glue you can bake and eat. Frank was impressed. Standing on a chair, with an apron tied beneath his chin, he turned out a thousand grubby pastry men with burnt sultana eyes. Gilbert was expected to eat most of them. Olive pretended she couldn't manage because of her teeth. So Gilbert changed the recipe, introduced sugar, ginger, butter and eggs, until Frank was producing an honest biscuit.

Flushed with success, Frank turned from the mystery of the biscuit to the secret of the sandwich. He stuffed bread with anything he could reach on the shelves and all the scraps he found on the floor. His sandwiches were explosive mixtures of fruit, honey, cheese, pickles, hair, beads and bacon rinds. He tasted everything. And when he felt too sick to eat he built boats from fingers of toast or carved faces from old potatoes. One afternoon he dusted his face with flour and made a necklace from noodles which he wore like a rope around his neck. He thought he might become a waitress. But Gilbert hadn't finished his education.

He taught Frank how to slice onions, dice carrots, shred cabbage and make stew. 'A good stew is like a good sandwich,' grinned Gilbert as he watched the vegetables boil on the stove. 'It should always be full of surprises.' He dropped a frankfurter into the brew and stirred it around with a spoon.

'What else?' said Frank, searching the floor for scraps.

'Fetch that bucket,' said Gilbert, waving his spoon at the kitchen table.

Frank hurried to the table where a big plastic bucket stood among the pots and pans. He tried to reach for the handle. But the bucket toppled and caught his face. He hit the floor with a shout. There was blood! His hand and face were running with blood. His hair was black with blood. There were fat, purple clots of blood slithering slowly under his shirt; evil, wobbling bubbles of blood that felt heavy and horribly cold. Frank closed his eyes and screamed.

'Don't worry – they're only pigs' kidneys,' shouted Gilbert, running to wipe Frank's face with a towel.

'They smell,' spluttered Frank in disgust. It was the first time he had encountered vital organs. He had thought pigs were nothing but bacon and hot, crisp sausages. These were bags of raw flesh that stank of murder, urine and blood.

Gilbert plucked a kidney from the boy's collar and gave it a sniff. 'There's nothing wrong with them,' he said with a frown. 'They're as fresh as daisies.'

Frank moaned and shivered with horror. 'But they're kidneys,' he sobbed. It wasn't right. Olive had kidneys she washed out with water and liked to keep warm in a vest.

'They're full of nourishment,' explained Gilbert, rolling a kidney in the palm of his hand. He stared affectionately at the organ and gave it a little squeeze. He couldn't understand Frank's fear. 'I've known men who like to swallow 'em raw – Sam used to say they slip down a treat – smooth as oysters.'

'You can't eat them,' wailed Frank.

'You can eat almost anything,' said Gilbert, collecting the kidneys up in the towel. 'And there's no waste on a pig,' he added proudly. 'You can eat their brains and ears, livers, trotters, entrails, all sorts. It's a remarkable animal.'

Frank wasn't listening. He had staggered away to ask Olive to wash him. There were bloody footprints on the kitchen floor.

The kidney stew appeared at the supper table but Frank wouldn't touch it.

'What's wrong?' asked Olive.

Frank shook his head and left the room.

For a long time afterwards he would eat nothing that came from the slaughter house. He lived on bread and potatoes, fried eggs and toasted cheese. Gilbert anxiously tried to tempt him with soft, white chicken and little morsels of sweet pork pie. But Frank refused to open his mouth and forgive him.

'It's delicious,' grumbled Gilbert.

'It's dead,' shuddered Frank and the noodle necklace clacked like a chain.

'What have you done to him?' complained Olive one

evening as she waited for Gilbert to climb into bed.

'Nothing,' snorted Gilbert, pulling at the buttons on his shirt. The shirt gasped open and his stomach bulged. He slapped the bulge with the flat of his hand.

'It was the kidneys,' said Olive, turning her face to the wall as Gilbert shook out his pyjamas. 'What did you tell him?'

'I told him they were delicious. Gently poached in mustard sauce. Splash of vinegar. Salt. Pepper. Lea and Perrins. I've known men who'd kill to get at my kidneys.'

'Well something happened to frighten him,' sniffed Olive, closing the neck of her nightgown. 'One day he was perfectly normal. The next day he was a vegetarian.' She shrank into her pillow, wriggled down, until the bedclothes covered her chin. 'It's the brain. When they're growing it affects their brains.'

'Nonsense.'

'I don't know,' sighed Gilbert, crawling carefully under the blanket. 'Try him with a cold sausage – he always liked sausage.'

'He won't eat it. He says he's a vegetarian.'

'Hitler was a vegetarian,' muttered Gilbert, snapping out the light.

'You're a bad influence on him,' said Olive, shrinking away from the hands that searched for a breach in her nightgown.

'It's not my fault,' wheezed Gilbert. 'I didn't turn him soft. I told him. If you don't eat red meat your teeth fall out. If you don't drink gravy your blood turns to water. It makes no difference.'

'I don't like it. He's got such queer ideas in his head,' complained Olive. She found one of Gilbert's hands between her knees and carefully extracted it.

'I taught him everything he knows,' muttered Gilbert as he turned away.

'Sometimes I think he knows too much,' yawned Olive. 'You'll make him unhappy – filling his head with nonsense.'

Gilbert grunted. What nonsense. He had hardly begun to explain the world to Frank. Olive didn't understand. Her world was the size of the Hercules Café. He wanted to tell Frank about the desert at night, stars as big as grapefruits, dogs wailing, the scuttle of scorpions, the smell of smoke from a scrubwood fire. He wanted to tell Frank about the forests, black with shadows, milky with steam, where monkeys sang in the rafters and fish, ugly as gargoyles, were hauled from the mud of yellow rivers. He wanted to tell Frank about the pure, carnal pleasures of life. There was so much pork and crackling in the world. Olive didn't understand. He wasn't going to let a spot of kidney trouble stop him.

But Frank was stubborn. Despite Gilbert's encouragement, he continued to refuse red meat and survived on bowls of biscuit and fruit. And this lack of gravy did nothing to stunt his growth. He was growing so fast that Olive had trouble finding clothes for him. His shoes, which had once seemed so big that no human foot would fill them, were splitting at the seams. His shirt sleeves looked too short for his arms and his head wouldn't fit his favourite hat. He was sprouting in every direction and as he grew bigger so Olive seemed to shrink. She was dwarfed by the saucepans and kettles, smothered beneath mounds of sandwiches and exhausted by the weight of food she carried between tables on her great metal tray.

Frank came to her rescue and when he wasn't in the kitchen, listening to Gilbert, he was out in the dining room helping Olive take orders, clear rubbish and sweep tables. But Olive always looked tired. Her hair had lost its curl. Her face was grey. She shuffled and sighed and forgot to darn her underwear. Frank and Gilbert watched her grow old in the heat of one short summer. As the days lengthened the sunlight made her sweat like a cheese, warped her legs and twisted her hands. Steam rose from her skull. The colour was boiled from her skin. When she dried out she shrivelled into an old woman. Her teeth looked too big for her mouth. Her bones clicked when she walked. The days darkened and the rains arrived. It was October. Frank was ten years old.

Gilbert baked a cake the size of a dustbin. Frank wore a fresh noodle necklace and for a few hours Olive came back from the dead. She wore a clean apron and danced around the kitchen, laughing and clicking her bones.

'We'll eat until we explode,' said Gilbert cheerfully. While he opened a bottle of sherry Olive hacked the cake to pieces with a bread knife.

'Give him a small glass,' scolded Olive as she watched Gilbert slosh the sherry into tumblers. 'He's only a boy.'

'It's his birthday,' boomed Gilbert. 'Boys are always sick on their birthdays.'

Frank grinned. They sat at the table and began to stuff themselves with cake and sweet sherry. For a little while Olive seemed restored but on her second slice of cake she started to moan and blow crumbs.

'What's wrong?' asked Gilbert, frowning at the ruined cake. He gave it a nasty prod with his spoon.

'Oh dear, I feel as drunk as the Lord,' wheezed Olive. She threw up her arms and bandaged her eyes with her hands. Her elbows hit the table and rattled the plates. The sherry bottle jumped in surprise, fell over, rolled across the table and splashed between her knees.

Frank looked appalled. He stood up, sat down, stood up, sat down and looked to Gilbert for help. Olive had crumpled and was slowly sinking under the table.

'Catch her arms!' cried Gilbert. He kicked away his chair and tried to snatch at Olive as she disappeared from view.

Frank peered anxiously under the table and watched Gilbert crawl around on his hands and knees. 'Is she hurt?' he whispered into the shadows.

'She fainted,' said Gilbert. 'It must have been the excitement.' It certainly wasn't the drink – she had barely raised the glass to her lips.

He dragged Olive out by her feet and arranged her in the middle of the kitchen floor. She lay there with her mouth open and her eyes closed. Her apron glistened with sherry.

'I don't like it,' whimpered Frank from the safety of the larder. He sat down and stuck a thumb in his mouth for comfort.

'Don't worry,' sighed Gilbert. 'She'll be fine.' He smiled across at Frank. 'We'll soon have her in bed.'

He scooped her up in his arms and kissed her tenderly on the nose. For a moment he looked as old as Olive. His face sagged and his dark eyes were full of fog. Then he threw her over his shoulder like a dead lamb and carried her up the stairs. She wasn't heavy. She felt warm and loose in his hands. During the ascent her slippers broke free and somersaulted into the darkness. He didn't turn to retrieve them. He manoeuvred her through the bedroom door and laid her to rest on the bed. She started to snore. He untied the wet apron, peeled off her dress and teased her from her underwear. It was the first and last time he saw her naked. He covered her with a blanket and made her comfortable. When he went back down to Frank he found the birthday boy had been sick in the sink.

The next morning Gilbert opened the café and Frank had helped him cook a dozen breakfasts before Olive came down to the counter. She looked exhausted. Her face was creased and her eyes were swollen. She shuffled back and forth like an ancient sleepwalker. When the customers called her name she ignored them.

'How do you feel today?' asked Frank, relieved to see her risen once more from the grave.

'Why?' frowned Olive, fighting with her apron.

'Gilbert had to put you to bed.'

Olive dragged the apron over her head and peered at him suspiciously. 'I must have come over queer,' she said absently. 'I'm sorry if I spoiled your birthday.'

'I don't mind,' said Frank. 'We saved you some cake.'

'Thank you.'

'You looked terrible,' ventured Frank. 'We thought you were dead.' He gathered up her apron strings, drew them gently around her waist and fashioned a clumsy knot.

'There's nothing wrong with me,' said Olive.

'I was as sick as a dog,' said Frank proudly. But Olive had already turned and lurched away.

'We'll have to get some help,' declared Gilbert as Frank returned to the toaster. 'Poor old Olive can't manage alone.'

'Me!' volunteered Frank. 'I'm good at tables. I'll be a waitress. ''Thanks, Frank, but you haven't finished growing.' Frank looked disappointed. He stood and scowled at the smoking toast. He wasn't a child. He was ten years old.

'And, besides, I need you in the kitchen,' added Gilbert gently. Frank nodded. It was true. Gilbert couldn't be expected to keep the kitchen working without him. The toast curled and burst into flames.

'We need some fresh blood in the place,' murmured Gilbert. 'Someone young and strong.

'Who?' coughed Frank.

'I don't know. We'll advertise,' said Gilbert, pulling the plug on the toaster.

But when Gilbert explained his plan to Olive she didn't like the sound of it. 'I work hard,' she barked, slapping her apron. She cocked her head and glared at him. 'I don't need your help.'

'You deserve a rest.'

'I can rest when I'm dead. Help costs money,' she growled, dismissing him with a flap of her hand.

'But we can afford it,' argued Gilbert.

'What will I do with myself?'

Gilbert was silent. He blew out his cheeks and frowned. He shrugged. It was a very difficult question. 'You like to watch television,' he said hopefully.

'I haven't seen it for months.'

'You never miss the wrestling – I've heard you shouting at Giant Haystacks.'

'I can't spend the rest of my life watching television,' said Olive fiercely. 'It sends you daft.' She rolled her eyes and crouched against the wall, her head full of terrible phantasms. 'If it's not a lot of Jessies jigging around to music it's a lot of adverts shouting at you about all sorts of stuff you don't want. They think you're ignorant. Damn nonsense. They dress up as tubes of toothpaste and doughnuts. I've seen them.'

'Nobody watches the adverts,' growled Gilbert. 'You're just trying to be difficult.'

'Well, when they're not singing about dog biscuits there's a man in a wig on the news telling you about bombs and murders and babies lost in fires and planes crashed in the sea. It frightens you to death. One moment there's a woman with a duster in a bathroom the size of a ballroom and the next moment there's an earthquake. You don't know what to believe.'

Gilbert had regarded television as an innocuous sedative for the bed-ridden and feeble-minded. Olive looked like she needed an exorcist. 'Forget the television,' he exploded. 'You don't have to watch it.'

'What else can I do?'

'You could finish your knitting.'

'It hurts my fingers.'

'Ask Frank to find you a book in the library. There are millions of books in the world. You could learn something.'

'Books!' laughed Olive bitterly. 'I don't trust books. They're not healthy. They give those library books to people in bed with nasty diseases and then the germs get on to the pages and when you open them the germs rub on to your fingers. You could catch anything. You never know what you'll find in a book.'

'There must be something you can do with your time,' insisted Gilbert. 'We'll just have to find it.'

'Why?'

'Because I want you to relax and enjoy yourself.'

'I enjoy the work,' she shouted impatiently. She couldn't understand why he wanted to replace her on the counter. She was only forty. He must be fifty but thinks I've forgotten just because he doesn't look it.

But Gilbert was determined to find some help. He placed a card in the café window.

WAITRESS WANTED. GOOD FOOD. OWN ROOM. APPLY WITHIN.

The first girl to respond to the advertisement was a tall German with a leather suitcase. Her eyes were blue and her fingernails were red. She sat at the table beneath the window and listened in silence while Gilbert explained the position. She nodded and smiled and stared into the street. She didn't understand the half of it. She thought he was trying to rent out a room.

'Thank you,' she announced while Gilbert was describing the history of the Hercules Café. 'Now I think, I will look at the room.'

Gilbert was puzzled. He hadn't explained her duties. But he took her upstairs and led her to a room at the back of the house.

'It has a bad smell,' she complained, striding through the door and throwing her suitcase on the bed.

'Well, I've not cleaned it out,' confessed Gilbert as he watched her kick off her shoes. He'd imagined that whoever he hired would need a few days to make arrangements before she settled into her quarters. This one came complete with a suitcase. Wouldn't be surprised to find an apron under her coat. Big girl. No complaints. Huge hands. Frighten the customers.

'Where is the bathroom?' she demanded.

'The green door at the end of the corridor,' he said, walking from the room and pointing a finger into the gloom.

'Thank you,' she said and shut the door in his face.

'Is *she* the new waitress?' asked Frank when Gilbert returned to the kitchen.

'I don't know,' said Gilbert nervously.

He waited for an hour and then returned to the room. The door was locked.

'What's happening in there?' he shouted through the keyhole. 'We're waiting for you downstairs.'

'I am asleep,' bellowed the girl.

'Are you decent?'

'Excuse me?'

'Parlour view on glaze?' roared Gilbert.

There was a long pause. 'I am asleep,' the girl shouted again. Gilbert swore beneath his breath. 'We want you to come downstairs,' he bellowed, shaping each word slowly enough for her to catch the sense of it. 'We want you to look at the kitchen. We always wanted a waitress who can't speak English.'

'Kitchen?'

'Yes.'

'No, I shall eat in my room tonight, I think. Bring me some cold meat and salad. Do you have German beer?'

'No, I don't think you understand. We want *you* to look after the customers,' Gilbert shouted. He was growing impatient. He slapped the door with the flat of his hand.

'Customers?'

'Yes.'

There was another long pause. 'Men?' the girl asked suspiciously.

'Yes, some of them are men. Customers. You can meet them.'

'My God!' shrieked the girl. 'Some of them are *not* men?'

'Men, women, dogs, children, all sorts,' shouted Gilbert.

'I am asleep! You are mad! My boyfriend is a policeman! I am asleep!'

'Who sold you that damn phrasebook?' Gilbert exploded. He wrenched at the lock until the handle came apart in his fist.

'Keep out! I have a pistol! I have a German passport!' screamed the girl.

When Gilbert broke through the door he found the room empty and the window open. His new waitress, half-naked and clutching a suitcase, was scrambling to freedom over the rooftops. Gilbert couldn't understand it.

The second girl to approach Gilbert was a frazzled dwarf who claimed to have served in some of the worst hotels in London. Her name was Ivy Murdoch but her friends called her Speedy. She had been a skivvy in the first Britannia and slopped out rooms in the old Palaestra. She had lost her teeth and one of her thumbs. She looked old enough to be Olive's mother.

'Is *she* the new waitress?' whispered Frank as they watched her stagger to the door.

'No,' Gilbert said gloomily.

The third girl was called Veronica Yardley. She was hard and lean and luminous. Her face was white, her eyes were grey and her hair, which was blonde and badly cut, stood out from her head in frayed spikes. She was wearing an army greatcoat and a pair of worn-out high-heeled shoes. She said she was seventeen and working at the Heavy Hamburger. She didn't like it. She grinned. The slope of her nose and the curious curve of her eyes made her look like a hungry cat.

Gilbert was enchanted. He bragged about the café, praised the kitchen, blessed the customers and apologised for Olive, who was glaring at them from a corner of the counter.

'Do you think she'll like me?' the girl asked doubtfully.

'She'll love you. There's only one thing wrong with her: she's slow, she's clumsy, she can't cook, she can't carry and she's not quite right in the head. Apart from that she's fine,' said Gilbert. 'Look, she's smiling,' he said as Olive bared her teeth.

'Does he belong to you?' asked Veronica, nodding at Frank who was watching her from the kitchen door. He was wearing his necklace and a tea-towel turban.

'Yes,' said Gilbert. 'We found him under one of the tables.' He liked to tell the truth because he knew that no one believed him.

Veronica winked at Frank who grinned and blushed and walked backwards into the kitchen.

'Is *she* the new waitress?' he asked hopefully when the girl had gone.

Gilbert nodded. His big, moon face was shining. 'She starts on Monday,' he said and combed his hair with his hand.

5

Veronica arrived at the Hercules Café with a canvas satchel, a shaving mirror and a doughnut. Gilbert took her up to her room while Frank and Olive waited anxiously downstairs at the counter.

'It's rather small,' he observed as he opened the door. He stared critically around the room at the flaking walls, the simple wardrobe, desk and bed, as if he were looking at it for the first time.

'There's a funny smell,' Veronica said as she swept past him and walked to the window. She turned around and wrinkled her nose.

'Disinfectant. I cleaned the place out and washed the floor and there's no lock on the door because I haven't had time to fix it. The bathroom is at the end of the corridor.'

Veronica pushed the satchel under the bed, placed the mirror on the desk, sat down and ate the doughnut.

'You'll need an apron,' said Gilbert, glancing down at the shine on his shoes. He was wearing a fresh apron, with plenty of starch, a clean blue shirt and Brylcreem. Olive had been cruel about this extra spit and polish but appearances were important. He wanted to make a good impression.

'I never wear aprons,' said Veronica. 'I brought my Heavy Hamburger uniform. I thought I could wear it here…'

'Fine,' said Gilbert. 'Where is it?'

'I'm wearing it,' she said. She stood up and pulled off her coat.

'That's a uniform?' whispered Gilbert. She was wearing a white shirt with a black elastic bowtie, a cheap red skirt and black stockings. Her legs were as thin and glossy as liquorice sticks.

'Yeah. Well, there's supposed to be a red jacket and a white paper hat but I didn't like 'em. Anyway, the jacket had Heavy Hamburger written all over the front of it. ' She bent down suddenly, narrowed her eyes at the shaving mirror and ruffled her hair. The tissue-paper skirt gave a shiver and floated out in the draught. 'So what do you think?'

'Is it warm enough?' said Gilbert.

'I keep moving.'

'I'm not surprised,' said Gilbert. He took her downstairs and gave her to Olive. 'If you have a problem you'll find me in the kitchen. Olive will take care of you,' he said hopefully and disappeared to the safety of his stove.

Veronica stood behind the counter and patiently waited for her instructions.

'I don't know what he wants me to do with you,' grumbled Olive. 'There's no work.' She glanced sideways at the elastic bowtie, blinked and then continued staring morosely over the counter at the empty dining room. In one corner an old man sat nursing a mug of Bovril.

'I'll clean the tables,' volunteered Veronica.

'Waste of time.'

'Why?' said Veronica.

'Customers mess them,' sniffed Olive.

'Fill the sugar bowls?'

'Customers steal them.'

'Fold the napkins?'

'Don't use them.'

'Anything?' said Veronica.

'Nothing,' said Olive.

But it wasn't true. At lunch time the café was crowded and Olive, bewildered and belligerent, soon retired wounded and set Veronica to work. The girl danced among the tables with her arms full of trays and her red skirt spinning. She worked fast and without mistakes. She was careful with the food and clever with the customers. Gilbert watched from the kitchen door and clapped his hands with pleasure.

It was evening before Frank found an opportunity to introduce himself. The café door was locked and Gilbert had gone to put Olive to sleep. The dining room was quiet and dark. Veronica was cleaning the counter so Frank found a broom and pretended to sweep the floor.

'I heard they found you under one of the tables,' Veronica said as she slapped the crumbs from her rag.

'Yes,' said Frank.

'Which one?' she said, leaving the counter and walking out to him.

'I think it was that one,' said Frank, leaning on his broom and blushing as he nodded at a near-by table.

Veronica smiled. Her blonde hair shone in the gloom. 'I suppose that's why you're so small,' she said. She bent down and searched among the table legs.

'I'm very tall for my age,' murmured Frank as he followed the flutter of her skirt.

'Yeah, but you're all skin and bone. You look like you need feeding. Come on, I'll make you a sandwich.'

She led him into the kitchen and fried him a rasher of purple bacon. 'Eat your crusts and I'll give you a kiss,' she said as she pushed the sandwich into his hands.

Warm fat leaked through his fingers. The rasher peeped from the slices of bread like a fat and drooling tongue. Frank stared at the bacon. He stared at Veronica. He ate the sandwich.

Olive remained cantankerous but by the end of the week even she was eating from Veronica's hand. The girl worked so hard it made Olive feel tired and she went to bed in the afternoons. The little café looked prosperous. The windows shone, the counter gleamed and customers, once driven away by Olive's clumsy table manners, crept back again.

'Where did you find that one?' said Horace, squinting at the waitress through greasy spectacles. He'd repaired a cracked lens with Elastoplast.

'Advertised,' said Gilbert proudly.

Horace nodded and sucked on his sandwich. 'Is she still infectious?' he said at last, wiping his mouth on his sleeve.

'What are you talking about, you daft bugger?'

'They cut your hair like that in hospital,' sniffed Horace.

Gilbert ignored him. The girls from the beauty parlour arrived, giggling, shrieking, hungry for gossip and doughnuts. The Greek grocer brought his family down for lunch. The café was crowded.

But among the old, familiar faces he began to see strangers: young men with cunning eyes who sat and gloated at his waitress. They would arrive, two or three at a time, and sprawl at a centre table. Sometimes they bought coffee. Sometimes they bought nothing. They would smoke and brag and whistle at Veronica when she tried to serve them.

'They don't eat,' brooded Gilbert one night while the family were gathered for supper. He had baked an enormous pie stuffed with onions, mushrooms and chicken. Potatoes clustered against its flanks, soft, plump and. sweaty with butter. 'They sit around but they don't eat.' He punctured the pie and glowered at a wisp of escaping steam.

Veronica shrugged. 'I'm not going to coax them with a spoon,' she said quietly.

Frank sucked a mushroom and grinned.

'I don't like it,' growled Gilbert. 'They're watching you.'

'I can't help it,' said Veronica.

'Sell tickets,' snapped Olive.

'We're not running a damn circus.'

'Mind your language.'

Gilbert grunted and poked at his pie. He wasn't happy. She's only a child. Doesn't understand. Wear an apron. That's the answer. Hide those lovely liquorice legs.

'You should wear an apron,' he said quickly, hunched at his plate, mashing potatoes with his fork.

'Why?' said Veronica. She stopped chewing. Her cheeks bulged. She lifted her head and stared at him.

'Why?' said Olive suspiciously. She turned to Gilbert and peered at him.

'Why?' said Frank. He looked at Gilbert and frowned.

Gilbert blushed to his ears. He opened his mouth and closed it again. He raised his fork and banged it down against his plate. 'I don't like it,' he muttered.

'They don't worry me,' said Veronica.

'Good,' said Olive. 'Ignore them.'

'You shout if they try to interfere with you,' said Gilbert.

'How do you mean?' asked Veronica.

'You know – interfere with you,' hissed Gilbert. He glanced nervously at Frank.

'I can look after myself,' said Veronica.

Gilbert finished the supper in silence. Women don't know. Parade about in the next to nothing. Men turn nasty. Trust your instincts. Say nothing. Wait for trouble.

It happened on Saturday afternoon.

The café was quiet. Olive was asleep. Frank had gone to the library. Gilbert was sitting in the warmth of the kitchen filling tomato ketchup bottles. He had a gallon drum of the sweet, red glue and was carefully pouring it into the bottles. He was so absorbed in his work that he paid no attention to the drone of voices from the dining room. And then someone laughed. It was an ugly, barking laugh that made Gilbert slip with his bottle. He swore beneath his breath. They were back again. He tried to concentrate but his hand trembled and covered his knuckles with ketchup. He reached for the towel. Someone hooted and whistled. Gilbert tortured the towel in his fists. Ignore them. Say nothing.

Veronica screamed.

Gilbert bellowed and jumped from his chair. He blundered through the open door, smacked the counter with his belly, bounced and staggered across the dining room.

Two young men were sprawled at a table. One was small, sharp, bright as a weasel. He was wearing a long, leather coat and cracked army boots. The other was tall and slow with a stupid, flat face. They stared at Gilbert and grinned.

'What's happening out here?' he demanded, turning to Veronica.

His waitress was standing a little distance from the table, anxiously stroking her legs. Her hair stood out in electric spikes and the bowtie hung by a thread. 'He put his hand up my skirt,' she sobbed.

'Which one?'

'That one,' sniffed Veronica, pointing at the tallest of the two intruders.

'You love it,' he jeered and raised one finger in salute.

'Stupid tart,' growled the small one.

'Get out,' said Gilbert softly.

The little one twisted in his chair and stared at Gilbert in silence. Then he swung out his legs and kicked the table with his boots. 'Cheeseburger!' he shouted. He looked at his companion. 'You want a cheeseburger, Charlie?'

'Get out,' repeated Gilbert.

'Fuck off and get the cheeseburgers,' ordered Charlie. The blood drained from Gilbert's face. He raised his fist and stuck out his stomach. He was holding a loaded bottle of ketchup.

'The old fart's got a bottle,' said the one in the leather coat. He snatched something from the table, leapt forward and waved a knife across Gilbert's stomach.

'Push it up his fucking arse,' suggested Charlie. He leaned forward and caught Veronica by the wrists.

Veronica shrieked. Gilbert bared his teeth. The killer grinned as he plunged with the knife.

'No one argues with Harry Nutter,' he hissed as he struck the old man's stomach.

Gilbert gasped. The blade bent against his apron. Harry Nutter grunted, stared at Gilbert and frowned at the knife. The blade had buckled like cardboard.

'Made in Korea,' said Gilbert mildly. Polished alloy. One twenty a dozen. It had always been his opinion that people who ate Porkies and Burgers could not be trusted with real knives and forks.

'Pick a window – you're leaving,' snarled Nutter. He threw away the knife and grabbed Gilbert by the apron strings.

'Leave him alone!' screamed Veronica. She struggled from Charlie's grasp and threw herself at Harry Nutter. She knocked him down, held him firmly between her knees and began to uproot his hair.

Charlie tried to push past Gilbert and rescue his friend. But

Gilbert caught him by the collar, swung the bottle and cracked his skull. He stumbled forward a few paces and sank to his knees. His mouth hung open. His hair was oozing a thick, red pulp. He wiped his face and stared at the gore on his hands. He couldn't tell the difference between the blood and the ketchup. He tried to taste it, pushed his fingers into his mouth, rolled his eyes and croaked. He was sucking broken glass. He started to cough and spit on the floor. A string of red bubbles dangled loosely from his chin.

'All right! Forget the cheeseburgers!' shouted Harry Nutter. He had thrown off Veronica and was crouching behind a table, watching Gilbert splash across the floor with the broken bottle in his hand.

Veronica groaned, hauled herself into a chair and looked around at the damage. One of the tables had been overturned. A chair had suffered a broken leg. The floor sparkled with glass and the windows were spattered with ketchup.

'I think I'm bleeding,' gasped Charlie, clutching his face in horror.

'You're lucky we didn't kill you,' snarled Veronica.

'Get out,' sighed Gilbert, leaning, exhausted, against the counter.

Harry Nutter stood up and grinned, combed his hair, brushed down his coat and swaggered to the safety of the door. Charlie staggered after him. He was bleeding ketchup from his ears.

'Did they hurt you?' said Gilbert, turning to Veronica.

'No,' she said. She hung her head and quickly wiped her nose on her sleeve.

'If they touch you again,' growled Gilbert, 'I'll murder them.' He raised his fist and stared proudly at the broken bottle. He felt huge. He was a dangerous man.

'I'm sorry, it was my fault,' said Veronica, chewing a ragged fingernail. 'I should have worn the apron.'

'Nonsense,' grinned Gilbert. 'I like the uniform. Are you going to let people push you around?'

Veronica smiled again. 'I'll fetch a bucket and wash down

the floor. It looks like we've butchered a pig. Olive will go mad if she finds this mess.'

They found rags and brushes and while Gilbert wiped the windows Veronica scrubbed the floor.

'You looked so fierce,' she said as she squatted under a table with her chin between her knees. She pushed on the brush. The ketchup frothed around her shoes.

'I was angry,' admitted Gilbert as he sloshed at the window.

'You nearly knocked his head off,' she grinned and banged her brush against the bucket.

'I didn't hurt him,' Gilbert said carefully. The ketchup had dried into small dark blisters. He picked at them with his fingers.

'I nearly wet myself,' chortled Veronica. 'I thought his brains were running out.'

Gilbert shuddered. Is it true? Blood excites them. Hand up skirt. Rough and tumble. Torn stockings. Rum business. Some girls like it. Olive wouldn't.

A woman walked into the café and pulled at Gilbert's sleeve.

'What happened to *you*?' she said.

'Nosebleed,' he said.

The woman looked disappointed. She sat down and asked for a coffee.

'Sorry,' he said. 'We're closed.' He waved her away and locked the door. 'Have you finished?' he said, turning again to search for Veronica.

She grunted and crawled from under a table. 'I'm covered in bruises,' she complained, lifting her skirt and frowning down at her legs.

'That's bad,' said Gilbert. He looked at her legs and stroked his chin. 'Come into the kitchen and I'll have a proper look at you.'

She followed him into the kitchen and took off her shoes and stockings.

'Make yourself comfortable,' he said as he washed his hands.

Veronica sat down and pulled up her skirt. One of her knees

was turning blue. Gilbert knelt down, laid his hands upon the knee and blessed it. 'It's swollen,' he whispered, closing his eyes as he measured her leg with his fingers. Her skin was soft and wonderfully hot.

'It's growing like a balloon,' she said proudly. She raised her leg and licked the knee with her tongue.

Gilbert soaked a towel in cold water and wrapped it gently around the bruise. His fingers were shaking. He couldn't control them. She had lifted her skirt to expose her thighs.

'How does it feel?' he inquired, pressing the towel with the palms of his hands.

'It hurts,' she complained, jerking back her knee and trying to look beneath the bandage.

'Don't move,' he said. He stretched out her leg and clasped the small, white foot in his hands, his thumbs gently working to massage her toes. 'We're waiting for the bruise to come out.'

Veronica sat back in the chair and closed her eyes. 'How long does it usually take?' she murmured.

'It's rum,' said Gilbert. 'You never know with a bruise.' And as he spoke he stroked her leg, pinched her calf, rubbed at her thigh, as if he needed to consider the knee from every angle and direction. His face was glowing with concentration. He clenched his teeth. His nostrils flared.

'Finished?' she said, after a long time.

'Finished,' he sighed. He squeezed the towel. A trickle of water rolled down her leg and collected in beads between her toes.

Someone rang the bell.

'It's the police!' gasped Veronica and pulled down her skirt.

'It's Frank,' said Gilbert, glancing at his watch. He groaned, stood up and went to unlock the door.

Frank marched impatiently into the dining room with his arms full of library books. 'You're closed,' he said in surprise.

'Yes,' said Gilbert. 'Watch your step – the floor is wet.'

Frank slithered through a puddle, skated across the room, hit the counter and ran upstairs. A few moments later he was standing in the kitchen.

It was too quiet. Gilbert was sitting at the table, pretending to fill ketchup bottles. Veronica sat beside him, eating a stale slice of chocolate cake. A cupboard creaked on its hinges. A fly prickled across the ceiling.

'What happened?' demanded Frank. He stared at Gilbert and scowled.

'I had a little accident,' said Veronica, but her words were muffled with cake.

'What?' said Frank.

'A little accident!' shouted Gilbert.

'What?' insisted Frank.

'I fell down,' said Veronica, avoiding his eyes.

'Where?' said Frank.

'Go and ask Olive if she wants some milk,' said Gilbert, pointing at the door with his bottle of ketchup.

'She's still asleep,' said Frank.

This scrap of news seemed to galvanise Gilbert. He banged the table with his bottle. 'It's time to get back to work,' he shouted. He pushed back his chair and lumbered into the dining room. Veronica jumped up and followed him. Frank stood alone in the kitchen and stared at the stockings draped on the back of her chair.

Gilbert never told Olive about the fight. It was a secret to share with Veronica. In the days that followed he chased her around the café, trotting at her heels like a foolish old dog. He wore clean shirts and worked every day in his best Sunday shoes. He baked elaborate pastries which he wrapped in ribbon and left in her room. He was bewitched. When she laughed he glowed like a lantern. When she frowned the light was snuffed from his face. The days became dreams through which Veronica beckoned him with a glance, a smile and a flick of her skirt. One night, burning with fever, he called out her name in his sleep.

'Wake up!' screamed Olive. 'Wake up!' She kicked off the blankets and pulled him out of his dreams by his ears.

Gilbert, eyes closed, half-unconscious, leaned across and tried to nurse her in his arms. 'What is it?' he mumbled. 'It's only a nightmare… I'll fix your pillow… go back to sleep.' He sat up in bed and searched for the bedclothes.

'Don't touch me,' howled Olive, shrinking from the sweep of his hands.

Gilbert opened his eyes and blinked. 'What's wrong?'

'You've been fiddling,' sobbed Olive. She seized the pillow and pulled it roughly into her arms.

'I haven't touched you,' said Gilbert.

'No,' she howled. 'You've fiddled with that waitress.'

'Veronica?'

'Yes,' sobbed Olive. 'Veronica.' She trapped the pillow with her elbows and knees and buried her face in the feathers.

'Fiddled?'

'How could you do it? Sleeping next to me and your head full of thoughts. Grunting all night like a dog. Tossing and turning with a mucky grin on your face. How could you do it?'

'Don't be silly,' soothed Gilbert. 'I haven't touched Veronica. And what makes you think she'd take an interest in me? She's only sixteen.'

'Seventeen.'

'She's only seventeen. She wouldn't want an old rascal with a big belly and no teeth. '

'You've still got your teeth,' said Olive, flustered.

'I look after them.'

'Exactly,' sniffed Olive. 'It's time you started to act your age. I don't blame the child. I blame you. You're as bad as my father – he chased women. It was idolatry killed my mother.' The memory made her shake her head and burst into tears. She punched the pillow until it shrank with a gasp between her thighs.

'You've been dreaming,' said Gilbert gently. He tried to reach out and stroke Olive's neck.

'Don't touch me!' she howled. 'You give me the willies!'

'Olive…'

'Go away! Leave me alone! Where are you going?'

Gilbert was on the floor and groping for his slippers. 'I've had enough,' he growled.

He took a blanket from the floor, dragged it downstairs and made a bed beneath the counter. No one tried to stop him. He lay down among the crates and bottles and glared into the gloom. What was he doing here? Why had he waited? Why had he wasted? So many years at the Hercules Café. Time past. Count the winters. What happened? Nothing happened. Sam Pilchard kept walking. France, Spain, across Gibraltar and down the coast of Africa. He worked for a time in Nigeria. Letters from Lagos. Onionskin paper. Settled at last in Bilharzia.

Write him a letter. Don't wait. Buy a ticket and join him. Count the winters. Fifty years old. How much more time to serve? Ten. Twenty with good behaviour. Time to look after yourself. A man should begin with a good night's sleep.

He wrapped the blanket over his shoulders and shuffled sadly to the window. Out there, beyond the Hercules Café, far away, past the endless rain, there are pygmies hidden from the night among the stems of giant orchids, faces painted with bone-ash and blood. Serpents coiled around the knees of sleeping elephants, baboons dancing, wild dogs screaming, panthers grinning at the moon. Girls prancing naked to the sound of drums, breasts bouncing, buttocks swelling, feet stamping the red dust. Out there, somewhere, Sam Pilchard, happy, drunk and fat as a walrus, asleep in a heathen's hammock.

It's cold. Dark. Cruel draught under the door. Rattles the window. This blanket smells funny. What is it? Mothballs. A man can't sleep like a dog on the floor.

At dawn he crept back into the bedroom, dressed himself in his one good suit and hauled a suitcase from the wardrobe. Shirts, shoes, socks and vests. Olive woke to find him packing recipe books.

'Where do you think you're going?' she demanded. Her face looked crumpled and her eyes were pink with sleep.

'I've finished,' he said quietly. 'I'm going away.'

'Where?'

'Who cares?' he shrugged. No time to argue. Slip away before Frank wakes up and asks questions. Don't look back. Boat train from Victoria Station. Find a bed in Paris tonight.

'Where?'

'I'm going to look for Sam Pilchard.' He snapped the locks on the suitcase and carried it to the door.

'But you haven't seen him for years. You don't know where he lives – he could be dead,' she said, scowling at him suspiciously.

'I'll find him,' said Gilbert.

'You won't find him in *those* slippers,' said Olive. Gilbert swore and searched for his shoes. When he reached the stairs Frank and Veronica were waiting for him.

'Are you going away?' said Frank. He was wearing baggy striped pyjamas that hid his hands and feet. He raised an arm and wagged his sleeve at the suitcase. He looked baffled.

'Yes,' said Gilbert.

'When will you be back?' said Veronica, wrapped in a church-white dressing gown.

'I don't know … I might be gone for a long time,' he mumbled.

'Take me with you,' urged Frank.

Gilbert looked down at the boy and his heart began to break. The tears bubbled into his eyes and blinded him. He sniffed and wiped a hand across his face. He wanted to snatch Frank into his arms and kiss him, find his hat and steal him away.

'Sorry, Frank. You have to stay and look after Olive. When I settle down I'll write to you and then, perhaps, you can come out and visit me.'

'Where are you going?'

'Africa,' said Gilbert, pulling at his suitcase.

'Africa?' hooted Veronica. 'How are you going to Africa?'

'Walking,' shouted Gilbert as he hurried downstairs.

'Good riddance!' screamed Olive.

'Stop him!' pleaded Frank.

But Gilbert was already marching through the dining room towards the shuttered door and the street. 'Too late,' said Olive, as they heard the door slam behind him.

'How are we going to manage without him?' asked Veronica.

'You'll learn,' sighed Olive.

Frank couldn't believe it. He knew he was dreaming. He pattered up and down the corridor, waiting to wake up in the warmth and safety of his own bed.

'I'll look after the kitchen,' announced Olive. 'Frank can help at the counter. Go and get dressed and we'll sort everything out.'

The café opened as if nothing had happened. Olive worked in the kitchen, spoiling soup, burning bacon and slicing her fingers into sandwiches. Veronica stalked the dining room. Frank sat under the counter and refused to come out. A strange silence hung over them. Veronica haunted the tables, scribbling orders and juggling plates with a look of absolute doom on her face. Frank was too shocked to speak or even pick at the plate of broken biscuits that Olive put down for him. Olive, alone, seemed unconcerned by Gilbert's escape. She crashed and smashed around the kitchen as if the poor man had never existed. Frank was furious.

'When will he come home?' he demanded whenever Olive passed the counter. He didn't understand what had happened to Gilbert but he felt that Olive was somehow to blame.

'I don't know, Frank,' she snapped back at him. 'Forget about it and do some work.'

Frank sat and sulked. He knew Gilbert wouldn't want to leave him alone with Olive. He would send a message, a signal, and find a way to help him escape. He had a notion that Gilbert's sudden departure was part of some marvellous secret plan. At any moment someone would walk into the café, search him out and press a scrap of paper into his hand. Follow this man. Eat this message. Gilbert. But at four in the afternoon and still no word he began to grow desperate.

'Let's go and look for him,' he whispered to Veronica.

'He's gone to Africa,' she said.

'But he's walking,' said Frank. 'He can't be far away.'

Veronica bent down and stroked his face. 'Don't worry,' she whispered and kissed him.

That night they gathered at the kitchen table to eat burnt

hamburger. Olive remained unrepentant but she looked tired. Her ankles were swollen and she had managed to slash a thumb. The rag she had used to bind the wound was oozing soup and gravy. In a few days she would be swaddled in dirty bandages.

'What happens if he *never* comes back?' complained Frank as he crunched morosely on his hamburger. 'What happens if he gets murdered in Africa and nobody finds him and we wait and wait for years because we haven't heard about it?' The tears were brimming in his eyes. He began to choke. Veronica slapped his shoulders.

'Oh, shut up, Frank!' shouted Olive. 'I don't care what happens to him. He's not going to Africa. It's all a pigment of his imagination. I've had enough of the silly old devil. I wouldn't have him back if he came crawling through that door on his hands and knees. And it's time you were in bed. I want some help tomorrow.'

Frank went to bed but he couldn't sleep. He kept thinking about Gilbert walking down the street to Africa. It didn't make sense. He hadn't taken his frying pan. He must be in trouble. Something must be wrong. If he hadn't returned by morning he would have to go out and find him.

Gilbert came home at midnight. He was drunk. He had lost his suitcase. He managed to unlock the café, stagger into the dining room and collapse among the tables. There was a crash of sugar bowls. Olive and Veronica flew down the stairs in a moment, their faces mad with moonlight, their dressing gowns open and beating like wings. They dragged him into the kitchen, pulled off his clothes, one, two, three, wrapped him in blankets and left him to sleep on the kitchen floor.

'Welcome home,' whispered Frank in the dark, smiled and fell asleep.

6

That summer Gilbert repainted the Hercules Café. He restored the sign with several coats of yellow enamel and painted the window frames blue. He wrote Delicious Hot or Cold, on the glass, in thick, black letters and edged the words in gold. He scoured the drainpipes, cleaned out the gutters and changed the locks on the door. When he had finished with the view from the street he mounted an attack on the dining room. He painted the chairs red and turned the tables green with a cheap and evil-smelling paint that refused to dry and marked his customers for life. He whitewashed the ceiling and scrubbed the walls as if he were trying to scratch through to the sunlight.

At night Olive watched him prowl the house, planning assaults on the furniture. He knocked down cupboards and bathroom cabinets, built loose shelves and tilting wardrobes, raised floors, lowered ceilings, and turned the doors around on their hinges.

'You'll do yourself a mischief,' she warned him.

But Gilbert snorted, swung his hammer and continued to rebuild the scenery. If you can't change your life change the wallpaper. Build your own castle. Every man a king in his own backyard.

'You'll cut off your fingers,' said Frank as he watched Gilbert hack at a length of skirting board with a long, blue chisel.

'They'll grow again,' said Gilbert cheerfully.

'That shelf is crooked,' said Veronica, squinting over his shoulder as he struggled to engage the final screw in a mess of crumbling plaster.

'Nothing wrong with the shelf,' said Gilbert. 'I blame the wall.' He made mistakes but they didn't worry him. If a shelf was crooked or a cupboard twisted he was happy to knock it down and start again.

It was a puzzle to Frank how a man who fried hamburgers in a kitchen all day found the strength to work around the house at night. And Gilbert never stopped working. Long after midnight, when Olive was safe and snoring under the bedclothes, when Veronica was soaking in the bath, when the café was empty and only cats roamed the dark and silent streets, Frank would go downstairs to check the doors and find Gilbert on his hands and knees in the dining room, painting a box or building a bench. Then they would sit together drinking coffee and talk about the world. Gilbert would smile and yawn until his eyelids drooped and his chin sank slowly against his chest. But Frank could never persuade him to put down his tools and rest. It was a mystery how the man found the time to sleep.

The answer was simple. Gilbert didn't sleep. Olive took to her bed without him and he was already working in the kitchen before she was awake. Sometimes his pillows were rumpled but often they remained untouched. If Gilbert ever closed his eyes she never caught him. She scolded him for his neglect but she was happy to be left alone. It seemed they had reached an understanding and she was thankful for it. No more monkey business with those great hands everywhere pinching and pushing birthdays and Christmas any excuse and you wake to him moaning and trying to feel you under your nightdress never so much as a please or thank you enough to turn a woman's stomach it can't be healthy so much poking despite what they say on the television I'm too old for all that nonsense and whatever happened to soften his sausage thank the Lord and don't ask questions.

Gilbert continued to hammer out his frustrations and gradually his work improved. Doors stopped sticking. Floors stopped creaking. Varnishes dried and screws retained their threads. Success gave him confidence and that made him ambitious. At the beginning of November and before anyone could stop him he moved the ovens, knocked down the larder and started to rebuild the kitchen.

The customers sat at tables covered in rubble and honked complaints above the sound of the sledgehammer. The soup was peppered with nails. The eggs were scrambled with plaster flakes. Olive took fright.

'They don't eat – we don't eat,' she shouted, searching for Gilbert through a haze of brick dust.

'Patience,' he roared. 'I'll soon be finished.'

He liked to boast that the Hercules Café had remained open throughout the alterations and it was true, although for nearly a fortnight they had served nothing but coffee and Veronica's toast. No one complained. The toast was such a success that when the kitchen was ready for business again nobody wanted a proper cooked meal. Gilbert blamed the dining room.

'They can't see what's cooking,' he concluded. 'We've got to work on their appetites.'

'What's wrong with my toast?' said Veronica sharply. She was proud of her work and pleased she had made Gilbert jealous.

'There's no money in toast,' explained Gilbert. 'If we want to succeed we've got to make them feel really hungry.'

'They can look at the blackboard,' said Olive. She stared mournfully at the board behind the counter.

Sink Your Teeth in the Famous Hercules Hamburger.

'That's no good,' growled Gilbert.

'What's wrong with my board?' said Frank. He had spent hours composing the message in a long and complicated scrawl of red and blue chalks. He thought it was rather good.

'Most of the buggers can't read their own names!' shouted Gilbert.

'There's no need to fly off the angle,' said Olive.

'He's right,' said Veronica. 'You've got to make 'em hungry. At the Heavy Hamburger they used to have a giant revolving hamburger in the window. A big, fat bastard running with ketchup and cheese. At night it used to light up and swell and throb and make a pathetic little squelching noise. People couldn't believe it. That hamburger used to hypnotise 'em. They walked into the place with their mouths open and we used to stuff 'em with food. Easy.'

'You can't force the food down their throats,' argued Olive.

'But you've got to show them what's cooking,' insisted Gilbert.

'You mean you're going to carry your frying pan to their tables,' scowled Olive, slapping her apron.

'No. But instead of letting them just sit there, picking their noses and watching their coffee grow cold, we'll show them the food.' He marched across the room, waved his hands at the counter and sketched an imaginary mountain of food. 'A big display. They'll walk into the place, sit down and there'll be a big display staring at them. They'll soon get the idea.' He stared around the dining room, rubbed his head and grinned.

A few days later he had replaced the wood and metal counter with a second-hand display cabinet, bright, shining and chilled to a frost. Behind its heavy, sliding doors food sat and shimmered in trays.

There were trays of cheese and hard-boiled eggs, tinned salmon, corned beef slices, chicken pies, steak pies, beans and porkies. Olive spent hours patiently arranging the food according to its shape and colour. She guarded the cabinet with a jealous pride, wearing the key on her apron string, as if she were curator of a strange museum. And, as Veronica had predicted, reluctant customers quickly recovered their appetites and exercised them on Gilbert's cooking. Gilbert, excited, laughing, belly big as Buddha, put away his hammer and chisel and returned to the kitchen. The oven roared and the windows steamed. They were back in business.

To celebrate the renovations Gilbert created a hamburger special he called Enola Gay: a glistening tower of hamburger, oozing relish, that concealed a bomb of mustard pickle and red pepper sauce so powerful it made strong men blister and glow in the dark.

As the café prospered so Frank began to grow again. He was now as tall as Gilbert. His shoes were splitting like chestnuts. His voice began to crack.

'You're sprouting whiskers,' whispered Veronica, standing close enough to make him blush and trying to tickle his chin.

'It's my age,' squeaked Frank and a button burst on his shirt. Veronica smiled. 'You'll soon be getting notions,' she crooned.

'What sort of notions?' frowned Frank.

'Mind your own business.' She grinned and turned away in a flutter of skirts.

The next morning Frank borrowed Gilbert's razor and made a bloody attempt to shave. He spent the rest of the day with a plaster under his chin and his shirt drenched in Bay Rum cologne. Veronica gave him a wicked smile whenever she passed the kitchen.

Olive, who had now cautiously accepted Gilbert's return to the bedroom on the understanding he sleep in a separate bed, was disturbed by Frank's development. She lay awake at night and brooded. 'He's growing too fast,' she complained in the dark. 'It's not natural. You ought to have a word with him.'

'I can't stop the boy growing,' growled Gilbert from the far corner of the room. They don't stay puppies for ever. What did she want him to do about it? Cut him down with a pruning knife?

'You'll have to say something,' insisted Olive gloomily.

'I don't know what you mean,' yawned Gilbert. He heard the mattress wheeze as Olive sat up and slapped her pillows.

'You know what I'm talking about,' she hissed across the room. 'You ought to tell him the facts of life.'

'Which facts?'

'All the nasty ones,' shuddered Olive. She closed her eyes and pretended to sleep.

Gilbert grinned and continued to stare at the darkness. Carnal knowledge. That's what she's talking about. The pleasures of the flesh. The thumping, bumping, belching, squelching, knee bending, teeth-grinding, belly bouncing, pleasures of the flesh. How to explain? Send him to the brothels of North Africa. That's what they did in the old days. Finished off their education. Leave him alone and he'll find out. Ignorance is bliss. Nobody gets away with it. Veronica will wet his whistle.

The months slipped away and Frank continued to grow. Gilbert kept watch and found nothing wrong. He was strong and healthy. He washed every day and shaved once a week. He certainly knew he was now a man: he blushed at the flirtatious laughter of the women customers, stammered when he spoke to them, avoided their eyes and hurried away at the least excuse; yet when Gilbert searched his face he saw nothing there but innocence.

And then, one night, Frank woke up in the dark. It was two o'clock in the morning. He slipped from the sheets, startled, holding his breath, staring wildly around the room. Something was scuttling under his bed. He knelt down and pressed his ear against the floor. The noises came from the kitchen. He knew Gilbert was asleep. He could hear him snoring. He knew the doors to the street were tight. He'd made it his business to lock them. Were the windows closed? He couldn't remember.

He felt defenceless in his pyjamas. He crawled across the floor, groped for his shoes and fumbled to knot the laces. There was a muffled crash of glass from the kitchen. He shivered and searched for the stairs.

The café was in darkness. Frank reached the dining room and crept slowly along the wall. There was someone prowling in the kitchen. He could hear them breathing. He tiptoed forward, following the edge of the wall until he had reached the open door. And then he paused. Had they heard him? Were they waiting? Knives. Axes. Broken bottles. Too late. Don't stop. He stretched out an arm and snapped on the light.

Veronica was squatting in the middle of the kitchen floor. She was using her fingers to sweep glass into a dustpan. She scowled impatiently at the glare from the lights but she didn't look surprised.

'Oh, it's you,' she said, glancing at him as she picked at the glass. 'Help me clear up this mess or Gilbert will throttle me in the morning.'

'What's happening?' demanded Frank. 'I thought someone had broken into the place.'

'The great sandwich robbery,' smirked Veronica.

'They'll steal anything. I thought they were taking the place apart.'

Veronica narrowed her curved, grey eyes and studied him for a moment.

'Is that why you're wearing your shoes?' she inquired.

Frank couldn't think of a sensible answer. He looked around the kitchen at the open cupboards, the torn carton of milk, the scattered biscuits and half-eaten sandwich. The waitress was raiding the larder.

'Don't just stand there, Frank. Come and help me,' said Veronica. She shook the dustpan to make it rattle, stood up and walked away to empty it. She was wearing an old shirt. Frank stared at the long, pale stalks of her legs. The shirt barely covered her buttocks.

'What are you doing in the kitchen? Do you know what time it is? It's two o'clock in the morning,' he complained.

'I'm starving.'

'It's nearly time for breakfast. Why didn't you eat before you went to bed?'

'I wasn't hungry when I went to bed and stop trying to look through my shirt.'

'I wasn't,' said Frank, staring at the shirt. His ears were hot. His face stung with embarrassment.

'You're doing it again.'

'It's my age,' said Frank. 'I can't help it.'

'I suppose little boys are *born* with turds for brains,' said Veronica sardonically.

'You should have put on your dressing gown!' retorted Frank.

'I didn't know I was going to be spied on by a nasty little boy. Jesus! I'm old enough to be your mother,' hooted Veronica. She found the half-eaten sandwich and pushed it greedily into her mouth.

Frank, who could name all the spiders to be found in wild pineapples, tried to check Veronica's claim of maternity with some rapid mental arithmetic and failed. 'I'm nearly fifteen,' he said at last.

'So what?'

'It's two o'clock in the morning, Veronica. I was going to call the police.'

'I'll call 'em if you don't stop staring at me,' she said, spitting crumbs.

'You're crazy,' said Frank.

'I've caught you watching me, trying to look up my skirt,' she said, waving a piece of crust at him.

'When?' said Frank. He blushed and scowled and turned away. Everyone tried to look up her skirt. Men threw their spoons on the ground when she passed near their tables. Gilbert polished floors until they shone like mirrors. Dogs howled and pushed their snouts between her knees. He wasn't going to be blamed for it.

'You watch me when I'm working. You think I haven't noticed?' she said, arching an eyebrow. 'I can *feel* you trying to undress me with those big, brown eyes. And they think you're so innocent! They should keep you on a chain. You're dangerous.'

'Are you coming to bed?' demanded Frank impatiently.

'What do you mean?' she snapped. Frank shrugged. As he walked to the door she grabbed him by his pyjama jacket, spun him around and watched him jump from his shoes. He lay, stunned, on the floor and let Veronica tread on him.

'I mean why don't we go back to bed?' wheezed Frank. 'It's two o'clock in the morning.'

'Don't threaten me,' said Veronica, as she kicked him. 'I'll scream. I'm not afraid of you.'

He wriggled and caught her foot in his hands. It was soft and surprisingly warm. He cradled it gently with his fingers, staring along the length of her leg towards the swell of her shirt tails. 'Calm down,' he panted. 'You're crazy.'

'Don't touch me!' she hissed. 'Look at the size of your hands. It's frightening.' She managed to twist herself free of his grasp and fell against the wall. 'You'll grow into a strangler,' she gasped. 'Those hands aren't natural. You've been cursed with stranglers' hands!'

Frank whimpered and tried to hide his hands inside his pyjamas. Olive said he grew in his sleep. Some mornings he hardly recognised himself. He would go to bed in full working order and wake up with ears that had unfurled like wings or hands the size of paddles dangling from strings he had once thought were arms. His body had become a monstrous burden of crawling skin that changed its size and shape around him.

'I don't want to fight,' said Frank. 'I just want to go to bed.' He glanced towards the safety of the door but Veronica leapt on him. She sat astride him, her knees cracking his bones, her ankles sharp as spurs.

'Listen – if you tell Gilbert I was stealing food I'll kill you. Understand?'

'Yes,' croaked Frank.

She caught his wrists and held them above his head. Her breasts shivered under her shirt. Frank squirmed. He felt suffocated. His head was ringing. Trapped painfully in his pyjamas his penis felt as hard as a carrot.

'I'll tell him you tried to *interfere* with me.'

'Interfere?'

'Don't you know what it means?' whispered Veronica gleefully. Her eyes blazed. Her hair, cut with bacon scissors, stood out from her skull in ghostly spikes. 'I'll tell him you pushed me down on the kitchen floor. I'll tell him you pulled up my skirt and exposed yourself!' She grinned. Her tongue poked between her teeth.

'But it's not true!' wailed Frank.

'So what?' said Veronica. 'He'll believe whatever I want to tell him. No one would trust a nasty lecherous little boy who creeps around in the dark like a strangler.'

'That's terrible.'

'I know,' sighed Veronica. The shirt fell open at the neck. He followed the long cords of her throat to the shadows in her clavicles and then swept down, staring into darkness in search of her breasts. He could see nothing. He was blind. He rolled his head in despair.

'Where do you get such terrible ideas?'

'Oh, I get all my best ideas from the magazines in your room,' she said, lifting herself slightly from his body and bouncing down again with a cruel slap of her knees.

'What magazines?' bleated Frank. His face was scarlet with excitement and fright.

'You know what I'm talking about. You didn't get *those* from the library!' she said, struggling to hold his hands as he made a last desperate effort to escape.

Frank surrendered. He lay helpless beneath Veronica and closed his eyes. He had found the magazines on a chair in the dining room. Three thumbed copies of *Wobble*. When he thought no one was watching, he had pushed them under his shirt and smuggled them into his bedroom. There, under the bedclothes with his Mickey Mouse torch, Frank had seen his first naked women. It was a shock. They were quite unlike anything he had managed to conjure up in his imagination. His own fantasy women were small, white and smooth as statues. The women from *Wobble* were pink and swollen and hairy. They wore masks and high rubber boots and rolled around the dog-eared pages like a troupe of demon acrobats, legs over arms, hands clutching feet, breasts hanging loose as pastry. They were so different from the women he saw every day in the street that Frank suspected they might be a special race of women, held captive by the magazine. He liked to dream that one of them would escape and seek safety at the Hercules Café. Frank kept her in the wardrobe where she slept by day and ventured to his bed at night dressed in her mask and rubber boots. He fed her seed cake and flasks of coffee.

'What were you doing in my room?' he demanded.

'Looking for magazines, stupid,' said Veronica. She stood up suddenly and pulled down her shirt. Her face was flushed. Her knees looked bruised. While Frank continued to sprawl on the floor Veronica began to bustle about the kitchen sweeping up crumbs and locking cupboards as if nothing had happened. Frank remained where he had fallen for several minutes but, it was no good, Veronica had finished with him.

After that first encounter she kept Frank simmering on a low heat. She contrived to leave the door unlocked when she took a bath so that Frank came blundering into the room in search of a toothbrush or razor, caught a glimpse of her soapy breasts before she blinded him with the sponge. She brushed against him while he worked in the kitchen until he blushed or scalded his hands.

The succuba he invited to his room at night no longer looked like the women from *Wobble*. The creature he conjured from bed sheets and shadow was a small-breasted sprite with curved grey eyes and badly cropped hair. Somewhere on the outskirts of sleep she would visit him, whispering, laughing, mocking him through the darkness. He prowled his nocturnal underworld with the lust of a panther. When she grew too bold and stepped within reach he would tear her clothes apart with his hands, smother her screams and feast on the luminous flesh. During the day she might feel secure and shrug off his love-sick glances. But at night, when she locked herself in her room to sleep, Frank was a few short yards away, mad-eyed, growling, savagely rutting with her kidnapped ghost. No cruelty was beyond him. No form of assault left unexplored. He tortured her until she surrendered and eventually, since this was the only conclusion that pleased him, no matter what outrage he cared to inflict, she would cry out with pleasure and confess her love for him.

Each morning he searched her face for some echo of the violation she had been made to endure in his sleep. But he was always disappointed. She remained untouched by his dreams. The more he yearned for a word or a smile the less she seemed to notice him. She might ignore him for days at a time. And then, when he felt so rejected he no longer cared to pay her attention, something would happen to rekindle his desire.

Once, passing her room at night, the door flew open and she pulled him roughly into her arms. She was stripped to her shoes and underwear. Before he knew what was happening she had squeezed him, kissed him, spun him around and leapt to safety on the bed.

He stood on the carpet and stared nervously around him. The room was warm and smelt of cloves. A thin piece of curtain had been drawn across the window. Beside the window stood a plywood wardrobe painted white, the doors embellished with magazine pictures of dogs, cats and mountain ponies. Against one wall stood the desk she used as a dressing table. The desk top was covered in rubbish. While he waited for something to happen and to keep his eyes away from a pair of gleaming stocking tops which, since Veronica was standing on the bed, were now at a level with his face, Frank stared at the rubbish. He counted a box of cotton-wool, a strip of Codeine, crumpled Kleenex, a few sticks of cheap lipstick, an empty perfume bottle, a shaving mirror, hairbrush, comb, a piece of novelty soap in the shape of a rabbit, a wristwatch, Elastoplast, small cotton brassière, gold bracelet and half a biscuit. The brassière made him blush. He stared at the ceiling.

'There!' she called suddenly, pointing at something beneath his feet.

'What?' said Frank, peering at his slippers.

'A spider!' yelled Veronica. She trampolined across the bed with excitement.

Frank jumped. 'It won't hurt you,' he said. A tangle of long black legs scuttled for cover under a chair. Frank stepped on it.

'I didn't tell you to squash it,' said Veronica in dismay. She stopped bouncing and fell down among the pillows.

'I wasn't going to eat it,' said Frank cheerfully, examining the stain on the carpet.

'Poor little thing,' pouted Veronica.

'You hate them,' said Frank.

'Oh, get out!' she shouted, pulling off a shoe and throwing it at him.

Another time, when he had smacked his hand with a hammer, Veronica came running to nurse him with unexpected tenderness.

'Come here,' she said as he staggered about the room, swearing and clutching his wrist. 'You might have broken something.'

He sat down and gave her the damaged hand. She spread his fingers into a fan, as if to count them, frowned, selected the index and slipped it slowly into her mouth to draw the bruise.

The clasp of her lips and the hot suction of her tongue was enough to send Frank fainting. He closed his eyes and groaned. The world rocked dangerously.

'Does it hurt?' she said, pulling the finger from her mouth.

Frank shook his head. His ears burst into flames. His face shone with sweat. Veronica grinned and returned his hand. When she had gone he stood up and looked for himself in the mirror. His teeth were bared. His eyes were wild. The Devil's own finger stuck like a spear through his apron.

The Devil gave him courage. The following day he confronted Veronica, declared his love and threw himself on her mercy. She smiled mysteriously and said nothing. Frank felt encouraged. Sometimes, when they were alone, he would pull her into a hurried embrace. She did not resist but when he tried to kiss her she would only laugh and push him away. Baffled and humiliated, fighting back tears, he would sit alone and sulk. Then Veronica would creep behind him, cover his eyes and plant a kiss behind his ear. As Gilbert suspected, she was helping to give Frank an education.

7

The year Frank became eighteen the Hercules Café had reached the peak of its popularity. At lunchtimes there were queues at the door for soup and sandwiches. At night the tables were always crowded. Olive, perched on a high stool behind the glass cabinet, sat all day and glowered at the customers, Veronica worked the tables. Frank cooked in the kitchen. Gilbert, triumphant, bustled and bullied and dreamed of the Hercules Hamburger Chain. The future seemed secure until, one morning in early September, a stranger walked into the café. He was a large man in a small brown suit and carried a scuffed leather briefcase. He sat down at an empty table and winked at Olive. He had yellow eyes and a small, hooked nose like a cashew nut.

'What have you got that's good and hot?' he demanded when Veronica arrived to serve him. He pulled a tobacco tin from his pocket and started to roll himself a cigarette.

'Egg, bacon, bean, sausage. Hamburger. Fishburger. Beanburger. Cheeseburger. Pork pie. Steak pie. What d'you want?' said Veronica.

He sighed, threw back his head and stared softly at the ceiling. 'A clean bed, a strong drink and the love of a good woman.'

'White or brown bread?' said Veronica.

'Coffee and doughnuts.'

'Anything else?' asked Veronica as she scribbled the order into her pad.

'I don't know,' he said. He poked the cigarette behind his ear. 'Let me have a look at your legs.' His hand shot out and flicked up her skirt. Veronica squealed and danced across the floor.

'Touch me again and I'll knock your teeth out,' she snarled.

'You're too late,' he said. His fingers flew to his mouth and plucked out a set of square, china teeth. He placed them on the table beside his knife and fork. Olive shouted for Gilbert.

What happened next was so unexpected that Olive nearly fell off her stool. Gilbert thundered from the kitchen with a broom in his fist and murder in his heart. But when he saw the stranger he dropped the weapon and threw out his arms in surprise.

'Parker!' he laughed. 'It's Parker!'

'Gilbert Firestone!' howled Parker as he jumped to his feet. 'I thought you were dead.'

'I can't find the time,' confessed Gilbert.

'Can you find the time for a drink?' asked Parker, scooping up his teeth.

'Time enough,' cried Gilbert.

And without wasting another moment the two men clasped arms and swaggered into the street.

'Where's Gilbert?' shouted Frank from the kitchen. 'There's something wrong with the freezer.'

'He's gone!' gasped Olive. 'He just walked out.' Frank stumbled into the dining room and wiped the hair from his eyes.

'What happened?' he said.

'I don't know,' said Olive. 'He found one of his old cronies.' She was hunched on her stool, knees up, head down, eyes staring at the open door. 'He just walked out.'

Frank turned impatiently to Veronica. 'Where did they go?' he demanded.

'I hope they've gone to Hell,' she snarled and stalked away.

Ten minutes later the two men were comfortably established in the Armistice Bar at the Volunteer. It was a long, damp hall of stained glass and smudged brass. The walls had been painted with brown enamel. The floors were polished with beer. It was dark, silent and as cold as a monastery: a place where men could sit in peace and reflect upon the storms of the world. Gilbert drank Guinness. Parker drank whisky laced with ginger wine.

'Do you remember the Coronation Hotel?' asked Gilbert, wiping a fleck of froth from his chin. 'Paddington. Sam Pilchard was breakfast and I was dinner. Brown soup and mutton stew. It was mostly bones and potatoes. No food after the war. Some nights it was so cold we slept in the kitchen under the ovens.'

'A long time ago,' sighed Parker with the ghost of a smile. The light from the window stained his face with a diamond pattern of red and green shadows. 'When was it? Nineteen hundred and fifty something. 1950. Yes. There was the sugar ration, I remember that. I never liked the Coronation. There were always too many stairs.'

'You were the head waiter – you didn't have to think about stairs.'

'Yes, I was the head waiter. But the maids, you'll remember, slept in the attic.'

'Ah, there was a maid – large girl – generous nature – now what was her name?'

'Annie. Mouth like a howitzer. Bum as big as a Welsh pony.'

'Annie,' said Gilbert. He shook his head. Whatever happened to Annie? He picked up his glass and stared wistfully into his Guinness.

'My God, but she wanted some attention. It was room service three times a week. Regular as clockwork,' grinned Parker. He winked and tapped his cashew nut.

'She gave Sam a pair of her knickers for his birthday. Expensive. Nylon. Soaked to the frills in perfume.'

'Did he wear 'em?'

'No. He gave them to me. I used them as a bouquet garni to give the soup some flavour.'

'There were some fine antics and no mistake,' said Parker. He belched and pulled his jacket open to let his belly breathe. 'Do you remember Mary?'

'Mary?'

'A tiny scrap of a girl. Green eyes. Red nose. She liked to sing hymns.'

'I don't remember.'

Parker scratched his scalp and found the cigarette tucked behind his ear. He examined it closely and put it in his mouth. 'Yes,' he said, striking a match and sucking at the smoke. 'The manager caught her stealing bread and stopped her wages for a month.'

'They were hard times.'

'He was a hard man. But we fixed him. One night he ordered a special supper. He was entertaining some fancy woman. A nasty piece of work called Thelma Millet. She was a part-time tart from the Balls Pond Road. But he didn't know it. He thought she was a countess. Anyway, he wanted the best of everything sent to his room. So when it was ready and you were straining the vegetables Sam took Mary into the pantry and made her piddle in the gravy boat.'

'No!'

'I'll never forget it. I served that dinner with particular pride. There were chops, carrots, turnips, dumplings and all of it swimming in Mary's own gravy.' Parker laughed. He laughed until he choked and had coughed himself black. He yanked a handkerchief from his pocket and spat an oyster into the rag.

Gilbert turned his eyes away. He looks old. What happened? Yesterday he was chasing Annie. Today he looks ready to drop down dead.

'It all changed when you and Sam walked out,' said Parker when he had recovered his breath.

'The world changed,' said Gilbert.

'Annie married a motor mechanic. I went to work at the Gladstone. But it wasn't the same. I went on the road in '59. Salesman. Yes. I've sold everything in my time. Pots, pans, soaps, brushes, liver salts for the bilious woman, bicycles for the common man. Encyclopedias are the worst. It's the weight. These days I travel in biscuits. Placebo Slim Bakes. It's a biscuit with nothing in it. No starch, calories,, vitamins, minerals. Nothing. No nutrition guaranteed. Fat women love 'em. Doctors recommend 'em. If you ate nothing but these biscuits you'd starve to death. Isn't that wonderful? That's science. They cost nothing to produce, sell for a fortune and every woman thinks she needs them. This briefcase is full of 'em. And it's light, light as a feather. Here. Take some home for the wife.' He wrenched open the scuffed leather bag and pulled out a packet of biscuits which he rolled across the table to Gilbert.

'Thanks,' said Gilbert, pushing the packet into his pocket. 'Olive likes the odd biscuit.'

'It's a marvel to think you married,' chortled Parker, shaking his head.

'It's not easy,' growled Gilbert. 'You think you're going for beer and skittles and you wake up to find that it's all blood and sawdust.'

'Milk puddings,' said Parker. 'That's marriage. Milk puddings and no crusts on your sandwiches. Warm slippers and a bum to finger in front of the fire.'

'You can't imagine,' said Gilbert darkly, drowning the sorrow in Guinness.

'It makes a man soft,' said Parker.

'I can still look after myself. Sam and me went to France after the Coronation,' Gilbert reminded him. 'We worked our way down to Africa.'

'A remarkable journey,' admitted Parker.

'Yes,' said Gilbert. 'We were in Algeria when it turned nasty so we pushed across to Morocco and down the West Coast.'

'You must have seen some sights,' nodded Parker, cigarette wagging, eyes closed against the smoke.

'The birth of nations. The end of empires,' said Gilbert, raising his glass. 'They were dangerous times. We boiled rice for beggars and the very next day they were kings.'

'You had to be careful,' said Parker, sucking his cigarette.

Gilbert nodded and dreamed. 'We sold crocodile stew on the Congo riverboats for a couple of seasons.'

'No.'

'It's true.'

'Fancy.'

'When we grew tired of the river we went into the forest and learned to brew palm wine. We might have made a fortune but we couldn't find the bottles.'

'There was always a snag in the best of schemes,' said Parker. 'Is that why you came home?'

'I don't know,' sighed Gilbert.

'It's a grand café,' suggested Parker helpfully.

'I'm comfortable,' said Gilbert. 'We work hard. I can't complain.' The Guinness had started to warm his blood. He closed his eyes. His feet floated above the floor.

'And you don't get notions to travel again?'

'I'm comfortable,' said Gilbert. He shrugged. Olive hates the idea of travel. The last time she left home was during the war. Evacuated. She must have been eight, nine years old. A frightened, skinny girl with a label tied to her coat. Sandwich in her pocket. Gas mask in a brown cardboard box. Thousands of them at Waterloo Station. Trains steaming. Sirens wailing. Crushed against the carriage windows, watching the rain sweep empty fields. When the train reached the end of the line she was offered, door to door, until someone gave her a bed. Forced to live among strangers. Fed on porridge and cocoa.

'A man needs roots,' said Parker. 'Do you remember Lucky Gordon, the baker with the business on the Edgware Road?'

'The one with the wife who went mad?'

'No, that was Harper.'

'His wife went mad and tried to cut her throat.'

'Yes, but it wasn't his wife. We found out later that he lived with his sister.'

'They slept in the same bed,' protested Gilbert. 'They had an idiot son that was born with no eyes. They wrote about it in the *Daily Sketch*.'

'Harper,' confirmed Parker. 'Lucky Gordon was a big Scotchman with tattooed hands and an old-fashioned walrus moustache.'

'I remember him. Yes. He used to suck it when he was angry.'

'That's right,' said Parker. 'Stuck his head in the oven. No family. No prospects. No roots. No one went to the funeral.'

'Sam had no roots,' said Gilbert. 'I heard he died in Ghana during the Independence celebrations of '57. But a few months later he wrote from Togo. He stayed there for a few years and then, after Sylvanus Olympio was murdered in '63 he went to Nigeria. I don't know. I lost touch. The last time I heard he was in Bilharzia. He could be dead.'

'Olympio?' said Parker, sniffing the air. 'That rings a bell. Wasn't he at the Coronation?'

'No,' growled Gilbert impatiently.

'He was a little Italian,' insisted Parker. 'Wore a wig and lifts in his shoes.'

'Olympio was the ruler of Togo after the French,' said Gilbert.

'Ah,' said Parker, losing interest. 'No, I never met him.'

'And what happened to Sam?' asked Gilbert sadly.

'That's easy,' said Parker. 'I'll give you his address.'

Gilbert banged his Guinness against the table. 'You know where to find him?'

'Yes,' said Parker.

'Where?' shouted Gilbert.

'He's here,' said Parker, slapping his pockets. 'Where? I've lost him,' he frowned. 'No, I think he's in my briefcase. I never like to lose a friend.' He pulled an address book from the biscuits, found a pencil and scribbled on a scrap of yellow paper.

'Have you heard from him? Does he write to you?' demanded Gilbert. He was too excited to read the address. Wait. Look. Something, something, Bilharzia. Yes. He was right. The old dog was still alive.

'I tried to sell him Bibles for the heathen but he wasn't interested. When was it? I can't remember. I think it was after the encyclopedias.' He drained his glass and whistled wetly through his teeth. 'This whisky tastes like Mary's own gravy. Finish your drink and we'll go across to the Hungry Fiddler.'

'I ought to get back for lunch,' wheezed Gilbert, trying to pull himself free of the chair. Crocodile stew on a bed of cassava. Boiled yams and sweet potatoes. Smoked mudfish. Dust and sunlight. The smell burning your nostrils. The heat melting the prongs on your fork.

'You can have lunch at the Hungry Fiddler,' said Parker. 'We'll order the Business Special. You'll enjoy that.' He leaned forward and blew smoke into Gilbert's ear. 'The girls who serve the food walk around with their mammies hanging out,' he whispered.

'What's the time?' frowned Gilbert. He pulled at his sleeve, searching in vain for a wristwatch.

'Mammies!' hissed Parker. He clawed at the front of his shirt and tweaked his nipples.

'While you're sitting at the table?' frowned Gilbert.

Parker nodded and grinned. 'Dangle while they serve the soup. Mammies everywhere. You need eyes in the back of your head.'

Gilbert blinked and tried to gather his thoughts. 'They walk around in the nude?'

'No, they're not nude,' scoffed Parker. 'You wouldn't want 'em stark bollock naked while you're stuffing yourself with pork and cabbage. They wear little aprons. It's very tasteful. Artistic.'

'How do you know about it?'

'It's a club,' explained Parker. 'I know all the clubs. The Pillow. The Garter. The Nunnery. There's a lot of entertaining in my game. A lot of business done in the dark. You'd be surprised.'

'Do they serve steamed pudding?'

'Bugger the pudding,' said Parker. He laughed abruptly, turned on Gilbert and playfully poked his stomach. 'I'll introduce you to Maureen. She runs it. Quiet girl. Good family. Educated. Mammies hang like a couple of fruit bats.'

'A celebration!' roared Gilbert.

'That's the spirit.'

'We'll drink until we swell like balloons,' boomed Gilbert.

'After lunch we can go down to Paddington.'

'Search out the old Coronation.'

'Puke on the carpet.'

'Piddle into the gravy boats.'

Frank was in bed with the women of *Wobble*.

He knew it was going to be a long night from the moment that Mandy had entered the room. She was wearing a black rubber playsuit. The tall blonde smiled at him with a wicked gleam in her big round pale blue eyes. Her lovely young face was flushed. Her long golden hair was loose. He saw she was naked under her playsuit. 'I've been watching you,' she said as she paused to unleash the gorgeous globes of her firm yet enormous breasts. 'And I'm going to teach you a lesson.' The sensational sensitive pert pink nipples stiffened deliciously as she cupped the luscious white orbs with her hands and began to continued on page 27.

Frank flicked the pages. The ancient magazine had grown so tattered that the staples had worn through the pages. He gathered the loose edges and carefully pulled them together.

Shandy came into the room, pulled off her school blazer and let it fall to the ground. 'You've been watching me,' she smiled with a cheeky toss of her pigtails. 'Now *you're* going to follow a lesson.' While he watched, she peeled the navy blue skirt over her long golden thighs to display the soft silky mounds of her hot plump sweet innocent young buttocks. A small gasp of pleasure escaped from his mouth as she wriggled to the bed and let his hands explore the pert pink continued on page 32.

Frank grinned and settled deeper into his pillow, the blanket drawn beneath his chin.

Sandy locked the door with the stolen key and turned around to face him. He looked dangerous. The big brunette stopped laughing and gasped in startled surprise. Her dark brown eyes were open wide. She began to tremble with excitement. 'I've been following you,' she sizzled as he roughly unbuckled the full force of the massive breasts that were bulging proudly from the red satin corset. 'And I want you to teach me a lesson.' The long delicate nut-brown nipples suddenly stiffened as he weighed the pendulous teats in his hands continued on page 35.

Frank moaned and rattled the pages.

Brandy kicked open the door and strutted proudly into the room. Her green eyes flashed with excitement. She was stripped to her peek-a-boo scanties. She smiled as he squeezed both gigantic bouncing breasts in her hands. 'You've been watching me,' she said and pulled what was left of the scanties over her full fat hot ripe pale pink thighs to reveal the glorious globes of her eager quivering…

Frank blinked, slapped shut the magazine and tried to stuff it under the sheets.

Olive opened the door and shuffled slowly into the room. She was wearing pyjamas, a dressing gown and gloves. Her eyes glittered and her nose looked raw.

'What are you reading?' she asked without interest.

'Nothing!' barked Frank.

'You'll go blind,' she sniffed. 'All that reading ruins your eyes.' She sat down at the foot of the bed and stared at him mournfully.

'What's the time?'

'I don't know.'

'Where's Gilbert? Has he come home?'

'No.'

Frank was silent for a moment. 'Would you like a hot drink?' he asked, shivering, pulling his knees beneath his chin, trying to work *Wobble* under the bedclothes.

Olive sniffed and shook her head. 'I think he's gone,' she whispered, wiping her nose with a length of lavatory paper.

'It's not the first time he's stayed out all night,' said Frank. He wondered if he should wake Veronica.

'That was years ago,' snuffled Olive. 'And that was different.'

'He came home,' insisted Frank.

'Last time he didn't have one of his blasted old cronies to take him boozing,' argued Olive.

'He'll be fine,' said Frank. 'Drunks look after their own.'

'I didn't like the look of him. You can't trust that sort. Crafty. Did you see what he did to Veronica?'

Frank shook his head. She gasped and closed her eyes as the stranger pulled her to the floor. Her small but perfect rose tipped breasts poked proudly through the gash he had torn in her shirt.

'Anything could have happened – he might have done himself a mischief,' moaned Olive.

'He's indestructible,' smiled Frank.

Olive shuddered. He's old and fat and full of beer. 'I think we should ring the hospital,' she whispered. Heart attack at his age and there's no hope when you fall down in the street because policemen laughing think you're drunk as you lie there twitching your arms and legs until the ambulance arrives too late and then they send for you to take away the clothes shoes count the money in the pockets sign here sign there go home hold out your hand while the doctor gives you something to sleep and the shock alone enough to kill you.

'Wait for another few hours – it's almost morning – he'll come home when he wants his breakfast,' said Frank.

'I don't know,' said Olive doubtfully.

'Yes,' said Frank.

'He'll come home with his head full of fancy ideas, that's the trouble. He'll want to buy a camel and become an Arab or some silly nonsense like that. I need him, Frank. And I need you.'

'I know,' whispered Frank. He reached out and took her hand. It felt small and brittle through the worn-out glove.

'He saved this café,' said Olive. 'It was a struggle in the early days.'

'I remember,' said Frank. He thought of the pitted metal counter and the gravy-coloured walls.

'No,' said Olive. 'I'm talking about the days before you were born. We lived from hand to mouth. You can't imagine.'

'You both worked hard.'

'It was Gilbert who knew the business.'

'But he couldn't have done it without you,' insisted Frank. He stared at the sleeves of her dressing gown. The cuffs were stained and badly scorched. A seam that had opened was silted with toast crumbs .

'Gilbert did everything.'

'He loves you,' said Frank.

Olive wiped the lavatory paper over her face. 'He's never satisfied,' she sniffed. 'He gets restless. He thinks he's missing something. He's always talking about life as if it were a sort of journey. It's not. He thinks it leads somewhere. It doesn't. You'd think he'd be happy to have four square meals a day and a roof over his head. There's enough misery in the world without going out to look for it.'

Frank might have wondered how Olive knew of this misery since her view of the world was no bigger than the café window but he didn't question the truth of it. She saw each cracked egg, every slice of bread gone stale, as a tragedy: overwhelming evidence of a cruel and hostile world. And Frank had learned to accept this jaundiced view as easily as he accepted Gilbert's dreams of a lost paradise. The real world lay somewhere between them: simple, solid and safe. Gilbert would be home for breakfast. Gilbert would come home for breakfast because it was impossible to imagine anything else.

'He'll come home,' he said and trod the *Wobble* women under his feet.

Fried eggs with black lace skirts skating on cracked china plates. Bitter coffee belching bubbles. Blistered bacon. Wrinkled mushrooms. Grilled tomatoes oozing seed.

'Open the ovens,' cried Olive.

'Open the windows,' bawled Frank.

The kitchen smoked and the windows flapped until the whole street was wrapped in the fragrant smoke. Gilbert came through the door as the first slices of bread jumped from the toaster.

'I can smell breakfast,' he said cheerfully.

He sat down at the kitchen table, closed his eyes and sighed. He reeked of stale beer and he needed a shave, but he didn't look too bad. There was a broken packet of biscuits wedged inside a jacket pocket.

'I went for a drink,' he said, grinning at Olive.

'We can smell it,' she snapped, scooped a breakfast from the oven and dropped it carelessly onto the table.

'It was old Parker. I haven't seen him for years. He was a waiter at the Coronation,' smiled Gilbert, turning to Frank.

'Imagine,' said Olive, slamming the oven door.

'I thought he was dead,' sighed Gilbert, wiping his fork on his sleeve.

'Life is full of surprises,' said Olive coldly.

Gilbert fell silent and chewed on bacon. He wanted to tell Frank about finding Sam Pilchard's address, about the food at the Hungry Fiddler and the girls with breasts that quivered like aspic; he wanted to tell him how they had gone, afterwards, to see a conjurer in a silk top hat who swallowed swords and breathed fire and the noise and the crowds and the wine that smelt like turpentine, he wanted to tell Frank about all the dirty alleys and hell holes, the miracles of life and the gutters full of stars; but he glanced at Olive and bit his tongue.

'Where did you leave him?' said Frank, pouring himself a mug of coffee.

'Chinatown. He had to see a man about a boat.'

'You said he was a waiter,' said Olive.

'Yes, but that was years ago,' Gilbert explained. 'These days he's a real businessman. Fingers in all sorts of pies.'

'Hands everywhere,' said Veronica. She was leaning against the door, arms folded, legs apart, her face a mask of sarcasm.

'He had a lot of interesting ideas,' Gilbert said quietly. He began to feel tired and depressed. The exhilaration he had felt at walking home through the city at daybreak, the beauty of empty streets, the buildings washed in the clean, cold light, the optimism of dawn, the energy he had gathered, leaked away. The kitchen was hot. The food turned to acid in his stomach. He wiped his face with his hands.

'What sort of ideas?' said Frank, to encourage him.

'The Hercules Hamburger Chain,' he said at last, leaning back and picking his teeth with a matchstick.

'What?' grunted Olive. She was down on her hands and knees, counting eggs at the bottom of the fridge. She turned to look up at him. Her hair was touched with frost.

'Yes,' said Gilbert. 'I've been thinking about it and we need to expand. A string of cafés to stretch across London. Pancakes and milk shakes. Free balloons. Proper uniforms. Imagine it!'

'It's all nonsense!' barked Olive. She stood up and kicked the fridge closed. She was clutching an egg in her fist.

'You've got to keep moving to change with the times,' said

Gilbert stubbornly.

'Why?'

'Because that's progress,' declared Gilbert. 'You work to make things better.'

'But things *don't* get better,' said Olive. 'They change but they don't get better.'

'Here?' frowned Gilbert, looking around.

'Anywhere,' said Olive, waving at the world.

'Five hundred years ago you died of toothache,' growled Gilbert, pulling the matchstick from his mouth. 'That's progress.'

'These days you die of the heartache. Toothache. Heartache. What's the difference? There's no end to suffering.'

'The Hercules Hamburger Chain will help people to suffer in comfort,' said Gilbert, winking at Frank. 'We'll make simple food for the common man.'

'We don't have the money,' objected Frank.

'That's easy,' said Gilbert. 'The banks are full of money.'

'And you're full of baloney,' snapped Olive. 'We'll be paupers. You'll borrow money we can't afford and we'll have to sell the furniture.'

'You have to take a few risks,' admitted Gilbert. He stretched and arched his spine. A dull pain began to clot in his neck.

'I don't want to take risks! You're always looking for trouble!' shouted Olive. The anxiety and confusion of the night erupted now in a spurt of anger. 'What's wrong with you?' she screamed. She raised her arm and threw the bomb at his head.

The egg broke above Gilbert's left eye. He cried out in surprise and twisted away. The shell slipped from his face on a snail's trail of slime and puddled his shoulder. He touched his eye with his fingertips and turned to Olive, his mouth open, the eye socket full of translucent jelly.

'The next time you go out drinking don't bother to come back,' she sobbed and fled from the kitchen.

There was silence. Gilbert hung his head and stared at his plate. A long string of egg yolk swung from his nose.

8

Despite Olive's gloom, at Christmas they felt prosperous enough to close the café for a week. Gilbert bought a tree and planted it in the dining room. Frank hung the walls with bunches of holly and looped paper lanterns from the ceiling.

On Christmas Day Gilbert cooked a special dinner. He was in the kitchen before first light, cutting swedes and scrubbing parsnips, his slippers covered in potato peel. For hours there was nothing but steam and the blue smoke of bacon but early in the afternoon the house had filled to the rafters with the smell of roast turkey.

Frank laid the table and trimmed it with enough tinsel and ribbons to decorate a wedding feast. He sported a wristwatch with a crocodile strap and felt obliged to pause at intervals to read the time or polish the glass against his sleeve. Veronica, wearing a necklace of mistletoe, helped Gilbert serve the food. Olive, wrapped in a new dressing gown and wearing a Christmas cracker crown, sat at the top of the table, surrounded by her adopted family. They ate and drank and laughed and stripped the bird to its skeleton.

'I stuffed the turkey with its own guts and giblets,' Gilbert announced proudly. He forced a spoon into the carcass and drew out a pile of soft, black worms. 'Here, Frank, they're full of nourishment,' he said as he emptied the spoon on Frank's plate.

'Veronica?' He pushed the spoon back into the turkey and gave it a twist.

'No thanks. I don't like 'em.'

'Giblets?'

'Yeah.'

Gilbert looked astonished. He stared at Veronica. He stared

at the spoon. 'Have you ever tried them?'

'I don't like the look of 'em,' said Veronica.

'You don't know what you're missing. Try everything in life at least once,' said Gilbert, flicking the worms on to his own plate. 'Except suicide and grapefruit,' he added quietly, licking the spoon.

Afterwards there was a Christmas pudding, fat as a Turk's head, shimmering in a halo of brandy flames.

'I've eaten so much I'm fit to bust,' said Olive. She belched, blushed, and began to laugh. And, because Olive laughed, Gilbert threw back his head and he began to laugh, and so Frank laughed because Gilbert laughed and next Veronica laughed so that everyone laughed and then Olive began to cry. There was no warning. One moment she was beaming and the next she was bawling. She choked and dropped her fork. Her face crumpled. The paper crown fell over her ears.

'What's wrong?' whispered Veronica, pressing a napkin into Olive's hand.

'It's the brandy,' said Gilbert. He sucked a tooth and stared ruefully at the broken pudding.

Olive wiped her face and snorted into the napkin. 'I was thinking,' she sobbed. 'This could be our last Christmas together.'

'Why?' said Frank. 'What's happening?' He looked at Gilbert for an answer but Gilbert only shook his head.

'You're a man,' wailed Olive.

'It's my age,' said Frank. He looked bewildered.

'You'll want to make your own life,' sniffed Olive. 'What can we offer you? Nothing. You'll get restless living here and then you'll move away and we'll never see you again.'

Frank was silent. He had never imagined that, one day, he would have to leave the café. The prospect startled him. He saw his life as already complete. He was set in perpetual motion between kitchen and table, the days counted in soup bowls and coffee spoons. Why should anything change?

'But I belong here,' he said quietly. 'I don't want to leave.'

There was another silence. He stared at Veronica who stared

at her plate. He watched her fingers twist the mistletoe against her throat. A berry, fat as a pearl, broke from the necklace and fell between her breasts.

'Frank, we've been thinking,' Gilbert suddenly shouted, leaning in a dish of buttered parsnips. 'We want you to have the café when we're gone.' He slapped his hands against the edge of the table and made the tinsel tremble. There. It was simple. He grinned and glanced at Olive for approval.

'Where are *you* going?' demanded Frank suspiciously.

'Nowhere, you daft bugger!' shouted Gilbert. He waved his arms hopelessly as if trying to measure the distance between heaven and hell. 'I mean when we're *dead* and gone.

'We want you to have the café,' continued Olive. 'And we'd like Veronica to stay and help to look after everything – if she wants. We've been thinking about it and that's what we'd like for you.'

'But you're no age,' protested Frank.

Olive stared at him. He's still a child despite all the talk and tall for his age with his heavy bones but I don't know I think he's started to outgrow his brains. She picked up her spoon and sighed. 'Yes,' she said. 'I'm sorry, Frank. Eat your pudding.'

'It sounds like you're expecting to drop dead tomorrow,' sulked Frank.

'Any time,' grieved Olive. 'You're young. You think you're going to live for ever. You'll learn.'

'I don't want anything to change,' insisted Frank fiercely.

'Eat your pudding,' said Veronica. They finished the dinner in silence.

It was a cold January. Snow blew down from the north and settled silently over the city. Blood froze in veins. Milk froze in bottles. The city burned its lights at noon. When the snow had drifted as deep as the windows, men were seen with leather shovels cutting trenches through the streets. Babies howled and steamed like puddings. Birds fell from trees. Old ladies, wrapped in blankets, cradled their dogs and cats for warmth. As the storms lifted the sun shone cold from a bitter sky. The snow hardened as it turned grey and perished. The gutters crunched with clinker. At the Hercules Café customers sat in overcoats scalding their mouths with peppered pea soup. Hands cracked with frost. Feet stamped and puddled the floor. It was so cold that Olive could not leave her bed. Frank wore a vest and Gilbert tried to cook in gloves until one morning, making toast, he managed to set his fingers alight. He ran around the kitchen with flames spurting from the tips of his thumbs. Frank went to the rescue and plunged the gloves in a dish of tomatoes.

Veronica worked the tables dressed in her army greatcoat and a pair of bright green high-heeled shoes. The coat, tightly buttoned from her ankles to her ears, gave her the look of a furtive stripper running from parlour to draughty parlour in a crowded Soho street. A man brave enough to break the buttons might find nothing beneath but little sequins sewn to the living skin. Frank made a similar suggestion and she hit him with a tray. She was too depressed and cold for games. Her teeth chattered. Her grey eyes set as hard as ice.

'I've had enough,' she suddenly announced one evening as they were closing the café.

'What's wrong?' said Gilbert. He was sweeping puddles on the floor. He paused for a moment and leaned on his broom.

'It's the customers,' she complained. 'They're fine when they first arrive but once they've got a pint of hot soup inside 'em they start to thaw out.' She pulled a towel from her overcoat pocket and wrapped one end around her fist.

'That's the idea,' grinned Gilbert.

'But they stink!' shouted Veronica. 'Some of 'em haven't been outside their clothes for a month.' She raised the towel and slapped the nearest chair. Crack. The chair jumped in surprise.

'Well, it's too cold for a wet flannel,' argued Gilbert.

'Wet flannel?' she shouted. 'You'd need a blow torch to get some of 'em clean. I swear they *sleep* in their clothes!' She was so furious she began to flog the chair. Crack. Crack. The chair bounced across the room and fell down with its legs in the air. Veronica kicked it.

'It's not that bad,' said Frank gently, picking up the battered chair.

'You don't have to serve 'em,' scowled Veronica, pulling off her shoe. She licked a finger and used it to wipe the scratched green leather.

'Wait until the summer,' said Gilbert.

'They're ripe *enough* for me,' muttered Veronica. She dropped the shoe and tried to spear it with her foot.

'It will be different in the summer,' said Gilbert. 'We'll attract a better class of customer. I thought we might open a fancy fish restaurant. I'll put tables outside on the pavement and big umbrellas for the shade. And we'll serve prawn cocktails in little glass buckets. And fresh sardines when we can get them. And potted shrimps and crab salads…' He gazed around the dining room and smiled. He saw office girls at summer tables, sunlight shining through their skirts. He saw windows open, lobsters curling, ice creams melting into rainbows.

'We could serve whitebait in baskets,' suggested Frank brightly.

'Yes,' said Gilbert. 'And fresh grilled trout.'

'Cockles and clams,' said Frank.

'Whelks and winkles,' said Gilbert.

'I could wear a straw hat and a long rubber apron,' dreamed Frank.

'And we'll buy Veronica a long frock with plenty of lace on the sleeves,' murmured Gilbert.

'What does Olive think of this idea?' asked Veronica suspiciously.

'I don't know,' said Gilbert. He looked surprised. 'I haven't mentioned it to Olive.'

'Why?'

'I've only just thought of it,' shrugged Gilbert. A paper lantern fell from the ceiling and hit the floor in a plume of dust.

Veronica sighed and walked away.

'Are you really going to leave?' whispered Frank, later, as he met her at the bathroom door. She smelt of toothpaste and talcum powder but she was still wearing her overcoat.

'I'm twenty-five years old, Frank. I don't want to spend the rest of my life squeezing hamburgers.'

'But where will you go?' he demanded anxiously.

'I don't know.' She pulled at her collar and looked away.

'But remember what they said at Christmas,' he whispered urgently. 'In a few years – when Gilbert wants to slow down and take it easy – we can run the place for ourselves. It could be different. We could turn it into a proper restaurant…' He stared up and down the gloomy corridor, searching the walls for a glimmer of hope.

'Look, Frank, when I was a kid I wanted to be a man. That was my ambition. It may sound crazy but it seemed like a good idea at the time. Then I started to grow. I couldn't stop growing. So I decided, if I had to be a woman, I wanted to be a beauty queen. Why fight it? I wanted to walk around in a silk sash that said First Prize and a stupid grin on my face. So I did exercises. I prayed. I bought a Mark Eden bust developer. I stopped growing. Next I wanted to be a dancer. I broke a leg. I wanted to be a hairdresser. I broke out in rashes. After that I just wanted to be married with a lot of little noses to wipe. Nobody ever made me an offer.'

'What are you trying to tell me?' whispered Frank, frowning and rubbing his ear.

'I'm trying to tell you that I never wanted to be a waitress. I wanted to be a lot of things but I never wanted to be a waitress. Nobody *wants* to be a waitress.'

'But things could be different,' he said desperately. He didn't understand. He had never wanted anything but the Hercules Café. Life was food and smoke and steam. He shuffled in his slippers and glared at the floor.

'You're beginning to sound like Gilbert,' hissed Veronica and swept past him to the safety of her room.

That night Frank lay awake in his bed and stared through the window at the flying, grey snow. His world, the café, that had once seemed so strong and buoyant, now felt shallow and dangerously small. What would happen when Olive and Gilbert were gone? How would he manage without Veronica?

He could take to the road as Gilbert had done so many years ago, pockets full of biscuits and a frying pan strapped to his back. But Gilbert had walked with a man called Sam Pilchard. The man who drank bleach and swallowed raw kidneys. The man with a razor concealed in his boot. How could he hope to manage alone? Run away with Veronica. She wouldn't want him. Old enough to be his mother. Nobody *wants* to be a waitress. One day she'll pick up her satchel and vanish. No. Impossible. Nothing must change.

At six o'clock he dressed and stumbled downstairs to warm the kitchen for Gilbert. The air was so cold it hurt his teeth. His breath feathered against his face like a damp and milky ectoplasm. He shivered and kicked at the kitchen door. When he switched on the light he found Olive. She was slumped against the great blue stove. She wore her Christmas dressing gown. The cord was twisted on the floor. Her head was floating in a pan of meat soup.

9

It was the end of the Hercules Café Gilbert drew the curtains and Veronica cancelled the milk. The doctor and later the hospital said that Olive had collapsed and drowned in the soup. But why she had struggled from her bed to meet death in an empty kitchen at five o'clock in the morning would always remain a mystery. She had slipped away in a dream, tiptoed past Gilbert helpless and snoring, along the dark corridor and down the stairs to an early grave.

Frank was sick with shock. He tried to hide himself away and refused any offers of comfort. He had stared death in the face and nothing could ever be the same again. In taking Olive, death had found *him* and entered his name on the waiting list.

Gilbert was lost. He carried his grief about the house, endlessly walking from room to room as if Olive might be found again.

Veronica was silent. She cooked meals that no one touched, blew her nose into paper towels and spent long hours scrubbing the kitchen floor with buckets of hot disinfectant.

Olive was calm. The hospital pulled out her stomach, rinsed it, dropped it into a dish and passed it among twenty young medical students. Three of them fainted. The others were sent home to write about it. At the end of the day she was quickly repacked and sent, on Gilbert's instructions, to the funeral parlour of Freddie Farouk. He had found the name in the Yellow Pages. Freddie Farouk your Friend in Grief. A Gift of Flowers in our Chapel of Rest.

The day of the funeral the snow melted and all the drains were singing. Frank and Veronica helped Gilbert into a borrowed black suit and led him into the sunlight. Horace the barber closed his shop. The street turned out to watch the procession. At eleven o'clock in the morning, after three verses of 'All Things Bright and Beautiful' and a quickly mumbled prayer, Olive, locked in a plywood box, was sunk to rest in the London clay.

Gilbert took to his bed. The room dark. The sheets pulled over his head. So lonely to be left alone. Olive gone. Stubborn to her last bad breath. Ten. Twenty. Thirty. Forty. Stick out your thumb and that makes fifty. A lifetime counted on your fingers. It's nothing. No time. She was too slow. The world spins so fast. God! It's cold. The silence. Terrible. What's left? There's Frank. What will happen to Frank? He's young. He'll forget. Learn to live without. Funny. All those years I dreamed of leaving. Tomorrow. When I wake up there's nothing to stop me. What? Nothing to stop me. What? Nothing to stop.

The snow retreated and the rain arrived. A curtain of cold Atlantic rain that danced and crackled in the narrow street. It hammered loose the slates on the roof, bent the gutters and washed into chimneys, clipping clots of wet soot that fell, smacking to the grates beneath. It rained for three days and nights and Gilbert never stirred from his bed.

'When are you leaving?' asked Frank on the morning of the fourth day as he pushed through the chairs in the empty dining room.

'Why?' said Veronica. She was slouched at a table, dressed in her long army greatcoat, watching a mug of coffee steam.

Frank shrugged. 'I thought you'd be anxious to get away now that the café is closed.' He kicked out a chair and sat down at a separate table.

'Don't be silly. I can't go now. You'll need me around for a while,' she sighed and contrived to look disappointed.

Frank stared at the window. Overnight, someone passing in the street had sprayed: ЯƎSSOT A SI YƆƆiS on the glass in aerosol paint. The words wept long, thin tears. 'Do you think we'll open again?' he asked quietly.

'Ask Gilbert,' said Veronica. She jerked her head towards the ceiling.

Frank frowned and pressed his fingertips along the table edge. 'I don't know what to say – I don't want to disturb him.'

'He'll understand – he's your father,' said Veronica. She raised the mug to her face and closed her eyes against the steam.

'No, I don't think he's my father,' said Frank.

Veronica opened her eyes. 'And Olive?'

'I don't think she was my mother,' Frank confessed.

'You mean they actually found you under a table?'

'Yes,' said Frank. He looked surprised. 'I told you.' He pointed a finger. 'That one.'

Veronica whistled. She tilted the mug against her mouth and began a little pecking motion, sip, swallow, sip, swallow, while she stared at Frank. 'So where are your parents?'

'I don't know,' grunted Frank.

Veronica looked exasperated. 'Don't you care? Don't you want to know where you came from and what happened and why they couldn't keep you and where they are now and if they still think about you sometimes and if they want to see you again and everything?'

'No,' said Frank.

'That's horrible, Frank. Absolutely horrible.'

'Why?'

Veronica glared at him. 'I don't know,' she muttered.

'What about your family?' demanded Frank.

'That's different, I hate mine. I never want to see 'em again. But at least I know where they live and what's happening to 'em.'

'This is my family,' Frank said doubtfully, waving his arm at the empty room.

'Are you going to ask him?'

'Tomorrow.'

'He's been sitting in bed with a blanket over his head for nearly a week. We've got to talk to him, Frank. We can't live on fresh air.'

'Has he eaten anything?'

'I cut him sandwiches every morning and put them outside the door. He writes notes and leaves them on the empty plates. Yesterday he wanted a pineapple.'

'Do we have any pineapples?'

'We don't have anything.'

'He'll come down when he's ready. It takes time.'

'I'm sorry. But if you can't talk to him I'll have to do it for you.'

'Tomorrow, said Frank wearily.

But the next day Gilbert was back in the kitchen, flames in his frying pan, hands glazed and dripping with fat.

'What's cooking?' sniffed Frank as he came through the door.

'Liver and bacon,' said Gilbert cheerfully. 'Want some?'

'No,' said Frank.

'The bacon's bad but there's plenty of liver,' said Gilbert.

'I'll have some toast,' said Frank. He yawned and scratched his head.

'There's no butter,' said Gilbert. He emptied the frying pan on to a plate and sat down at the table. When Veronica arrived he waved his fork and smiled.

'Are we going to open today?' she asked hopefully, glancing at Frank.

'Liver and bacon,' said Gilbert.

Veronica stared at his plate. The bacon glowed with a queer phosphorescence. The liver resembled a knob of charred wood. Gilbert stabbed it with his fork and made the wood bleed. 'No thanks,' she said. 'I'll just have coffee.'

'There's no milk,' warned Gilbert.

'You told me to cancel it,' said Veronica.

'That's right,' said Gilbert.

'Have some orange juice,' said Frank, peering into the fridge.

'Why?'

'There's a gallon of the stuff in here.' He poured some into a mug and offered it to Veronica who drank, frowned and wrinkled her nose.

'I've been thinking,' said Gilbert. 'We can't stay here for the rest of our lives, like toads under some damn stone. We're getting out while there's still time. There are places out there you can't imagine. There are places out there you can't even pronounce. Wonderful places. Wild places. You're too young to hide yourselves away. And I'm too old.'

'What's wrong with it here?' said Frank.

'It's not healthy now Olive is gone. If you stay you'll end up with your head in a saucepan. Is that what you want to happen? Do you want to spend the rest of your life trailing up and down here, up and down, day after day, with Olive's old apron tied round your neck?'

Frank found that, under the circumstances, he couldn't confess to such aspirations but, yes, he would be happy to spend his life in the warm fog of this kitchen with Gilbert shouting, Veronica swearing and the world demanding nothing from them but hamburgers and doughnuts.

'No,' said Gilbert. 'It's finished. We should be out in the world.' He folded a slice of bread in his fingers and used it to wipe his plate clean.

'It's raining,' said Veronica.

'We'll get wet,' said Gilbert. 'I'm selling the Hercules Café.' He pushed the bread into his mouth and sucked his thumb.

'How are we going to eat?' demanded Frank.

'Do you remember Sam Pilchard?'

Frank nodded. He had known Sam Pilchard as long as he could remember. He had grown up with Sam Pilchard stories. The name had become as familiar to him as Ali Baba and Rumpelstiltskin. 'The man who ate dogs,' he said. 'You worked with him in Africa.'

'That's right,' said Gilbert. He paused to belch and wipe his chin. 'Well, I found his address and wrote to him. He's still out there. He runs an hotel in Bilharzia. It's a big place, fifty bedrooms, fancy restaurant, night clubs, you wouldn't believe it. He says it needs a few repairs but that's nothing. The climate does horrible things to the timber. It's the heat. Anyway, he wants me to join him. He wants all of us to join him.'

'How long have you known?' asked Veronica.

'Some time,' said Gilbert. 'I didn't tell Olive because she hated abroad. Now... we could sell everything and go tomorrow.'

'What sort of hotel?' asked Frank.

'Here,' said Gilbert. 'He sent me a picture of the place. It's not very good but it gives you an idea.'

He pulled an envelope from his trouser pocket, flicked it open and pulled out a dog-eared photograph. He glanced at it lovingly for a moment and then placed it on the table.

Veronica stared. She saw a length of breeze-block wall cut by a tiny Moorish window. Crates and bottles and canvas sacks had been piled against the wall. Above the wall ran a stripe of blue sky. 'It looks like a cattle shed,' she concluded scornfully. 'It looks like a cattle shed with fancy windows.'

'That's the local architecture,' explained Gilbert patiently.

Veronica bent closer to the table. 'There's a nig-nog,' she said with renewed interest.

'Where?' said Gilbert.

'There.'

'That's not a nig-nog,' said Gilbert. 'That's Sam.'

Frank picked up the photograph and held it to the light, as if he suspected a counterfeit bank note. The nursery rhyme giant, the man who ate dogs and beetles and babies, the man who could shrug off flames and shave with broken glass, looked improbably shrivelled and old.

'And he wants us to go out there and work for him?' said Veronica.

'Yes,' said Gilbert.

'What sort of food do they serve?' asked Frank.

Gilbert grinned. 'Lobsters,' he said, licking his lips. 'And tiny shrimps the size of eyebrows. Swordfish. Fat fish the colour of rainbows. Yams. Peppers. Sweet potatoes. Egg-plants. Greens. Giant tomatoes. And the fruit! Pineapples. Bananas. Mangoes. Pawpaws. Coconuts. Pomegranates. Everything grows. You'll be amazed.'

Veronica snorted. 'When was the last time you saw this character?' she demanded.

Gilbert gave her a brief account of his days at the Coronation Hotel, the march across Morocco and life aboard the Congo riverboats. But he saw that Veronica wasn't impressed.

'It's probably changed,' she objected. 'You'll feel like a stranger.

'Everything changes,' said Gilbert. 'But we can learn. We can start again.'

Frank remembered Olive. Yes. Everything changes but everything remains the same. There's no end to the suffering. 'They're starving in Africa,' he said.

'That's true,' said Gilbert. 'But they're also living from the fat of the land. It's big, Africa. North to south it's as far as London is from Bombay. You could drop the entire United States of America into the Sahara Desert and make it disappear. They're not all starving or fighting or running around in stove-pipe hats with bones through their noses.'

'I don't know,' said Veronica. 'There's a famine in Ethiopia, I saw it on television. They're trying to raise money to send 'em food.'

'That's because they grow sand in Ethiopia,' said Gilbert.

'It's drought,' said Frank.

Gilbert shrugged. 'They cut down the trees, suck all the goodness from the land and let the soil blow away like dust. They're growing sand. It's their biggest crop.'

'How can you talk like that when millions of 'em are starving to death?' said Veronica.

'It's the truth,' said Gilbert mildly. 'They're digging themselves a graveyard. It was happening thirty years ago. You can't stop 'em.'

'I'm not going,' Veronica snapped.

'I'm not *taking* you into the desert,' insisted Gilbert. 'We're going to the forest.'

'What happens if something goes wrong?' said Frank.

'What?'

'Well, if we don't like it,' squirmed Frank.

'We'll come home again.'

'But you're going to sell it,' said Veronica.

'We'll make another home. It's not the end of the world. It's the chance of a lifetime.'

'He's mad!' said Veronica, turning to Frank.

'It's an idea,' said Frank.

'A mad idea,' snapped Veronica.

While Frank and Veronica argued Gilbert wrote himself a shopping list, milk, bread, bacon, butter, wrapped his head in the *News of the World* and went off into the rain towards the Greek grocer.

'I can't believe it,' said Veronica, shaking her head. 'I can't believe it's happening. He's gone crazy.'

Frank stood and stared at the rain through the dining room window. Someone had sprayed ЯƎƧƧOT A ƧI YƆƆIƧ on the glass in soft black paint. 'I'd like to see Africa,' he said wistfully.

'It's not that easy, Frank. You can't just wander through the world with a grin on your face and a slice of cake in your pocket. Everywhere you go you need passports and permits and permission just to blow your nose.'

'Don't worry, Gilbert will find a way.'

'He'll find a way to get thrown into prison,' said Veronica pessimistically. 'And if we don't starve to death or die of some revolting disease, you'll be murdered and I'll be raped in my shoes.'

'You don't want to go,' said Frank.

'Brilliant!' screamed Veronica.

All day they talked and argued as the light failed around them. Towards evening the rain feathered into snow. Gilbert, growing tired and finding Olive in every shadow, returned to the safety of his blanket lair. Veronica warmed a little sweet milk with brandy, for the comfort of it, went to her room and locked the door. Silence pressed down on the old café. Frank paced the kitchen for a long time and then, reluctantly, took to his bed. In the frosty darkness he lay awake listening to the cries and whispers of a tropical night. Between his ears the apes barked, panthers coughed, frogs warbled and fireflies throbbed.

He tried to picture himself standing in the local market at dawn, picking through a pyramid of chrome-yellow fruit, while all around the babble of black faces, the screech of caged parrots, the smell of perfumes, spices and smoke, swirled about him like a magic cloak. He fancied standing at dusk on the hotel veranda, Gilbert and Veronica beside him, watching the sun sink into the mountains as great cats called in the distant forest. Everything pleased and excited him. He was excited by the thought of buying a suitcase, owning a passport and taking flight. He was excited at the prospect of encountering all the fabled creatures of Gilbert's bestiary. And he was excited because he knew suddenly that he had always been going to Africa with Gilbert and, despite his greatest endeavours to save it, life with Olive at the Hercules Café was finished and now he must leave the past behind him. He could not tell if he was running for his life or merely running to escape his death. But he knew he would follow Gilbert.

He was nearly asleep when he heard the floorboards start to creak, first one and then another, along the length of the corridor. He sat up in bed and fumbled for the light. But before his hand had found the switch he felt a sudden, chilling draught as the door swung open in the dark.

'Who is it?' he whispered from under the bedclothes.

'I'm freezing,' growled Veronica. 'There's no heat in my room.'

Frank uncovered his head and spoke to the phantom. 'Do you want me to fix it for you?'

'No, it can wait until tomorrow,' she whispered, creeping to the edge of the bed.

'Have you thought about Africa?' he said.

'You know what I think,' she said, pulling at the blanket.

'That's no answer,' he insisted.

Veronica said nothing but climbed into bed beside him. She brushed his face with her perfumed pyjamas, wriggled down and curled herself into a knot. 'If you're stupid enough to follow Gilbert I suppose I'll have to go and look after you,' she whispered. 'Anyone *that* stupid shouldn't be left alone.'

'You're cold,' grinned Frank.

'Shut up and go to sleep.'

The next day Gilbert knocked a table apart and painted FOR SALE on the worn wooden boards. He hammered the sign above the door. The following week the business was sold. To everyone's amazement the Hercules Café was a very desirable property. The man who bought the café was a pale youth in a green polyester suit. He had orders to turn the place into a Chunky Chicken Counter. There was a little plastic chicken pinned to the pocket of his polyester jacket. 'There's big money in Chunky Chickens,' he told Gilbert as they signed the forms. 'Believe me, in twelve months you're going to find Chunky Chickens all over the country. Everybody loves them and I'm not surprised. We spent five years at Consolidated Chemicals perfecting the colour and flavour.' He had the face of a very young hamster. His eyes twitched and he had a way of squashing his nose with his thumb whenever he grew excited. He was excited by the thought of Chunky Chickens. 'Every morsel melts in the mouth. Every bite is beautiful. It's a shame you're selling out.' Gilbert didn't argue with him. He shuffled through the papers and signed his name. He could hardly believe his good fortune.

The passports turned out to be more of a problem. Frank had never needed a passport. Veronica claimed she had once owned a passport but thought it might have been stolen. Gilbert's passport was hopelessly out of date. They sat for photographs in a booth at Woolworth and scribbled out their applications. Frank was given his birth certificate wrapped in a sheet of greaseproof paper. Gilbert sent Veronica to fetch it from the bottom of Olive's underwear drawer. When it arrived it smelt of lavender. Frank didn't want to look at it. He folded it into his application and licked down the envelope.

While they waited for their passports they made carpets from maps and spent the evenings on their hands and knees, searching the corners of Africa.

'Where's Sam?' called Frank, one foot in Lagos and the other planted on the shores of Lake Chad. He stared across the borders of Cameroon into the heart of Bilharzia.

'South, south-east, in a town called Plenti,' said Gilbert, sweeping up through Zaire. 'It's somewhere near the Congo border.'

'But there's nothing there,' protested Frank, approaching

from the Atlantic and cutting through Equatorial Guinea. 'Everything is green. It's nothing but forest.' He met Gilbert in the capital, Batuta, and together they stared at a yard or more of blank green paper.

'There are cannibals in those forests,' Gilbert said softly. 'And dwarf elephants and deserted cities and temples without gods and rivers with no names.'

'Plenty of nothing,' said Veronica from her castle in Gabon.

'There are roads,' argued Gilbert.

'Three of them,' said Veronica, picking out the tiny, yellow wriggles.

'Where there are roads there are towns,' said Gilbert.

'I don't see any towns,' admitted Frank.

'We need a proper map,' said Gilbert. 'A bigger map with everything marked.' He was already crawling into Angola, his nose pressed against the paper as if he could smell the jungle.

'We need proper work permits,' said Veronica, interrupting his reverie.

Gilbert smiled. He had everything planned to the smallest detail. Nothing had been forgotten. 'Sam will fix the work permits,' he said. 'And as soon as we get the passports I can apply for the visas. You worry about the shots.'

'What shots?' said Frank.

'Oh, cholera, typhoid, yellow fever,' said Gilbert. 'Whatever you fancy.'

Veronica looked pale. She crawled across Gabon and settled herself in mid-Atlantic. 'What happens if we don't have shots?' she asked quietly.

'You die,' said Frank.

'I'll take the chance,' Veronica said quickly and then, remembering Olive, felt ashamed and bit her tongue.

'You don't get into Africa,' corrected Gilbert. 'You need the paperwork for your passport.'

'I thought you said you knew about passports,' said Frank.

'I don't remember having shots,' scowled Veronica and clutched her arms.

'We can't do without them,' said Gilbert gently. 'But we'll go together and it won't seem as bad.'

So Frank made the arrangements and the following week paid a doctor to fill their arms with dilute diseases. Veronica dragged herself around the house until finally cholera put her to bed. Frank fell victim to yellow fever. Gilbert was the last to surrender; he snorted and steamed like a wounded buffalo, quivering with indignation, until typhoid brought him to his knees. While they nursed each other and cursed the needle another letter arrived from Sam.

Dear Gilbert,

So your coming out!! Bring Bovril! Weather good. Temperature eighty plus. Short rains next month. Tell Hank and Veronica that their all ready the talk of the town and Boris plans a special supper. River soup and jungle pudding. (ha ha) Remember the old days?'

'Who's Hank?' demanded Frank.
'He means you!' crowed Veronica in delight.
'Who's Boris?' asked Frank.
'I don't know,' said Gilbert, scratching his head.

'You ask how will you get here? Listen. Trust me. When you book your flight to Batuta buy an onward ticket for Malabo (eg). They like to know your leaving as soon as you arrive so a cheap ticket to nowhere (eg) saves a lot of difficult questions. Etc. Then they forget. Good hotels in Batuta. Stay the night…'

'eg?' interrupted Veronica. 'eg what?'
'Equatorial Guinea,' explained Gilbert.
'But we want to stay in Bilharzia,' said Frank innocently.
'We're going to stay in Bilharzia, you daft bugger. The Malabo tickets are just to make 'em think we're not planning to stay for ever.'
'So they'll treat us like regular tourists,' said Veronica.
'Exactly,' said Gilbert, pleased that she had grasped it.
'Because we don't have any work permits,' continued Veronica sourly.
Gilbert sighed and wiped his face with the palm of his hand. His arm felt stiff and the puncture marks burned. 'Sam said he'd

make the arrangements. We can sort it out when we get there,'
he said impatiently.

'I'm not going anywhere without a work permit,' grumbled
Veronica.

*An express train for Bolozo Noire leaves Batuta every day at noon and
costs about CFA 3300. Boris says it takes 10 hours. At Bolozo Noire
find a driver you can trust (bargain the price or they rob you blind) and
he'll take you on good roads to Bolozo Rouge and as far as Koto and
Nkongfanto. Their you'll stay at a place called Grand Safari Lodge. It's
clean and comfortable. I'll send someone to meet you. So everything is
ready. Boris says will Hank help in the kitchen. I tell him wait until
Gilbert helps in the kitchen. Then he'll learn something. (ha ha) Yours
as ever. Don't forget the Bovril.*
Sam.

As soon as he found the strength, Gilbert went out and
bought three suitcases, large, medium and small. He gave the
largest to Frank because he was the youngest, and told him to
pack up his life. He gave the second to Veronica and kept the
smallest for himself.

Frank tried to pack everything. But the suitcase bulged and
sprang its locks. After hours of pushing and squeezing he was
forced to abandon most of his books, the puppet with no head,
the robot with the rusty clockwork, Basil the tap-dancing bear
and a picture of Wendy from *Wobble,* a fat girl in a black wig
who, in the interests of art, had managed to pull a large measure
of her left breast into her own mouth where she sucked on it
contentedly. Frank concluded that Basil was too old for travel
and Wendy wasn't dressed for it. The suitcase closed with a
snap.

Veronica, who had arrived at the Hercules Café with all she
possessed in a canvas satchel, filled her suitcase with an inch to
spare. Since the funeral she had hung up her uniform in favour
of cheap printed frocks, loose squares of cotton with holes cut
out for the arms and head. Her favourite resembled a white flag
decorated with raspberries. She wore these frocks with a small
elasticated belt that sported some sort of fancy buckle, although

Frank never caught much more than a glimpse beneath her army overcoat. She continued to stagger and strut in a variety of high-heeled shoes but wore them now with knitted socks to help against the cold. She packed everything in tissue paper and wrote her name on the suitcase.

Gilbert was reluctant to pack anything but jars of precious Bovril. He claimed there was nothing he wanted to save and grumbled when they bullied him.

'The past chains you down, drags at your ankles. It's different for someone like Frank. He's young. But when you reach my age there's so much behind you and it gets so heavy you find you can't move your feet. I don't want it,' he barked. 'I can't afford it. 'But finally they persuaded him to pack a few clothes, his shaving tackle and toothbrush.

When the task was complete Veronica was sent into the snow with Olive's few possessions and told to come back without them. They amounted to nothing more than a box of old rags, the new dressing gown with the soup-stained collar, shoes, a few postcards, an empty autograph book and a bag of knitting she hadn't finished. Veronica went out in the morning and returned at dusk with a bunch of early daffodils which they placed in a jug beside Olive's bed.

PART TWO

And Away

10

'hat's happening?' whispered Veronica. She was strapped into an armchair with her satchel clutched between her knees. It was not yet dawn. A wind howling over the city. The black sky churned with ice and rain. The lights flickered. The floor rumbled beneath the armchair. Veronica grabbed Gilbert's arm.

'Don't worry,' said Gilbert. 'Try a treacle toffee.' He rummaged through his pockets until he found a bag of melted toffee lumps. He tried to separate the lumps but found the toffee was glued to his hands.

'Can you see anything?' asked Veronica anxiously, turning to Frank.

Frank pressed his nose against the window and saw the ghost of his face staring back at him. 'No,' he said. 'It's raining.'

'Is that bad?'

'I don't know.'

The engines roared until the rivets rattled. Veronica moaned and closed her eyes. The armchairs gave a shudder, the aircraft lurched and catapulted into the sky.

'Jesus,' said Frank.

'Christ!' said Veronica.

Gilbert sucked his fingers and smiled. They were free.

Breakfast in Paris. Sunset over Africa. Why had he waited? All those precious, wasted years. God bless Sam Pilchard. Clear the tables. Here we come!

The aircraft thundered into the clouds. There was a grinding noise as the landing gear retracted and locked into the fuselage. The satchel fell through Veronica's knees.

'Can you see anything now?' she inquired miserably, turning her face into Frank's shoulder and trying to hide her eyes.

'It's getting light,' he reported with his face squashed against the window. His reflection faded. The darkness was blowing away like smoke. The world tilted. The engines went quiet. The aircraft filled with sunlight.

'Take off your coat,' said Gilbert. 'Make yourself comfortable.' He stretched his legs and yawned.

'I think I'll wait,' said Veronica gingerly. She wasn't convinced they would stay aloft. She stared at the cabin ceiling, concentrating, helping it hang in thin air. When she closed her eyes, relaxed for a moment, she saw the aircraft falling, bodies burning, wax dripping from melted wings.

'You look terrible,' said Frank, staring at her for the first time.

'Thanks.'

'What's wrong?'

'Nothing,' she muttered. 'I always look like this when I'm pulled from a warm bed in the middle of the night, driven out to nowhere and shot from a cannon.'

'Curl up and try to sleep,' said Gilbert, squeezing her hand. 'When you wake up we'll be in Paris.'

Veronica nodded, crouched down in her seat and closed her eyes. Wreckage scattered over the city. Engines, wheels and blazing armchairs. Suitcase bombs exploding on houses. The sky raining corpses. Men and women falling in flames. False teeth. Wallets. Wedding rings. Shoes found with feet inside them.

'I'm hungry,' said Frank.

'They'll feed us on the next flight,' promised Gilbert, picking toffee from his fingernails.

Frank returned to the window. They had left the café under cover of darkness, locked the doors and thrown away the key. And now, for the first time in his life, sitting above the clouds, the sun on his face and the sound of thunder in his ears, he found he had lost tomorrow. The thought of the future defeated him. He began poking at the seat pocket in front of him, pulled out a copy of the flight magazine and thumbed the pages. He found the safety instructions and spent several minutes on the use of oxygen masks. He counted the doors and felt for his life jacket with his feet.

'These seats are a bit of a squash,' muttered Gilbert, rubbing his knees. 'It's not like the old days. Imperial Airways. There was room to move around in a flying-boat. They had promenade decks and proper old-fashioned picnic hampers and waiters to serve the coffee.'

Frank smiled. He peered under his elbow and found an ashtray, flicked it open and shut, open and shut, absurdly pleased with the discovery.

'I'm hot,' complained Veronica, wiping her face.

Frank stared at the ceiling, reached up and wrenched a plastic nozzle. He was rewarded by a thin draught that ruffled his hair.

Veronica groaned and rolled her eyes.

'Do you feel sick?' asked Gilbert, frowning, holding her face in his hands.

Veronica nodded.

Frank turned to his magazine.

Toilet areas. Toilets are located on each aircraft as follows:
Concorde: One at the front, three in the middle of the aircraft.
747: One on the upper deck, two at the back of the first class cabin, four in the middle of the aircraft and six at the back.
737 *and Trident:* One at the front of the aircraft, two at the back.
Super One-eleven: Two at the back.
757: Two at the front, two between the centre and rear cabins.
748: One at the back.
Please be patient if there is a queue...

'I'm going to die,' groaned Veronica and belched mournfully.

'Wait for another few minutes,' urged Gilbert as the aircraft roared and dropped through the clouds.

Charles de Gaulle airport was wrapped in a fog of fine rain.

They helped Veronica into transit and tried to revive her with strong, black coffee.

'OK?' said Frank.

'Fine,' said Veronica, searching her satchel. 'It's nothing. I felt queer but I think it's gone.' She pulled a lipstick from the satchel, grinned morosely at a little mirror and spent a long time painting her mouth.

'I thought you were going to faint,' said Frank. 'You looked dreadful. What was it? Why were you so frightened? Nothing went wrong.'

'I wasn't frightened,' growled Veronica. 'I felt sick.'

'There was no reason to be frightened. It's safer than crossing the street. I'm not frightened. I loved it,' prattled Frank. He pulled his passport from a pocket and admired it in silence for a few moments. 'Anyway, there's nothing you can do about it. I mean, if there's a crash you won't know anything. It's all over in a few seconds. So it's silly to sit there and worry…'

'Leave her alone, Frank,' said Gilbert gently.

'I was just trying to help.'

Gilbert sat smiling in his Sunday-best suit, hair oiled and shoes polished, holding his belly like a prize pumpkin. 'We'll feel better after lunch and a couple of drinks,' he promised.

'I wasn't frightened,' insisted Veronica as she took his arm.

'I know,' said Gilbert.

'I'm ready for anything,' she muttered, scowling at Frank. But an hour later, strapped in the tail of an Air Afrique 747 bound for Batuta, she started to shake and burst into tears.

'Quick!' said Gilbert. 'She's gone again.' He pulled a flask from his jacket and while Frank struggled to hold Veronica's head, gave her a large dose of brandy.

'Don't worry. We'll look after you,' whispered Frank, wiping her chin with his hand.

Veronica sobbed, closed her eyes and prayed until she fell asleep.

The aircraft creaked and swayed, its belly dragged upon the peaks of tremendous clouds. A seat-belt sign began to flicker. The smell of hot food drifted from the galley kitchens.

'Where are we?' said Frank.

Gilbert tugged on a sleeve and squinted at his watch. 'Spain,' he said. 'Or it might be Morocco.'

'You went to Morocco,' said Frank.

'That's right,' said Gilbert. 'Sam found us work in Casablanca.'

'What's it like?' asked Frank. He pressed his face against the window and peered down at the mountains of cloud.

'It's not like Africa. We're the wrong side of the Sahara.'

'Will we see the desert?' asked Frank hopefully.

Gilbert smiled and stretched his feet. 'Wait until you see the forest. You'll be amazed. You wake up in the morning and it's like the beginning of the world. You can't hear anything but the echo of monkeys calling to each other through the mist. When you step outside it already feels warm and the earth smells sweet as Christmas pudding. And just for a moment, as the sun comes up through the trees, you feel like you're the only person in the world. I can't explain. But Sam knows what I'm talking about. He'll show you.'

'I'm hungry,' said Frank.

Lunch was delivered by a plump girl with a square head and a smile stitched to her face. She pulled three trays from a metal trolley, thrust them forward and hurried away. Frank and Gilbert unhooked the little shelves that served as tables and carefully arranged the food. They tried to shake Veronica awake but she refused to open her eyes.

'It smells good,' said Gilbert, exploring the nest of plastic cups and bowls. There was a cup containing a thick and doubtful fruit juice. A second cup held a water biscuit sealed in a cellophane envelope. Between the cups a small dish held a pale bread roll and, wrapped in foil, a yellow lump of glue called cheese. The largest dish contained a slice of soft, white meat and a stew of unknown vegetables, decorated by creamed potato, machine moulded into a flower. Finally there was a plastic carton containing a sweet, yellow sludge stamped with a sugar button and sprinkled with desiccated coconut. The sludge tasted slightly of butterscotch.

The cutlery was wrapped in a paper napkin which, when it unrolled, revealed a curious number of spoons. Gilbert chose a fork, a small knife without teeth and deliberately set to work.

For a time the aircraft became a long canteen, filled with the clickety clack of tethered prisoners striking their trays with plastic spoons. Across the aisle an old woman wearing fake hair and a jacket made from squirrel skins was making a lot of noise with her butterscotch. Beside her a little man, soft and pink as a baby, was tugging at the wrapper on his ration of cheese. The woman turned and looked at Frank. She gave him a long and hungry smile.

'You'll feel better if you eat something,' said Frank as Veronica's face emerged from the collar of her .coat.

'What is it?' she grunted.

'I don't know. I think it's chicken,' said Frank.

'Is it?' said Gilbert, looking surprised. 'I thought it was veal.'

'I'm not hungry,' groaned Veronica.

'No, it doesn't taste like veal,' said Frank, poking his bowl.

'It doesn't taste like chicken,' said Gilbert.

'Is it turkey?' said Frank.

'It doesn't smell like turkey,' said Gilbert.

'We could ask someone,' suggested Frank.

'They won't know,' growled Gilbert. 'They'd tell you anything just to keep you quiet.'

'I don't believe this is happening!' shouted Veronica. 'I'm strapped to a chair five miles high in some damn fireball the size of a supermarket flying to God-knows-where and *you* want me to eat God-knows-what with a plastic spoon!' She snatched at her paper napkin and threw the cutlery over the floor. Gilbert produced his opium flask and plugged her mouth. She sucked greedily. Open your mouth. Close your eyes. Cover your ears to stop the noise. Engines screaming. Flames eating along the wings. Fire. Smoke. The cabin filled with poisonous fumes. Hair scorched. Skin glowing. Spoons melting in clenched teeth.

When the meal was finished people began to yawn and scratch and fall asleep. The old woman with the fake hair snored into her squirrel skins. Her companion picked half-heartedly at the cellophane on his wafer biscuit. Frank sat quiet with his arms wrapped protectively around the bundle of over-coat in which Veronica had made her bed.

Gilbert sat and sucked his teeth. He thought of Sam at work in the kitchen making plans for their first supper. Apricot tart or fruit dumplings. He was always a devil for hot puddings. Women loved him for it. The smell of him seemed to make them hungry. Animals. Cannibals. All over the world. Feasting. Strong women soaked in rum, stuffed with raisins, glazed with treacle. Soft women rolled in butter, filled with chocolate, burning with brandy. Feast or famine in those days. Did he ever take a wife? Not likely. He would have mentioned it in his letters. Remember to ask him.

The aircraft hissed through the freezing sunlight. Frost sparkled on the edge of the wings. The air conditioning whistled.

'What's the time?' asked Gilbert.

'Three twenty,' said Frank.

'Good.'

'When do we land?' said Frank.

'Four fifteen,' said Gilbert.

'It feels like we've been flying for ever.'

'Can you see anything?' asked Gilbert.

'No,' said Frank, peering through the little window.

Gilbert grunted and settled down to sleep with his head on a polythene pillow.

Frank looked over the rows of narrow seats, set straight as cemetery headstones. Occasionally a hand or the top of a skull would rise above a seat for a moment before sinking back into its grave. He yawned and rubbed his face. He felt tired and uncomfortable. Last night he had fallen asleep in a bed in the corner of a room in a house in a street in a city already a thousand miles away and tonight, by some miracle of navigation, he would fall asleep in another bed in the corner of another room in a hotel on a street in a city he had never seen. And how such things were made possible, why they were thought necessary and why no one else seemed surprised by them, exhausted him and hurt his head.

While they sat in the great machine pretending to eat and sleep as if nothing unusual were happening the whole world was changing around them. Spinning. Spinning. Riches to rags. Princes to pumpkins. The coins in his pockets were now worthless tokens. The keys he carried were just souvenirs. Tonight he would open his mouth and speak in a foreign language. Tomorrow he would be a stranger.

A fat child ran shouting down the length of the aisle pursued by its angry mother. Veronica cringed at the sound of their feet. It starts with a shout and a scuffle. Mad soldiers disguised as women. Rifles slipped beneath their skirts. Bombs strapped to their bodies like breasts. The moment arrives. They throw off the mask. Reveal the secret face of terror. Something snaps. Something goes wrong in their heads. They scream. They laugh. They fire their rifles at the sun. And then the silence. Blood. Bone. Scraps of hair. Crimson petals floating to earth.

The aircraft staggered and sank. The engines growled. A stewardess made an announcement in three languages that no one could understand. There was a clatter of seat belts. The wings were engulfed by cloud.

'What is it?' Veronica shouted through the uproar. She turned to Gilbert and squeezed his arm.

'We've arrived,' he grinned, trying to button his jacket.

The clouds broke open and the earth rushed to meet them.

'I don't believe it!' gasped Frank with his face pressed against the glass.

'What?' yelled Veronica. 'What?'

'Africa,' said Frank. He turned and smiled, his eyes bright with excitement.

'Where?' she demanded, leaning across him to chance a glance through the window. But the aircraft was already sinking towards the airport across a grey sweep of concrete waste.

11

It was a smell that Frank would remember for the rest of his life. He stepped from the cool, machined air, through a cabin door and was caught in a suffocating blast of heat, dust, smoke and aviation fuel that carried him down the steps and into the African afternoon. He staggered in the sunlight, screwed up his face against the glare and saw Gilbert marching Veronica across the apron towards the airport buildings.

'Follow me!' he shouted back at Frank. 'Follow me and say nothing!' He speared Veronica in the armpit and raised her slightly from the ground so that she danced on tiptoe beside him. Her head wobbled dangerously in its socket.

They reached the immigration hall and joined the beleaguered caravan of pale travellers in crumpled clothes, clutching tickets and bottles of duty-free Scotch. The woman in the squirrel skins nursed a large, rubber doll in her arms. The doll wore a lunatic grin and a pair of canvas shoes. Beside them a tall man in a wrinkled blue suit held an electric toaster against his chest.

Frank, bewildered by the heat, the noise and the crowds of black faces shouting in French, stood meekly in Gilbert's shadow and hoped that no one would notice him. They shuffled slowly to the desk with their passports open like prayer books. When each had been blessed with a small rubber stamp they were free to search for their luggage.

At the customs shed they unbuckled the suitcases and cheerfully flaunted their underwear. Veronica's tiny brassieres excited less interest than Gilbert's Bovril and he was obliged to leave several bottles behind him as a goodwill gesture.

'Have we got everything?' said Gilbert, once they had repacked and found their way back into the sunlight.

Veronica nodded.

'What next?' said Frank, squinting around him. Africa was a car park, a bank of grass and a length of dusty road.

Gilbert was about to confess that he hadn't been told what should happen next when an old man with a face the colour of blood sausage climbed from a battered Toyota and beckoned them forward.

'What does he want?' hissed Veronica suspiciously.

'Passengers, you daft bugger,' said Gilbert, hoisting his suitcase on to his shoulder and stepping into the road.

'How do you *know?*' demanded Veronica.

The old man walked around his car, kicked the tyres, opened the doors, spat in the dust and clambered into the driving seat.

Gilbert, Frank and Veronica squashed into the back of the car and settled their legs around their luggage. It was hot. The seats burned their skin. The roof glowed like an oven. Gilbert immediately broke out in a sweat that filled his ears and drenched his collar. Veronica struggled to pull open her overcoat but the heat and the brandy had taken her strength. She flopped and gasped like a suffocating fish while Frank tried to break her buttons. When they thought they were certainly going to die, poached to death in their own juices, the driver turned and offered a blood-curdling smile. Gilbert gave him a slip of paper on which he had written the name of a hotel and they drove the eight kilometres into Batuta without another word between them.

Veronica didn't open her eyes again until she was standing in the air-conditioned twilight of the Hotel Napoleon. Her room was a pure, white cube, the windows sealed, the air sweet and perfectly chilled. When she was sure that the door was locked and the floor wouldn't move beneath her feet she pulled off her clothes and fell on the bed exhausted.

It was an hour or more before she felt sufficiently interested to explore her surroundings. Africa was a blue carpet, an empty wardrobe, a glass bowl of tropical flowers. She walked around this clean, cold world with a shivering pleasure. When she went to use the bathroom she found herself squatting in a pharoah's tomb, a fancy chamber of hand-painted tiles, with a bath like a marble sarcophagus. She sat on the bowl for a long time, elbows propped against her knees, watching herself in the endless mirrors; and for the first time that day she felt comfortable and safe.

In the next room Gilbert and Frank were already planning tomorrow. After breakfast they would need to change their money, check out of the hotel and find the central railway station. The express train left at noon. They should reach Bolozo Noire before midnight. Gilbert studied Sam's letter and tried to trace their route on the map.

'It's a shame we can't stay here for a few days,' sighed Frank.

'Sorry,' said Gilbert. 'We don't have time. And, anyway, we can't afford it. At this place it costs you a fiver to fart.'

'It's enormous,' said Frank, looking through a copy of the hotel brochure he had found beside his bed. There were pictures of a swimming pool, a tennis court and something that looked like a shopping arcade.

'It's certainly handsome,' said Gilbert. He had expected mosquito nets and moonlight, bleached walls and wooden verandas, fans whisking the torpid air. But his disappointment had turned to astonishment. Here they had found a fortress of steel and glass, push-button music and climate control.

'It says here that the Napoleon has three hundred and twenty-seven bedrooms,' said Frank. He had noticed that the woman who splashed in the pool looked remarkably similar to the woman who walked on the tennis court who might easily be mistaken for the woman who strolled through the shopping arcade. Turning the page he found her again, sitting in one of three hundred and twenty-seven bedrooms, and smiling into a mirror.

'I'm not surprised,' said Gilbert. 'The old Coronation had nearly ninety and that was built before the war.' He strolled across the room and plucked a banana from a bowl of polished fruit, carefully arranged on a marble table. He studied the banana for some time, searching for a blemish or the sign of a bruise. The banana proved to be perfect.

'Breakfast leisurely in your room or the Coffee Shop,' read Frank. 'Soak up some sun at Poolside, play hard at Tennis or browse the beautiful Gardens. After a day of business or pleasure you will enjoy grilled meats and other international specialities cooked to perfection at the Restaurant Napoleon.' He put down the brochure and gazed about the room. 'Do you think Sam's hotel will be anything like this?' he inquired hopefully.

'Well, he talked about a night club...' said Gilbert. He skinned the banana and squashed it slowly into his mouth.

'If it's anything like the Napoleon we'll need street maps to find our way around,' said Frank.

Gilbert grinned and licked banana from his chin. 'Find us somewhere to eat,' he said.

Frank returned to the brochure. 'We could try the Supper Club, the Restaurant Napoleon, the Coffee Shop or the Café Polynesian.'

'The café what?'

'Polynesian.'

'No,' sniffed Gilbert. 'It sounds like gammon and pineapple rings. What about the Supper Club?'

'It's a picture of a woman in a diamond necklace smiling at a candle,' retorted Frank.

'We could try the Restaurant Napoleon,' said Gilbert doubtfully.

'Are you hungry?' said Frank, rolling the brochure into a tube.

'No,' said Gilbert. 'Are *you* hungry?'

'No,' said Frank. He placed the tube against his eye like a telescope and used it to survey the floor.

'And we don't have to worry about Veronica because she still can't get her mouth working.'

'That's true,' said Frank. 'Let's forget it.'

'Yes,' said Gilbert. 'We'll have an early night. There's another long journey tomorrow.'

At dawn the telephone rang. Veronica woke up and scrambled from bed in a fright. She had dreamt she was home at the Hercules Café.

'Good morning,' said Frank, when she picked up the phone. 'Come and have breakfast.'

'Frank?' she whispered. 'Frank?'

'Yes,' said Frank.

'What's the time?'

'Six something.'

'Where are you?'

'Africa,' said Frank. 'We've had breakfast brought to the room. There's coffee and toast and fruit and boiled eggs and some little sponge cakes full of sultanas. Come and get it while it's hot.'

Veronica pulled on her dressing gown and tiptoed along the corridor to the next room.

'Where's Gilbert?' she said, when Frank opened the door.

'He's gone to find out about the train to Bolozo Noire.'

Veronica settled herself in an armchair and let Frank wrap her knees in a napkin. 'I didn't think it would be like this,' she murmured peacefully. She threw back her head and yawned like a cat.

'What?' said Frank as he served her a cup of thick, black coffee.

'Any of it,' said Veronica. 'I mean, I've never stayed in a *real* hotel. It's like a palace.' She accepted a cake and nibbled at the sultanas .

The door rattled and Gilbert appeared.

'Is it arranged?' said Frank.

'The trains aren't working,' complained Gilbert. Veronica watched him stamp across the room in search of coffee and toast. He was wearing a linen jacket with a dozen useful pockets and a pair of loose trousers that were strapped to his stomach by a green elastic belt. The trousers billowed and flapped around his legs. Beneath the trousers she caught sight of a pair of heavy walking shoes. He looked dressed for a fortnight of camping. She felt sure that, asked to empty his pockets, he would produce a compass, a bar of chocolate and a Swiss army knife.

'What's wrong with the trains?' asked Frank.

'I don't know,' grumbled Gilbert. 'I couldn't understand half of it.' He wiped his hand across his skull, scratched an ear and sighed.

'So we'll have to stay here,' said Veronica, picking at another cake.

'No. We can reach Bolozo by road. I was talking to someone at the front desk and his brother drives a truck and he can give us a ride into Bolozo this morning. It takes longer by road but it's cheap and his brother speaks English. It won't be so bad.'

'When do we leave?' said Frank.

'Nine o'clock,' said Gilbert. 'The truck will be at the hotel gates.'

So they locked their luggage and surrendered their keys and said goodbye to the Hotel Napoleon. It was a hot and brilliant morning. The sky stung their eyes. The ground burned their feet. But when they reached the road they found no one waiting for them. No driver. No truck. Nothing but sunlight and heat and silence.

They sat on their suitcases and tried to shelter in the shadow of the gate posts. After a while a man floated past on a bicycle. He wore a black suit, leather sandals and gloves. He shouted to them in French. Gilbert laughed and waved his hand.

'What did he say?' asked Veronica.

'No idea,' said Gilbert, settling back to watch the road. A lizard perched on the gate post and stared suspiciously down on him. A flock of grey birds squabbled in some thorn bushes.

'It's past nine,' said Frank, digging in the dust with the heel of his shoe. His shirt was wet. His eyebrows glistened with sweat.

'Patience,' said Gilbert.

'You can fly to Bolozo in forty minutes,' muttered Frank.

'We won't see anything of the country if we fly there,' said Gilbert. 'That's why we wanted to take the train.'

Frank scowled at Veronica but she only smiled and hitched up her skirt to let the sun admire her legs. She had abandoned her army greatcoat in favour of one of her new cotton frocks, a brief blue article printed with poppies. Her legs looked very lean and white.

And then they heard a growl of thunder that rattled the gravel under their feet; the birds took fright, the lizard fell from its perch and a truck appeared on the road. It was an empty beer truck. An old German beer truck with scoured paintwork and a buckled hood. It shuddered to a halt at the gates and stood trembling, belching smoke. A little man climbed down from the cab, walked over and grinned at them.

'Mr Gill Bear?' he asked Gilbert. Gilbert nodded.

'You're welcome,' said the driver. 'My name is Al Bear.' He took Gill Bear's hand and shook it vigorously.

'Bolozo Noire?' said Frank.

Al Bear turned and shook Frank's hand too. Then he smiled shyly at Veronica, picked up her suitcase and threw it in the cab.

The cab was hardly large enough for all of them but they squirmed and wriggled and somehow managed to close the door. Veronica sat on Frank, Gilbert sat with his feet on a suitcase and Al Bear sat with his elbow stuck through a window.

'Are you comfortable?' he shouted above the noise of the engine. The ceiling rattled, the floor smoked and the beer truck rolled away. A rubber Virgin Mary, hanging by a thread from the driving mirror, began a mournful little dance as they drove through the outskirts of town.

'Are the roads good?' asked Gilbert as the truck lurched and swerved through the streets.

'Yes. The roads today are good,' said Al Bear cheerfully. He had a neat polished face and his smile showed the tips of his small, gold teeth. 'But, you know, the rains wash them away. In a few weeks they will be rivers of mud!' He shook his head and laughed helplessly. 'Rivers of mud!'

'How do you manage to drive in the mud?' inquired Frank.

'You must not ask me horrible questions,' said Al Bear, wiping his eyes.

The streets were full of cars, buses, trucks and bicycles, forced between buildings, bleak as barrack blocks, with rusting corrugated roofs. Here and there Frank saw figures standing in the gloom of workshops, surrounded by bottles, crates and tyres. Dust. A woman shuffled past with an empty oil drum on her head. Pot hole. Dust. Bar Dancing. A donkey cart loaded with bricks. Coiffeur. Cactus hedge. A yellow dog. Beaufort Bière. Six men, sitting on a wall, staring at their feet. Dust. Heat. Noise. Dust.

'Are you American?' asked Al Bear as they left the town.

'English,' said Gilbert.

'London,' said Al Bear. 'Ox Four Street. Totton Core Row.'

'Yes,' said Frank.

'I had a brother once who worked in London,' said Al Bear. He laughed again and shook his head.

Frank watched the road. After a few kilometres they passed the wreck of a large white Peugeot abandoned in the bushes. It had been torn completely in half, the doors missing and the front wheels gone.

'Nasty business,' murmured Gilbert as the truck rumbled past squirting smoke.

'There are many accidents on the road,' smiled Al Bear.

'Why don't they clear them away?' asked Frank when they came upon the skeleton of an overturned truck.

'Nobody wants them. Who wants to drive a wreck?'

'But it's dangerous,' argued Frank.

'Oh, yes,' laughed Al Bear, flashing his teeth. 'It's very dangerous on the road.'

'I'm thirsty,' complained Veronica. They had been riding for nearly an hour. Gilbert unbuttoned one of his useful pockets and pulled out a small and slightly withered orange.

'We shall stop here,' declared Al Bear, swinging the truck from the road towards a collection of sheds. As he switched off the engine a man appeared through a hole in a wall and waved at them. Al Bear clambered from the cab and disappeared. He was gone for a long time.

'Where are we?' moaned Veronica. The temperature inside the cab began to soar. The seats gave out a peculiar smell. She leaned across Frank and hung her head from the window.

'Nowhere in particular,' shrugged Gilbert, staring across at the sheds.

'We'll never get anywhere,' said Frank impatiently, as Veronica stabbed him with her elbow.

'He's in no hurry,' confessed Gilbert, nodding at Al Bear who had ambled from one of the sheds and was now sitting in the sun with a bottle of beer.

And it was true. Every few kilometres Al Bear found an excuse to interrupt their journey. First he stopped to inspect the engine, walking slowly around the truck and pausing to urinate over a tyre. Next he stopped to eat a slice of smoked fish he unwrapped from a newspaper parcel. Once he stopped to secure the tail-board. Another time he stopped to buy some fruit.

In the afternoon they drove through a palm plantation and then the forest closed around them. The road became a corridor between dark and silent trees. The sunlight splintered. The sky turned to steam. Gilbert unbuttoned another pocket and pulled out a small Instamatic. He held the camera against his eye and began to take pictures through the dusty wind-screen. Snap. Trees. Snap. Trees. Snap. Trees.

'Take my picture!' shouted Al Bear and grinned. 'Take a picture of the driver!'

Gilbert turned and took a picture of Al Bear's gold teeth. Snap. Al Bear obscured by the Virgin Mary. Snap. Al Bear driving the truck through a ditch. Snap.

'Thank you!' laughed Al Bear, fighting to keep control of the wheel.

'You're welcome,' said Gilbert.

A few minutes later they passed a man by the side of the road. He stood, motionless, holding a wooden pole in his fist. A pair of dead monkeys were tied to the pole.

'We shall stop here,' said Al Bear. He jumped from the cab and walked back to the man. After a brief exchange, during which several tattered bank notes were unfolded and counted, he took possession of the little carcasses and brought them back to the truck. He threw them down on the floor where Gilbert tried to take pictures. They looked like grotesquely shrivelled babies. The eyes were open and the lips pulled back to expose the fangs. A large, blue fly emerged from one of the monkey's ears and settled on Gilbert's shoe.

'When do we get there?' demanded Veronica as the truck lurched away. She stared in disgust at the dead monkeys. The sun had already disappeared and it was growing dark inside the cab.

'Tomorrow,' said Al Bear, leaving the road and steering the truck down a rough dirt track.

'What?' roared Frank.

'We've been driving all day,' protested Gilbert. 'How far is it?'

'Far away. Far away,' smiled Al Bear. 'Tonight we'll stay with my sister. Nice food. Clean beds. Good price. And then, tomorrow, Bolozo Noire.

They were too tired to argue with him. Hungry, bruised and bleached by dust, they clung grimly to the seat as the truck bounced into the shadows. The track went black. It began to rain. Al Bear drove in silence, his mouth open and his eyes fierce with concentration.

'Here,' he shouted suddenly. The track had melted away. The truck was trapped in a cobweb of ferns and giant grasses. Al Bear smiled and switched off the engine. 'We have arrived.' He jumped from the cab and urged everyone to gather their luggage and follow him up a slippery bank of mud. The moon blinked through a torn cloud. Thousands of frogs were singing.

Beyond them, lit by the flares of hurricane lamps, stood a cluster of shacks. The smell of wood smoke drifted towards them. An old man squatted over a puddle, washing his arms in the green water. Gilbert sniffed the air, gulping down the smells of wet jungle, cooking meats, rags, rubber and rain. They walked past the shacks, through a hedge of banana palms and reached a crumbling wooden mansion with a peaked iron roof.

'Jesus, what's that terrible smell?' said Veronica as she grabbed Frank's hand.

'It smells like shit,' said Frank, wrinkling his nose.

'I know it's shit,' hissed Veronica. 'But what have they *done* to it?'

'Follow me please,' whispered Al Bear. He led the party on to the veranda and through a metal door.

They had entered a large, bare room with a wooden counter set against one wall. A collection of torn armchairs had been placed in the centre of the room. They stared around at the circle of chairs, the mildewed carpet and the empty walls. A sudden gust of rain rattled on the roof. The floorboards swayed beneath their feet.

There was a woman behind the counter. The woman was huge and wearing a long red frock printed with bunches of acid-green flowers. Her hair was wrapped in a turban which she prodded with her fingers as Al Bear approached.

'How now?' beamed Al Bear. 'Chop don ready?'

'Smol tam,' said the woman. Al Bear gave her the two dead monkeys and she shook him warmly by the hand.

'Her name is my sister Alice,' Al Bear announced proudly.

Alice nodded at the strangers, pulled some glasses from a bucket of water and wiped them over with a piece of cloth.

'Guinness,' called Al Bear as he led them towards the armchairs. And once they were comfortable Alice lumbered forward with the Guinness on a battered tray. She made a little performance of opening the bottles and pouring the beer, snapping off the caps with an opener tied by string to her wrist.

'This is my favourite place,' explained Al Bear proudly. 'A lot of visitors like to stay here.'

The beer was a bitter, mahogany syrup, so strong that their ears began to ring. Gilbert nodded, smiled and tried to smother a yawn. Frank hung his head. Veronica looked dead.

After a while the curtain rustled behind the counter and Alice appeared again with her tray. She set it down on the table before them. There were spoons, bowls and a dish of hot peppered chicken.

Gilbert watched her waddle away. By thunder, but she's a big girl. Royal buttocks. You have to be careful with big women. Dangerous when excited. Strong as elephants. Lose control and they stamp you to death. That's why you see them with tiny men. Small. Nimble. Fast on their feet.

'Good,' grinned Al Bear. He laid out the bowls and began to fill them with stew. But it was too late for food. Frank couldn't find his mouth with the spoon, Veronica began to snore and even Gilbert, who could have sworn he was ready to eat a horse, found the chicken too much for him.

'You like it?' demanded Al Bear as Gilbert set down his unfinished bowl.

'Very good,' said Gilbert gravely.

Al Bear belched and gargled with Guinness. He looked happy and immensely pleased with himself. He sat back and picked at his teeth with a fingernail. Time passed. Rain crackled against the roof. The shell of a spider rolled across the floor on a draught. No one spoke. Frank closed his eyes and settled deeper into his chair. You can fly to Bolozo in forty minutes.

And then a girl appeared through the curtains. She was no more than twenty years old with a long, narrow face and hair that was tied into tight little knots against her scalp. She wore a translucent blue cocktail dress copied from an old French *Vogue* and cut from something that might once have been a nylon rain-coat. The sleeves and the collar were gone but the buttons and belt remained. Her legs were bare. Her shoes were suede brogues with black rubber heels.

She shuffled forward, perched on the arm of Gilbert's chair and grinned at him. Her dress strained its buttons. She smelt profoundly of patchouli oil.

'Dis man he big plenti,' Al Bear warned her as she toyed with Gilbert's ears.

'Ousey you kom out?' she asked Gilbert.

'He don kom out England,' said Al Bear.

The girl laughed and moved away. She spoke to Alice who spoke to Al Bear who composed a translation for Gilbert.

'My sister Alice has asked me if this woman is your wife?' he said, pointing an accusing finger at Veronica who was sprawled asleep with her mouth hanging open.

'Yes,' said Gilbert. 'She is my wife.'

Al Bear looked disappointed.

'And this man,' he said, turning to Frank. 'Is he your son?'

'Yes,' said Gilbert. 'He is my son.

When these things were explained to Alice she growled and

dismissed the girl. Al Bear shouted something in French, shook his head and laughed.

'Wat you problim?' snapped Alice.

'Notin!' said Al Bear, wiping his eyes and trying to hide his smile.

'Jakas!' barked Alice. She took a swing at his head with her fist but Al Bear was quick and caught her arm, pulling her forward into the chair. She staggered and fell like Babylon. The chair overturned. Al Bear hit the floor and Alice sat on him. 'Kis ma bak seid!'

Al Bear cursed and coughed and, in the confusion, worked his hand beneath her frock. Alice grunted and looked confused. Al Bear squeezed. Alice howled. She pulled open the neck of her frock and peered into her underwear. While she tried to fish for the hand Al Bear wriggled loose and scuttled to freedom.

'What was all that about?' whispered Frank as Alice crawled to a chair and pretended to tidy her turban.

'They're fighting over us,' said Gilbert.

'Why?'

'You'll learn,' yawned Gilbert. He looked at Frank and smiled.

'Are you tired?' asked Al Bear cheerfully, as he slapped the dust from his clothes. 'You can go to bed. My sister Alice will show you the room.'

'Good idea,' said Gilbert.

'Ok, dem go silip,' Al Bear announced.

They picked up their luggage, shook Veronica awake and let Alice guide them through the counter curtain. They walked down an unlit corridor and into a room filled by six iron beds. Each bed had a blanket and a pillow. An oil lamp stood on a metal table. Beneath a shuttered window, a water pipe and a big bucket. Alice pointed at the beds, the bucket and the bolt on the door.

Without further ceremony Veronica lay down and fell asleep in her clothes. Frank turned and smiled politely at Alice. 'Thank you,' he said as he set down his suitcase. She stared sadly at him for a moment, wagged her head and lumbered away.

'Where do you think Al Bear will sleep?' asked Frank as Gilbert tinkered with the lamp.

'I think he sleeps with his sister Alice,' murmured Gilbert and the floor creaked as he crawled into bed.

Frank lay down and waited for his own dreams to carry him to safety. The rain had stopped and Gilbert was already snoring. But when he closed his eyes he found himself back in the beer truck, trapped in the smoke and dust and sunlight. It seemed like weeks since the Hercules Café. A different life. They were lost. It was gone. He thought again of the man standing on the edge of the forest with the monkeys strung on a pole. The smell of death in the warm afternoon. Did Alice eat them? How did she cook them? Ask Gilbert. He knows. Skin them, clean them, stew them like babies. Something ran across the wall above his head. What's that! Cockroach? Yes. Probably. Cockroach everywhere. Eating the world. Thousands of them, crawling from the woodwork, running around the room in the dark. Switch on the light and find a living, twitching carpet of beetles. Don't think. Close your eyes. Pull the blanket over your head.

At dawn they woke up sweating and thirsty. Alice brought them a breakfast of bread, fruit and thin, boiled coffee and led them to the lavatory. Al Bear was waiting on the veranda. He grinned when he saw them, blew his nose between finger and thumb and wiped his hand on his shirt.

'Did you like it?' he asked as they walked away from the house.

'We'll never forget it,' said Veronica. Her hair bristled. She was wearing a pair of plastic sunglasses.

Al Bear looked puzzled. 'A favourite place with visitors,' he chirruped.

They walked to the truck and threw their luggage aboard. The sun burned in an empty sky. The undergrowth steamed in the heat. They clambered into the cab and sat and sweated patiently while Al Bear settled down to work. He rolled up his sleeves, cleaned out his ears, growled in his throat and spat, twice, through the window. He scratched his chest, picked his nose, wiped his knees and pinched the Virgin Mary. He poked and preened and finally, at the very moment when Veronica thought she might lunge and pull out his heart with her teeth, he started the engine and steered the truck, very slowly, back along the track towards the forest road.

'Do you have friends in Bolozo Noire?' he inquired as he swerved to avoid a passing truck.

'No,' said Gilbert.

The truck roared past with its horn blaring and wrapped them in clouds of oily smoke.

'No one? Where will you stay? Do you have a hotel?' asked Al Bear. He looked baffled. He couldn't understand them.

'We don't want a hotel,' explained Frank, rubbing his chin. The skin felt sore and he needed a shave.

Al Bear shook his head. 'I have a sister,' he said cheerfully. 'She will look after you.'

'Another sister?' said Veronica.

'Yes.'

'It's a big family.'

'Oh, yes!' said Al Bear. He laughed and shook his head. 'And you will like this hotel. Nice food. Clean beds. Good price. Air conditioned. Music and dancing every night. Do you like to dance? Don't worry. I can arrange it.'

'We're not staying in Bolozo Noire,' shouted Gilbert impatiently. 'When we get there we want to find another truck leaving for Bolozo Rouge. We're trying to get to the Grand Safari Lodge at Nkongfanto.'

Al Bear fell silent. He frowned and sighed and sucked his teeth. The truck rattled over a bridge. Beneath them a river of brown water oozed between banks of scrub. A car was parked in the river. A group of men were gathered about it, soaping and scrubbing the paintwork.

'Can you help?' said Frank.

'I think I have a brother,' said Al Bear slowly and gave them another golden grin.

'We were depending on it,' said Veronica.

'If we can find him he will take you to Nkongfanto.'

'When?'

Al Bear shrugged. 'The roads are dangerous and it's far away.' They reached Bolozo Noire in the afternoon. It was a small, neat city concealed in the folds of the hairy hills. Al Bear guided his truck through busy, tree-lined streets, grinning and punching the horn with his fist. They passed a hospital and a cinema, bars, hotels and bone-white concrete office blocks. They drove through the centre of the city and turned into a dusty square full of wagons and trucks.

'Stay here,' said Al Bear. 'I must find my brother.' He jumped from the cab and disappeared into the crowd. When he returned he was followed by a tall man in a green vest and a polished trilby hat.

'Mr Gill Bear, this is my brother,' announced Al Bear proudly. 'His name is Renoir. He is a very good driver.'

'Does he speak English?' asked Gilbert. He looked doubtfully at Renoir. The man had a wet cigar butt stuck to his mouth, a fat nose and a blind eye.

'Not often,' admitted Al Bear.

'French?'

'Not often.'

'He sounds perfect,' sighed Gilbert.

'He is a very good driver. Very fast. Very brave. You will like him,' Al Bear said enthusiastically.

Renoir stood in silence and shuffled his feet in the dust.

'Nkongfanto,' said Frank.

Renoir grunted. The cigar butt stuck to his lip like a scab.

'Does he know where we're going?'

'I have explained everything,' said Al Bear.

'Grand Safari Lodge,' said Veronica.

Renoir turned and tried to stare through her dress. His bad eye shone like a peeled boiled egg.

'Is he all right?' frowned Frank.

'Oh, yes. He thinks slow but he drives fast. Very fast. Dangerous. I know you will like him.'

While Frank and Veronica tried to persuade him to carry their luggage Gilbert and Al Bear sat down in the shadow of the truck and discussed the problem of money. At first Al Bear demanded thirty thousand francs for the journey from Batuta but after some elaborate calculations, made entirely on his fingers, declared he would settle for eighty dollars. Gilbert, once it had been established that Alice was included in the price, offered fifty and Al Bear promptly accepted. Gilbert was taken by surprise and had a suspicion he might have been robbed. But it was too late to argue. He paid the price, shook hands and followed Frank and Veronica to Renoir's truck.

'I have a brother in Bolozo Rouge,' Al Bear shouted after them. 'He works at the Maison du Tourisme...' But Gilbert had already climbed aboard and Renoir was driving away.

Beyond the city the forest closed around them. Veronica fell asleep on Gilbert's shoulder. Frank stared from the window. There were moments when he fancied they were riding through an English wood in the heat of a summer's afternoon. He saw familiar treetops, broad grass ditches and the twist of birds in a brilliant sky. But sometimes the forest grew darker, crowding in upon the road and touching the walls of the truck. Then they drove through a humid twilight. On every side the trees, raised up on monstrous claws, spread canopies to shut out the sun. The silence pressed down on them. The heat became a suffocating stink. When the forest broke open they found themselves riding through a monotony of cocoa and palm plantations.

On the outskirts of Bolozo Rouge they followed in the smoke of six lumber trucks crawling towards the plywood factories. The trucks contained carcasses of massive trees, cut down, shorn and held in chains.

'Look at that!' shouted Gilbert. 'We've only just arrived and they're already taking the scenery down!'

Three children squatting in sawdust throwing stones at a sleeping dog. Two French priests on a bicycle. An empty wheelchair on a pile of oil drums. The forest swallowed them again.

At Koto they paused while Renoir went off on some mysterious errand.

`Goodbye and thanks for the truck!' shouted Gilbert as they watched him wander away. Renoir grunted and rolled his bad eye. Half an hour later he returned with beer on his breath and his trilby forced down over his ears.

It was dusk when they left the town. Fifty miles south lay the jungles of the Congo. Renoir turned east on a red dirt track and carried them into the night. Huge moths danced in the glare of the headlamps, their wings casting long and morbid shadows. Baffled by light they hit the windscreen in huge puffs of brown velvet and fell back into the undergrowth. The track skirted boulders and dropped into gullies, twisted, turned and disappeared. The forest swept them into a tunnel, sucked them down into its darkness. And then, when it seemed impossible to continue, as the trees all around became a cage and the wheels slithered and lost their grip, the track returned and led them safely into the moonlight.

They were on the crest of a hill. Before them, set in a patch of rough lawn, stood a small hotel with a red iron roof. A naked lightbulb hung like a jewel from the rotting veranda. Nothing stirred. No one came to meet them. Renoir switched off the engine and climbed from the cab. He stood on the grass and beckoned them toward the house.

When they stepped through the door they found themselves at an empty counter. The smell of old carpets. A faded noticeboard. A guestbook with curling pages. Behind the counter, shoulders propped against the wall, a moth-eaten gorilla stared at the ceiling with a pair of blue glass eyes.

`I think we've arrived,' whispered Gilbert.

12

On the fourth day Frank woke up in a sweat. His head was aching. His hair was wet. He rolled from the sheets, fell to the floor and lay there for a long time, too weak to raise himself again. He stared at the cracks in the ceiling. The air was thick and stale. A cluster of flies were nailed to the lightbulb.

`Are you awake?' asked Gilbert brightly.

Frank groaned and crawled to his knees. They were in a small, square room. The walls of the room had been washed with a lime-green paint. There was a piece of lino on the floor. The room contained a metal wardrobe, four beds, a table with a telephone and lamp.

Gilbert was sitting on one of the beds with a banana in his hand. `You were moaning and groaning in your sleep,' he complained as Frank emerged. Sitting there, naked to the waist, belly rolling and nipples swelling like raspberries, there was something pagan and wild about him. His face and neck were red with dust. His beard sparkled. His skin had the shine of wet clay.

Veronica was sitting in the next bed. She was still wearing her frock, the front stained with dirt and sweat. Her hair was a tangle of ginger spikes.

'Jesus, you look like you've been pulled from a river,' said Frank.

'I know. I think I drowned in my sleep,' she said miserably, fanning herself with a magazine. 'These sheets are soaking.'

'There's an air conditioner over there but we can't get it working,' grumbled Gilbert, waving his banana at something that looked like an old truck engine hanging from the wall above the window.

But Frank wasn't listening. There were knives cutting under

his ribcage, twisting his stomach, hacking his entrails. The pain caught his breath and paralysed his face. 'My stomach!' he wheezed. He jerked forward and wrapped himself in his arms.

'Diarrhoea,' said Gilbert. 'It's the heat. You'll get used to it.'

'I bet it's snowing in London,' sighed Veronica.

Frank staggered along the wall, found the bathroom and locked himself inside.

'We're going out to look for breakfast,' Gilbert shouted through the door.

Frank groaned, sickened by the stench of his own putrefaction. Squirting. Straining. Nothing solid. Filthy. Yellow. Thin as soup. Burns. Try to control it. That's better. No, it isn't. What happens if something serious? You die. Shit yourself to death. Buried with your knees tucked under your chin. Here it comes again. Knives chopping under the ribs. The strain turns you inside out. It can't last for ever. No food. Empty stomach. Nothing left to lose.

When it was finished he stood trembling under the shower, gargled in the tepid water, washed his hair, let the dust drain to mud at his feet. Then he found fresh clothes and went to join Gilbert and Veronica who were sitting at a table on the long veranda.

'Where is everyone?' he asked, pulling up a chair.

'I think we're it,' said Gilbert.

'And him,' said Veronica, glancing over her shoulder. The head of a lion hung morosely from the wall of the house, cobwebs knitted into its mane, glass eyes watching the edge of the forest.

'Do you think he died here?'

'There aren't any lions in the forest,' said Gilbert. 'He must have come down from the north.'

An old waiter in a greasy red jacket came creaking towards them bearing a big tin tray. He left them a jug of muddy coffee, tumblers of fruit juice the flavour of soap, crusty bread rolls with moist grey interiors, white butter, maroon-coloured jam.

'Do you think we'll see any animals?' asked Frank as they set to work on the food.

'They've probably eaten 'em,' said Veronica. 'Remember the monkeys?'

'I used to have a recipe for monkey,' said Gilbert, breaking open a bread roll. 'They take a long time to clean but they don't taste too bad when they're fresh. You have to be careful with bush-meat. Nothing stays sweet in this heat.' He pulled the soft, grey pulp from the roll and tucked it neatly into his mouth. He began to talk about rats, bats and the livers of dogs.

'Who's that?' Veronica interrupted. Beyond the veranda a tall figure in a trilby hat was sitting on a pile of logs peacefully picking his nose.

'I think it's Renoir,' said Gilbert, squinting into the sunlight. 'He's waiting for me to pay him.' He drained his cup, wiped his mouth and set off briskly across the lawn.

Veronica yawned and stretched her arms. 'I stink,' she said proudly, sniffing the seams of her frock. 'I'm going to wash.'

Frank sat alone and stared at the forest. The heat made him tired. The coffee bubbled in his stomach. After a while the old waiter returned to clear the table. His dark face was pitted with pox. His hair was a tuft of coarse grey wool.

'Where are the animals?' demanded Frank as he watched him stick his thumb in the butter.

The waiter smiled. 'Crocodile,' he said.

'Crocodile?'

'You see the crocodile?'

'No,' said Frank.

The waiter put down the tray and led Frank along the veranda to the back of the hotel. In the corner of a yard, behind a stack of breeze blocks and a pile of rubbish stood a narrow wooden cage. It was a coffin nailed from boxes and crates. Through the bars of this prison a long tail protruded like a cracked leather sausage.

As Frank watched, the waiter picked up a broomstick and thrashed the top of the cage. The crocodile flicked the tip of its tail.

'Crocodile!' shouted the waiter. He laughed and performed a little tap dance.

'Is that it?' said Frank.

'Crocodile! '

'Yes,' said Frank sadly. He stared at the reptile in the box, the flies swarming, the stinking rubbish and the baked, red earth. He hung his head. A terrible weariness seemed to press down on him. And for the first time he felt afraid. Where were they going? What would become of them?

'Where are the other animals?' he asked when the old man had finished his dance.

The waiter frowned and wiped his face. 'We have a donkey,' he said anxiously. 'We have a donkey but he gone died.'

In the afternoon they sat in the shade of the veranda and drank many pots of hot, weak tea. Veronica read through old copies of the *Watchtower* she had found beneath her bed. When will the Kingdom come? What does God want with me? Frank dozed in his chair. Gilbert kept watch on the forest. It was as if he expected, at any moment, to see Sam Pilchard come stumbling through the undergrowth, shouting, hooting, arms thrown open to greet him. As they came closer to Plenti so Gilbert grew more excited, embraced everything, laughed like a child with each new discovery. The wall of the forest reminded him of his days on the Congo riverboats. The smell of wood smoke from the hotel kitchen put him in mind of lost tribesmen, squatting naked under the stars, roasting meat in the camp fire's ashes. He was returning to some lost and distant country that Frank could not penetrate. Where Frank found only heat and dust Gilbert could see the gates to a tropical paradise. When will the Kingdom come?

Late the next morning a car came for them. The driver, a lugubrious African wearing a cardigan and elasticated winkle-pickers, found his way into their room and tried to walk out with their luggage.

'How do we know he's from Sam?' demanded Veronica as they chased him around the room.

'He must be from Sam,' reasoned Gilbert. 'Everything is arranged.'

'Well, why didn't he phone?' complained Veronica. 'How

does he know we're here? We could have been delayed or anything. We could be anywhere.'

'We *were* delayed,' said Frank. 'We should have been here days ago.'

'It's not my fault,' shouted Veronica. She ran into the bathroom, collecting up washbags, towels and a precious sliver of perfumed soap. 'What day is it?'

'I don't know,' said Frank in surprise. 'I think it's Friday. What do you think? Is it Friday?'

'I don't know,' said Veronica as they followed their luggage into the sunlight.

When the car was loaded the driver paused, hunted through his cardigan and gave Gilbert a little note.

'This bastard is Happy,' Gilbert read aloud. 'Watch him. He farts. Waiting for you. Boris.'

'Why didn't Sam write?' asked Frank suspiciously as he climbed into the back seat. The car was hot and smelt of human decay.

'He's probably too busy,' said Gilbert, sitting himself next to Happy. 'He left Boris to make the arrangements. Nothing wrong with that.'

Veronica settled down next to Frank and opened the window. 'He could have phoned,' she insisted.

Happy farted and drove them away. They skidded and bounced down a narrow track cut through the silent forest. A tunnel of dust in the green sunlight. They drove for an hour and then had to stop to let Frank empty his bowels in the bushes.

'How do you feel?' said Veronica when he staggered back to the car.

'I don't feel so good,' he confessed. He was white and shaking. His neck was shining with sweat.

'Can't we rest for a moment?' she pleaded, turning to Gilbert. 'Frank looks worn out.'

'It's nothing!' barked Gilbert. 'He'll get used to it. Let's get going before it's dark.' He stamped impatiently on the floor and urged Happy to start the engine again.

'You've waited years and years,' snapped Veronica. 'What

difference are another few hours going to make to anyone?'

'There's nothing wrong with him,' insisted Gilbert. He swung round and glared at Frank. 'Nothing serious.'

'How do you know?'

'It's the heat. I've seen it before. It happens to everyone.'

'It hasn't happened to me,' argued Veronica stubbornly.

'You're not human.'

Frank moaned and closed his eyes. Veronica pulled him down against her breasts and suffocated him. 'He doesn't look normal,' she said, staring into his ear. 'His skin has gone a funny colour.'

'When we get there he can go to bed. He's not going to improve sitting out here, in the middle of nowhere, while we shout at each other,' shouted Gilbert. 'I can't work miracles.'

Veronica held Frank's head and sulked. They were going to drive through this heat for ever. The forest would lead them in circles. For ever and ever. Amen.

Happy farted and the car sprang forward.

'We're nearly home,' said Gilbert, settling back into his seat. He scratched the top of his head and grinned into the driving mirror but Veronica ignored him.

They reached Plenti in the afternoon. At first it was no more than a leak of rubbish along the jungle road. The rusting bulk of a truck, broken bottles, paper, rags. Then the road spread as the forest shrank and they were driving through a small town. On either side of them a confusion of houses and workshops crowded down upon the road which filled, at once, with chickens, dogs and naked children. A few of the buildings were made of timber and stone, others were no more than crude shelters the size and shape of packing crates. Men sat in shadows, talking, scratching, drinking beer. A radio blared. At one end of the town a line of fat and silent women stood patiently at a water pump.

'I think we've arrived,' Veronica whispered into Frank's ear. He opened his eyes and struggled weakly to pull himself from her embrace; but when he looked from the windows the town had gone.

The forest smothered them again. For a few kilometres the road became a narrow ledge of rock that seemed to roll dangerously among the tops of trees, then it plunged into a gravel trench that slithered and sank beneath them.

'Where's the hotel?' asked Veronica anxiously. She peered into the twilight. The trees were wrapped in succulent skirts of undergrowth, mosses, ferns and red wax flowers. Cobwebs hung on invisible threads. The earth steamed.

'There!' shouted Gilbert, pressing his face against the windscreen.

They climbed a ridge and broke into the sunlight. Happy grunted and stopped the car with a fart.

It was a shabby building with a deep veranda and walls the colour of mud. The word HOTEL had been daubed on the roof in thick, white paint.

As the car stopped a figure moved from the darkness of the veranda and walked out towards them. He was dressed in a grubby cotton jacket and a pair of shapeless black trousers, worn to a shine at the knees. Beneath an old straw hat his face was the colour of boiled ham. Gilbert ran to meet him.

'You're Boris!' he boomed, snatching at the man's hand.

Boris grinned. 'Mr Gilbert!'

They shook hands, laughed, slapped each other on the shoulder, shook hands again.

'And Miss Veronica,' declared Boris as Veronica stepped from the car.

'And this must be Hank.'

'Frank,' said Frank, falling over his feet.

'Are you tired?' asked Boris. 'Did Happy behave himself? Good. Good. Well. I show you the rooms we prepared. Everything is ready. You want to wash? You hungry? You like something to drink? Maybe. Happy can bring the luggage.'

Boris began to move away. Gilbert climbed the veranda and followed him into the hotel, Veronica leading Frank, Happy farting with the strain of the suitcases. They crowded into the entrance hall and stood, uncomfortably, blinking into the gloom. An old chintz sofa with greasy arms was sprawled in a corner. A table cluttered with books and magazines ran the length of one wall. *The London Pageant. Ideal Home. Baxter's Book of Mountain Memories.* Where the spines had broken yellow pages sprang apart and curled like brittle fans. A mottled mirror, blind with dust, hung by a chain above the door.

They stared at each other for a few moments, waiting, excited, baffled by the silence. Frank and Veronica sat down in the sofa. Gilbert steamed with excitement. He kept looking around, grinning and nodding his head. The sweat rolled down his neck and stained his collar. His hands trembled.

'Where's Sam?' he boomed.

Happy looked scared. He dropped the luggage, made a dash for the daylight and clattered off down the veranda.

'All in good time,' said Boris. 'Let me show you the rooms.'

'Bugger the rooms!' roared Gilbert. 'It's time I took a look at Sam. Where is the old devil? I want to show him the children. He drags me halfway around the world and then plays hide-and-seek. Is he here? Where is he?'

'Yes,' said Boris. 'He's here.'

'Bring him out!' laughed Gilbert.

'He's in the garden,' said Boris.

He led them through the empty hotel and into a courtyard protected by a fat, mud wall. A chicken scratched in the dust. A stack of chairs stood creaking in the blistering heat. They walked past a kitchen block and a store room, to the far end of the yard where a small plot of earth was marked by a barbed-wire fence.

'There,' said Boris. He pulled off his hat and gripped it tightly in his hands. He seemed reluctant to approach the fence.

'Sam?' whispered Gilbert. He ran forward, stumbling, catching his coat on the line of barbed wire.

The plot had been destroyed. The ground was trampled and where once all kinds of plants might have flourished now there were only broken bundles of wilted leaves kicked and thrown in every direction. It looked like the work of a madman or perhaps some marauding animal. The garden had been dug out and nothing was left but a mound of fresh earth.

Gilbert stared at the mound. The kettle of flowers. The wooden cross. Flies swarmed around him, drawn down to the stink of rotting cabbage. He stared at the mound and then raised his eyes, looking out towards the forest.

'How did it happen?' he said softly.

'The fever,' said Boris.

'When?'

'A few days ago. We wanted to keep him until you arrived but we couldn't risk it in this heat. I'm sorry.'

Gilbert nodded. An eagle drifted from the treetops and hung, motionless, in the darkening air.

13

Frank leaned back in his chair and gazed out at the night forest. The air was warm and hissing with insects. Fifty yards away the trees appeared as frozen fountains, fantastic shadows against the sky. Through the feathered peaks of these shadows he watched stars drifting like sparks blown from a brilliant fire.

Veronica, beside him, was talking to Boris. She was talking about Olive and the Hercules Café, about Gilbert's stories of Sam and how, when she was flying, she thought she would die. She spoke in a whisper, afraid of disturbing the sleeping forest, and kept pausing, frowning, searching for words while Boris listened, soft as a priest.

'I'm glad you've come,' said Boris gently, when Veronica had finished. He sat with his back to the forest, shoulders pressed against the veranda and a bottle of brandy in his fist. A moon the size of a dinner plate hung in the darkness over his head. 'You've come. I shall stay. You want to see the hotel? Yes. Tomorrow. Don't take long. No one here. Empty rooms.'

'You're closed,' said Frank.

'What?'

'You're closed because of Sam.'

'We never closed,' exploded Boris. He laughed and sloshed the brandy into glasses. 'Sam said we was like the Windmill. We never closed but somehow we never looked open. We had problems. Difficulties. It hasn't been easy these past few months.'

'What went wrong?' asked Veronica.

'Don't matter,' sniffed Boris. 'Finished. Sam said Gilbert would fix it. Sam always had plans for the place. Sam was like that. Crazy bastard. God rest him.' He took off his hat and fitted it tightly over his knee. His hair was long and bleached by the sun. He wiped his nose. The hat had left a yellow crease on his burnt red skin.

'God rest him,' said Veronica.

'I'm glad you've come. You sitting there. Me sitting here. Sam sitting at the bottom of the garden. Let's drink to Gilbert.'

He pressed his glass against his mouth, jerked back his head and the brandy disappeared. He snorted and sucked air through clenched teeth. Frank and Veronica tried to imitate him.

'It goes to my head,' wheezed Veronica. She laughed and coughed and wiped the tears from her eyes.

'It's French,' said Boris, as if that explained everything and he gave the bottle a little shake.

'Lovely,' gasped Veronica.

Boris nodded. 'I save this bottle for something special. Drank the others when old Sam died. Poor bastard. Broke my heart. He loved brandy.' He carefully refilled their glasses and replaced the bottle between his boots.

Frank thought again of Gilbert standing over the grave of his friend. For a long time he hadn't moved, he hadn't spoken, but stood pressed forward against the barbed wire. When they had helped him away his face looked grey and swollen. His clothes were torn. There were flies crawling over his hands. It was one of the few times in his life that Frank had seen him defeated, as if all the sorrow and disappointments, the little pains and defeats of twenty years had squeezed with the strength to burst his heart. Boris had pulled off Gilbert's shoes and helped to put him to bed. He had looked at them. He had said nothing. They drew the mosquito nets around him and waited until he had fallen asleep. Where had he gone in that sleep? Had he hurried back to Olive or was he running out to Sam? He had closed his eyes against the living and slipped away to be with his ghosts.

Frank felt a pain in his stomach. He squirmed in the chair, pulled up his knees and hunched his shoulders, trying to smother the slashing knives .

'What's wrong, Hank?' asked Boris.

'Nothing,' whispered Frank. He pulled back his head and tried to smile. The brandy splashed his knuckles.

'It's his stomach,' said Veronica.

Boris stared at Frank. His eyes flashed in the lamplight.

'It's my stomach,' said Frank.

'You shouldn't be drinking,' Veronica snapped.

'I can't eat,' complained Frank. 'I've got to drink.'

'Have you taken something for it?' asked Boris.

'We don't have anything,' said Veronica.

'No medicines?' said Boris.

'No,' confessed Veronica. 'Nothing but Paludrine for the malaria.'

'No medicines,' said Boris, turning to Frank. He retrieved the brandy and poured himself another glass as if he were trying to recover from shock.

'Gilbert says it's the heat,' said Frank miserably.

'I'll get Happy to bring you something,' declared Boris. 'Where is that lazy bastard?' He hammered on the veranda and bellowed until Happy came running from the house. 'Medicine box!' he barked.

'Do you think it's anything serious?' asked Veronica.

'No,' said Boris. 'Sam was fever. Hank is hot. The sun does something to the stomach.'

'It hasn't happened to me,' said Veronica.

When the medicine box was produced Boris rummaged through a jumble of bottles and cardboard cartons. Most of them seemed to be commercial samples. He selected a packet of tiny white pellets and gave them to Frank.

'Try a couple,' he said. 'Let me know what happens.'

'What are they?' asked Veronica, pulling the packet from Frank and trying to read the label.

Boris shrugged. 'We'll soon find out,' he said. He grinned and winked at Veronica.

'Your hair is white and my hair is white,' he said after a while.

'Yes,' said Veronica.

'His hair is dark.'

'Yes,' she said. She laughed and licked her teeth. She looked comfortable in this strange place with this peculiar man. She crossed her legs and balanced the glass on her knee.

'What do you think of the old place?' he said, returning to his brandy. He waved his glass at the house. 'It was built by a German missionary. Came out. Want to save the world.'

'What happened to him?' asked Veronica.

'Cannibals come creeping out of them trees one night and eat him,' said Boris. 'Perhaps he went mad or the fever got him. I don't know. It was a long time ago.' He grinned and reached for the bottle. His jacket hung open. His chest was covered in thick, grey hair. A crucifix hung from his throat.

'It's smaller than we imagined,' ventured Frank.

'We got ten bedrooms here,' said Boris. 'We got the biggest place south of Bolozo Rouge.'

'Sam wrote letters,' explained Veronica. 'He said there were fifty bedrooms and a night club and everything.'

'Dreams,' sniffed Boris. 'Sam was a terrible man for dreams.'

Frank was silent. He sprawled in the chair, eyes fixed on his empty glass, and felt the world swelling and falling around him. Bruised by fatigue and confused by the brandy, he sensed Veronica was flirting with Boris. He gloats. She laughs. He drinks. She watches him. What happens if the drink turns him nasty? No escape. Nowhere to hide. Nothing but fear and darkness and forest. Watch him. Don't let him touch her. They say you can smell fear. Why doesn't she pull down her dress?

He tried to catch their conversation but he couldn't unravel the words; he heard someone call his name but he found he couldn't answer them. He tried to stand up, sagged, staggered, and then they were helping him to his room, pulling off his clothes and folding him gently into the bed.

The next morning he woke up to find himself in a small, square box of sunlight. A window. A wardrobe. His suitcase at the foot of the bed. He groaned and closed his eyes. He had dreamt that he was home at the Hercules Café: his room damp and filled with shadows, beyond the window the sound of traffic squelching through the wet street, a draught from the keyhole strong enough to lift the lino, Olive upstairs shouting, Gilbert downstairs laughing and, above everything, the smell of fried eggs, tomatoes, sausages, hamburgers, bacon smoke, burnt toast and fresh coffee.

There was a knock on the door and Boris appeared with a breakfast tray.

'Are you awake? You've been asleep. Look, I've brought you some breakfast.'

Frank sat up and shivered. A fan in the ceiling churned the air, sucking at the mosquito nets.

'How is your stomach?'

'Empty,' said Frank. He stared at the tray. There was coffee, bread and a large banana. The coffee came with a biscuit and a little jug of condensed milk.

'Is Gilbert awake?'

'Yes,' said Boris. He smiled. 'And Veronica. She is washing. You can wash. I will show you. When you are ready. I shall be waiting.'

He walked towards the door and then paused, turned and glanced under the bed.

'Look in your shoes,' he advised gravely.

'Why?'

'Spiders,' said Boris.

Frank stuffed his mouth with bread, rolled on to the floor and peered suspiciously into his shoes. When he was satisfied they were empty he dressed and went out to search for Gilbert. He found him following Boris around the compound. The sun was already burning, high in a blue, blank sky. He stepped forward into the heat, shielding his eyes against the glare.

'Good morning,' shouted Gilbert as he approached. 'Boris is showing me over the place. Come and look at the kitchen.' He smiled and wrapped Frank's shoulders in the hook of a fat, damp arm. His breath smelt of death and toothpaste.

The kitchen was no more than a large shed with a dirt floor. The ceiling had been papered with the colour pages of magazines: advertisements for airlines, vitamins, beer and baby food. The walls were thickly coated with blue enamel paint. There were shelves and benches around the walls, a zinc tank with draining boards, a Kelvinator, a big wooden barrel and a cast-iron stove. The stove was an old wood-burner with a pot-bellied oven. The air stank of boiled eggs and blood.

Happy was working at a bench, cutting up a goat with an axe. He had reduced the beast to a pile of hair, offal, legs and bones. The goat's head lay on the floor and stared up at Happy with hard, astonished eyes. The bench was shining with blood.

'These flies must be a problem,' said Gilbert, slapping at the air with his hands.

Boris frowned. He stared around the kitchen, as if he were looking at flies for the first time. He seemed puzzled by them. He tried to catch one with his fingers.

'You bastard!' he bellowed at Happy. 'Clear out those bones!' Happy flinched and farted. He gathered up the scraps and tossed them through the open window.

Frank leaned from the window and squinted into the sunlight. At the back of the kitchen a great heap of rubbish was spreading slowly into the forest. It was an oozing porridge of skin, skulls, beaks, claws, bones, feathers, tails and teeth. Here and there a plastic bottle or drum stuck through the crust like flotsam caught in a petrified sea. Above the rubbish a shroud of grey steam was whisked by flies.

'Where's the dog?' asked Gilbert, peering into the big, wooden barrel. The barrel lay on its side in a corner of the shed. It contained a pillow and a dirty, army blanket.

'No dog,' grinned Boris.

'What have you got in the larder?' asked Frank, staring at a wall of open shelves. The shelves sagged beneath the weight of buckets, baskets and bowls.

'We got cooking oil, rice, onions and soap,' said Boris, scratching his neck. 'We got tomatoes, dry fish, plantain and peppers. What else we got? We got sugar, salt and yams. We got eggs. We got tinned milk, cornstarch and coffee. We got bread. We got beer from the truck when the road is open. Today we got goat from the market in town.'

'Do you bring vegetables up from town?' asked Frank.

'Yes. We got no garden since we planted Sam.'

'I brought him Bovril,' said Gilbert sadly.

'What's that?' inquired Boris.

'Bovril? Bovril is Bovril. Alas my poor brother. You know. Bovril. It's a sort of beef gravy,' said Gilbert.

'Can you eat it?' asked Boris.

'Yes.'

'Is it good?'

'Yes.'

'We'll have to lock it up in the store,' grumbled Boris.

Gilbert fetched his suitcase and Boris led them into the maze of sheds and cabins that clung, like a little shanty town, against the main walls of the kitchen block. In one of the sheds an old German generator cursed and thundered, straining at its rusted anchors, sweating pearls of hot, black oil. Boris stopped before something that looked like an ammunition store with barbed-wire garlands on the roof and a heavy padlock on the door.

'Security,' he said. 'Don't trust anybody.' He poked the padlock with a key and rattled a length of chain.

'You have to be careful,' said Gilbert, to humour him.

Boris nodded. The door creaked open and he ushered them into a hot gloom. The store room was packed from floor to ceiling with food. There were cases of canned cocktail sausage, bales of cornflakes, bundles of fruit cake and a thousand tinned apricots in heavy syrup. Everything was stacked in original factory cardboard. It might have been the hoard of some demented grocer.

'What's this?' said Gilbert. He cocked his head and tried to read along the side of a carton.

'Emergency rations,' said Boris proudly. He sniffed and pulled on his big, meaty nose. 'Top quality. No rubbish.' He pushed a finger into one nostril and bent his nose out of shape.

'But where did you find it?'

'Food agents,' said Boris. He unplugged his nose and watched nervously as Gilbert knelt down to open his suitcase.

'Do you have any sardines?' asked Frank hopefully when they had donated their Bovril to the hoard.

'It's emergency. Special. We don't touch it,' barked Boris. He looked angry. He looked threatened. He bundled them out and quickly chained the door.

'I'm sorry,' said Frank. 'I didn't mean to upset you.'

'They're all thieves,' grumbled Boris. 'Don't trust nobody.' He pushed the key back into his vest and glared across at the kitchen. 'You got to keep stuff for special.'

'The boy's sick. You get queer appetites when you're sick. I'll look after him,' said Gilbert gently.

'I give him sardine. What happens? Pretty soon every damn bastard want a sardine. Pretty soon we got no rations.'

'That's right,' said Gilbert.

'I got to look after these things,' seethed Boris.

'You're the best man for it,' said Gilbert.

'They don't steal nothing from me,' insisted Boris.

'They wouldn't dare,' said Gilbert.

'I teach the bastards a lesson,' growled Boris.

'They wouldn't forget it,' said Gilbert.

Boris nodded and looked mollified. 'You want the car today?' he inquired suddenly.

'No,' said Gilbert.

'Good,' said Boris. He pulled off his hat and examined the brim. 'I got business in town. You want something? Ask Happy. Nothing happens.'

Frank and Gilbert watched him hurry away.

'That's a rum business,' said Gilbert, at last. He searched among the pockets of his jacket for a scrap of something to eat. He found a broken biscuit and picked at the crumbs.

'He's mad,' declared Frank. 'No wonder the hotel is empty.'

'I suppose Sam must have had his reasons,' said Gilbert doubtfully.

'I'm sorry about Sam.'

Gilbert discovered a sultana at the bottom of a pocket. He offered it to Frank. 'Let's collect Veronica,' he said.

They walked back into the shadow of the silent hotel and found Veronica in her room. She was sitting on her bed, counting shoes and underwear. She had filled a little wardrobe with frocks. Her empty suitcase was thrown on the floor.

'Have you had breakfast?' said Gilbert. He looked around in the hope of a crust. It was a large, bare room with pictures from the life of Christ on the walls. *The Nativity. The Sermon on the Mount. The Last Supper.*

'Boris brought me coffee,' said Veronica absently. 'There's a shower at the end of the corridor.'

'Did he seem strange to you?' asked Frank, peering through the window at the great forest.

'Who?'

'Boris.'

'No,' said Veronica. 'He's Dutch.'

'He told me he was Hungarian,' said Gilbert.

They waited until Veronica had finished counting her clothes and then wandered aimlessly up and down the hotel corridors.

'That's the shower,' said Veronica.

They paused. It was a tiled cell with a crucifix nailed above the door.

'That's my room,' said Frank as they turned a corner. He tapped the door with his fingernails.

'And this is my room,' said Gilbert, opening his door and waving them inside. There was a bed, a window and a painted wardrobe. Pictures from the life of Christ: *Healing the Sick, Walking on Water.*

'All the rooms look the same,' said Veronica.

Gilbert smiled. He sat on the bed and clasped his knees. 'Look in the wardrobe,' he said.

'You don't need a wardrobe,' laughed Veronica. 'You didn't bring any clothes with you.'

'No room for clothes,' grinned Gilbert.

Frank pulled open the narrow, plywood doors. The wardrobe had been fitted with shelves and on the shelves there were twenty large, black, telephones. They had been carefully arranged in rows, catalogued and numbered, like prehistoric knucklebones.

'What are they doing here?' murmured Frank.

'Waiting,' smiled Gilbert. 'Waiting to be connected. One day we'll be able to call anywhere in the world.'

'I knew there was something wrong,' sighed Veronica as she caught sight of the hoard. 'I knew there was something missing.'

'Why aren't they working?' insisted Frank. It puzzled him. He thought Boris must have hidden them. I give him a telephone. What happens? Pretty soon every damn bastard want a telephone. Pretty soon we got no telephones.

'We're a long way out,' Gilbert explained patiently. 'The lines haven't reached this far into the forest. But the telephones are here. And that means, one day, we'll be able to use them!'

'Brilliant!' hooted Veronica. 'Until then we'll use cocoa tins tied to a piece of string!'

'I thought you'd be pleased,' said Gilbert impatiently, rubbing his knees.

'But what happens if there's an emergency or something?' demanded Frank. 'How do we get help?'

'Shout,' said Veronica.

'There's a post office in town,' said Gilbert. 'They'll have a telephone.' He jumped up, closed the wardrobe doors, and pushed them from the room.

'I'm sleeping next to Boris,' said Veronica. 'You're sleeping next to Gilbert. There are six empty bedrooms.' She counted on her fingers. 'Where does Happy sleep?'

'I think he sleeps in the kitchen,' said Frank.

'Boris keeps him in a barrel,' said Gilbert.

They strolled into the yard and sat in the shade of the mud wall. The air dazzled them. Wisps of dust smoked from the baked earth.

'No one's stayed here for years,' sighed Frank, staring up at the house.

'Have you seen the dining room?' asked Veronica. 'It's the big room at the front. The room that opens on to the veranda.'

'What's it like?'

'There are birds building a nest in a hole in the ceiling.'

They fell silent. Frank scratched the earth with a stick.

Veronica closed her eyes. Gilbert sat and studied his shoes.

'Are we going home?' said Frank, at last.

'Do you want to go home?' Gilbert asked him.

'I don't know.'

'Do you want to go home?' Gilbert asked Veronica.

She shrugged and opened her eyes. 'What are we going to do here? We've reached the hotel at the end of the world.'

'We could make something of it,' said Gilbert.

'What?'

'We could make a few changes here and there,' said Gilbert. 'Fix that roof. Paint these walls.'

'Pull it down and start again,' said Veronica.

'It's not that bad,' said Gilbert.

'But who would find us here?' demanded Frank, waving his arm at the forest. 'We're lost. We don't even have a telephone.'

'There's a town at the bottom of the hill,' said Gilbert. 'A town needs an hotel.' It was obvious. If they didn't want a bed they would come for the food and the beer. Bring out the tables. Light the candles. Supper under the stars. Yes. You have to start somewhere.

'I thought it would be different,' said Veronica miserably. She stretched out her legs until her feet stuck from the shadow and caught the heat of the sun.

'It could be different. Sam would have wanted us to stay. He had plans. We could turn the place into something special. Look at this yard. It could be a huge garden. Everything grows in this heat. You could stick an umbrella in the ground and the bugger would root. Imagine. It could be beautiful. The place doesn't look too good at the moment. But we can make it work. And once we've settled down – word gets around – people will start to search us out.'

They were discovered sooner than he expected. At dusk Boris returned with the car and announced his arrival by leaning an elbow on the horn. He had two white men with him.

'Patron!' he shouted as Gilbert appeared on the veranda. 'Patron, we have some friends for supper.'

The two men grinned and waved at Gilbert. One of them

wore a crisp, blue safari suit and spectacles. The other was dressed in a brown city suit and leather sandals.

'Good evening,' shouted Gilbert as he waited for them to climb the steps. He beckoned Frank and Veronica from the sofa in the lobby where they had been trying to make sense of Sam's account books.

'Maurice Grey,' grinned the one in the blue safari suit as he reached for Gilbert's hand. He had a long, pale face and smelt of too much aftershave. He squeezed Gilbert's hand like a piece of wet flannel.

'Oscar Stamp,' smiled the one in the sandals. He was smaller than his companion and had a face like a potato.

Everyone shook hands and nodded and smiled. Then Boris led them through the hotel into the compound where Happy had arranged a table and chairs.

Maurice Grey introduced himself as a baby-food man from You-Kay. He said his company was very big in bottled baby-care products. He had been working in Batuta but had been sent to the forest to investigate new opportunities in the powder milk market. He looked disappointed. Nobody wanted his powder milk. He said the darkies preferred their teats. They suckled their babies for years. It wasn't natural. You couldn't teach these people anything. He blamed the teat. He said if women didn't have teats he'd be a happy man. Pardon his language. He was finished with Africa. He was going home to You-Kay.

Oscar Stamp said he was a tractor man. The forest needed his tractors. He said one day they would succeed in clearing out the forest with proper tractors. He had been in Africa for seven years and he also wanted to go to You-Kay but first he had some business in Lagos.

When they were settled at the table Happy came running from the kitchen. He was wearing an apron splattered with blood. He brought peanuts and bottles of ice-cold beer.

'Where are you staying?' asked Gilbert as they sucked at the bottles. A lantern on the table had attracted a cloud of pinhead moths. They floated like sequins above the flame.

'He's staying with me,' said Oscar, nodding at Maurice. 'I've got a house in town. The company looks after me. I can't complain in that department.'

'Why don't you stay out here at the hotel?'

Oscar laughed and shook his head.

'He got a woman. She cook. She clean. Look after him,' said Boris.

Veronica snorted and spat peanut shells.

'She likes to see me comfortable,' admitted Oscar. Happy staggered through the darkness carrying a cauldron of hot goat stew. He had mixed the meat with tomatoes, peanuts and peppers.

'You've taught him to cook,' marvelled Maurice as he sniffed up the steam.

'Is he still farting?' asked Oscar.

'The bastard don't stop,' muttered Boris.

'You should change his diet,' said Maurice. 'What are you feeding him?'

'Nothing,' said Boris indignantly. 'Scraps. He steals what he want.'

While Boris served the stew Happy scuttled away and returned with bowls of yam and fried plantain.

'Sam could take a goat and make it taste like a baby lamb,' sighed Oscar.

Boris nodded sadly. He picked up his bottle of beer, turned towards the garden and gave the grave a salute.

'I'll miss old Sam,' said Maurice, looking at Frank. 'Did you ever meet him?'

'No,' said Frank.

'He was my friend,' said Gilbert proudly. 'We walked across the whole damn country after the war.'

'It's changed a lot since those days,' said Oscar.

'Sam was a character,' said Maurice.

'He drank me under the table,' said Boris with considerable admiration. A large beetle with scarlet wings fell from the sky and landed in the bowl of yam. He pulled it out, cracked it with his thumb and threw it away.

'You're fresh from You-Kay,' said Oscar.

'Yes,' said Gilbert.

'What are you doing here?'

'Sam sent for me.'

'Too bad,' said Maurice. 'Are you staying on?'

'Yes,' said Frank. He couldn't decide when he had made this decision but, confronted with the man's expression of incredulity, he felt determined to stay with Gilbert and make it work.

'You're keeping the hotel?'

'Yes,' said Veronica, glancing at Frank. 'We're keeping the hotel.'

'I'll give it six months,' said Maurice.

'Twelve if you're lucky,' warned Oscar.

'Why?'

'It's no damn good. Nothing happens. Nothing works. You'll learn,' said Maurice.

'It's a flea-bitten, God-forsaken country,' said Oscar. 'The place is jumping with jiggers.'

'There's worse than jiggers,' said Boris mildly.

'You're right,' said Oscar, waving his fork. 'There are flies that crawl up your nose while you sleep and lay their eggs in your sinuses. Then the maggots hatch out and eat your brains.'

'I don't believe it,' grinned Frank.

'It's true,' said Boris. 'I heard of someone. He died from it.'

'It's the heat,' complained Oscar. 'It slows you down and wears you out. You arrive and you think you won't make the same mistakes. But it gets you in the end.' He fell silent for a minute and contemplated a mouthful of gristle, turning it over with his tongue.

'Look what happened to Sam,' said Boris.

'It's the darkies,' said Maurice. 'The darkies drive you mad. You can't teach them anything. They suckle their babies for years and years. Can you believe it? They've all grown teats like cucumbers. Pardon my language.'

'Why do they do it?' asked Frank.

'Birth control,' said Maurice. 'They think it works like birth control .'

'It sounds perfectly sensible to me,' said Veronica.

'Birth control?'

'Yes.'

'It isn't natural.'

'Why?'

'I'm a baby-food man,' said Maurice. He shook his head, stunned by the absurdity of the world into which he had fallen. His spectacles flashed in the lamplight.

'I can't wait for You-Kay,' said Oscar, grinding gristle between his teeth.

Maurice sniffed and took a swig from his bottle. 'You know what I miss about You-Kay?' he said.

'Tell me,' said Oscar.

'It's clean and cold and everything works.'

'Which part of You-Kay you from?' demanded Oscar, turning to Gilbert.

'London.'

'London!' crooned Maurice. He rubbed his rough potato face and grinned.

'How is it?' asked Oscar.

'Fine.'

'Oxford Street on a wet November afternoon.'

'Selfridges blazing with Christmas lights.'

'Egg and bacon.'

'Apple pie and custard.'

'Sweet Jesus.'

'I just want to get to Heathrow,' said Maurice. 'I just want to get to Heathrow and you know what I'm going to do?'

'Tell me,' said Oscar.

'I'm going to fall down on my knees and kiss the ground.'

'You don't miss it, I mean you don't appreciate it, until it's taken away from you,' said Oscar.

Gilbert thought of London and tried to see it as the golden city of the cold, blue north. He could see only gloomy office blocks, collapsed Victorian tenements, dirty streets and gimcrack bazaars. The people looked grey, their clothes smelt dirty, there was sickness in the sulphurous rain. The old city, throne room to an empire, had become a bear-garden for tourists, a diorama, a tuppenny peepshow. He wanted to explain these things to the visitors but he knew they wouldn't hear him. The London they had carried with them across the length of Africa was a lost world, made miraculous by memory.

'I feel sorry for you, stuck in this hole without Sam,' said Maurice. 'Don't get me wrong. I hope it works out. But it makes me feel sick just thinking about it.'

'It's no life,' said Oscar.

Gilbert said nothing. The man was a buffoon. It's no life in London. The noise. Bedlam. The squalor. Nasty. Women locked away at night. Afraid to walk the streets. Anyway. People don't have lives any more. They have television.

'Have you got an English cigarette?' said Maurice hopefully, when they had finished the stew.

'Sorry,' said Gilbert.

'Nobody?'

'They got no medicines neither,' said Boris scornfully.

'Isn't there a doctor in town?' asked Veronica.

Oscar laughed. It was a queer, high-pitched yapping noise like a little dog. 'There *was* a doctor. He was a Frenchman. Drank himself to death on palm wine. Poisoned his blood. Legs like balloons. Remember him, Boris?'

Boris nodded. 'He was a bastard.'

'Darkies make their own medicine. It's the whites who suffer, 'said Oscar. He sighed and stared at his bottle. 'It makes no difference. The town is finished. We don't need a doctor. There's no one left. You and me. Henry left last month.'

'It's a shame,' said Maurice. 'It used to be a good town. There were a couple of dozen families here at one time. French and German. Women and children.'

'Why did they leave?' asked Gilbert.

'Different reasons.'

Veronica shivered, glancing out at the dark forest.

'It's Agassou. He's the problem,' said Oscar. 'You come out here and build a factory and as soon as you get it working old man Agassou throws you out and steals the business. He stole the rubber. He stole the coffee. And now he's trying to steal the trees.'

'Why don't they do something about him?' asked Frank innocently.

'He's the president,' said Maurice.

'Why don't they get rid of him?' asked Veronica, who wasn't sure she understood.

'It's a one-party state. The *parti démocratique de Bilharzia*. They hanged the opposition after the last election,' explained Oscar.

'Which election was that?' asked Maurice.

'There was only one election,' said Oscar.

'It's not so bad,' growled Boris. He leaned across the table and touched Veronica's arm. 'Don't listen. The sun turn their brain soft. They leave. Others arrive.'

Oscar smiled. 'He's right. We're tired. It's time we went home.' He stood up and yawned. 'How much do we owe you for supper?'

Gilbert looked at Boris who looked away with a vague, distracted expression on his face.

'You're our first guests,' said Gilbert. 'Compliments of the Hotel Plenti.'

'Thanks.'

'You're welcome.'

Boris shouted for Happy.

'Good luck,' said Maurice. He grinned at Gilbert and belched.

'We'll see you in You-Kay,' said Oscar.

When they had finished shaking hands Happy took them to the car and drove out into the darkness. The noise of the engine was swallowed by trees. The compound was silent. The lantern flickered and started to smoke.

'We clean the tables,' said Boris, offering Frank an empty bottle. 'The patron must sleep.'

Gilbert staggered to his feet and let Veronica lead him away. He felt heavy and uncomfortable. The beer had muddled his head.

'We'll make it work,' he said to no one in particular. Frank and Boris watched them retreat.

'Hank' said Boris as he stared after Veronica. 'Yes?'

'Your hair is dark.'

'Yes.'

'Her hair is white.'

'Yes.'

'Are you her brother?'

'No.'

Boris nodded and studied the guttering lantern flame. 'Boris.

'Yes?'

'My name is Frank.'

14

Gilbert lost his hair. It happened in the first week at the Hotel Plenti. He found it on the pillow when he woke in the morning and clinging to collars when he undressed at night. When he washed he found it stuck to the soap like torn, grey fur. It rubbed from his scalp in untidy patches, revealing sections of shining skull. As the days passed he began to take on the appearance of a monstrous child. His head was a smooth, pink globe of flesh. His ears stuck stiff from the sides of his skull like a pair of germinating wings. It happened so quickly and appeared so shocking that no one spoke about it. Boris found him an old bush hat to stop him burning in the sun. Gilbert lumbered about the yard with the hat pulled down to his eyebrows but the heat and the sweat made him itch and he finally threw the hat away.

He spent his time sniffing under beds and measuring windows, tapping walls and squinting critically at the roof. He studied the rotting hulk of his jungle hotel until he knew every knot in its timbers. But how to transform it into a palace continued to escape him. Sometimes he went missing for hours. Then he could be found in Sam's bedroom, sitting in a green cane chair, surrounded by books and piles of old clothes. Although Frank and Veronica never questioned him, they guessed he was searching for a message; a letter or diary that might give him reason and hope. But he found nothing to help him. The worn-out clothes, cracked spectacles and tattered carpet slippers were the remains of a strange old man that Gilbert had not known. The Sam Pilchard of his youth, brave, laughing, toast of the Coronation, hero of Frank's nursery, had not lived in this room. This Sam Pilchard was a poor, mad crow who chewed cola nut and never changed his vest. Gilbert sat, with his big, bald head in his hands, and tried to make sense of it.

Frank spent his time in the kitchen. At first Happy was frightened. Frank made him fart. But he soon settled down and began to take a pride in his knowledge of soups and stews. He showed Frank how to make fufu from maize flour and pounded yam and the trick of eating with his fingers: pulling at a piece of fufu, rolling it into a sticky ball, dipping it into a bowl of gravy. He showed him how to scrub the sand from dried river fish and pull off the heads for a nourishing broth. He helped Frank make small chop from fried ripe plantain and introduced him to palm wine. He kept a bottle in a bucket beneath the table. He called it the white stuff. It tasted sour and strong.

At the crack of dawn, while it was dark and Frank was still asleep, Happy emerged from his barrel, swept the floor, counted the eggs, checked the shelves for snakes and fetched wood for the pot-bellied stove. He drew water from the tank, washed, gargled and boiled coffee. While he waited for the coffee he liked to sit on a stool and stare at the ceiling. He had papered the place with his favourite pictures. He loved the man who grinned and held out a bottle of bright, yellow beer. The man wore an embroidered shirt, gold cufflinks and a large, silver wristwatch. Happy was amazed by the size of this wristwatch. It fascinated him. He thought the man was probably the president. Next to the man who grinned at the beer bottle he had pasted the picture of a beautiful woman holding a huge, pink, laughing baby. The woman was Chinese. Happy had heard that the Chinese eat babies. He wondered how to cook them. Life was full of mysteries.

Frank usually arrived in time to drink the coffee and help Happy make breakfast. When breakfast was finished they began, at once, to prepare the supper. They soaked rice, scrubbed yams, peeled plantain, ground peanuts, gutted fish, plucked feathers and pulled entrails. They made a stew from whatever they found available, set it on the stove to simmer and, finally, unless Boris caught him, Happy crept away to sleep in some dark, secluded corner through the hottest part of the day.

Happy spoke pidgin and, since this was the language of the

kitchen, coaxed Frank to talk by training him like a tame parrot.

'You go mek?' asked Happy.

'You go mek?' echoed Frank.

'A nopa mek notin,' said Happy.

'A nopa mek notin,' echoed Frank.

Happy would laugh and dance about the kitchen and stop for a swig of the white stuff.

Veronica did nothing. She was in the business of taking orders and, since there were no orders, there was no business. She sat in the sun and cooked her legs. They also serve who only stand and wait. After breakfast she would make a raft of blankets in a corner of the compound, pull off her frock and sit for the sun in her underwear. Frank made up a mixture of kitchen oils, for the sake of her skin, and scolded her for taking risks in the heat. She sat, smiling and shining, while he polished her shoulders with fat.

'You'll die in this heat,' he grumbled, as his fingers slithered across her back. 'It's hot enough to melt marble.'

Veronica snorted. 'It's not done anything for me.' She held out a pale and slender arm. 'Look. I'm as white as bread.'

Frank leaned over her shoulder, pretending to study her arms and dared to look instead at her breasts. Her bra was loose, the cups had sagged and her nipples stood exposed.

'You could at least wear something to make yourself decent,' he complained, watching a nipple stiffen and grow.

'I am decent,' Veronica said impatiently, pulling the bra into place.

'What happens if Boris finds you?' argued Frank.

'He's in town.'

'And what happens if he comes back and finds you sitting around half-naked?'

'I expect the excitement will kill him,' she said scornfully. She stretched out and lay on her stomach, bunching the blanket beneath her chin. 'Now go away, Frank. I'm concentrating.'

It was while she soaked in the sun that Chester emerged one morning from a pile of logs. He was an old, mad-eyed chicken. A bundle of straw and broken feathers. He tiptoed forward, eyes rolling, head bobbing, and settled down beside her on the blanket.

Chester was the last of the chickens of Plenti. There had once been dozens of them, scratching a living from the dust. But, one by one, Boris had caught and butchered them, snapping their necks in his fist. Chester survived because he was cunning and even when Boris, frustrated beyond reason, had set down poisoned grain, the old bird would not be caught. He had retired at last to the log pile and lived there quietly with his loneliness and lice. No one could explain why he fell in love with Veronica. But once he found her he wouldn't leave her alone. He became her most devoted admirer. He followed her around the compound and sometimes ventured inside the hotel.

'That Chester a bad chicken,' warned Boris one morning as he drove Frank and Veronica to town. 'You wait. You find out. What a bastard. Peck out your eye for a cockroach.'

But Veronica only grinned and cradled Chester in her arms. 'He's like a kitten,' she said, blowing the dust from his feathers. And Chester, hypnotised with pleasure, whistled softly through his beak.

It took nearly an hour to descend the slippery slope. Beyond the hotel the jungle sucked them into the twilight while Boris struggled for control of the wheel. The trees swallowed them. Frank hung his head from the window and looked for the road. He found himself staring down a wet, green throat. There was an overwhelming smell of growth and collapse, life wriggling from decay, the smell of the forest eating itself. There were cucumbers, heavy as human corpses, hanging from curious aerial vines. There were trees that looked like sticks of giant celery and others that might have been sprouting bones. There were gooseberries big as porcupines that burst and drowned in their own blood.

There were towering purple cauliflowers that filled the car with the stink of putrefying flesh.

As they reached the edge of town, sunlight broke through the forest canopy, the trees dwindled and lost some of their strength. The road turned to dust between clumps of thorn and yellow grasses, overgrown ditches and mud-block houses. Here and there small plots had been planted with ground nuts and raffia palms. A woman sat by the road holding a small and hairy pig. Boris hammered the horn and shouted at her through the window. An old man ran out and threw stones.

'Crazy bastard!' laughed Boris. He followed the road to market and stopped the car in the shade of a wall.

The market was a patch of waste ground where women came to sit beside baskets of vegetables, fish and fruit. They sat in silence, a circle of black buddhas in batik frocks. One of the circle, a young buddha with a blind eye, was guarding a cage stuffed with dead chickens. When she saw Veronica she looked angry and tried to wave her away.

'She thinks you've come to sell Chester,' grinned Frank.

'Best thing,' muttered Boris. He bought bananas and a dried mud fish. When he was finished he took them to the general store. They walked through the town with an escort of children and flea-bitten dogs. One of the children, a fat boy in torn pants and a Superman vest, kept the dogs at bay by smacking at them, now and then, with a stone tied to a short stick. Whenever he threatened to use the stick the dogs cringed, ran in circles and came back snapping at his heels.

The store was an evil-smelling shed with a hot, zinc roof. The shelves, lit by a single paraffin lamp, looked empty. There were a few blocks of Palmolive soap in sun-faded wrappers, a box of large size Vaseline and a carton of coloured plastic combs.

'These look good,' said Frank optimistically, picking up a tin of mixed fruit salad. He wiped the dust from the lid with his thumb.

Boris took the tin and gave it a shake. Then he grunted and pushed the tin away. 'All gone bad,' he said in disgust.

'Ask him if he has any biscuits,' said Veronica, nodding at the storekeeper who was asleep in a chair behind the counter. Pages from an old calendar had been pinned to the wall above his head. Miss January 1964 was a very pink girl in a swimsuit, smiling through a fall of fake snow.

'Chocolate biscuits,' said Veronica.

But Boris only scowled and would not wake him. 'He don't have nothing,' he said. 'We wait for the food agent.'

They had been living at the hotel for more than a fortnight when the food agent called on them. It was an afternoon of heavy, suffocating heat. Nothing moved. The air burned like acid. The shadows were caked with flies. Gilbert and Frank were sitting sweating on the veranda when a truck struggled up the forest road.

At first it was nothing but a glint of light, dancing through the dark trees. Then it became a roll of thunder followed by smoke. Finally a long, red truck roared into view and shuddered to a halt in front of the hotel. As they watched, a driver swung himself down from the cab and stamped his feet in the dust. He was a young Moroccan dressed in a fancy leather waistcoat, blue jeans and cowboy boots.

When Gilbert introduced himself as the new patron the Moroccan smiled and shook his hand. He said his name was Alley. He stepped back and invited Gilbert to inspect the cargo. But before Gilbert could make a move, Boris had appeared from nowhere, coiled his arm around the agent's neck and led him a safe distance from the hotel. They talked urgently together for several minutes. Boris spat, Alley laughed and money was exchanged. Then they walked back to the truck and unloaded a pile of cardboard cartons.

Frank and Gilbert sat on the veranda and watched them carry the supplies up the steps and into the hotel.

'Where does he get the money?' whispered Frank as Boris staggered past with a carton under his arm.

'Don't look at me,' shrugged Gilbert. He cocked his head and tried to read the legend on the side of the carton.

'Do you suppose Sam had money hidden somewhere?'

'Tinned grapefruit!' exploded Gilbert. 'The daft bugger has bought tinned grapefruit!'

Frank frowned and stared at Gilbert. 'How much money do we have left?' he asked suspiciously.

'Nothing,' said Gilbert.

'Nothing?'

'Well, we spent our savings on the tickets.'

'But what about the money from the Hercules Café?'

'Yes, we've got that coming. But it takes time, Frank. You don't just sell everything and wake up next morning with a suitcase full of dirty bank notes at the end of your bed. There's a lot of paperwork.'

'But it is coming?' insisted Frank.

'Oh, yes,' said Gilbert confidently. 'It's coming.'

'So how long will it take to get here?'

Gilbert shrugged again. 'I don't know. Three or four months. Five. No more than six.

'We can't wait six months.'

'It's not so easy, said Gilbert. 'They don't know we're here. We've got to find a way to smuggle the money into the country without anyone asking a lot of damn silly questions.'

'Because we don't have work permits,' said Frank. 'We're illegal immigrants. Isn't that the truth? If they catch up with us they'll throw us out.'

Gilbert nodded gloomily. 'I thought Sam could make the arrangements,' he said.

Then Veronica appeared, half-dressed, bare-foot, wrapped in a blanket. 'What's happening?' she demanded. She had been disturbed trying to sunbathe behind the store room. At the sight of Boris and Alley she had taken fright and made a dash for cover with Chester flapping at her heels.

'Boris is trying to corner the grapefruit market,' said Gilbert sourly.

'Have you seen where that stuff comes from?' said Veronica.

Gilbert shook his head.

'The Eurovision Famine Appeal. It's international famine relief. They're hoarding charity food.'

'I don't believe it,' scoffed Frank.

'It's true!' she shouted.

'How do you know?'

'Because it has Eurovision Food for Africa printed on every box, noodle-brain!' Her feet hurt. She wiped them, one against the other, as she talked.

'Well what can I do about it?' complained Gilbert.

'Stop them,' demanded Veronica. 'Go out and stop them.'

'I'll have a word with Boris when they've finished,' he growled. He rubbed at his skull. A pearl of sweat flew from his nose.

'It must be a mistake,' said Frank.

Veronica looked at him. She wasn't impressed. She gathered up her blanket and marched away with Chester scrambling in her wake.

'What do you make of it?' grunted Gilbert, as another load of grapefruit came stumbling up the steps.

'It doesn't make sense,' said Frank, shaking his head.

Once the supplies had been safely landed and locked away, Boris led Alley back to the veranda and sat him down with Gilbert and Frank. He looked immensely pleased with himself.

He produced a bottle of Johnnie Walker and a tray of greasy glasses.

'Where did you pick up your supplies?' demanded Gilbert, pointing a thumb at the truck.

'No problem, patron,' smiled Alley. He fetched a pair of mirrored sunglasses from his waistcoat pocket and made a little performance of polishing them against his sleeve.

'It looks like charity food,' ventured Gilbert. He glanced unhappily at Boris.

'First class,' smiled Alley. 'You wanna take a look? Check it out?'

'But you're selling supplies that were shipped out here by famine relief organisations,' protested Frank. 'It was meant to feed the starving and the homeless.'

'No one starving here,' said Boris.

'So how did he get his hands on it?' said Gilbert.

'Good and legal,' laughed Alley. 'It comes through on the black market. I pay cash for everything. I got anything you want. American hamburger. English biscuits. French sausage. Ask me. I got anything.' He stroked his forehead with a slender hand. He had a delicate face and an easy smile. His skin was the colour of hard, polished wood.

'I don't know. It's not decent,' said Gilbert. 'And, anyway, we don't need it.'

'We got to think of tomorrow,' said Boris. He opened his shirt and scratched himself savagely. 'We got to plan. Something goes wrong. Maybe. Something happens. We got to be prepared.'

'Feed the hungry. That's my business,' said Alley peacefully, sipping his Scotch. A silver bracelet swung on his wrist.

'Did Sam know about this business?' demanded Gilbert.

'Sam? Yes. He understood a thing or two,' sulked Boris. He gulped at his drink and glared out at the glittering trees.

'What happened to Sam?' inquired Alley.

'Fever,' said Boris.

'Bad?'

'Dead.'

Alley nodded and smiled at Gilbert.

'It doesn't feel right,' complained Gilbert, wagging his head. What's wrong? Mountains of food in Europe. An embarrassment of riches. Move mountains and feed the world. Fat chance. What happens? They send potato powder to people with no water. Wheat to people starving for rice. Sometimes they send food but no trucks. Other times they send trucks and no food. Tinned grapefruit! No man alive ever went hungry for a tin of grapefruit.

'I'm easy,' yawned Alley. 'Take it or leave it. No problem.' He stretched out his legs and studied the stitching on his cowboy boots. 'I've got customers screaming for the stuff.'

There was an uneasy silence.

'Look. Maybe tonight I break the rules,' suggested Boris uncomfortably. 'We have sardines. Some nice tinned peas. What you want?'

'Happy made a stew,' said Frank. 'We've already prepared supper.' He didn't want charity. Stuff the sardines. He stood up and walked out to the kitchen.

'Are you staying?' asked Boris.

'OK,' said Alley.

'We don't have a clean room,' said Gilbert, wiping his head.

'No problem. I sleep in the truck. What a baby! She's got everything. Night cabin. Foam mattress. Stereo. Air conditioning. You'd better believe it!'

'Stay and eat,' said Boris anxiously. 'We have a few drinks. We have a few laughs.'

So Alley made himself comfortable with a bottle of Scotch and when it grew dark Frank came out to serve the stew. Gilbert sat down with them but Veronica went to eat in her room.

'What is this muck?' demanded Boris. He poked the stew with his spoon, frowning and sniffing as if he expected to find a turd.

'Fish,' said Frank.

Boris choked with disgust and threw his spoon away. 'You call this food? It makes me sick in the stomach!' He bent his head and spat, fiercely, into his bowl.

'Eat,' said Gilbert. 'Eat and be glad of it.'

'Hah! You talk!' shouted Boris. 'Not so long ago. You want to open the store and steal every damn thing. Invite every damn bastard to one big supper. Now it's a different tune. Eat snot. Starve.'

'That was before we knew it was stolen,' said Gilbert quietly. He sat back in his chair and picked at his teeth with a fish bone.

'Stolen?' roared Boris. 'I pay good cash money for everything! This bastard rob me blind.' He turned to Alley and speared his ribs with a finger. 'Tell him. Tell him the price.'

Alley grinned. 'Quality don't come cheap, patron. You have to pay the market price.'

'And if you can't pay?' asked Frank.

'You don't eat,' said Gilbert. He shrugged. 'I'm going to bed.'

'You don't know nothing!' bellowed Boris, as Gilbert trudged off down the veranda. 'You don't know!'

'Leave him alone. He'll learn,' said Alley, reaching for the bottle of Scotch.

Frank remained on the veranda, watching them get drunk. It was a hot clear night. He sat, a little distance from them and listened to their conversation. They tried to refill his glass whenever he raised it to his mouth but, otherwise, ignored him.

They were talking about the border towns, the roads that were open, the roads that were closed, the trade in the north and the war in Chad. Boris was always eager for news. Alley had heard that the Libyans had bombed Ndjamena airport and the French were moving more troops to the city. Boris cursed and said they were always looking for trouble. The French everywhere. A soldier stuck in every pineapple.

Alley laughed. He plucked a Marlboro from his waistcoat pocket and offered the pack to Boris who began to smoke them, one after another, sucking greedily, flicking them away when they burned too small for his fingers.

Frank watched the butts gather in the darkness beneath the veranda like tiny, smouldering eyes.

At night the jungle gave out the damp, sweet smell of decay. Somewhere in the undergrowth an invisible beast began to bark at the moon.

Alley said that he wanted to get away from the forest before the rains washed out the road. He thought he might spend some time along the coast of Cameroon. Boris told him about a place in Douala called Club Saint Hilaire. There was a girl at the club called Temptation. He described her reproductive organs at length and with remarkable relish. His mouth hung loose. His chin was wet. Alley promised to give her a message.

'You say old Boris will be back. Collect her one day,' belched Boris. He staggered from his chair, wrenched open his pants and urinated over the edge of the veranda. The cigarette fell from his mouth and he bent to retrieve it. He was so drunk that he wet his shoes.

'We finished the whisky,' sighed Alley. 'And the whisky finished me.' He held up the empty bottle and gave it a little shake.

'I'll help Boris back to his room,' said Frank.

'I don't need no damn bastard to hold my hand,' wheezed Boris as he lurched down the veranda.

Frank reached out to him but Boris struck out with his fists, punching at the air like a decrepit boxer fighting shadows, turned, toppled and fell down the steps.

'Don't bother with him,' said Alley as they watched him crawling about in the dust. He took Frank's arm and drew him back against the wall. 'You wanna come to my truck?' He looked at Frank with a soft, flirtatious smile. His brown eyes shone in the moonlight.

Frank frowned. He shook his head, ashamed and confused. He twisted free and hurried away.

As he groped along the corridor towards the safety of his room he heard Boris singing on the edge of the forest. It was a foolish, sentimental song scored with a chorus of curses. He lay in bed and listened to the noise echo around the hotel, first loud, then soft, as Boris staggered in circles. Sometimes he heard him shout with rage and throw stones at the undergrowth. Sometimes he heard him stop to chuckle like a lunatic at some secret joke. And then there was silence.

Frank closed his eyes and tried to sleep. But sprawled in a sweat beneath the sheet he found himself counting the days. Monday. Tuesday. Wednesday. Thursday. Friday. Saturday. Closed on Sunday. Egg, bacon, sausage. Two egg, bacon, sausage. Cold in the morning. Rain spreading in the afternoon. Gilbert in his counting house, counting out the money. Olive in the parlour, eating bread and honey.

There was a scream, a frantic scramble, a series of screeches and Boris was shouting again. But this time the noises were more animal than human. Frank had dressed and was charging down the corridor before he had time to think about it. He reached Veronica's room, kicked open the door and flung himself to the floor.

Everything he most feared confronted him in that room. There were clothes and feathers everywhere. Boris, wearing nothing but shoes, was pinned against the wall while Chester flew and pecked at his face. Veronica crouched on the bed with her arms full of mosquito net. Her legs were trembling. She looked dumb with fright.

'I kill you bastard!' growled Boris. He thrashed out with his hands, trying to knock down the crazy chicken. But Chester, fierce as a basilisk, continued to screech and attack his face.

Boris shouted and cringed with pain. He was bleeding suddenly from the nose.

'What the hell is happening?' demanded Frank.

'What you think?' roared Boris. 'She call me. Boris. Boris. I show you something. I think she want me. Maybe. I come here. She sit there. Smiling. No shame. Next thing. Click-clack. This bastard fly at my face.'

'Liar!' screamed Veronica. 'He's drunk! He came creeping into the room and tried to get into bed while I was asleep. He didn't know I had Chester with me.'

'I kill you bastard!' thundered Boris, wiping the blood from his nose. 'Bastard! Bastard!' He gave the chicken a terrible punch to the head that stunned the bird and knocked it to the ground where it spun in circles on the tips of its wings.

Veronica burst into tears. 'Leave him alone,' she sobbed. 'Please don't hurt him.' She capsized and buried her face in the pillow.

'Now I kill you,' said Boris, glaring at Frank. He reached along the wall, unhooked *The Last Supper* and bent the frame in his hands. 'You watch. I break you.' He twisted the frame until the dry wood snapped and the glass cracked into daggers.

'Go to bed,' said Frank. 'You can kill me in the morning.'

'I snap your neck. Tell Happy. Bring a knife. Cut you into meat for stew,' growled Boris. He threw down *The Last Supper* and trampled the broken glass. He looked like a huge and dangerous ape dancing in a dead man's shoes. His arms were too long. His legs were bent beneath the weight of his body. The thick stub of his penis poked angrily through a mane of wild hair. He grunted and sprang forward. Frank attempted to jump away but Boris was quick and his fists were large. He caught Frank by the throat and started to strangle him. Frank tried to speak, to talk himself free of the monster's hands, but all his words had been squeezed to a rattle. His face turned purple. His tongue fell out. He clawed at his assailant's face, catching his nose, feeling a fresh flow of blood on his fingers. Boris tightened his grip and Frank, fainting, fell to his knees. The floor sank beneath him. The room was growing dark.

While Frank struggled Veronica jumped through the mosquito net and seized her chance to rescue Chester who had collapsed in a heap beside the bed. She picked him up like an odd cushion and carried him back to safety.

Boris watched her from the corner of his eye. He blinked. He belched. He unhooked Frank and staggered along the length of the wall until he came gently to rest against the side of the wardrobe. 'That woman. Ask me. I think she gone wrong in the head. Sleep with a damn chicken!' He gave a short, snuffling laugh and scratched his stomach.

'Get out!' hissed Veronica.

'She want a good shag,' he told Frank confidentially as he pushed his way to the door. He grinned peacefully and ruffled Frank's hair with his hand.

Frank managed to crawl to the door and press it shut. Then he sat on the floor and stared at the ceiling. A necklace of finger-prints burned on his throat.

'Did he hurt you?' whispered Veronica.

'Yes,' said Frank, without turning his eyes from the ceiling. 'Did he hurt you?'

'No,' said Veronica. 'But he nearly murdered poor old Chester.' She made a little clucking noise, picked up the chicken and squeezed it tight against her breasts. Chester scratched half-heartedly and paddled the air with his feet.

'I've had enough,' Frank said quietly. 'I want to go home.'

'We can't go home. We haven't started to do anything.' She let Chester wriggle from her arms. 'You'll feel different when we get the place working again,' she said hopefully, frowning at Frank.

Frank smiled and shook his head. He was very tired. 'It's not going to work, Veronica. We'll go mad. We'll die here and Boris will bury us in the garden with Sam.' He looked down at the floor. Jesus still sat at the overturned supper, arms outstretched, sunbeams crowning his long, pink face. The disciples smiled at their plates. Their nightgowns were sprinkled with flakes of glass.

'You're just feeling sorry for yourself because Boris took a swipe at you. He didn't mean any harm. He's drunk.'

'He's insane.'

'Go home if you don't like it!' snapped Veronica impatiently. 'I don't care. There's nothing to stop you.'

Frank stared at Jesus for a very long time. They were so far away. Outside the window a thousand miles of jungle. The beginning of the world. The end of the world. At night, in bed, the silence sometimes hurt his head. He felt crushed, deafened by the empty air. He caught himself listening for voices, footsteps, wheels, engines, the faraway drone of an aeroplane. There was nothing in the world but darkness and the sound of blood in his ears. The beginning of the world. The end of the world. 'We can't go home,' he said at last. 'We bought one-way tickets. This it it.'

'So what?'

'Don't you understand?' he shouted. 'Gilbert spent every last penny getting us here. The money from the café hasn't arrived. If anything goes wrong we're going to have to walk home!'

'When did you find out?'

'This afternoon…' He stopped and gasped for breath. He was surprised to find himself crying. He wiped his face and turned again to Jesus.

Veronica crawled across the bed and pulled open the mosquito net. 'Nothing will go wrong,' she said softly. 'Gilbert will think of something. You know how much he wanted to come here.'

'He used to dream of Africa,' whispered Frank. He looked towards the bed. She was crouched naked on her elbows and knees, watching him with her strange, green eyes. Her little breasts hung loose. The curtain was caught in the crease of her buttocks.

'Come and climb into bed with me and Chester,' she whispered. 'You'll feel better in the morning.'

15

Frank woke up to find Veronica asleep between his legs. She was sprawled on her back, snoring softly, her arms thrown over her face, hair sweated into yellow spikes. He opened his eyes and gazed at her for a long time. She was nothing but skin and bone. A beautiful scarecrow. Elbows sharp as flints. Hoop of ribs. Scoop of belly. A pin cushion between her thighs. Watching her sleep he felt huge, powerful, an ugly machine of muscle and blood. Her thin shoulders were speckled with freckles. Her breasts were no more than luminous buds, soft white ghosts where the brassière had saved her from the burning sun. He stared, feasting on these simple morsels, remembering how she had flirted with him behind the counter of the Hercules Café. The tortures inflicted by this nimble *frotteuse!* The squeezing, teasing, pinching and scratching he had endured in those days of burgeoning lust. Yet, despite all the pleading and promises, the sighs and whispers and fleeting kisses, he could count the number of times she had taken him to bed on the fingers of one hand. He reached down with the hand and used the fingers to trace a circle around a nipple. His penis ballooned against her throat. She stirred and grumbled and rolled away.

He turned his head and looked around the room. Africa glowed through the shutters, filling the room with narrow stripes of brilliant light. Chester was roosting on top of the wardrobe, one eye open, one eye closed, his feathers crawling with flies.

He pulled himself from the bed and searched for his clothes. Veronica continued to snore. He dressed quickly and slipped from the room. He half expected to find Boris waiting for him in the dark corridor. But there was only the silence and warm dust. He groped his way to the sunlight.

'A don mek wata fo kofi,' grinned Happy, when Frank appeared at the door to the kitchen. There was a smell of ripe bananas, onions and coffee. Happy was standing at his bench, wrapped in a fog of wood smoke from the pot-bellied stove. He was wearing his cardigan and a pair of khaki canvas shorts. His winklepickers were sitting on a shelf beside a bag of beans.

'Boris he don mek big troble las net,' said Happy. 'A don no silip.'

Frank sat down on a stool, rubbed his face and yawned. 'You an me togeda,' he sighed.

'Plenti palaba!' said Happy, shaking his head.

'You louk dis ting bifo?' Frank asked him, as Happy poured him a mug of coffee.

'Plenti tam bifo,' said Happy, wiping his hands on his cardigan. 'Won tam he don won kil Happy. Anoda tam he don won kil hiselef. He kos an holla. Holi Gost! A no lek dis ting.'

'It's the whisky,' said Frank. 'It turns him nasty.

'Daso,' said Happy. 'You lek to ex? A kouk am meselef.'

'No,' said Frank, peering at the basket of eggs. He didn't have the stomach for breakfast. 'A nopa chop notin.'

'Dey smel sweet,' frowned Happy, picking one up between his fingers and giving it a sniff.

Frank didn't have enough Pidgin to explain that Boris and Veronica had, between them, spent most of the night trying to throttle and suffocate him. So he just sat on the stool, nursed his bruised throat and smiled.

A little later Gilbert rolled up for breakfast. While he waited for Happy to boil the eggs he cut himself a huge plate of banana sandwiches and brewed another pot of coffee which he drank, very hot, with sweet tinned milk.

'Where's Boris this morning?' he asked, spitting banana at Frank.

Frank shrugged. He had been waiting to explain how he'd heard screaming and found Boris invading Veronica's bed. Last night? Yes. Drunk? Yes. And then what happened? Boris had tried to tear out his throat. Notice the bruise beneath the chin. Observe the thumb prints under the ears. And then what happened? Boris had retreated and left them alone. Why? No answer. And then what happened? Veronica stopped screaming. And then what happened? Nothing. Was she hurt? No. Did you look? Yes. What was she wearing? Nothing. What did she say? Nothing. And then what happened? Nothing. Nothing. Nothing happened. 'I suppose he's gone to town,' he said, avoiding Gilbert's eye.

Gilbert nodded and chewed thoughtfully for several minutes. A fly settled on his big, smooth skull. He brushed it away with his hand. 'How long have we been here?' he asked suddenly, as if he were late for an appointment.

'I don't know,' sighed Frank. 'A week? A month? It feels like a year.'

'Homesick?' asked Gilbert, cocking his head.

Frank nodded.

'It's natural,' said Gilbert. 'I'm sorry. It's my fault. We should have done this a long time ago.' He hooked a crust from his coffee mug and sucked it into his mouth. 'This is the life,' he grinned. 'Free food and plenty of sunshine. No television. No newspapers. No poison in the air. No crime in the street. The world could come to an end tomorrow and we'd be the last people to hear about it.'

'No customers,' added Frank. 'It's a long climb up here from town.'

'It's time we had that supper-dance. A real, old-fashioned supper-dance will bring in the crowds. We can hang strings of lightbulbs over the compound and set out the tables and chairs in a big circle to mark out a dance floor and we could build a pit for a fire and get Happy to roast a pig.'

'We don't have any music for dancing,' objected Frank.

'There's a gramophone in Sam's room,' said Gilbert. 'And a pile of old Frank Sinatra records I found in a box. We can sort them out. There must be something suitable. Sam used to love dancing.'

Frank tried to imagine the compound blazing with lights and music and laughter, a window cut in the forest's darkness. It wasn't impossible. They would need to clear the rubbish and fill the holes where the ground had cracked in the heat. A coat of whitewash for the walls. They could make it work. They must make it work. People would find them. Things would be different.

'How many tables do we have outside?' he asked.

'I don't know. We'll count them after breakfast. Some of them need a lick of paint. But that's no problem.'

'We could paint the walls too,' said Frank.

'Yes,' said Gilbert, his eyes shining. 'And find some new clothes for Happy to make him look more wholesome.'

'A uniform,' grinned Frank. 'With brass buttons.'

'Tell Happy the plan. Ask him what he thinks about it.'

Frank turned to Happy and tried to explain. 'Gilbert giv ba fo sing an dans toude afta toumoro. Plenti smol chop for glad pipli. Gilbert say you go be nomba won man fo kouk dis ting.'

Happy looked confused. He glanced up at his winklepickers, down at his dusty, bare feet and let out a tremendous fart.

'What did you say to him?' asked Gilbert, amazed.

'I don't know,' said Frank.

When Gilbert had eaten the rest of the sandwiches and filled his pockets with warm, boiled eggs, he took Frank out to inspect the tables and chairs. The furniture had been standing against the mud wall of the compound for a long time and was rusting into a scrap metal pyramid.

'Why do you think Sam left it out here to rot?' said Frank as they tried to untangle a clutch of chairs.

'It's a mystery,' said Gilbert.

They worked all morning, trying to dismantle the pyramid. Towards noon the metal burned so hot it blistered their hands.

They salvaged five tables and seventeen chairs. The rest of the furniture was good for nothing, although Gilbert thought he might straighten it out with the help of a hammer. They arranged the best of the tables and chairs around the compound and made another, smaller, pyramid from the remains.

When they had finished Veronica came strolling from the hotel with Chester under arm. She was wearing a white cotton shirt and a pair of plastic sunglasses.

'What's happening?' she demanded, pulling her sunglasses over her nose.

'We're sorting out the furniture,' replied Frank. He glanced apprehensively in her direction. She was standing by one of the tables. The white shirt dazzled his eyes. Beneath the shirt her bare legs gleamed with cooking oil. She was scrubbed, peeled and ready for roasting. She looked remarkably composed for a woman who had been attacked in her bed by a brawling drunk. She caught Frank staring at her legs, stuck out her tongue and gave it a waggle. Frank blushed and looked away.

'*Why* are you sorting out furniture?' she said, turning to Gilbert.

Gilbert stopped work and sat down on one of the chairs. His hands were red. His shirt was drenched with sweat. 'Because after we've knocked off some of the rust, you're going to paint it,' he said cheerfully.

'What colour?' she demanded.

'What sort of paint do we have in store, Frank?'

'Green paint,' said Frank, taking hold of a chair and sitting down beside him.

'Green,' said Gilbert. He pulled a boiled egg from his pocket and cracked the shell against his knee.

'I can't do any painting,' said Veronica indignantly. She sat down beside the men and stuffed Chester between her knees.

'Why?'

'This is my last clean shirt,' she said, shaking an arm in Frank's face.

'Take it off,' said Gilbert.

Veronica said nothing. She leaned back in her chair and studied the sky. She opened her legs and let Chester tumble from between her knees. She unbuttoned the shirt and slowly pulled her arms from the sleeves.

'Holi Gost!' whispered Frank.

Gilbert turned and looked at Frank and then peered at Veronica. 'You daft bugger,' he mumbled, stuffing his mouth with boiled egg.

'What's wrong?' asked Veronica. She wrapped her arms

around the back of the chair and stuck out her legs. She was stripped to a pair of little lace pants.

'Haven't you got anything else to wear?' demanded Frank, pretending to study his shoes.

'It's hot!' said Veronica. 'If you don't like it, don't look.'

'But what happens if Boris finds you like that?' said Gilbert. He stared at her thoughtfully, his cheeks bulging with egg.

'Like what?' murmured Veronica. She closed her eyes and raised her face to the sun.

'Like that,' said Gilbert. 'Walking around in next to nothing.'

She opened one eye and peeped at him. He stared brightly back with his old mischievous, crumpled grin until she felt flustered and raised an arm against her breasts. 'Don't stare!' she scolded. She snatched up her shirt and threw it at him. The shirt caught on his ears and covered his face like a veil.

'Anyway, I'm nothing special,' she added, glancing hopefully at Frank.

'I don't know,' said Gilbert, from under the shirt. 'I've seen the way Boris looks at you sometimes. Hungry. You shouldn't tease him. Men can turn nasty. Something inside them snaps.' He wiped his hands on his trousers and fished for another of Happy's boiled eggs.

'Men! You're such children. There's nothing wrong with Boris. He's always behaved like the perfect gentleman. Ask Frank.'

Frank whistled and shook his head.

The perfect gentleman returned at dusk with beer and fresh fruit. They gathered on the veranda to watch him unload the car. He waved when he saw them, threw a pineapple into the air and laughed.

'Hank, help me shift these bastard boxes!' he bellowed as he dragged a beer crate into view. He kicked the crate to rattle the bottles and paused to wipe his face.

Frank left the safety of the veranda and walked out to him. He had expected some kind of confrontation. But Boris looked neither guilty nor apologetic. He behaved as if the previous night's attack had been nothing more than a high-spirited game, something to be enjoyed and forgotten. There was nothing in his voice or manner that suggested he remembered anything about it. Frank was flummoxed. He helped Boris carry the crates to the kitchen and fill the fridge with beer.

Later, when they were assembled for their evening stew, Gilbert announced his plan for the grand supper-dance.

Boris beamed with pleasure. 'I go to town,' he said. 'Most days. Every day. I tell those bastards this hotel is under new management. Make them come for carnival night.'

'How many customers can we expect?' asked Frank.

Boris spread out his fingers. 'Fifty. A hundred. Maybe. Everybody want to drink. Everybody want to dance,' he said eagerly.

Gilbert looked surprised. 'Do we have enough beer for so many?'

'They drink the beer. They drink the palm wine. They drink any damn thing. Boris knows how it works,' said Boris.

'We could find some paper and make a few posters,' suggested Veronica .

'Posters?' grunted Boris. He stared at Veronica as if he were looking at her for the first time. He frowned and pulled his nose.

'Yes,' she said, glaring at him. 'You stick 'em up around town. It's called advertising.'

'The bastards don't read!' shouted Boris. He threw back his head and let out a great, explosive laugh.

Veronica squirmed and fell silent.

'It's a small town,' said Gilbert. 'The word will spread.'

'News spreads like fire,' said Boris. 'We make it a night they don't forget.'

So the next day they set to work. Veronica painted the furniture green while Frank whitewashed the walls. Happy dug a pit outside the kitchen big enough to roast a horse and Gilbert counted lightbulbs. At the end of the count he was forced to abandon his plan to fill the compound with electric light but found candles instead and declared them to be more romantic. Boris donated a box of Christmas decorations to use as bunting. Happy was sent into town for ten gallons of palm wine.

At the end of the week the hotel compound had been transformed. Long strings of tarnished tinsel fluttered on the perimeter walls. The tables and chairs were drawn into a circle. A dance floor had been cleared and swept of stones. The gramophone, an early German machine in a wooden suitcase, was brought out and cleaned. Everything was ready and waiting.

And then it rained.

All night the clouds came boiling and foaming out of heaven. Beneath the clouds the air began to rush through the forest, shaking the trees and banging on the hotel shutters. Dust devils danced in the compound. The tinsel broke loose and took flight. At dawn the sun came out like a bruise and, all around, the sky was a rumbling canopy of water.

The hotel felt cold. Gilbert woke up shivering, deafened by the drumming on the loose, metal roof. He dressed and went running for the kitchen. The compound was flooded. The ground bubbled beneath his feet. Tables rattled. Shrieking chairs bled rust.

'What a mess!' he shouted as he splashed through the kitchen door. He was fighting for breath, his stomach jumping beneath his shirt.

Frank and Happy were huddled against the pot-bellied stove, watching the rain as it seeped through the ceiling. 'All that wasted work,' moaned Frank.

'It will dry out,' Gilbert said cheerfully, stepping closer to the stove. His boots were squelching with mud.

'We can't dry that out,' said Frank, nodding at the floor. He had been too late to rescue the gramophone. It was sitting in a puddle of dirty water. The suitcase had swollen and started to split at the seams.

'It doesn't look too bad,' said Gilbert. He sniffed and wiped his head. The gramophone was ruined.

Frank didn't bother to argue with him. He tried to fight back his disappointment, squatted in the warmth of the oven and waited for Gilbert to speak again. But Gilbert said nothing. He looked worried. He paced about the kitchen, squinting up at the dripping ceiling.

Veronica arrived pursued by Boris. She scampered into the kitchen and danced about the floor with bare, muddy feet. Her nose was red, her spiky yellow hair washed flat against her skull. Boris had cut a polythene sack as a shawl for her shoulders.

'I think it's lifting!' she said breathlessly, shaking the water from the shawl.

'No,' said Boris. 'Getting worse.' He took off his old straw hat and beat the living daylights out of it against the edge of a table.

'How long do you think it will last?' asked Gilbert.

Boris grunted and shrugged. 'Two, three days. Maybe. A week.'

'We'll drown!' shrieked Veronica, laughing.

'Maybe. The rains come and everything drown.'

'Daso!' said Happy, very excited. 'De ren he fol. Notin dray. Smol tam we go be waka fo wata!'

'Be quiet you bastard!' roared Boris.

'Walker for what?' said Gilbert.

'Waka for wata,' said Frank.

Happy nodded and made swimming movements with his arms.

They cooked a hot breakfast and, one by one, set out again into the rain. Beyond the compound the trees were screaming. The forest had vanished behind a wall of water. Boris went to investigate the smoke that had been spurting through the planks of the generator house. Veronica went back to her room to try to repair the shutters that had blown from their hinges during the night. Frank followed Gilbert to the dining room to look at the hole in the ceiling. A thin yellow soup was splashing through the broken plaster and forming a pool on the floor.

'The roof is rotten,' said Frank furiously. 'There's nothing we can do about it.' He turned away. 'I'll bring a bucket.'

'Wait a minute,' said Gilbert. 'We'll have to plug that hole or we'll have the ceiling down on our ears'.

He sent Frank to fetch rags and hammer and, while he waited, dragged a table into position beneath the hole. He gingerly climbed aboard and poked his hand through the sodden plaster. A gush of soup caught his face and splashed the front of his shirt.

'You knew it would rain,' said Frank, squelching back into the room. He had raided one of the laundry baskets. His arms were full of dirty towels. 'Sam told you it was going to rain. He warned you in his letters.'

Gilbert made a sausage from one of the towels and stabbed at the ceiling. 'Yes, I knew it was going to rain!' he roared impatiently. 'I thought we could beat it. We only needed another few days. We could have done it.'

Frank offered him another sausage. 'It can't rain for ever,' he grunted.

'You heard Boris,' said Gilbert. He forced the second sausage into the ceiling and gave it a punch with his fist. 'Where's that hammer?' He took the hammer and used it to prod home the rest of the towels. 'This hole is full of bird shit!' he muttered, pausing to sniff his fingers. 'Anyway, it gives us time to make a few repairs. Once we've got this room sorted out we can bring in the furniture, make a proper dining room and forget about the damn weather. Paint the walls. Build a bar in the far corner. A big potted palm by the door to the veranda. We can dig one out of the forest. Dig out a dozen of 'em.'

He climbed down from the table. The Garden Restaurant. Wine and dine among giant jungle flowers. Try a cold beer and a charcoal grill. Meat to please you. Pleased to meet you.

Frank peered doubtfully up at the repair. The ceiling creaked and farted a string of evil smelling, wet, cloth sausages.

'It's no good!' bellowed Gilbert. 'Bring a bucket!'

All day the rain slashed at the forest until the hotel seemed to sink through a furious ocean of trees. The rafters rattled. The walls felt soft. The baked, red earth was a slippery pudding of mud. The log pile collapsed. The veranda broke loose from its moorings. There was a rush of water in the shanty town that knocked down Boris, swept under the kitchen floor, flooded the garden and drained into old Sam's grave.

As it grew dark the rain stopped and mosquitoes arrived. They swarmed against the doors and shutters, crawled through every chink and crevice, keyhole, knot-hole and floorboard; sizzled like tiny electric needles as they settled down to feast. Happy slept with the lid on his barrel. Boris got drunk to poison his blood and stumbled around in the mud, cursing and slapping himself with his hands . Frank and Veronica slept in their clothes with their heads buried under their pillows. Gilbert, sponged down with vinegar, retreated behind his mosquito net and watched the insects invade his room.

Look at them flitter. There must be a thousand. Specks of plague on gossamer wing. A man's blood, stolen in droplets, carried away in the night. Vampires. Men turning into mosquitoes. Ghosts of the forest. We only needed another few days. We could have done it.

At daybreak the hotel was hidden by a soft, grey fog. Gilbert hauled himself from bed and hurried out to the kitchen, anxious for bread and cake and coffee. The cold, damp air took his breath and tried to pull out his teeth. His boots slithered in mud. Beyond the compound, in the dripping forest, a solitary bird was hooting.

As he splashed towards breakfast he heard Boris shouting in shanty town. It was a long bellow of frustration and fury. A terrible rumble of thunder. He turned from the kitchen towards the maze of shacks and waterlogged cabins. In the darkness of the generating shed he found Boris raging, banging the works with a spanner.

'We got no oil. Finished. Bastard drink it. No lights. No power. Nothing,' he screamed when he saw Gilbert watching him. He was wearing a vest and a pair of greasy underpants. His arms were shining with mud and oil.

'Can't we get fuel in town?' frowned Gilbert.

'No good. No money. You got money? I got no money. What you want me to do about it?' roared Boris. He turned on Gilbert and threatened him with the spanner. His face was scarlet with mosquito bites. His mouth looked swollen. One of his eyes had closed.

'But you're always buying stuff in the market,' protested Gilbert. 'I thought Sam must have left you something...'

'Sam?' screamed Boris. 'What a bastard. He leave me nothing but trouble. He sit all day. Drinking and sleeping. Drinking. Sleeping. Watch the house fall down. People come out here. Want a room for the night? He scare them away. Shout and scream. Chase them around with a hunting knife. His brain gone. He think everybody want to hurt him. Pretty soon no one come out here no more. Pretty soon we got big trouble. What happen? Nothing. He just sit there. Drinking and sleeping until he take the fever and drop down dead. Bastard leave me nothing but trouble.'

'That's not true,' barked Gilbert, puffing out his belly. 'Sam was a good man. I trusted my life to him. He knew this country. And he loved the forest. There was nothing wrong with his head. He had a good head. He had plans. He asked me out here to help him.'

'You don't know,' shouted Boris. He threw down the spanner and kicked it away. His hair jumped. Foam gathered in the corners of his mouth. 'You think the sun shine out of his arsehole? You wrong. He was a mad old bastard. I work so my fingers bleed. He done nothing.'

'So how did you manage?' demanded Gilbert.

Boris collapsed against the generator and hung his head. For a while he said nothing. He was exhausted. He looked at his hands as if he expected to see them drip blood. 'I sell what we got left,' he said sadly. 'One day I sell a picture of Jesus. Maybe. Bring home a fish and a bag of beans. Another time I take a blanket, a few lightbulbs, whatever I find.'

'Here's my wristwatch,' said Gilbert suddenly, pulling at his sleeve. 'It's gold. How much is it worth?'

Boris wiped his hands on his vest and gave a hoick to his underpants. 'You want me to go down to town?' he said, taking the wristwatch and holding it against his ear.

'Yes,' said Gilbert. 'Will it get us out of trouble?'

Boris stared at the watch. 'Gold?' he said.

'Yes,' said Gilbert.

'Maybe,' said Boris. He picked at his nose. He didn't look convinced.

'We've got money,' said Gilbert, trying to reassure him. 'I sold everything I owned to come out here. We've got enough money to build the biggest damn hotel in Bilharzia. But we have to wait. Do you understand? It takes time. There's a lot of legal paperwork. When the rain stops and we get the money everything will be different. We can have anything we want. So we have to stay alive for another few weeks. We have to stay alive.'

Boris grunted, strapped the watch to his wrist, for safety, and splashed back to the hotel for a change of clothes. Gilbert followed him across the compound and went out to wait on the capsized veranda. While he leaned on the rail, staring down at the smoky, blue jungle, Frank came looking for him.

'Do you think he can make it?' asked Frank, when Gilbert explained what had happened.

'I don't know,' said Gilbert.

They watched Boris start the car and drive slowly away down the steep forest track. The engine spluttered. The wheels sprayed arches of fine, red mud.

'This weather will wash out the road' said Frank, shaking his head.

'It's not too late,' scowled Gilbert.

An hour later the car returned. The headlamps were shattered. The windscreen was caked with branches and leaves.

They ran down to meet it, legs loose as rubber, heads bent against the pelting rain.

'What's wrong?' shouted Gilbert as Boris clambered out and slammed the door.

'You bastard,' roared Boris. 'Mad as Sam. You want to kill me? The road all gone. Nowhere to drive. Nothing out there but mud and water.'

He tore at his arm and threw the gold wristwatch into the mud.

16

A storm swept over the forest, broke along the peaks of the hills and exploded. Rain clattered through the hotel roof, sprayed into windows and washed along floors. The ceilings sagged. Furniture floated. The bedroom walls changed colour and sweated an evil-smelling milk. All through the afternoon Frank and Gilbert ran from room to room, plugging the leaks and sealing shutters. Boris dug a trench through the shanty town to channel water away from the kitchen. Happy struggled to lash the veranda more securely against its moorings. Veronica went searching for Chester. Terrified by the belching thunder he had managed to scramble free of her arms and scuttle away to hide, wings out, beak snapping, tail feathers hanging in shreds. She wandered forlornly through the hotel, calling his name and clucking her tongue to attract his attention; but he would not answer.

It was night before the storm had blown itself out. The rain died away and the moon appeared. The silence startled them. On the edge of the forest frogs were calling.

'It's stopped raining!' shouted Gilbert. He ran outside and took a great gulp of the cold, calm air.

'But it's too dark to do anything,' grumbled Frank.

'Let's go to the kitchen. Find the lanterns. Light the stove. We can dry our bones and find something to eat before these mosquitoes bleed us to death,' said Gilbert. He screwed up his face and spat legs through his teeth.

They called everyone together and made their way across the flooded compound. The mud splashed their knees and squirted in worms through their toes. When they reached the kitchen Happy hung lanterns from the ceiling while Frank and Gilbert tried to fire the oven. Veronica and Boris searched the shelves for something to start a stew.

'I can't find anything,' said Veronica impatiently, rummaging among the pots and bowls.

'What have we got for the stew tonight?' asked Frank, turning to Happy.

Happy frowned and rubbed his chin. He looked up and down the kitchen as if he expected to see calves' heads, pigs' trotters, mutton pies and yards of peppered sausages come rolling out of the darkness. When nothing happened he looked disappointed. 'You lek bret?' he asked anxiously.

'Yes,' said Frank.

Happy nodded. Good. 'You lek frout?' he inquired.

'A chop am,' said Frank.

'OK,' said Happy. His face brightened and he looked relieved.

'For wat?' insisted Frank.

'We mek bret an frout chop patron,' said Happy in a low voice.

'What's happening?' demanded Veronica.

'He says we've got bread and fruit,' said Frank. He looked at Gilbert and shrugged.

'Nothing else?' said Gilbert.

'Kofi an korn,' said Happy. 'Res an souka.'

'You bastard!' roared Boris. He turned, rushed at Happy and tried to scalp him with a swift slice from his hand. 'You steal the food from our mouth? You got food here. Where you hide it?' he demanded.

Happy whimpered and cowered in a corner. 'Bifo ren he fol we don chop plenti tin. Mek mistik. Toude de kopot he empti. A kouk notin.'

And then, before anyone had time to stop him, Boris began to attack the shelves, throwing down the pots and pans, shaking baskets and smacking bags with his fists. 'Look here!' he shouted in triumph. 'I found an egg!' He waved it at Happy. He waved it at Gilbert. He managed to drop it.

'What else you got hiding?' he growled, pulling Happy from the corner. He took him by the scruff of the neck and shook him until he farted.

'Leave him alone!' barked Gilbert. He prised the two men apart and used all his great weight to force Boris back against the wall. 'We've got food here and you know it,' he said. 'You've put most of it under lock and key.'

Boris shrank along the wall and wagged his head in horror. 'It's emergency,' he moaned. 'We don't touch it. Top-quality rations.'

'Tomorrow we touch it,' hissed Gilbert, baring his teeth. 'As soon as it's light you're going to open those rations.'

The next day, at dawn, they assembled before the store and waited patiently in the mud for Boris to surrender the key. The sky smoked. The early rain was a shivering drizzle. Veronica was wearing her polythene shawl with an old flour sack for a hood. Frank and Happy let the rain soak them. Their faces gleamed. Their clothes clung like treacle. Gilbert, driven mad by the way the rain kept scrubbing his skull, was wearing a red, rubber bowl on his head.

'Do you think he'll do it?' asked Veronica.

'I don't care,' snorted Gilbert. 'I'm starving. If he doesn't unlock it I'll take it apart with my bare hands.'

'We could cut that barbed wire and climb down through the roof,' suggested Frank, surveying the fortifications.

'We'll give him another five minutes,' said Gilbert, glancing in frustration at his empty wrist. 'What's the time?'

'My watch has stopped,' confessed Frank sadly, looking at Veronica .

'I don't even know the day of the week,' said Veronica.

'Tuesday,' said Frank.

'Friday,' said Gilbert.

'Sondi,' said Happy.

When Boris finally appeared he was stripped down to his underwear. The vest sagged from his shoulders. His underpants drooped and filled with water that leaked, in a trickle, between his legs. He cursed the eyes of his audience, removed the padlock and dragged open the store room door.

The stink astounded them. It was the ammonia smell of condemned meat, the sickly scent of rotted fruit, the musty vapour of rancid fat and spoiled cereal. They were too shocked to speak or turn away. They stood, transfixed, and stared at the ruin. The tinned rations had exploded with the force of grenades and plastered their contents over the walls. Strings of poisoned cocktail sausages were hanging from shelves like guts. Shrapnel shone in the ceiling. The floor festered with a creeping carpet of black fruit salad.

Boris looked bilious. 'No, it all wrong!' he sobbed. 'This don't happen to me.' He fell down on his knees and burst into tears.

They stepped over him, picking through the odious porridge in the hope of finding something left fit to eat. Several times the smell threatened to overwhelm them, driving them back into the rain. But after ten minutes of fretful digging they managed to salvage a dozen tinned fruit cakes and carried them home to the kitchen. No one cared to comfort Boris. He wandered off through the rain and vanished.

They quartered a cake and stuffed themselves with it while Happy boiled the water for coffee. The heat from the stove began to warm and revive them. Their clothes steamed. Happy took off his winklepickers and hung them up to dry. Gilbert prised off his red rubber bowl which had made a groove around the top of his head.

'We can feed ourselves for a week!' said Frank gleefully. The cake was rich and dark and full of raisins. He filled his mouth until his cheeks bulged and he couldn't work his teeth, his tongue clasped tight in a soft knob of sweetness.

'It's not going to rain for ever,' said Veronica. She bent her head to dry before the heat of the stove. Her hair changed colour and sprang into spikes.

'No,' said Gilbert. He licked a finger and began collecting crumbs from his plate. 'It might rain for a couple of months. But it won't rain for ever.'

'We can't wait for months!' cried Veronica. She turned from the stove and stared in alarm at the row of cakes.

'I can't change the weather,' said Gilbert. 'We'll have to be patient. Anyway, it's not so bad. There's been a drought. The crops need the rain.'

'We don't have any crops,' said Frank.

'We could plant some,' said Gilbert.

'We'll starve!' spluttered Veronica. 'We can't do it. It's mad. I'm getting out.' She stood up and searched for her polythene shawl.

'Where?' asked Frank.

'Town,' she shouted impatiently. It was obvious. 'We've got to get into town.'

'The road is washed out. Are you going to *walk* through that jungle?'

She hesitated, glared at Frank and stopped looking for the cape. 'We have to do something,' she insisted, marching up and down the kitchen.

'We'll manage,' said Gilbert. 'The forest is probably full of food. Nuts and berries. Fish in the rivers. Fruit on the trees. You watch. We'll be self-sufficient in no time.' He picked up his plate and licked it clean. Enough meat on a crocodile to feed this circus for a month. First catch your crocodile. Sweet meat. Peel the tails like enormous lobsters. Make a necklace from the teeth. Something to give to Veronica. Frank wore a necklace. Threaded from noodles. Taught him to cook. Knows his onions. We'll manage. Dogs. Rats. Lobsters. Men. All the same. Eat anything. Thrive on filth. The Four Horsemen of the Apocalypse. Ate them in the war. Pantry hanging with horses' heads. A plague of gluttons sent to devour the land. Gobble the world. Squirt it out through your arse as shit. What's left? When it's finished. Rats to eat the lobsters. Dogs will eat the rats. Men to eat the dogs. Chinese cook chows. Meat like mutton. Men will eat each other. No doubt. Fat ones first. The fat will eat no lean. Fee fi fo fum. I smell the blood of an Englishman. Grind your bones to make my bread. The last man on earth. The last supper. Make a meal of his own fingers. Next. Nothing. A ball of shit as big as a planet spinning through eternal space.

Veronica continued to march around the kitchen, slapping the shelves in exasperation. 'I hate it. I hate the rain. I hate feeling hungry. My bed smells damp. The ceiling leaks. There are snails all over the walls!' she screamed.

'What sort of snails?' asked Gilbert.

Veronica was flabbergasted. 'Horrible, giant, monster snails with their eyes hanging out on stalks!' she shrieked.

Gilbert clapped his hands and laughed. 'We'll go and collect them,' he said, jumping up and wrapping Veronica in his arms. 'They'll make a stew.'

He danced her around the kitchen and backwards through the door.

'I'll take Happy and hunt along the edge of the forest,' shouted Frank as he watched them plunging into the rain. Gilbert waved and disappeared with Veronica still whirling in his arms.

Happy was already back in his winklepickers and dragging a parcel of greasy rags from a cupboard.

'What's all this?' said Frank, watching Happy lay the parcel lovingly on the table.

Happy grinned and rolled his eyes. 'You louk dis ting,' he said, unpicking the rags.

'Good grief! Do you know how to use it?' whispered Frank. He was looking at an old French army rifle, a survivor from the Second World War.

'Daso,' said Happy, lifting the weapon from the table and nursing it in his arms. 'No fia fo mek.' He curled a finger over the trigger and gave it a squeeze. 'Youselef?' he asked, looking hopefully at Frank.

Frank shook his head. It was the first time he had been in a room with a rifle. It looked dangerous. He thought he might learn how to fire it but he knew he could never hit anything.

Happy looked a little disheartened. He was no marksman. 'You kip dat nef,' he said, nodding at a heavy butcher's knife hanging from a hook on the wall.

Frank took the knife and wrapped it in the flour sack that Veronica had used for a bonnet.

'Na we go hunt fo kil dat bif,' said Happy, growling and stabbing at the air with the rifle barrel.

'Fo wat bif dat?'

Happy considered all creatures great and small. 'Mongi,' he

said, smacking his lips. 'Senek. Taygra. Bouch kao. Wata hors. Even dam ting. Dis gon he plenti big nof fo kil alafen,' he bragged.

'There aren't any elephants in the forest,' said Frank.

Happy grinned and rattled a box of cartridges.

They left the compound through a hole in the wall and forced their way through the undergrowth. As they entered the deeper forest the trees gave shelter from the rain. It grew silent. The air diminished to a humid twilight. Happy moved ahead of Frank, clambering over roots and boulders, slithering into ditches, fighting free of the clinging thorn, with the rifle held always above his head.

Frank followed with the knife hanging loose in his hand. He had folded the sack and tucked it under his belt, ready to bag whatever bush meat they could collect. He didn't have much faith in Happy's hunt for the buffalo and elephant but perhaps they'd be lucky and knock down a couple of birds. Anything to fill the pot. Gilbert said you could survive on snake and even grow fat on forest rats. He was breathing hard. His shirt was sticky with sweat. He supposed they were walking on a forest track but, when he turned to look over his shoulder, he saw nothing but undergrowth closing over him. The jungle drowned them. There was nothing to mark their progress through these secret passages and nothing to guide them out again.

It was an hour before Happy allowed them to rest. 'We go stop fo hia,' he declared and sat down among a pile of dead roots to watch the surrounding forest. The trees around them were ancient skeletons, the trunks crusted in flowering warts, the branches hung with long beards of lichen.

Frank wiped his face. He stuck the knife in a pad of moss between his feet and lay back among the roots. Nothing moved in the empty forest. He wondered if anything lived here but phantoms. It would be dark in another few hours. They should have carried a lantern. What happens in the forest at night? Light a big fire and sleep in a tree. They should have carried some matches. Perhaps he would search for some fruit and berries. Ask Happy to shoulder the rifle and help him. Something that looked like a soft, white crab fell from the leaves above his head and scuttled for cover under a stone. He sat up, startled, and stared at the ground. A party of ants crawled over his shoes.

'Sofri!' Happy whispered urgently. 'Sofri!' He cocked his rifle and pressed it firmly against his shoulder.

Frank stared along the line of the barrel as it pointed into the darkness. At first he saw nothing. But then his eyes, adjusting to the shadows, picked out a group of apes watching him from the bushes. They were a little Stone Age family, peering out from a primitive nest of green twigs and ferns. The largest ape, an old female, stared at Frank as she chewed at a piece of fruit. She looked tired and wet and hungry. She reminded him, for a moment, of Olive. There was something he recognised in her crumpled face, something familiar in the way she peeled the fruit and sucked at the sweet, red seeds.

'Won...to...tri...' whispered Happy. His fingers trembled. He farted quietly as he squeezed the trigger.

The ape looked at Happy, tossed the fruit away and wiped her hands on her knees. She sat, motionless and erect, as if posed to have her photograph taken. There was a terrible explosion and a rush of stinging, white smoke. Birds screamed from the treetops and hung in the rain like ashes.

When the smoke cleared the old ape was still sitting beneath the bush with her hands clasped to her knees. She had been decapitated.

'Chit!' laughed Happy. 'Chit!' He dropped the rifle and ran out to admire the damage.

Frank ran after him. He stared at the corpse and felt his skin crawl in horror. It was part human and part raw carcass, feet spread, fingers still clenched, hot blood pumping as the life drained away. He spent several minutes trying to push his sack over the ape's shoulders, working at the problem with infinite tenderness, as if trying to dress a crippled child in a badly fitting vest. But the ape was too large to be hidden and the sack began to split. He lifted the hairy body and carried it home in his arms.

The hunters said nothing as they retraced their steps through the forest. Happy's excitement at hitting a target had evaporated and he hung his head now, burdened by the weight of his guilt. Frank walked close beside him and cradled the slaughtered ape. The flies swarmed. The blood soaked his shirt and stained his skin.

It was dark when they broke through the undergrowth and reached the safety of the compound. It was a cool night, the sky still heavy and running with rain. They met Gilbert and Veronica splashing towards the kitchen with a bucket slung on a pole. Gilbert shouted in delight when he saw them, dropped the bucket and rushed forward to look at the meat.

'What a mess! Where did you find it?' he boomed. 'It looks like something tried to bite off its head.' He was very impressed.

'It was Happy,' explained Frank. 'We took out his rifle.'

Happy surrendered the weapon like a soldier exhausted and sick of battle. Gilbert examined it with fascination, felt the weight of it in his hands, held it up to his nose and gave it a sniff.

'What have you got in the bucket?' asked Frank.

'Snails! Hundreds of the buggers,' grinned Gilbert. 'We've been picking them all day. I think they must be falling out of Heaven.'

'There are lights in the kitchen,' called Veronica, who still stood guarding the harvest.

'It must be Boris,' shouted Gilbert.

'He'll be drunk again,' said Frank. He gently rocked the ape in his arms. She had grown very cold.

'I hope he hasn't hidden the cakes,' muttered Gilbert.

They hurried towards the flickering light, Gilbert leading them with the rifle, Frank following, Happy and Veronica trotting behind with the bucket swinging on the bamboo pole.

Boris greeted them with a roar of approval. He ushered the party into the kitchen and lurched among them, squeezing Veronica, hugging Happy and, to Frank's disgust, picking up the dead ape's hand and planting a kiss on the knuckles.

'You good people,' he burbled. 'We don't starve while Gilbert here.' He shook Gilbert by the hand until his teeth rattled. 'Sit down. We drink a few beers. You bring home the rations. I cook the stew.'

They made themselves comfortable by the blazing stove while Happy took care of the snails and laid out the ape on the butcher's block.

'What did you put in this stew?' asked Frank. The delicious vapours of peppered meat and vegetables poured from a pot on the top of the stove.

Boris sucked at a bottle of beer and grinned. 'I find a few things,' he belched. He wiped the neck and offered Frank the bottle.

'Where?' said Frank. He took the beer but he would not drink.

'Who cares?' said Veronica. 'It can't be any worse than snails — or that horrible creature.' She glanced towards the butcher's block. It was the first time she had mentioned the ape or even acknowledged its presence. She shivered and turned her face away.

'It's not a pretty sight,' admitted Gilbert. 'But wait until you taste the cutlets. I'll cook 'em so they melt in your mouth.'

They pulled off their shoes and sat to toast their feet by the warmth of the oven while Boris fetched bowls to serve the stew.

'Glori!' beamed Happy, when the stew reached his mouth. 'Dis fein chop, patron.' He looked flustered. It was a long time since anyone had cooked him a meal and he couldn't remember the etiquette. He adopted an attitude of fawning gratitude, half-afraid that Boris might change his mind and snatch the bowl away.

'It's hot,' hissed Gilbert, urgently sucking air through his teeth.

'It's chicken!' blurted Frank.

Veronica dropped her spoon. Her face changed colour, grew red, turned green and went a nasty shade of blue. Her nostrils trembled. Her mouth fell open and the stew fell out. She clutched at her throat and her eyes began to bulge, as if she were choking on bones. She stared at Boris. Her eyes speared him through the heart and lungs and held him pinned against his chair.

'You killed him,' she said in a tiny voice. 'You killed Chester!'

'That chicken no good,' said Boris. 'What a bastard. We got to eat something.' He filled his mouth with stew and chewed contentedly.

'He wasn't a chicken!' screamed Veronica. 'He was my friend!' She erupted in a fury of fangs and claws, spat poison, pounced at Boris and knocked him to the floor.

Boris laughed and grasped the top of her thistle head in one almighty hand. She scratched and spat but he was too strong for her and it only served to make him excited. They rolled across the kitchen and she found herself caught with her legs astride him, while he laughed and bucked and made little grunting sounds of pleasure.

'She try to kill me. Crazy woman. She want a good shag. You help me here,' he sang, wrapping an arm around her waist and driving her down against his groin.

'Leave her alone!' bawled Frank. He threw down his bowl and sprang forward, grabbing Veronica under her arms and trying to drag her free.

'She too good to waste on you!' complained Boris and slapped him hard against the side of the head.

'That's enough!' shouted Gilbert. He was standing in front of the oven, the rifle in his hands, his face puffed into a gargoyle of thunder.

'Look at the big man!' howled Boris. 'He got the gun!' He let out a great honk of laughter that tossed Veronica on to the floor. 'You think old Boris afraid of him?' He staggered to his feet and wiped his mouth. His eyes flicked around the room, searching for something to call a weapon.

'Don't move,' warned Gilbert.

'You watch,' grinned Boris, catching sight of a suitable knife. 'I poke out his eyes.'

He rushed at Gilbert. Veronica screamed. There was an ear-splitting bang and a spray of sparks as the kitchen vanished in smoke. Boris was blown through the kitchen door. He wasn't hurt. Gilbert had missed him and shot a hole through the roof.

But when the smoke had cleared and they looked for him, Boris was already running for his life through the mud and the rain, over the slippery compound wall and into the sheltering forest.

17

Gilbert lay in bed and tried to count the days. One two snail stew. Three four monkey's paw. Five six chop up sticks. Seven eight lick your plate. Nine ten a big fat hen. Roast potatoes. Buttered carrots. Plenty of gravy. Veronica stood in the rain and was sick. We ate Chester behind her back. She sulked. Angry. It can't last for ever. She'll learn. It's not all gammon and spinach. You forget. All over the world. The rain. Floods. The hotel floating over the treetops, down the coast and out to sea. Boris gone and good riddance. When the rains stop we'll have a celebration supper. That's the spirit. Roast a porker. All hands on deck. We need Sam to sort out the kitchen. Teach Frank the tricks of the trade. Learnt to survive at the old Coronation. Sam was breakfast and I was dinner. Brown soup and mutton stew. It was mostly bones and potatoes in those days. Bones and potatoes? Thought yourself lucky. No food after the war. Fancy. Some nights it was so cold we slept in the kitchen under the ovens. Is that right? Nothing changes. Olive talking. Nothing changes. You'll learn.

Out in the forest Happy was shooting at shadows. Each morning he took the rifle and stalked away through the undergrowth. His hunting trips produced squirrels, rats and something he said were crocodile eggs. They were an odd shape but tasted good broken and boiled in the stew. Sometimes he returned with a bag of pink mushrooms, snails, bullfrogs or tree maggots. He dropped the maggots in boiling water, pulled off their heads and ate them like shrimps. He seemed to love them. No one else tried it.

Frank stayed at home with Veronica. They built umbrellas from bamboo canes and banana leaves and patrolled the mud kingdom, waiting for Boris to return from the rain. They thought he would creep back to murder them but neither liked to admit it.

'How long do you think he can stay out there?' asked Veronica, looking towards the shrieking trees.

'A couple of days,' said Frank. 'If he doesn't poison himself or break his neck something else will put an end to him.'

'It's been more than a week.'

'He must be dead,' said Frank hopefully. 'Nothing could survive in these conditions.'

'Perhaps he found his way into town. Perhaps he'll come back with a gang of his cronies.'

'Why?'

'I don't know. He's mad. Perhaps he'll come back for me. Maybe he'll come back to murder Gilbert. He could do anything,' she said nervously. The wind tore through their umbrella and whistled as it looked up her skirt.

'The road has gone,' said Frank, trying to comfort her. 'He might be mad enough to come crawling back here on his hands and knees but he's not going to persuade anyone else that it's worth the trouble.' He looked across at the remains of the car, still standing where Boris had abandoned it. The tyres were flat and the windscreen shattered. A green vegetable tripe was creeping over the blistered paintwork, feeding itself on the rust.

'I think he's still out there. I can feel him watching me,' she said, poking her skirt between her thighs. A rifle shot rang from the forest.

'Happy's not afraid,' said Frank, turning his face into the rain.

'He's got the gun,' said Veronica.

At night they slept together in a canvas tent hooked from the ceiling above Frank's bed. It was warm and dry and gave some protection from the mosquito storms. They lay in the dark and listened to the noise of Gilbert snoring through the wall behind their heads. More than once they heard him wake up with a shout and call for Olive. Then he would laugh and moan and mumble to himself until the sounds faded and he sank again into sleep.

'Do you think?' whispered Veronica one night, raising her face from the pillow.

'What?' grunted Frank.

'Gilbert,' said Veronica.

'Yes,' said Frank.

'Do you think he looks different?'

'I don't know,' frowned Frank.

'Bigger,' she said, sitting up in the dark and pulling the sheet from his head. 'I think he's getting bigger.'

'He was never a small man,' said Frank.

'But he's growing enormous,' insisted Veronica. 'It's like the rain has started to germinate him.'

It was true. When Frank looked at Gilbert again he saw that the old man had split his shirt. His boots had burst. His trousers clung by a thread. His belly stuck out through the rags like some monstrous tuber. Everything was swollen. His flesh was fermenting. The chins quivered and multiplied, folded one against the other, until it looked as if his face might be swallowed by the bulging fat. His nose and mouth were small as buttons. His dark eyes strained against the weight of his forehead. The red rubber bowl appeared screwed to his head.

Frank tried to find him some clothes but nothing could support his weight. When his trousers finally fell apart Gilbert stamped about in his vest and underpants until Veronica took pity on him and cut a blanket into a cape. He wore the cape proudly around his shoulders, tied at the neck by a piece of string. He used his shirts to bandage his feet.

A month of rain fell on the forest. They learned to forget to guard against Boris and devoted their energy to the drudgery of finding food and trying to keep warm. For a time they seemed to prosper in this flooded, twilight world. But gradually, without them even knowing it, their strength was seeping away. Veronica, weakened by mysterious bouts of bleeding and diarrhoea, shrank to a skeleton. Happy was punished by rotting teeth. Frank cut his thumb and poisoned his arm.

Gilbert, exhausted by the work and too tired to drag himself around, took to sitting in corners and talking to himself. He joined them at night to share out the stew but liked to spend the daylight hours beyond sight of them, sheltering alone, absorbed in his own private miseries. He became fascinated with the spread of decay, a morbid chronicler of the creeping mud, the drowning rooms, the secret sorrows of the hotel. Sometimes, seized by diabolical energy, he would jump up and take a party of ghosts on a tour of inspection, pointing out the damage as if it were a feature of some grand and mysterious architecture. When Frank or Veronica caught him, standing in the rain, absorbed in one of these flights of fancy, he would stop and look startled, pretend to sing or clear his throat. Then he would become furtive, speak to his ghosts in a murmur, answer their questions with the slightest nod or shake of his head. Finally he would grow lethargic, retreat to a corner and fall silent again.

One evening Happy found him collapsed in the compound. He was shivering with fever and his ears were full of mud. They managed to get him back to his room and laid him out on the bed. His burning body made the blanket steam. Frank cut the bandages from his feet and tried to wrap him in towels while Veronica ran for the medicine box.

They searched the bottles and cartons but nothing looked familiar, the drugs were stale, the descriptions printed in French or German, and they were afraid of making a mistake and poisoning him.

'It's hopeless!' said Frank impatiently, throwing the box to the floor.

'We could make him sweat it out,' suggested Veronica. She wiped Gilbert's face with her hands. 'That's what they used to do in the old days. They used to cover 'em with blankets and make 'em swim in their own sweat.'

'Why?'

'I don't know. Perhaps it acts like a disinfectant or something.' They sent Happy to look for blankets and wrapped Gilbert into a hairy, woollen parcel. He was too weak to protest. They kept him a prisoner for two days and two nights, watching him stew in his own juices. He grew so hot that he bubbled and boiled. He puddled the floor and steamed the window. His sweat dripped down from the ceiling. They took it in turns to sit by his bed but they didn't know how to nurse him. At first he found comfort in their simple vigil but soon grew confused, failed to recognise them, rolled his eyes and shouted at them to leave him alone. On the second night he shouted so hard that he fainted and when he woke up the fever was gone. He lay beneath the blankets, boiled white, drained and cold.

It took him a long time to recover. He was too feeble to hunt for food so he sat in the kitchen and stirred the stew. The rain continued. They struggled through the days, silent and starving, the last people on a God-forsaken earth.

And then, one morning, Frank found a little parcel of leaves hanging from the rafters of the veranda. He gazed at the object, transfixed, unable to believe his eyes. When he raised the alarm Happy appeared with his rifle and ran up and down the veranda, shouting abuse at the forest. Gilbert and Veronica stared up at the packet in silence. They were dumbfounded. It was a wad of fresh leaves, hanging by twine like a grub on a long silk thread. As they watched, it began swinging, gently, in the draught of the rain.

'What is it?' asked Veronica. She felt frightened and sick at the thought of unknown eyes watching them from the forest.

'Open it,' ordered Gilbert. 'It's not going to bite you.'

'It's too high,' said Veronica quickly. 'I can't reach it.' She wrapped herself in her arms and stepped back against the hotel wall. No one else volunteered.

'Do you think it was Boris?' said Frank.

'It doesn't make sense, you daft bugger!' growled Gilbert. 'Why should he come creeping around the place and hang big green turds from the woodwork? It's not Christmas!' He glared at Frank and whistled angrily through his teeth.

'What do you think?' said Frank, turning to Happy.

'Haiden medesin,' said Happy. He looked surprised that they needed to be told these things.

'What?' shouted Gilbert impatiently. 'What?'

Happy glared at him in disgust, snorted, honked and spat at the rain.

'I don't know,' said Frank, rubbing his ear. 'I think he said it's heathen medicine.'

'Daso,' said Happy, amazed at their stupidity. 'You wait pipli no savi dis ting?'

'You mean it's some sort of witchcraft?' wheezed Gilbert. He reached up and plucked the little parcel from its string.

'Don't touch it,' pleaded Veronica, retreating to the end of the veranda .

'Gently does it,' breathed Gilbert. He held the object to his nose, gave it a sniff and then carefully laid it down on the floor.

'Is it alive?' said Frank when Gilbert failed to drop dead or be seized by demons.

'What is it?' said Veronica.

It was a blue toothbrush. When the leaves were pulled apart they found themselves squatting on the floor, heads tucked between their knees staring down at a blue, plastic toothbrush.

Frank was the first to see the pygmies. When he stood up and turned again towards the forest he saw a tiny figure standing in the rain about twenty yards from the hotel. It was the figure of an old man the size of a child. He was naked but for a large fur hat and in one hand he held a spear. He stood and stared at Frank without moving, silent, expressionless, while the rain danced on the top of his hat. And then other figures emerged from the forest. They gathered silently before the veranda and laid a mildewed suitcase down in the mud.

'Who are they?' whispered Veronica, clutching Frank's hand.

'Forest people,' said Frank.

'What do they want here?' she demanded. She surveyed the little group of wet naked pygmies with morbid curiosity. She tried to measure the distance between herself and the nearest open window.

'Speak to them,' said Frank, turning to Happy, who had dropped his rifle and was staring out at the forest with his mouth hanging open. 'Ask them what they want.'

Happy tried a few words of Bamileke and pronounced a greeting in Fang but the pygmies ignored him. They were staring at Gilbert.

'They're looking at you,' said Frank.

'Yes,' said Gilbert. It must be a dream. Six little men with a suitcase. How did they get here? They must have come out of the trees. Want a room. Large double. Sleep three in a bed. It must be a dream. Hold your breath. Close your eyes and open them again. They're still down there. You can see through ghosts. Cannibals have pointed teeth. Why did they leave a toothbrush?

'That one is holding a spear,' hissed Veronica. She was edging slowly towards her chosen window. 'And the one next to him has got a bow and arrow.'

'Don't do anything to scare them away,' said Gilbert gently. 'I'll go down and talk to them.'

He wrapped the cape around his shoulders and clambered cautiously down the veranda steps escorted by Frank who struggled bravely to hold a banana leaf umbrella over his head. He walked slowly and with great dignity towards the silent pygmies and stopped before the group elder who, he decided, must be the one in the fancy fur hat.

The pygmies stared at him without a flicker of life in their faces. They looked as if they had been carved from wood. Gilbert held out his hand. The old man blinked at Gilbert. He looked at the fat, white hand. Then he reached up, shook it and grinned. His face crinkled with pleasure and he began to laugh.

At once all the pygmies pressed about Gilbert, pulling open the sodden cape to touch and stroke the great, pale bulk of him. One of the younger men, a dubious youth with a torn ear, began to act out an intricate pantomime, pretending to eat the tips of his fingers, squeezing his stomach and gesturing towards the hotel. Gilbert was enchanted. While the performance was repeated for the benefit of Frank, the other pygmies opened the big, mildewed suitcase and squatted beside it, directing Gilbert to look inside.

'What can you see in this suitcase?' said Gilbert, bending forward and staring with bright, astonished eyes.

Frank took a long time to reply. 'Toothbrushes,' he whispered at last. 'Toothbrushes and soap and razor blades and toothpaste and tins of shoe polish and bottles of hair tonic.'

'That's what I thought,' said Gilbert. 'Do we have any meat?'

'A couple of rats and the rest of last night's squirrel,' said Frank.

'Go and tell Happy to bring them out,' said Gilbert, stroking his chins.

They exchanged the rats for new toothbrushes and a large tube of toothpaste and, because they were large rats with plenty of meat on them, Veronica was allowed to choose a small bar of soap and Frank bargained for a razor blade.

When the business was complete the pygmies shut up their shop, took it in turns to shake Gilbert ceremoniously by the hand and slipped back into the forest.

As soon as they were out of sight Veronica ran back to her room as if the Devil were chasing her. She locked the door and hid the precious bar of soap beneath a loose floorboard at the foot of her bed. She stayed in the room for the rest of the day for fear that the others might come and discover the hiding place. She sat behind the door, exhilarated and vigilant, giggling with delight, waiting for footsteps in the corridor outside. But no one came. Frank had found his razor and spent a long time shaving himself before a piece of mirror, watching his face emerge from his beard. Gilbert spent hours just standing in the rain to scrub his mouth with pink worms of toothpaste. It stung his tongue and foamed on his wrists. He scrubbed until the mud around his bandaged feet was floating pink with toothpaste bubbles.

Only Happy was less than pleased with the bargain. He had lost the meat he'd been saving for supper and his rotting gums were too tender to bear the touch of his toothbrush. Frank offered him the razor but he preferred to sit in the kitchen and sulk.

Towards dusk the rain lifted and the clouds rolled apart for the moon. As it grew dark there was laughter and shouting on the edge of the forest. When Gilbert went to investigate he found the pygmies had returned with their friends and relations, women and children. He sat on the veranda with a jug of palm wine and watched them build a camp fire of brushwood pulled from the undergrowth.

The fire smoked and exploded into a ball of flames. While the women cooked rats and spinach, the men sat with their feet buried in the warm ashes and sang sad, sentimental songs. After the food had been eaten the warrior in the fur hat stepped forward and beckoned Gilbert to join their circle. Gilbert threw off his cape and went down to them with the palm wine.

At midnight Frank stepped out to find Gilbert hunched before the fire like an old, melancholy bear, surrounded by naked, dancing goblins. When he went to the rescue a woman approached him with a selection of postcards. *Pygmy Beauties Bathing. Brave Pygmy Hunters. A Secret Pygmy Ceremony.* Frank gently pushed her away, took Gilbert's hand and led him back to his room. The pygmies continued to sit by their fire but in the morning they were gone.

18

The rains retreated. Each day the sun burned brighter through the collapsing columns of cloud. In the hotel compound the mud lost its shine, shrivelled, cracked and flaked into dust. The jungle steamed and stank.

Frank and Veronica spent their time scrubbing the kitchen and trapping cockroaches. Happy managed to mend the roof with metal salvaged from the old store room and embrocated the walls with fresh blue paint. Gilbert surveyed the property, counting beds and spoons and doorframes, as if he feared the bad weather might have robbed him of something. He scribbled his conclusions in a curly notebook which he kept beneath his pillow.

When they weren't working they sweated and squabbled and rooted for food. The stew, which had boiled thick and strong throughout the long rain, began to taste thin and lacked fresh meat. They tried to revive it with spinach, pepper and wild garlic, but nothing could disguise its poverty. The stew was exhausted .

As the heat returned Frank found himself watching the forest road. At every opportunity he slipped away and sat among the trees, listening for the distant sounds of moving trucks, men shouting, machines growling, anything that might tell him the road was open and he could make the journey into town. They had nothing left he could carry for trade. But if they could catch enough bush meat he could sell what they didn't eat; take it to market and bring home coffee, sugar, rice and eggs. Gut and smoke it. Rats the best. String them on a long pole. Ask Happy to build snares and set them around the hotel perimeter. Bait them with fruit. Soak the fruit in palm wine.

Despite Frank's careful watch of the road it was Veronica

who first heard the engine. It was early one morning and she had gone out to search for lizards drowsing in the undergrowth. She had taught herself to catch them in a net fashioned from a stocking on a wire coat hanger. Whenever she caught one she took it back to Happy and the butcher's block. He had the knack of skinning them and breaking off the tails for the stew.

When she heard the sound of the engine she dropped the net and went flying into the compound, shouting and waving her arms in a frenzy of excitement.

'The road is open!' she shrieked. 'There's a truck on the road!' They ran out and stood in the sun, watching the road as a funnel of dust approached through the trees. It was a big green motor wagon. The wagon was covered in canvas stretched on iron hoops in the manner of a gypsy caravan. It wasn't until it had rattled to a halt beneath the veranda that they recognised the driver. He'd had his hair cut and he was sporting a smart black nylon suit but it was the familiar boiled face of Boris who grinned up at them.

'You good people I come home!' he bellowed. 'You think I forget? Look here!' He waved at the wagon. 'We got supplies. We got fuel. We got a pork and bean supper. Special occasion.'

They looked at him in bewildered silence. They thought he was dead. They thought he was buried. He certainly looked dressed for a funeral. When Gilbert recovered from the shock of this unexpected resurrection he stepped down and peered suspiciously at the wagon. Frank limped after him and stood scowling at his old adversary. Veronica stayed behind, sheltering in the shadows.

'The rain! What a bastard. Knock down everything,' laughed Boris, throwing open his arms to embrace them. 'You look bad. Happy don't feed you. Bring him out and I kick him around.'

Frank looked at Gilbert. His blanket was dappled with dust and gravy. His toothbrush dangled on a cord at his throat.

Gilbert looked at Frank. One hand was still wrapped in a bandage. His knees had worn through his trousers and all the buttons were gone from his shirt.

They turned and looked at Boris.

'You take a look here. Make your heart glad. We got everything,' he grinned, walking them to the back of the wagon. He tore open the curtain and urged them to dip their faces into the spicy darkness.

There were bales of bananas, pouches of peas, satchels of soap, scented and household, kettles of klipbok, shovels of sugar, strings of onions, bowls of beef belly, buckets of beans, pails of peanuts, hampers of herons, barrels of buffalo cured in salt, pottles of plums, firkins of figs, whiskets of widgeon, basins of bacon, baskets of biltong, yards of yam, carboys of cucumber pickled in vinegar and bottles and bottles of bright, sparkling beer.

But it wasn't the sight of this staggering cargo of food that caught their eye in the canvas cave. It was the sight of the woman. On a mattress of millet, wedged between drums of sweet milk, tar and kerosene, sat a woman as round as an elephant god. Her face was yellow and pink enamel. Her hair was a pile of sticky, black curls. She stared out at them and raised an eyebrow. She had hard, shiny cockroaches for eyes with lashes that drooped like so many dangling legs.

'Look at this lady!' crooned Boris. 'Her name is Charlotte. A very good friend to me. You wait. Charlotte make it work!'

Charlotte raised a pale, imperial hand and two smaller women, no more than girls, seemed to hatch from the folds of her skirt.

'This here my girls,' she said in a rumbling voice. 'This one Comfort. This one Easy. They good girls the both of them.'

The two girls blinked sleepily into the sunlight. Their clothes were crushed and stained with sweat. Their faces were dark as molasses .

'Here, Frank, help the girls down,' said Gilbert. 'You've arrived at a bad time – the rain washed us out – but we'll soon make you comfortable.'

He held out his hand to pilot Charlotte gently from the back of the wagon. It took time and patience to guide her out through the bottles and barrels. When she was free she stood in the dust and stared thoughtfully at the derelict hotel. She was dressed in a long black frock festooned with lace hanging from ivory buttons. It was an old, sad frock, gone grey fighting with her belly and breasts, rubbed to a shadow on the battleground of her buttocks, worn out, defeated, surrendering at every seam.

'A very superior residence,' she declared, turning her smooth, enamel face on Gilbert. 'A very lovely property.'

'Yes,' said Gilbert. His mouth fell open and he wagged his poor head with pleasure.

'You got nice rooms for me?' she rumbled. 'My girls need nice rooms.'

'You've got the best rooms in the house,' said Gilbert. He rubbed his hands anxiously on his blanket. 'Don't worry about anything. We'll make you feel at home.'

It took them all day to unload the wagon. When they had safely landed the food they uncovered trunks of clothes and clean bed linen. Charlotte counted the trunks and went to inspect the bedrooms. She installed Comfort in the room opposite Frank, Easy in the room next to Boris and chose to settle herself in the room opposite Gilbert. Boris insisted on taking his old room next door to Veronica. She didn't argue since she was still sleeping with Frank but she was frightened someone would enter her room and find the hidden treasure of soap.

'Who are they?' she whispered when she caught Frank alone.

'Friends of Boris,' he said simply.

'But what do they want?' she demanded. 'What are they doing here?'

'It's a hotel,' said Frank.

Veronica wasn't convinced. When the wagon was empty she followed Gilbert back to the kitchen where she stayed and watched Happy cook supper. The girls sat in the sun and sipped beer with Boris. Charlotte kept Frank to unpack her clothes.

'What's your name?' she said when she had settled herself on the bed. The mattress groaned beneath her weight. She plucked a handkerchief from her sleeve and began to fan herself with a little pecking motion, stirring the lace around her breasts.

'Frank,' said Frank as he knelt down to explore the trunk. He turned the key in the lock. When the lid sprang open he found frocks the size of silk pavilions, sprays of petticoats bright as fireworks, satin stockings, rubber girdles, slips, stays and bloomers dripping with wreaths of crepe flowers. Enough clothes here to fill ten wardrobes. What did she want him to do with them? Grown too fat to reach her own buttons. Cut her out of that long black frock. Sponge her down with a bucket of water. Feed her stew from a long wooden spoon. He arranged the clothes neatly in piles on the floor.

'What's wrong with your hand?' she demanded as she watched him unfold her bloomers.

'It's gone bad,' he said, pausing to look at his tattered mitten. The bandage was filthy. 'It won't heal properly.'

Charlotte grunted and held the handkerchief up to her nose.

At the bottom of the trunk there were boxes of paint and bottles of perfume that leaked heliotrope, frankincense, musk and rose. These she made him arrange on the table beside the bed.

'You got religion?' she said when he had finished. She unscrewed a bottle and sprinkled scent on the pillows.

'No,' said Frank. He looked surprised. 'Do you want a Bible?' Charlotte said nothing. She sat motionless with her dark cockroach eyes concentrated on the wall behind his head.

'You sure you got no religion?' she said after a while.

'Yes.'

'There's a lot of religiosity here for people who don't have God,' she said suspiciously.

Frank turned and looked at the wall. She had been staring at a picture of Jesus walking on water with a dinner plate behind his head. 'It used to be a German mission,' he explained.

'People don't like it,' said Charlotte.

'Religion?'

'Picture of Jesus lookin' down on them,' she growled, shaking her handkerchief at Him. 'It makes them feel bad.'

'Do you want me to take it away?'

Charlotte smiled and thrust out her stomach. 'It don't bother me,' she said and dapped again at her breasts.

That night they gathered in the dusty moonlight to dine on a cauldron of pork and beans. Charlotte sat on a throne of beer crates with Comfort and Easy curled at her feet. Gilbert sat on a drum of treacle with Frank and Veronica close beside him. Boris sprawled on the ground behind Charlotte, pulling bottles of beer from her skirts. Happy ran in circles, farting and dropping plates.

'It tastes good, eh?' said Boris, waving his spoon at Gilbert. 'Not so long ago we starve. You lucky people to have a friend like Boris. Believe me. I was afraid to find your bones.'

'We didn't starve,' said Gilbert proudly. He dropped beans down the front of his blanket and picked at them with his fingers.

'We managed to look after ourselves,' said Frank. 'Happy went hunting.'

'Catch anything?'

'Plenty.'

'And we picked fruit and mushrooms and snails and stuff,' scowled Veronica. 'Happy didn't let us go without.'

'Happy!' barked Boris. 'What a bastard!' He tossed an empty bottle at Happy who yelped and scampered to safety.

'We couldn't have done without him,' said Gilbert indignantly.

'What you done?' sneered Boris. 'You done pull down the place. Looks to me.' He belched and wiped his chin on his sleeve.

'Now that you're here what are you going to do about it?' snapped Veronica. She wanted to throw her bowl at him but she was too hungry to waste good food.

'You wait,' grinned Boris. 'Charlotte fix everything.'

'Do you think you can help?' asked Gilbert.

Charlotte raised her hand to her head and let her fingers flutter through the tower of black curls. 'Did you ever happen to visit Ndjamena?' she inquired. She fluttered her lashes and pouted at Gilbert, her mouth as fat as an apricot.

'Chad,' said Gilbert the man of the world.

'Yes,' she said.

'No,' said Gilbert sadly.

'The next time you visit Ndjamena you must visit the Chari Palace Hotel,' said Charlotte. 'A very exclusive residence. Chicken counter. Dance hall. Hygienic bedrooms. I bought it from a man called Mangarios. He was Lebanese. He said I would suffer. He feared to sell me the property but I knew he needed the money and I had some very big ideas. I made changes. I worked hard. When I left it was a palace. The Chari Palace Hotel. The most famous residence standing in town.'

'Why did you leave?' demanded Veronica.

'Did *you* ever visit Ndjamena?' asked Charlotte, without turning her eyes from Gilbert.

'No,' said Veronica.

'The war spoils everything. Curfews. Killings. Shortages. The French soldiers have no respect.'

'Soldiers in the hotel?' said Gilbert.

Charlotte nodded. 'A very bad sort.'

Comfort, who had been watching with hypnotised eyes while Frank licked his plate and spoon, began to snigger at the thought of soldiers. Charlotte gave her a poke with her foot.

'One morning I woke up and knew it was time for Charlotte to leave,' she continued. 'I always wanted to travel. So I sold the Palace and took my girls into Cameroon. We worked in Douala for a little time and then we moved to Batuta. Did you ever visit Le Paradis Bar on Avenue du Général-de-Gaulle?'

'It's been so long,' said Gilbert. He closed his eyes and frowned, as if trying to sort through a thousand dance halls and beer parlours. 'Le Paradis Bar. Avenue du Général-de-Gaulle?' No, I don't remember it.'

'There was a big electric sign on the wall,' she said helpfuly. 'A blue palm tree of my own design.'

'No,' confessed Gilbert. 'No, I've forgotten.'

'A very lovely location. But so expensive. And the paperwork! These days they want a permit for this and a licence for that. They want money for sunlight. Every week the chief of police came to inspect me. You wouldn't believe it.'

Comfort sniggered again and prodded Easy. Charlotte bent forward and cuffed the girl across the head.

'I had already sold the premises when Boris told me about you in the forest. It's true to say I thought he was mad. But then he explained how you had come here and how the town needs a proper hotel and I knew that Charlotte could help,' she said.

'You're a long way from the bright city lights,' said Gilbert. 'I'm afraid you'll be disappointed.'

'Tomorrow you show me the works,' smiled Charlotte. 'You tell me everything.' And she licked her lips as if she could taste him.

That night Gilbert lay in bed and thought of the woman in the opposite room. She looks Chinese. Tiny feet. Buffalo buttocks. The girls are African. Did you ever visit the Chari Palace? I never had that pleasure. The place needs the touch of a good woman. They have an instinct for the little comforts. Clean carpets. Velvet cushions. Fresh flowers on all the tables. Tell me everything. Show me the works. Allow me to lick you into shape. Sam would be pleased. Sam loved the touch of a fat woman. He liked to feed them on milk and sugar. He loved the forest and he loved fat women. There was nothing wrong with his head. Nothing. He had plans. The most famous residence standing in town. An electric sign of my own design. That's the idea. High on the roof. The Hotel Plenti. Blinking. Winking. An electric star. Down in the town they see the star shining over the top of the great night jungle. Navigation light. A star to guide them. How do they work? Ask Charlotte. She'll know. Stout woman. Mother of invention. Feed something off the generator. Gallons of fuel thanks to Boris. Daft bugger. Don't understand him. Thought he was dead. Show him a rifle and he comes back with food to feed an army. Gun law. Taught him a lesson. No more trouble. Sleep safe in our beds tonight. It's hot. Belly aches. Pork and beans are a shock to the system. Tell me. Show me everything. See how it works tomorrow.

At first light he woke Charlotte with fruit and coffee and steered her through the ruined hotel. He showed her the dining room with the hole in the ceiling. He took her out to Sam's grave and through the wreckage of shanty town. Charlotte took an interest in everything. She inspected the latrines and the generator shed, tapped the water tank and probed the oven. When she asked him questions about the kitchen he ran to fetch his pillow book and proudly provided the most detailed answers. Knives forty-seven. Forks sixty-nine. Surviving saucepans eleven.

As she made her grand tour she made him collect all the religious ornaments and carry them back to her room. Framed scenes from the life of Jesus ten assorted eight in full colour. Crucifixes five. Bleeding hearts one painted plaster.

'People don't like it,' she growled at him. `Pictures of Jesus don't make 'em feel good.'

Gilbert didn't argue. Charlotte knew what belonged in a palace. Frank helped him hang the pictures around her walls and nail the crucifixes above the bed. They screwed the bleeding heart to the wardrobe.

`It looks like a funeral parlour,' Frank told Veronica that night as they sat in his bed and fed each other biscuits by candlelight.

'What's the idea?'

'She says Jesus upsets the customers.'

'We don't have any customers' she objected.

Frank grinned and filled her mouth with biscuit. `Have you spoken to Comfort and Easy?'

'No,' she mumbled 'They just sit around in the sun with Boris and drink warm beer and stare.'

'I suppose they'll start work when we're ready to open again,' he said, but he didn't sound convinced. Nothing worked in the rain. Nothing worked in the heat. They would probably never be ready to open.

'Open? We're nearly full!' She protested. 'There are only three bedrooms left in the place and they're fit for nothing.'

'Charlotte must know what she's doing or she wouldn't have come here.'

'She's enormous,' said Veronica.

'Yes,' said Frank, sucking his fingers, 'And Gilbert. They're like a pair of circus elephants.'

In the days that followed Charlotte set out to prove herself as Gilbert's mother of invention. She was a seamstress and a barber, a butcher and a dentist. She could bake bread, brew wine and make her own herb medicines. She boiled a poultice to draw the poison from Frank's bad hand and mixed a paste for his ears when they were sunburnt and peeling. As soon as she heard Happy complain of his teeth she filled him full of hot whisky, sat on his chest and attacked his mouth with a pair of pliers. He gurgled as his throat filled with blood and fainted. When he woke up it was dark and he found four teeth in his cardigan pocket. She offered Veronica sweet herbs for the sake of her stomach and a green leaf tea against the bleeding. But Veronica would have none of it.

'There's nothing wrong with me,' she barked running around the yard, a bundle of bones in torn knickers. It might have been Olive.

Charlotte smiled and shook her head and turned her attention to Gilbert. He was still weak from the fever, rose late, retired early and liked to sleep through the heat of the afternoons. Charlotte nursed him. She cooked his meals and cleaned out his room. She burned his blanket and dressed him in a set of her own pyjamas, a black satin jacket with a scarlet collar and a huge pair of matching pantaloons. She stopped him working and tried to confine him to bed. But he rolled around the property, giddy with pleasure, his toothbrush stuck in his jacket pocket and the pantaloons blowing. The place needs the touch of a good woman. That's the idea. Maddened by desire to see the jungle palace he urged Boris to start the generator.

Boris grunted and ignored him. 'Charlotte tell me when it's time,' he said.

'It's time!' roared Gilbert. 'What's wrong with you?'

'Charlotte tell me,' insisted Boris and glared at him with a yellow eye.

But that night the generator rumbled into life. Charlotte had already tucked Gilbert into bed when the fan creaked above his head and sent cobwebs spinning around the ceiling. The Kelvinator shuddered in a corner of the kitchen. All over the Hotel Plenti the lights flickered, blinked and glowed once more against the walls of the forest.

19

Gilbert sat in bed in his satin pyjamas and let Charlotte feed him. She stuffed him with cakes and soaked him with beer and spun him stories of palace life. She turned a Chari chicken parlour into a pleasure pavilion of stupendous proportions. She told him that the bedrooms had glass floors, the courtyards were cooled by marble fountains and a little monkey, dressed as a waiter, carried drinks on a silver tray. She told him that all the princes of Persia came from the east to stay at the palace and pashas and pharaohs came from the north and blue-skinned men from the desert. She told him that there were peacocks stewed in honey served on nests of wild rice, turtles roasted in their shells, brandied figs and coloured sherbets. And poor, fat, befuddled Gilbert, because he wanted to believe it, because he needed to believe it, gorged on her words and stared at Charlotte with love in his eyes.

'We'll build a jungle palace,' he wheezed as she fed him on lumps of banana cake. 'I worked the Congo riverboats. I've seen something of the world. Everything grows in the forest. When we're established we'll sit here and feed from the fat of the land.'

'Cushions stuffed with peacocks' feathers,' she purred, wiping his mouth with her fingertips. 'Living carpets of forest flowers.'

'And a star on the roof?' he said. 'A star on the roof to shine at night?'

'Bright as the moon,' she said.

'The others don't understand. They're children,' he whispered, pulling his heavy head from the pillow. 'You're a woman of the world. You understand. You've had the experience.' He tapped his nose and fell back on the bed exhausted.

'It's not good for a man to live with children,' said Charlotte.

'I brought them here,' sighed Gilbert. 'I brought them here and I've made them suffer.'

'They're strong,' said Charlotte. 'And children like to suffer. It makes them feel romantic.'

Gilbert shook his head. 'They share all the hardship but they don't share the dream,' he whispered sadly. 'They look but they don't see anything. They listen but they don't hear anything.'

'They're children,' said Charlotte. 'And a man needs the touch of a woman.' She offered him more banana cake but Gilbert had fallen asleep.

Meanwhile Boris began to decorate the hotel according to Charlotte's instructions. He scrubbed out the little entrance hall, polished the mirror and stuffed the broken sofa with most of *Baxter's Mountain Memories* and pages from *The London Pageant*. He swept out the dining room, repaired the ceiling with cardboard and embellished the walls with posters. The posters were grey with age and featured a set of impossible, naked, Hollywood girls. They were all laughing. Their hair was bright as ribbon. Their breasts were hard and polished like fruits. One of the girls was stepping out of a bath in search of a towel. Another was kneeling on the beach with her swimsuit held in her hands. They were advertising something called Sweetheart Beer.

'Real American!' he roared indignantly, when Frank dared to look doubtful. 'Top quality USA.'

'But this is a dining room,' objected Frank. 'People are going to want to eat here.'

'Makes me hungry just lookin' at women,' muttered Boris and he threw himself at the wall, licking the nearest available breast with his tongue.

'Gilbert isn't going to like it,' warned Frank.

Boris ignored him. He knocked out the door to the veranda and hooked a string of paper lanterns around the walls. 'You people as bad as Sam,' he grumbled as he screwed home the lightbulbs. 'He sit around all day complaining. Do nothing. Watch the house fall down. People come out here. They want a nice place to drink. They looking for comfort.'

Comfort was usually on the veranda. The two girls sat out every afternoon, dressed in their Sunday-best satin frocks and a wealth of bent wire jewellery. Comfort was a beautiful, mad-eyed girl with long limbs and a face as black as an olive. Her mouth was full and curved like a knife. Easy was less lovely but a good deal friendlier with big breasts and buttocks too heavy for her bandy, pipe-cleaner legs. She sat around drinking beer or strutting up and down the veranda in plastic high-heel shoes. They provided themselves with a constant babble of music from a tape machine the size of a suitcase. The music they favoured was reggae and old love songs from the Nigerian hit parade. They danced together in a lazy shuffle, leaning forward, arms loose, heads bobbing, feet scrubbing the floor. They called out to Frank and laughed whenever he passed them but he was too busy with the kitchen work to give them much thought.

'Dem pipli mek plenti troble an no mistik,' complained Happy as he helped Frank cut onions for the evening stew. 'Fos tam a louk am a no lek am,' he said, shaking his head. The juice from the onions stung his eyes and he had to stop to blow his nose in a rag.

'They haven't done anything,' said Frank. That's the trouble. They appear from nowhere, make themselves at home and then sit around all day waiting to be fed.

'Dat won he nem Easy,' gasped Happy. 'He don mek Happy louk he big bak seid.'

'What?' said Frank. He didn't believe his ears. He tossed the onions into the pot and stirred at the stew with a stick.

'Daso,' confessed Happy. 'He don tek he clot and pout for op – kouik kouik – an mek a louk he neket bak seid!' He bent forward, hitched up his cardigan like a skirt and waggled his rump in the alr.

'When did this happen?'

'Plenti tam.'

'More than once?'

'Fo, feif tam,' said Happy, wiping his eyes in his rag. 'Ma blod he run col.'

There was a crash of saucepans and Boris broke into the kitchen. 'What's happening?' he shouted at Frank. 'You make this bastard work for a living?' He turned to Happy, slapped him playfully around the head and sent him spinning into a corner. Happy farted and fell on the floor.

'Happy works hard!' barked Frank. 'Leave him alone.'

Boris grinned and swaggered to the stove. 'What you got cooking you bastard? It smells like a turd.'

Before Frank had time to stop him, Boris snatched up a spoon and sampled the stew. He rolled it around his mouth. He sieved it through his teeth. He sucked. He chewed. He sprayed it across the kitchen wall.

'It makes me sick in the stomach!' he roared. He brushed his teeth with a dirty finger and spat a string of bubbles on the stove. 'I bring you special rations. What happens? You cook me a turd.'

'Get out!' shouted Frank. 'This is my kitchen and that's my stew. If you don't like it you can make your own arrangements.'

For a moment he thought Boris was going to reach out and strangle him. He watched the big, boiled face begin to swell with blood, the eyes glitter, the fingers curl and claw at the air. Frank watched and was ready for him. Kick the stove. Drench the bugger in boiling stew. Burn him. Blind him. Bang his head on the butcher's block. Cut his throat to stop him screaming. What happened? Couldn't save him. Fell down drunk. Bled to death on the bacon knife. Shame to waste him. Ask Happy to skin and bone him. Frank watched and waited but nothing happened.

'You think you know something?' growled Boris. 'You don't know nothing.' He laughed abruptly and waved his hand around the kitchen. 'Charlotte make some changes around here and you bastards kiss goodbye to everything.'

'Gilbert gives the orders,' said Frank quietly.

'Gilbert!' hooted Boris. 'He makes me sick in the stomach.' He turned and staggered back towards the sunlight. 'Gilbert like your stew,' he shouted from the doorway. 'He full of turds.'

'Holi Gost!' muttered Happy, ran across the floor and into his barrel.

That evening, before Charlotte had time to stop him, Frank took Gilbert his supper in bed. While the old man sat propped among the pillows and gobbled the stew, Frank seized the chance to complain about Boris.

'Why did he come here?' he demanded. 'We don't want him. He's nothing but trouble.'.

Gilbert licked his spoon and stared at Frank with lugubrious eyes. 'He brought back supplies,' he said. 'He got the generator working again.' He looked up at the fan in the ceiling. His bald head flashed in the lamplight.

'We could have managed without him,' insisted Frank.

'And he brought Charlotte here,' said Gilbert, poking the air with his spoon. 'He listens to Charlotte. If he gives you any trouble she'll sort him out.'

'He slapped Happy this afternoon,' complained Frank. 'He's crazy. He's not allowed back in the kitchen.'

Gilbert sighed and licked his chin. 'He doesn't mean any harm. He's trying to help. Charlotte has great plans. She can see the opportunities.' He laid the dish on the curve of his stomach and stared dreamily about the room.

'And what about Comfort and Easy?' said Frank.

'Charlotte's girls?'

'Yes,' said Frank. 'They don't do anything. They sit around all day waiting for me to feed them.'

'They're only children. They probably feel lost out here. Remember how difficult you found it for the first few days. I'm depending on you, Frank, to make them feel at home.'

'They feel at home with Boris,' grumbled Frank. 'He keeps them up drinking all night.'

'That's good,' said Gilbert. 'It shows they're beginning to feel comfortable. It takes time.'

Frank shook his head. 'I don't like it,' he muttered. 'There's something wrong.

'What does Veronica think about it?'

'I don't know. She spends most of her time hiding out in the trees. She creeps into the compound after dark and I have to go out and bang her dinner bowl and call her home like a cat.'

'She'll settle down,' said Gilbert. 'Charlotte has some wonderful ideas. You'll be surprised. You won't recognise the place when she's finished. Has she redecorated the dining room?'

'Yes,' said Frank.

'And the lights?' said Gilbert. 'Has she managed to hang up the lights?'

Frank nodded.

'I wish Sam was alive to see it,' grinned Gilbert. He belched and closed his eyes. The spoon slipped from his fingers. When Frank reached out to rescue the soup dish Gilbert was asleep.

'He's besotted,' said Frank later as he sat in bed with Veronica. 'He's besotted with Charlotte.'

Veronica was trying to break into an orange, scratching at the leathery skin to get at the flesh. 'He'll get over it,' she grunted.

'And he spends all day in bed,' worried Frank. 'He hasn't been outside his room for days. The hotel could fall down and he wouldn't know about it.'

'The hotel *has* fallen down,' Veronica reminded him.

'And have you seen what Boris has done to the dining room?' continued Frank. 'It looks like a Chinese massage parlour.'

'I don't care what he does to the place so long as he doesn't bother me,' shrugged Veronica.

He scowled at her in disgust. And then, as he watched her picking at the orange, his disgust turned into a creeping horror. Her sunburnt skin had a queer, phosphorescent pallor. The corners of her mouth looked caked with blood. There were faint green circles around her eyes. 'What's happened to your face?' he whispered.

'Nothing,' she said sharply.

He reached out to hold her chin in his hand but she recoiled from his touch and turned her face away. 'You've painted it!'

'So what?'

'Why?' he demanded. What was happening? 'Why have you painted it?'

'Mind your own business,' she retorted, sucking viciously at the fruit. 'I wanted to paint it. Comfort let me use her make-up. Jesus, Frank, what's wrong with you?'

Frank snorted and snapped out the light. She's gone mad. She looks like a trollop. Why did she want to paint her face? It doesn't make sense. When was she talking to Comfort and Easy? She spends all her time in the trees.

But as the days passed he noticed that she stopped running to hide in the forest and began to hang around the hotel, drinking and laughing with Charlotte's girls. They painted her face and curled her hair and buttoned her into a short, satin frock. She no longer came to his room at night but returned to her own bed to sleep.

'It's not safe,' he insisted. 'It's not safe to sleep alone.'

'You mean you want me to sleep with *you*,' said Veronica contemptuously.

'No,' said Frank. 'I mean I don't want to have to come running every time Boris takes a fancy to you and tries to kick down the bedroom door.'

'I can take care of myself,' she said.

'And I think you should take Gilbert his food sometimes,' he added.

'Why?'

'He'd like it.'

'Charlotte looks after him.'

'She's an outsider. He ought to have his family around him.'

'Charlotte is part of the family,' said Veronica. 'What has she done to upset you? You've been difficult ever since she came here. Would you rather we were starving and scratching around in the rain?'

Frank had no answer. He tried to talk to her again but she contrived to avoid him. He could only watch helplessly as she drifted into the camp of strangers.

'Why she leave you?' grinned Boris as he watched her walk the veranda. 'She want a proper shag. Look. See. She beg for it. Boris make her beg for it. Bite her teeties. She grunt like a hog. Too good to waste. You wait. You watch. Boris make her hot for shagging.'

'I need Veronica in the kitchen,' Frank complained. 'I need her to share all the extra work.'

'Don't be so jealous,' growled Charlotte. 'She needs to be with other women. You can't keep the poor creature locked away. Look how she laughs. See how she shines since my girls arrived.'

20

Frank retreated to the kitchen. In the sour heat of the long shed he molested marrows, butchered yams and wreaked havoc on the vegetable kingdom. He made stew as hot as molten lead, brewed soup that scorched and blistered the tongue, boiled coffee into creosote and baked bread into ashes.

At the end of the week Boris took the motor wagon into town and returned with a cargo of customers.

'I come home!' he bellowed through the afternoon dust. 'We got our first paying guests!'

Half a dozen men clambered down from the wagon and stood, grinning bashfully, while Boris unloaded two fat, excited, girls. The girls shrieked when Boris squeezed them. They wore bright nylon frocks and plastic shoes. The men were smartly turned out in boiled shirts, flared trousers and sandals. One of them carried a rolled umbrella and another sported a trilby.

'We do hot business tonight!' laughed Boris. He led the party into the dining room and set Happy to work, serving peanuts and beer. When everyone had a drink he shouted for silence and introduced Charlotte. She was sitting in a nest of pillows and cushions, whisking the air with a paper fan. She wore a grey cobweb sewn with glass beads. The thickly powdered face and swollen body made her look like a giant moth. When she had shaken everyone by the hand and welcomed them to the Hotel Plenti, she sent Happy out to search for Frank.

'These young ladies require rooms for the night,' she said when Frank came running from the kitchen.

Frank looked at the girls sitting at a corner table surrounded by silent staring men.

'Do they have any luggage?' he said.

A man hooted and clapped his hands. The man in the trilby sniggered.

Charlotte smiled coquettishly at Frank and tapped a bouquet of bank notes against her breasts. 'No luggage,' she said.

So Frank took the girls along the corridor and showed them the empty rooms. He opened the shutters and wardrobes, checked the towels and water jugs and drew the mosquito nets on the beds.

'I hope you'll be comfortable,' he said. The first girl grinned and licked her beer bottle. The second girl shrieked and kicked off her shoes.

When he returned to the dining room he found Happy serving another tray of beer. The men were sitting around the room, shouting and drinking and laughing among themselves. Charlotte sucked on a small cigar and beckoned Frank through the smoke.

'Do you think you can find our guests something for supper?' she said.

Frank looked doubtful. He glanced around the room, attempting some rapid mental arithmetic. Fifteen mouths to feed. Sixteen if you counted Gilbert. He saw Veronica standing on the veranda, drinking beer with Comfort and Easy.

'I don't know,' he said slowly. 'I could make small chop to stretch the stew…'

'Whatever you think,' she said and dismissed him.

Frank left the room and marched across the compound with Veronica running behind him.

'What do you want?' he shouted as they reached the kitchen.

'I'm a waitress, noodle-brain. I'm supposed to serve the food.'

'You look ridiculous,' he said, glaring at her buttered curls and rouged cheeks.

'Look, Frank, I'm trying to help.'

'I don't want your help,' he said as Happy scampered past with more bottles of beer. But, despite his protests, he made Veronica carry the food and was glad to have her working with him.

Charlotte encouraged her guests to eat and drink and enjoy themselves. The stew made them sweat and the beer made them brave. They began to bray at Comfort and Easy, dancing together on the veranda. As it grew dark the paper lanterns filled the hotel with a flush of red light. Happy continued to run about with his arms full of bottles. He clutched them like babies snatched from the flames of a burning building. His cardigan squelched with beer. His eyes were hard and swollen. Boris skulked around the compound sucking a bottle of palm wine and talking to himself. The sounds of reggae thundered under the hotel roof. The shouts of the supper guests frightened the forest.

'What's happening out there?' said Frank, frantically frying a basket of plantain.

'They're eating,' snapped Veronica as she hurried away with a bucket of stew.

'How long are they going to stay?' he demanded, desperately trying to skin a yam.

'Until they've finished,' she shouted impatiently, dashing back to refill the bucket.

They worked for an hour. When all the food had been served and Veronica was safe in the kitchen sitting, exhausted, against Happy's barrel, Frank slipped out to look at the dining room.

The air in the room was hot and stale. There was a stink of sweat and smoke and perfume. Empty bottles rolled on the floor. Through the fog he could see Easy standing in one corner of the room, smoking a cigarette and staring at the cracks in the plaster. She was bending forward, hands pushed flat against the walls and her legs planted wide. During the excitement her frock had been pulled up over her shoulders, where it hung in a curious hump of cloth. A man stood behind her and stared at the hump. He kissed it while he fingered her buttocks.

Comfort was entertaining another of the guests by dancing with a third, who was so drunk he had to follow her around the floor on his knees. She shuffled in a circle, advancing, retreating, spinning her partner by his ears. Frank watched him fall in a heap and stare in astonishment at the ceiling. Comfort shouted something above the music and the second man laughed. She squatted over the drunk's face, hitched up her skirt and hissed through her teeth. The poor man grinned, stuck out his tongue and fainted.

One of the fat girls from town was dancing with the man in the trilby. He led her briskly around the floor, his sandals slapping in time to the music, his black face shining like treacle. His hat flew off and the fat girl kicked it under a table.

Charlotte sat splendid among her cushions with a steel cash box in her hands. The box was stuffed with bank notes. She was chewing her cigar and counting the dinner money. During the meal one of the diners had crawled forward and become entangled in the long strands of her web. He lay, exhausted now, with his head crushed white between her knees and his body stretched out on the floor at her feet. He was spreadeagled in an attitude of divine surrender. His shirt was leaking gravy.

'How did they like the food?' shouted Frank.

Charlotte turned her head and squinted at him through the gloom. 'They enjoy the food. They enjoy the music. And now they enjoy themselves. Everything is perfect. The Hotel Plenti is back in business,' she shouted. She smiled and snapped shut the cash box.

'I'll go and fetch Gilbert,' shouted Frank. 'He'll want to be here.'

'No,' thundered Charlotte. She pulled the cigar from her mouth and stared at it thoughtfully for a moment, as if surprised by its discovery. 'Leave him alone and let him sleep tonight. We'll tell him the news tomorrow.' She returned the cigar to her mouth and let smoke leak through her teeth.

Frank didn't argue. He was already creeping towards the door. 'If there's nothing else…' he yelled above the music.

'Where's Veronica?' shouted Charlotte.

'She's working in the kitchen.'

Charlotte looked irritated. She shouted something at Frank but her words were lost in the uproar.

Frank turned quickly and collided with the missing town girl as she stumbled into the dining room followed by a sweating, excited admirer. His affections seemed fired by her tiny breasts which he coddled in his hands like eggs. When the girl saw Frank she wriggled free of the embrace and pushed the man away. Frank tried to reach the door but she slipped her arms around his waist and began to dance across the floor, bumping and grinding herself against him.

'You go be may man tonet,' she announced in his ear. She danced him against a wall where she kept him amused by squirming softly against his groin.

'I've got to work,' insisted Frank, grinning, glancing anxiously about the room. It was wrong. She was a child. She couldn't be more than thirteen or fourteen years old. The man she had spurned was now fighting for a share of Easy's fat, brown buttocks.

'Fos tam a gif you plenti everi tin fo notin,' she promised.

Frank yelled with pain and surprise. Her fingers had sneaked their way into his pants. She began to pull roughly on his penis as if she were trying to work a cow's teat.

'That's very generous of you,' gasped Frank. 'Did you enjoy the meal?' Comfort pushed past them, wearing a dirty, beer stained trilby. His legs began to buckle. He slipped slightly against the wall and the girl leaned her shoulder hard against him, afraid he might escape. Her breath blew hot on his neck. Her hair stung his face like brambles.

'A fok you so you hola,' she grunted.

Frank, held fast by the short and curlies, tried to look enthusiastic. 'It sounds like fun,' he winced.

'You lek me?' she demanded, after trying to milk him for two or three minutes. His penis was shrinking away from her hand. She stopped its retreat with her fingernails.

'Yes,' he moaned. 'Yes.' Her fingernails brought the tears to his eyes. The fat girl, encouraged, gave a mighty pull on his parts and sank her teeth into his neck.

Frank let out a sneeze of pain that blew them apart and, while the girl paused to recover her balance, he had lurched to the door and escaped. The honking of Charlotte's laughter followed him into the compound.

'What's happening?' asked Veronica when he appeared again in the kitchen. 'Have they finished?' She was eating from a tin of mixed fruit salad, fishing for the cherries with a bent fork.

'We're living in a brothel,' said Frank, sitting down to recover his breath.

'What's that supposed to mean?'

'They're tarts!' he laughed. 'Charlotte's girls. They're tarts.' It was obvious. He should have guessed what was happening that first evening when Charlotte had called him to unpack her trunk. She was a brothel keeper. He wondered if Gilbert had guessed the truth. Where was the man? Why didn't he do something to restore law and order?

'It's your imagination, Frank. You've been on heat ever since they arrived here.'

'It's not my imagination. Ask Happy what happened to *him*. They're tarts,' insisted Frank.

'Daso,' crowed Happy from behind the stove. He bent forward and flapped his cardigan at Veronica.

'They're doing things out there you wouldn't believe,' said Frank.

'I don't believe it,' said Veronica. She speared a pineapple chunk by mistake and flicked it on the floor in disgust. Her lipstick was leaking from the corners of her mouth.

Frank shrugged. He was defeated. Why should she believe it? He had just had his penis pulled by a squelching, belching, fat fourteen-year-old with death in her eyes and beer on her breath and *he* didn't believe it. He felt numb with horror and excitement. 'Go and have a look for yourself,' he said wearily. 'I don't care.'

'I can't!' shouted Veronica. 'Boris is out there and he's drunk again.' She nursed the tin against her chest and threw him a faintly demented look.

'Dear God, what's happening here?' he marvelled. 'We're hiding in the kitchen like frightened rabbits while Boris is swaggering around out there as if he owned the place!' He jumped up and walked to the door. 'I'm going to talk to him.'

'No, don't leave me. Wait until the morning,' pleaded Veronica. She caught him by the sleeve and tried to drag him back to safety.

Frank pushed her away. 'I'm tired of being kicked around,' he shouted. 'If Gilbert isn't going to do anything we'll have to sort it out for ourselves.'

'Boris took the rifle,' croaked Veronica, hugging the fruit tin. 'What?'

Veronica nodded. Her eyes were brimming with tears. 'He's out there with the rifle. We couldn't stop him.'

Frank paused. 'I don't care. Sleep in the kitchen with the cockroaches if that's what you want. I'm going to bed,' he said quietly and walked out into the compound.

There was no sign of Boris as he made his way to the house. The music had stopped and the lights had gone out. When he passed the dining room he heard a scuffle and scratching, a shriek, a sigh, a rustle of whispers.

He was creeping down the corridor when a bedroom door opened and a small, naked, man stepped out to challenge him.

'What you want?' he said, scowling at Frank. 'This one taken. I paid my money.'

'Yes,' said Frank.

'So what you want?' demanded the stranger.

'I live here,' said Frank, pushing past him to reach his room.

At dawn Boris swept silently through the hotel and collected his cargo of customers. He led them, shivering and yawning, to the waiting wagon and carried them back to town. Their pockets were empty but their hearts were full. He left them in the market square and went off to spend his day in the bars, searching for trade. Frank spent the day with Happy, cleaning out the bedrooms. Veronica scrubbed the dining room floor. Charlotte fed Gilbert and washed him down with a wet flannel. Comfort and Easy appeared, late in the afternoon, and danced lethargically on the veranda. At dusk Boris returned with a wagon full of fresh recruits. The lights flickered. The beer and the gravy overflowed. And so it continued.

Late each night, when the dancing finally stopped and the

fire was gone from the pot-bellied stove, Frank would lie awake in his room and listen to the song of the mattresses. As the girls set to work he could hear the beds groan, wheezing and gasping under the strain, flexing their springs and calling to one another through the bedroom walls. All through the night they clanked and rattled until the hotel itself seemed to come to life, grinding its jaws in the moonlight.

One night, when business was poor, he heard his door creak open and someone shuffled into the room. Through half-open eyes he watched Comfort approach his bed. She was wearing a white cotton brassière and a pair of fancy boxer shorts. For a long time she stood and stared down at him. Frank didn't move or make a sound. She whispered his name but he didn't answer and finally she shuffled away.

For a long time afterwards he lay and waited for sleep. Egg, bacon, sausage. Two egg, bacon, sausage. But sleep refused to shelter him in the way that it chose to favour Gilbert. For as long as he could remember, whenever Gilbert had felt overwhelmed by the sorrows of the world, he had promptly fallen asleep. When Olive had died he had taken to his bed and allowed his grief to flood him with all the speed of an anaesthetic. When he'd heard the news of Sam's death they had carried him to bed and watched helplessly while he buried himself in slumber. And now he was under the influence of that healing narcolepsy again, as if he were already mourning the death of his jungle hotel. Perhaps Gilbert had known, before any of them, that the dream wouldn't work, that there would never be anything here but memories and disappointment. Ashes to ashes. Heat and dust. What did he care now if Charlotte established the biggest bordello in Bilharzia or Boris knocked the place down and sold the timber for firewood? The old man no longer took an interest in the affairs of the hotel because he was no longer living in it. God knows where his dreams had led him. He could be anywhere. Frank felt determined to talk to him, reason with him, shake him awake. He crawled painfully from the mattress and groped his way to the corridor. The hotel was quiet. Comfort had returned to her room. He crept as far as Gilbert's room and gently opened the door.

The smell of oranges, incense and damp feathers filled his nostrils. Candles were smoking beside the bed. Deep among the greasy pillows, face as stiff as a painted mask, eyes set hard, mouth pulled open, Gilbert lay and stared at the ceiling. He was not alone. Charlotte was sitting astride his stomach. Her fat thighs engulfed him. Her big, dimpled belly spread over his chest. She was feeding Gilbert with tiny pieces of fruit, pulling the fruit apart with her fingers, pushing it deep into Gilbert's throat. She turned when she heard Frank open the door. She looked at him with her terrible, glittering cockroach eyes, bared her teeth and smiled.

21

Confined to his room, hidden from sunlight, the varnish peeled from Gilbert's face and his hands began flaking like scrubbed potatoes. Every morning Charlotte would take him breakfast and refill his jug of boiled water. She swept the floor, opened the window to change the air and, when everything was in order, liked to sit beside the bed and talk to him as she smoked a cigar. Sometimes she described the customers that passed in the night, the gossip they brought, the beer they drank. At other times she listened while Gilbert gave instructions to be carried to the kitchen. Spare the sugar. Pepper the stew. But something was wrong and, as the days passed, she saw him grow weaker and more confused. He began to dream of the Hercules Café and shouted for Olive in his sleep. Then Charlotte sat helpless, watching him moan and choke on his tears.

Frank knew nothing of Gilbert's decline since, whenever he asked, Charlotte insisted her patient was making a slow convalescence and shouldn't be disturbed.

'We could make a bed up on the veranda,' he argued. 'We could carry him out there and keep him cool with screens.'

But Charlotte shook her head. 'He's too weak to be disturbed. It's best for him to stay in his room.'

'Did he ask about me?' Frank asked anxiously.

Then Charlotte clucked and smiled. 'He wants you to work hard and not worry about him,' she said.

Frank only discovered the truth when he found Gilbert one afternoon, escaped from his room and squatting in the shade of the compound wall. He was crouched in the dust, poking at a cockroach with a broken stick. His pyjamas steamed in the heat. His skull shone with sweat. When he saw Frank he tried to hide the cockroach under his foot. An expression of terrible bewilderment spread across his piebald face.

'Who are you?' he demanded as Frank bent down to take the stick from his hand.

'Frank,' said Frank.

Gilbert looked relieved. 'Frank?'

'Yes.'

'Have you seen Olive?' he whispered. He struggled to rise but fell exhausted against the wall.

Frank tried to steer him towards the house. But the old man was heavy and Frank couldn't find the strength. He shouted for Happy. He shouted for Veronica. Charlotte came running and together they managed to manoeuvre Gilbert back to his room.

'What's wrong with his skin?' he complained as they rolled him into bed.

'It's nothing,' said Charlotte, smoothing the sheet over Gilbert's stomach. 'I'll make him some ointment.'

Frank pulled a kitchen rag from his belt and used it to wipe the old man's face. Gilbert grunted and closed his eyes.

'He needs to rest,' said Charlotte.

Frank nodded and turned away. 'He didn't recognise me,' he said softly.

'Sometimes he forgets his surroundings,' said Charlotte. She sat down in the chair and helped herself to a glass of boiled water.

'But I thought. You told me.'

'He don't sound so good no more,' confessed Charlotte. 'He don't seem to know himself.'

'He belongs in hospital,' protested Frank. 'We can't keep him here.'

'I nurse him with every attention,' growled Charlotte. She waved her hand impatiently. 'He wants for nothing.'

'He wants proper medical treatment,' said Frank fiercely.

Charlotte puffed out her chest and glowered at Frank. 'We're not in Lagos,' she barked. Her throat trembled like a turkey wattle. 'Don't you understand? It could take days to get him to hospital. We don't even know where to find a hospital.

The journey alone is enough to kill him.' She poured a little water into her hand and pressed the hand against her neck. She had been asleep when Frank had raised the alarm. She was wearing a dirty dressing gown and her hair was wrapped in cheesecloth.

'We've got to do something,' said Frank, sitting on the floor beside her chair.

'Yes. We've got to wait and be patient. And we have to watch him. If he gets out again he could hurt himself.'

Frank stared at the bed. Gilbert snored. The sun had broken through the shutters and filled the room with narrow blades of dusty, afternoon light.

'I could help you to nurse him. And we could ask Veronica to sit with him sometimes,' he suggested.

'Good,' said Charlotte. She smiled. 'I want you to work with me, Frank. We're depending on you.' She bent forward, making the chair creak, and squeezed Frank's shoulder. 'I need your help with the business,' she added confidentially.

'I don't know,' said Frank. He felt uneasy. She had stooped so low the dressing gown showed the tops of her breasts.

'Do you want us to fall into ruin? Do you think Gilbert would want us to close the hotel just because he don't have his strength?'

'No.'

'No. He'd want you to take charge of everything.' She ruffled his hair with her hand. 'He'd expect you to take command.'

'I can't do anything. No one listens to me,' he said cautiously.

'I listen to you and that enough,' she said and pressed his head against her knees.

In the days that followed Charlotte deliberately asked for his opinion on everything from the price of a room to the quality of Bilharzian beer. She had favoured Gala beer in Chad but thought the local Tusker was sour. Frank suggested they switch to Beaufort and she took his advice. He began to feel encouraged. They shared the work of the sick room and forced Veronica to reluctantly pay her respects.

'Jesus, he gives me the willies,' she said, when Frank took her into the room. 'What's gone wrong with his skin?'

'It's nothing,' said Frank confidently.

Veronica wrinkled her nose. The room smelt of home-made ointments, Jeyes fluid and the stale smoke of cheap cigars.

'How d'you know it's nothing?' she demanded. 'It could be serious. It could be anything.'

'What?'

'I don't know.' She frowned and turned away from the bed.

'Charlotte's treating him. She says he just needs to rest and build up his strength,' said Frank.

Veronica sneered. 'I don't trust her medicine,' she said, slouching against the wall. Her face was sticky with paint and she was wearing one of Comfort's frocks.

'She fixed my hand,' said Frank, to reassure himself. 'And she pulled Happy's teeth.'

'I wouldn't let her touch me,' declared Veronica.

'There's nothing wrong with you.'

'She uses herbs and stuff,' said Veronica. 'What kind of medicine is that?'

'We don't have any other kind,' said Frank.

'He ought to have a proper doctor,' she said stubbornly.

'We can't move him.' He glanced across at Gilbert, heaped upon the mattress. His eyes were closed but his jaw was working, grinding his teeth in his sleep.

'Frank, if we don't do something it could be too late.'

'We're doing everything we can to make him comfortable.'

'It's not enough. He looks terrible. He's big enough to burst,' she said angrily. She pulled herself from the wall and moved nervously about the room. Her spine had pressed a seam of sweat through the back of her dress.

'We'll watch him for another few days,' said Frank, feeling exasperated. 'If he doesn't improve we'll send Happy into town to fetch help.'

'What sort of help?'

Frank turned to the door. He didn't have the energy to reply to her questions. There wasn't a doctor for a hundred miles.

They had to trust Charlotte. 'It's important to keep him in bed. It's important to make him rest,' he said and hurried back to the kitchen.

But despite all their efforts, Gilbert continued to escape. One afternoon he slipped past Charlotte, asleep in the chair, wandered through the deserted compound and reached the rubbish tip at the back of the kitchen block. They found him covered in meat scraps and flies, hiding a chicken's claw in his fist. When Frank asked him what he wanted he said he was looking for Chester. Veronica broke down and sobbed. They scrubbed him clean and carried him back to his bed.

Two days later he escaped again by climbing through the window and disappearing into the forest. Boris found him sitting at the side of the road and brought him home in the wagon.

'What a bastard!' he bellowed as he dragged him through the hotel corridors. 'I don't fetch and carry him no more. First time. Last time. He want to die in the jungle. Boris say good luck. He nothing but trouble.'

Gilbert stumbled and fell to his knees.

'Be careful with him, damn you,' shouted Frank, running to the old man's rescue. At the sound of Frank's voice Gilbert raised his face and smiled.

'He don't feel nothing. Look. He grinning,' said Boris. He grabbed Gilbert by the collar of his pyjamas and tried to haul him to his feet.

'Treat him with some respect or leave him alone,' ordered Frank, trying to push between them.

'I leave him alone,' said Boris. He stepped back and let Gilbert fall to the floor.

'Thanks a lot. Now go and fetch Charlotte.'

Boris bristled. 'I tell you bastard! I don't fetch and carry no more!' he roared, stabbing at Frank with his fingers. 'Anyway. I see you hiding up Charlotte's skirt. You think I don't know? You want something? Maybe.'

'I want to get Gilbert to bed. He's sick. He needs help,' said Frank.

'You talk to Charlotte. Poison her head against Boris. You think you call for Charlotte. Help. Save me. Everything work like a dream.' He paused. His voice softened to a hiss of steam. 'You wait. Boris catch you. Nowhere to hide from Boris.'

At dawn the next day Frank went down to the kitchen to help cook breakfast and found that Boris had been there before him. He sensed the danger as he crossed the yard. An unfamiliar silence hung in the air and no lights burned at the windows. He missed the smell of smoke from the hungry stove and the clatter of Happy, still half-asleep, colliding with his pots and kettles. He ran to the door and waded into the shadows.

The kitchen had been ransacked. Shelves had been torn from the walls. Happy's barrel had been kicked from its corner. There were great bags of rice and precious white flour dropped like bombs on the dirt floor. Frank found Happy sitting under the bench with his winklepickers in his hands. He held the shoes pressed tight against his chest and would not surrender them. His eyes stared at nothing. His face was covered in blood.

'What happened?' whispered Frank, squatting beside him.

Happy blinked. 'Boris,' he croaked. 'He bin mek big troble fo Happy. He don wan kil me. Holi Gost. You louk may het. Hia. He don brok he.' He raised his hand and waved a shoe across his face.

'When did all this happen?'

'Diesno.'

'Where is he hiding?'

Happy shrugged.

'Don't move. I'll try and clean you up,' said Frank, searching for towels through the rubbish. A pan of water survived, untouched, on the stove. He washed the blood from Happy's face and gently searched for the damage.

'It's not too bad,' said Frank. 'I think it's just a crack on the nose? The nose was swollen, the nostrils plugged with congealing blood.

'A fia dat man,' gasped Happy miserably.

'He's mad,' said Frank. He stood up slowly and stared around him in disgust. He felt frightened and cold. He trampled to the barrel and fished for a blanket. .

'Plenti blod hia,' said Happy, sniffing and wiping his nose on his sleeve.

'How did Sam control him?' said Frank, crawling from the barrel.

'Sam?' said Happy, looking anxious. 'He don go day. Benegron.' He began to pull on his shoes as if he were planning to make a run for it.

'Yes,' said Frank. 'But when he was alive he must have given Boris orders and made him behave himself.' The blanket smelt of onions. He draped it over Happy's shoulders.

'Sam he don notin,' shivered Happy. He shook his head. 'Boris nomba won man hia.'

'You mean Boris ran the hotel?'

'Daso. He don tel pipli dis ples belong he.'

Frank was baffled. 'But why did he do this to you?'

'Fo wat?' said Happy, staring at Frank in surprise. 'Bikos you don wan gifloa hia lek Gill Bear. Boris no lek dis ting. He don tel me. He go kil you.'

22

Frank made a bed for himself among the sacks of grain in the kitchen and stored his few remaining possessions in a box which he hid in the wall behind the stove. Happy, who had never been permitted to sleep in the house, was glad of the company and made Frank welcome. He didn't ask questions. While Frank was there he felt protected from Boris.

Each morning, before the sun had reached the compound wall, they worked together at the stove, boiling water and feeding meat to the stew. While Frank washed and shaved, Happy went out with the breakfast trays.

Later Charlotte arrived to collect the day's rations for Gilbert. She insisted on preparing his meals, although she did little more than choose fruit and cake. It was several days before she noticed that Frank was living in the kitchen.

'You don't like your lovely room?' she said, puzzled by his new sleeping arrangements. 'It's a crime to waste a good bed.'

Frank tried to explain but she didn't look convinced. An empty bed cost money. That was the problem.

'You're not afraid of Boris,' she chuckled, when he had finished his story. She cut a slice of cake and wedged it into a chipped enamel bowl.

'He's dangerous,' insisted Frank.

'He doesn't mean any harm.'

'He nearly killed Happy,' Frank shouted indignantly.

'Is this true?' asked Charlotte, turning to Happy.

Happy nodded.

Charlotte frowned and sniffed at a pineapple. 'He drinks,' she concluded. 'Ration his beer.'

'I can't control him,' said Frank. 'He only takes orders from you.'

Charlotte laughed. 'That man got the brain of a yam. You think I listen to his nonsense? I keep him to frighten the customers — keep law and order about the place. You and me got the brains here, Frank.'

Frank bit his tongue. He saw with a rush of despair that Charlotte depended on Boris. She owed him everything. He had brought her to the forest, given her the hotel and provided her girls with customers. What was a mere kitchen quarrel compared to this fortune? He was a fool to trust her any more than he trusted Boris.

Charlotte smiled and squeezed his arm. He walked as far as the kitchen door and watched her waddle across the compound.

At noon the heat tormented him. He spent the afternoons sheltering with Happy in the darkest corners, exhausted, suffocated, lost in a kind of drugged sleep. Perhaps Veronica was right about Gilbert. They should get him away from Charlotte's quack medicines and find him a bed in a hospital. If they could smuggle him to safety the old man might recover his wits and take control of their lives again. Boris would be banished. Veronica would come to her senses. All their problems would vanish like smoke. He could lead Gilbert from his room and into the shelter of the trees at night. But he couldn't hope to get him as far as town. The old man was too feeble, he was confused and his legs wouldn't work. They needed the motor wagon. If he recruited Happy as driver they could load Gilbert aboard and drive him to safety. But they couldn't expect to steal the wagon without someone raising the alarm. Boris would catch them. And Boris had the rifle.

He squatted against the kitchen wall, head hanging, drenched in sweat, and tried to revive his sinking spirits. He had to find a way through the nightmare. There must be an answer.

As the darkness spread from the heart of the forest he stirred himself and ventured into the compound to watch the hotel come to life with light. The sound of reggae drifted towards the kitchen. He heard Boris shouting and the explosive noise of men laughing.

He waited outside until he saw Veronica leave the hotel and walk through the dusk towards him. He barely recognised her beneath the powder and paint. She was wearing a dirty yellow frock, very short and far too tight, with a bunch of paper flowers at the waist. It looked as if it might have been stolen from a child's birthday party. She was walking barefoot but her ankles were weighted with metal hoops and strings of plastic beads.

He stood at the kitchen door, watching her, hoping for some acknowledgment, but she ignored him, swept past and spoke to Happy. She loaded a tray with a big bowl of stew, fried plantain, dried fish and peanuts and started back again towards the house with Happy scampering in her wake. Frank waited for her to return but Happy came back to the kitchen alone.

'How many tonight?' asked Frank.

'Fo,' grunted Happy.

Frank shuffled miserably away and looked towards the trees. The moon had risen and the forest seemed to swell like a dark and fathomless ocean. It whispered to him on every side, pressed forward and surrounded him. A man could drown out there and his body never be recovered. Fifty paces from the hotel a man might lose his sense of direction. The forest would drag him down, hold him fast and choke him to death.

As he turned back to the kitchen Boris sprang out of the darkness and waved the rifle at his chest. When he recognised Frank he laughed, cocked his head and spat in the dust.

'You got to be careful. Boris mistake you for a stranger. Maybe. Blow your brains out through your ears.'

Frank shrugged and walked towards the light of the kitchen.

'We got to keep watch for trouble now we got Charlotte to make the place nice,' continued Boris, walking beside him. 'We got to keep law and order.'

Frank quickened his pace and said nothing.

'Why you hiding out in the kitchen?' demanded Boris when they reached the door.

Frank ignored him, turned his back and entered the shed.

'Maybe you hiding from that Veronica,' taunted Boris. 'She gone shag-happy. I heard she can't get enough of it.' He grinned at Frank and sucked a tooth. But he didn't follow him into the kitchen. He stood impatiently at the door until Happy ran forward with a slab of bread and a large bottle of palm wine. Boris tucked these provisions into his vest and returned to sentry duties.

That night Frank told Happy of his plan to save Gilbert and escape the Hotel Plenti. Happy thought there was a modern hospital at Bolozo Rouge. He knew there was a medical station at Nkongfanto, a few miles from Malabo. It was only two days drive when the road was open.

'We'll have to make the escape at night when everyone's asleep,' Frank whispered. 'You'll be driving. We'll be gone by the time they raise the alarm. Do you think you can do it?'

Happy's face was squeezed with excitement. He rubbed his nose with the palm of his hand. 'Daso,' he said at last. 'Happy tek do mota.' He nodded. 'No troble.'

'We'll wrap Gilbert in a blanket and carry him out,' continued Frank.

'We nopa mek dat Miss Veronica go back no place,' said Happy slowly. 'He lek dis ting hia.'

'I'll try and talk to her tomorrow,' said Frank. 'But if she won't see sense we're going to have to leave her behind. We can't take any risks.' He paused, shocked by this decision, and tried to imagine leaving Veronica to the mercies of Charlotte and Boris. He didn't believe she would want to stay. It was impossible. When the time arrived, when the moment came for her to choose, despite everything, she would be there in the wagon.

'Boris he go be vex,' said Happy, breaking into a sweat. 'Holi Gost. He go holla an cus. He go com fo Happy with he gon.'

'He won't get far without the wagon,' Frank reminded him.

Happy nodded and wiped his hands on his cardigan. He retreated into his barrel to ruminate upon the risks of their enterprise. He had a wife in a village west of Nkongfanto. There were children too, but he couldn't remember how many of them belonged to him. He hadn't seen his wife for years. He tried to imagine sitting behind the wheel of the big motor wagon, the engine vibrating, kicking out smoke, the sun in his eyes, the hotel shrinking away behind him, the road that stretched beyond the forest; he tried to imagine but failed.

'We mek smol mistik an he de go kil meselef day,' he muttered. 'He de go kil youselef day. Dat man Boris he sik in de het.'

Frank pulled off his shoes and made himself comfortable in the grain sacks. He lay awake for some time listening to Happy's doubts echo around the barrel. At first light he would talk to Veronica. She would have to be there to help when they loaded Gilbert into the wagon. He settled down and tried to sleep. Tomorrow he would tell her everything. They were stealing Gilbert. They were going to escape.

But in the morning Gilbert had gone.

Charlotte woke the hotel with a terrible scream. It was a huge bellow of rage that cut through the grey dawn and made the zinc roof sing. Happy came out of the barrel like a man shot from a cannon. He charged around the kitchen shouting and farting until he found the door and staggered into the compound. Frank was already racing ahead of him, towards the house and Gilbert's room.

He found Charlotte sitting on the edge of the bed with a pillow swinging loose in her hand. Beneath a vast, patchwork dressing gown she was wearing a pink rubber girdle and a pair of embroidered carpet slippers . A fat black sausage of hair lay curled upon one shoulder. There was no sign of Gilbert.

'He's gone!' she wailed when she saw Frank. 'He must have wandered off somewhere in the night.' She stared woefully at the ceiling and clasped the pillow against her breast. 'Someone should have been looking after him. Sweet Lord. Must I do everything myself? Am I never to sleep?'

Frank was stunned. He stared about the room and shook his head. He opened his mouth but found he couldn't make a sound.

'He don't get far in his pyjamas,' muttered Boris, limping into the room. He stood shivering in his underpants. His hair sprang out of his head like nails. His face was purple and creased with sleep.

'Don't just stand there!' barked Charlotte impatiently. 'Go

and look for him.'

'Where?' growled Boris. He pushed past Happy, who was trying to imitate a chair in a corner of the room, scuffed across the carpet, sniffing the wardrobe and punching the foot of the bed.

'Everywhere!' shouted Charlotte. She puffed herself out until her corset creaked. 'Go and look everywhere!'

'What a bastard,' seethed Boris. He turned and pushed his way back into the corridor. 'What a bastard.'

At once the room was crowded with gawping, chattering, half-naked people.

'Has someone been attacked?' asked a tall, elderly man with a scarified face. He fumbled with a pair of spectacles, hooked them to his ears and peered anxiously at the bed.

'It's nothing,' said Charlotte. She smiled and put down the pillow.

The old man looked disappointed and let Comfort lead him away.

'I heard screaming. No mistake. Something happen here,' said another man. He was wearing a pair of nylon bloomers. He looked at Charlotte and then scowled suspiciously at Frank. 'You make mischief, white boy?'

'Nothing has happened,' said Charlotte, standing up and brushing him away with her arms.

The man muttered under his breath and continued to glare at Frank but Frank didn't see him.

A few minutes later Boris returned. He had made some effort to get dressed and was carrying the rifle. 'He disappeared. I looked high and low. This place and that place. He must be out in the jungle, talking to the monkeys. Good riddance. What a stupid, goddamn bastard.'

'He's sick!' shrieked Veronica.

Frank turned and searched the faces that filled the doorway. He saw Veronica pressed between two sleepy men. She was wrapped from head to toe in a sheet. Her face was a rainbow of dirty make-up.

'We've got to find him,' she sobbed. She caught Frank's eye

and burst into tears. One of the men tried to comfort her but she cracked his ribs with her elbow.

'Boris, take Frank and search the perimeter,' said Charlotte quickly. 'Happy can give the gentlemen some breakfast and drive them back to town.'

There was a mutter of approval from the assembled guests. Happy crept from his corner and led them away with the promise of hot bread and coffee.

'I didn't have no breakfast yet,' complained Boris. 'You want me to search with an empty stomach? Old Gilbert out there. Dead some place. He don't care. He can wait until after breakfast.'

'Don't say that! He's not dead!' screamed Veronica. She collapsed into Easy's ample arms and had to be taken back to her room.

'You can eat when we've found Gilbert,' said Frank.

'Waste of time,' grunted Boris, but he followed Frank to the door.

They searched the compound wall past the kitchen block and into the jungle. The sun had risen and the warm air was spangled with flies. Boris walked behind Frank, chewing a cigarette and nursing the gun in his arms. They moved forward in silence, wading through ditches of giant cabbage, scrambling over rocks and boulders, into the darkness of the forest. They travelled in a wide circle, searching the undergrowth for signs of life.

At last, when Frank had all but given up hope, they found a narrow track driven through a thicket of fern. The damage looked fresh, flies swarmed where the trampled stalks still seeped a sticky, yellow milk.

'I don't understand,' murmured Frank, stepping into the tunnel. 'Why did he take off into the jungle?'

'He come out here to die,' laughed Boris.

'Shut up,' snapped Frank.

'You forget. I got the rifle,' growled Boris. 'I might shoot you. Leave you here. Who care about you no more? No one care about you. I break your neck. Maybe. Throw you in the river.

Good riddance. Nothing but trouble.' He prodded Frank between the shoulder blades with the barrel of the rifle.

'And then what?' said Frank.

'And then nothing.'

'What will you say to Charlotte? How do you think you're going to explain it?' Frank demanded as they trudged forward.

'I think of something,' grunted Boris.

After a time the forest floor became a tangle of roots clutching at the soil like claws. Above them the trees were crippled giants, diseased, rotting, branches dripping with thin, green beards.

Frank scrambled among the roots, falling and skinning his hands. Boris clambered after him. They followed the trail for an hour and came, at last, upon a clearing in the undergrowth. A shaft of sunlight pierced the high vaults and speckled the ground in a shimmering circle of light. Wasps droned in the silence. The clearing smelt sour with collapse and decay. They hesitated for a moment, drew breath, and then pushed forward through a grove of bamboo, tormented by clouds of tiny flies, until they floundered in a patch of razor grass where they stopped, astonished, unable to believe what they saw before them.

A few yards away, crouched on a bed of banana leaves, immense, naked, luminous in the half-light, belly clasped in his outstretched arms like a mighty ball of dimpled stone, Gilbert sat and stared at the trees.

For a long time Frank and Boris stood transfixed, staring into the magic circle. And then Boris blinked and jerked back his head. He snorted. His face turned black with fear and rage. Before Frank could stop him he was running into the clearing, screaming and firing the rifle. He held the weapon over his head and shot blindly at the tops of the trees.

Frank ran through the smoke, fell down and held the old man's hands. He peered into his face and whispered his name. Gilbert bared his teeth in a smile but his dark eyes stared through Frank, beyond the forest and into some far and distant place.

'He dead?' inquired Boris, peering doubtfully down at him. 'He look dead to me.'

'No. Not dead,' said Frank quietly. A giant centipede rippled through the leaves at his feet.

'Too bad,' said Boris.

'How did he get out here?' wondered Frank. 'Where was he going?'

'Savages catch him. Maybe,' growled Boris. 'This place full of savages.' He grinned and strutted up and down, waving his rifle at the surrounding darkness.

Frank wiped Gilbert's face with his hand. The skin felt hot and soft as sponge. 'We've got to try and move him,' he said anxiously when Boris grew tired, at last, and came to rest beside him.

'He's a big bastard,' said Boris, with something that approached admiration. 'I swear he swelling up while I look at him. We tie something around his arms and drag him. Maybe.'

'If we can only make some sort of sling to support him…'

'I don't like to touch him,' confessed Boris. But he took Gilbert by the wrists and struggled to drag him into the shelter of a fallen tree.

Gilbert groaned and his mouth fell open. They propped him up in the shade, straightened his legs and tried to make him comfortable, but he slowly capsized and fell forward with his head hanging over his stomach.

'I don't see no blood,' said Boris, frowning. He looked at his hands and wiped them roughly on the front of his shirt. 'You think something broken?'

'I don't know,' said Frank. 'But we've got to get him back to the hotel as fast as we can carry him.'

Boris collected some young bamboo and, while he stripped it, showed Frank how to make a kind of rope from pigtails of grass. They lashed the canes together with the rope and fashioned a crude harness for Gilbert's shoulders. It took a long time. When the harness was finished Boris slung the reins around his own shoulders and managed to drag Gilbert a few paces across the clearing .

'It work!' he shouted to Frank. He picked up the rifle and strapped it securely against his chest. He was trembling, sweating, already exhausted by the heat. 'You take his legs and we get him back to Charlotte.'

Frank took the weight of the old man's feet in his arms. Gilbert opened his eyes and smiled at the sun in the top of the trees. 'It's going to be all right,' Frank whispered. 'Everything is going to be all right.' He was talking to himself, trying to summon up his courage for the long journey home.

They carried him from the clearing and into the twilight of the deep forest. Boris bludgeoned his way through the undergrowth, cursing the thorns that tore at his arms and legs, while Frank walked behind and kept control of Gilbert's feet.

But Gilbert was heavy and the ground seemed to sink beneath them. After a few yards they were staggering, drenched with sweat, their progress reduced to a painful shuffle. More than once they lost sight of the track and found themselves plunging through hidden ditches of stagnant, rust-coloured water. Flies crawled into their hair and eyes. The grass ropes blistered their skin.

'Crazy bastard!' screeched Boris in a sudden burst of anger. 'I leave him here. I leave you both. Good riddance. No one care.'

Frank had no voice left to answer him. His mouth was dry and his throat began to burn with thirst. He wondered if they had the strength to reach safety. How long had they been out here? He didn't recognise this part of the track. He searched for familiar landmarks. Everything seemed different, twisted, as if he were looking at the jungle reflected darkly in a maze of distorting mirrors. Moss banks grew around them. Giant ferns sprang from the path like spouts of green water and broke, foaming, high above their heads.

'Crazy bastard. No one need you,' panted Boris. 'No one care about you no more.'

Frank stumbled and fell between Gilbert's knees. What happens if Boris breaks loose? What happens if he tries to leave them? Don't trust him. Catch him while he's still in harness. Knock him down and take the rifle. Encourage him. Reason with him. Press the gun against his head.

The light began to fail. The night was seeping from the forest floor, pulling at their limbs, submerging them, staining the air like soot. As the darkness spread the forest became a bedlam of noise. Above them, the treetops echoed with the screams of birds and the babbling, insane, laughter of apes. Far away, to their left, a panther roared, while all around them a vast orchestra of insects created a cacophony of wooden rattles, brass whistles, electric bells and sewing machines.

'He kill everyone before he finished,' gasped Boris.

There seemed no end to the nightmare. They waded through bushes knitted by spiders and groped through tunnels of living barbed wire. They dragged themselves forward, into the darkness, while Gilbert hung in the harness, silent, staring, his bloated body swinging between them like the corpse of a huge, white pig.

23

It was dark when they reached the hotel. Happy ran to meet them, hooting and shouting to raise the alarm. He held out a lantern as they hauled Gilbert home. Frank saw Charlotte appear on the veranda. She stood, stiff and silent, her eyes in shadow, her mouth a red wound in the pale, enamel face.

'What happened to him?' she growled as they laid him to rest at her feet. 'Why isn't he wearing his pyjamas?'

Boris threw himself into a chair. He groaned and rubbed at his face. 'No pyjamas. Boris find him like that. Save the old bastard. Waste of time,' he added, prodding Gilbert with his rifle butt. 'He good for nothing now.'

'Did you hurt him?' said Charlotte, fixing him with her cockroach eyes.

'I save him,' protested Boris. He squirmed in the chair and scowled at Gilbert. He had found the old fool and brought him back again. He had risked his life and missed his breakfast. What more did she want?

Gilbert lay on his back and stared at the ceiling. He was still wearing his bamboo harness. His stomach rumbled and roared like thunder.

Veronica ran from the house, glanced down at Gilbert and shrank, frightened, into Frank's arms. 'Don't leave him on the ground,' she pleaded. 'Somebody bring him a blanket. Lift him into a chair.'

Frank bent down and pillowed Gilbert's head in his hands. Gilbert blinked at him. His belly roared. He belched and blew bubbles.

'Help him!' Charlotte bellowed at Boris.

Boris left his chair with a curse and helped pull Gilbert to his feet. It was like moving a vast mattress of bulging skin. He sagged in their arms, sank, spread and threatened to engulf them. After a long struggle they managed to lever him up and balance him against the wall. Comfort and Easy came out to look at him, tittered and wandered away.

'What happened?' said Charlotte, peering into the old man's face. 'Did they hurt you?'

Gilbert leaned against the wall, his arms loose and his big belly full of thunder. He didn't see Charlotte. He was staring forlornly into the forest.

'He don't say a word,' said Boris. He shrugged. 'All the way home he don't say nothing.'

'Are you hungry?' said Charlotte. 'Do you want something to drink?'

Happy arrived with a blanket. Charlotte tried to throw it around Gilbert's shoulders but Gilbert shrugged her away. For a moment he seemed to return to life. He tottered forward and looked imploringly at Frank.

'Too late,' he whispered. 'Too late.'

He wagged his great head and shook the cobwebs that clung to his ears. His eyes glittered. The tears were rolling down his cheeks. As they watched he turned and walked away from them. He staggered to the end of the veranda, toppled forward and fell to the ground. His stomach gave one final trumpet of terrible despair.

For a long time no one moved. They stared at him as if they were waiting for something to happen, as if they expected him to perform some miraculous recovery, float from the floor and sail majestically into the air. But nothing happened. Gilbert was dead.

'He's gone,' declared Charlotte. She was the first to step from the trance. She went to Gilbert and stroked his face. Her hand rested on his skull for a moment, as if she had felt a slight flicker of life, but then she sighed and took her hand away.

'No,' whispered Frank. He stared at the body in horror. He couldn't believe that Gilbert had abandoned them. He wasn't dead. It was impossible. Everything depended on him. They were still living inside his dream.

Charlotte stood up and wiped her hands on her skirts. 'We'll bury him tonight,' she said briskly, nodding at Boris. She picked up the blanket and began to cover the corpse.

'Leave him alone!' screamed Veronica. She flew at Charlotte and snatched the blanket away. Her face was white with astonishment. She was trembling from head to toe, her teeth chattered and the bangles were clacking against her ankles. She fell down beside Gilbert and tried to cradle his head in her arms but he was too heavy and she collapsed, sobbing, against the veranda wall.

'He won't last in this heat,' Charlotte said impatiently. 'We can't leave him there – it's bad for business.'

'I want to take him home,' sobbed Veronica, nursing one of his outstretched paws. 'Give him to me. I'll take him home.' She raised his hand to her face, kissing the palm and wiping her tears with his fingers.

'I'm not digging no grave tonight,' Boris growled at Charlotte. 'I finished with it. Waste of time. Boris going to get himself drunk!' He jumped up suddenly and overturned his chair.

'I don't want you to touch him,' hissed Frank. 'I'll do it. Happy will help me. We'll put him next to Sam. That's what he wanted.'

'I don't care what he want. I don't care if you turn him into sticks of kebab. I need a drink,' shouted Boris.

'You can drown your sorrows after you've helped carry him into the compound,' said Charlotte.

'Sorrow?' barked Boris. 'I don't have no sorrow.'

'I'll give you plenty if you don't help,' Charlotte promised him.

So Boris helped Frank lift Gilbert up by the shoulder harness and carry him from the veranda. Happy and Charlotte managed the feet and Veronica held the lantern. They took him through the hotel and out towards the plot that Boris had used for Sam's grave.

The little garden, demented by so much rain and sunlight, had become a wilderness of cabbage and maize. They laid

Gilbert down on a tangled bed of beans, cut off the harness and arranged his hands upon his heart. When they had finished Boris stood over him and addressed the mourners.

'I hope he rot in Hell,' he announced solemnly. 'He was a mad old bastard. He come out here looking for Sam. Think the sun shine out of his arsehole. He was wrong. He don't know nothing. But he learn. I hope now he rot in Hell.'

He paused and licked his lips. He couldn't think of anything to add to this sermon so he hoisted his rifle above his head and fired a military salute. Then he spat, loudly, into the maize and lumbered away to the kitchen. They watched him dissolve in the darkness.

Charlotte bustled impatiently among the cabbages. 'I must go and attend to my girls,' she said suddenly. 'They'll want to know what happened.' She stumbled out of the garden and turned, with relief, to the house.

Frank and Veronica sat, huddled by the light of the lantern, and waited for Happy to find a pickaxe and shovel.

'We ought to read some words over him,' said Veronica, staring across at Gilbert.

'Do you know any prayers?' asked Frank.

Veronica shook her head. 'I don't know anything. I don't know what we're doing here. I don't believe this is happening to me.'

'I know,' said Frank softly.

He held Veronica while she sat and cried like a child. The tears flooded from her eyes and washed the make-up down her face. Her nose was running. Her little body shook with grief. She was weeping not only for Gilbert, but for Frank too, and herself especially, and for everything they had lost.

A few minutes later Happy trotted back with the tools.

Veronica wiped her eyes and, still sobbing, held up the lantern as Happy started work. Frank took the shovel and slashed at the undergrowth, filling the air with pollen and dust. They worked in silence. Frank cleared the ground. Happy sweated and swung the pickaxe. Gilbert lay back in the beans and patiently stared at the stars.

Beneath the riot of vegetation the earth had baked as hard as slate. They marked out a grave and were barely ready to cut the trench when Charlotte returned from the house. She was carrying a crucifix and the bleeding heart she had made Frank screw to her wardrobe door. She placed the plaster heart carefully in Gilbert's hands and planted the cross between his feet.

'He looks lovely,' she said, as she stood back to admire the effect.

Happy screamed and dropped his pickaxe. He was sinking slowly into the ground. It looked as if the earth had opened its mouth and was trying to swallow him, sucking him down by his legs. He thrashed out wildly, caught Frank's hands and hauled himself to safety. His cardigan was torn and he had lost one of his winklepickers.

'Did you hurt yourself?' asked Frank.

Happy shook his head. 'Chit!' he moaned. 'Chit!' He crawled into the grass, sweating and fighting for breath.

'What's wrong with you?' barked Charlotte. 'Don't you have no respect for the dead?'

'Lampo,' gasped Happy, pulling the lantern from Veronica's hands. He swung the light into the hole and gave a gurgle of horror. They had unearthed Sam Pilchard. At the bottom of the pit lay a broken skeleton dressed in the rags of a shirt and a pair of slimy, leather boots. The skull was tilted, one arm was raised, like a man swimming through a muddy sea.

Veronica stood on the edge of the grave and screamed. She stamped her feet, clenched her fists, threw back her head and howled.

'Shut your mouth!' shouted Charlotte. She grabbed Veronica by the shoulders and shook her so hard that she rattled. 'Shut your mouth!' But Veronica was seized by terror.

'Leave her alone!' yelled Frank, trying to pull Charlotte away.

The noise brought Boris from the kitchen. He staggered into the garden and roughly prised the two women apart.

'Let me handle it!' he snorted at Charlotte. 'I show you. He lifted Veronica up to his face. 'Boris make you scream,' he whispered. 'Boris make you wriggle.' He grinned and stabbed at her mouth with his tongue. She spat in his face and he roared. He tried to throw her over his shoulder and walk off with her but she managed to wriggle from his grasp and fell sobbing to the ground. Before he could catch her, she crawled into the beans and hid behind Gilbert. She had stopped screaming.

'That's enough!' snapped Charlotte. She pulled Veronica from the corpse, dusted her down and scolded her like a child.

Boris grunted and tried to embrace her again.

'Help them finish the burial,' Charlotte told him. 'I'll take this one and put her to bed.'

'You make her ready,' said Boris. 'I come and sort her out.'

Charlotte took Veronica by the wrist and led her away. Boris grinned at Frank. He grinned at Happy. He lurched about the garden and stopped, astonished, beside Sam's open grave.

'Waste of a good pair of boots,' he muttered to himself, peering down at the skeleton. He swayed dangerously on his feet. 'We drop the old bastard down here,' he said, turning to Frank. 'Big hole. Plenty of room. Sam look ready for him.'

'I've told you,' said Frank. 'I don't want you to touch him.'

But Boris had already removed his rifle and was pulling off his shirt, ready to conduct Gilbert on his last, brief journey across Africa. 'You keep him and the sun cook him. Next thing. Rats come out and eat him. What you want? You got no strength to dig no grave. We all drop dead before you finish scratching.' He gestured towards their own attempts at grave digging, turned on Happy and snatched the pickaxe from his hands. They watched him hurl the pickaxe into the darkness. It cartwheeled against the sky and fell into the bushes beyond the compound wall. Then he pushed past Frank with a grunt of disgust and trampled his way to Gilbert. He knelt down beside him and plucked the crucifix from between his feet.

'Leave him alone,' said Frank softly.

Boris hesitated. He stood up slowly and turned around. 'You think you scare me?' he growled.

Frank looked at Boris, standing there, swaying, with the crucifix held like a knife in his hand. He glanced down at

Gilbert, cold as the moon, waiting patiently in the bed of beans. He squeezed the trigger.

Boris bellowed. The force of the explosion wrenched Frank's shoulder, whipped the rifle from his hands and knocked him into the cabbages. When he recovered his senses and opened his eyes nothing seemed to have changed. Boris took a step towards Frank and then paused, raised his foot slightly and gave it a little shake. He looked puzzled. His shoe had disintegrated. The foot was a broken pudding of blood.

'You bastard try to kill me!' he gasped. He was so surprised that he laughed. He took another step forward and fell to his knees. Happy cracked his head with the shovel.

'Holi Gost!' shouted Happy. He dropped the shovel and farted.

Boris lay sprawled on the edge of the grave. His head was the wrong colour and his foot was pumping blood. Happy retrieved his lantern, scrambled from the cemetery and ran for his life.

24

The days were hot and filled with dust. The old hotel, grown fat with sunlight, settled deeper into the forest. Vines invaded the walls, clutching at crevices, sprouting from gutters, hanging in curtains over the windows. Frank restored the cemetery fence and planted the ground with jungle flowers. It was a quiet and private place, a garden in the wilderness, where Gilbert slept secure with Sam. In the months that followed Frank repaired the veranda and painted the grey wooden boards. He patched the holes in the zinc roof and tinkered with the generator.

Veronica spent her time in the kitchen, wrapped around in a giant apron, endlessly baking sugar biscuits or boiling thick, ferocious stews. She had grown tired of dancing with Comfort and Easy. While Frank repaired the buildings she built her own kingdom from buckets and barrels, baskets of fruit and smoked fish.

Happy took charge of the motor wagon and resumed the daily taxi service. He was soon a popular man about town. Everyone knew and trusted him. He had a knack of promoting Comfort and Easy with such astonishing hesitation, so many farts and grimaces, that he had men fighting to ride in the wagon. Charlotte bought him a new set of clothes and gave him a beer allowance. He strutted about the place in a big, blue suit and a pair of black rubber sandals. Frank found him a hat. Veronica donated her own sunglasses.

The Hotel Plenti prospered.

Sometimes a customer would ask after Boris and then Charlotte would growl and wave her hand and tell them Boris had gone away. No one spoke of that terrible night when they had carried him into the kitchen and laid him out on the butcher's block. Frank had managed to cut off his boot and stared at the wound with his hands dripping blood. The tarsal bones had been smashed and some of the toes were missing. They turned up the lamps and sterilised knives while Boris moaned and cried for whisky. Charlotte amputated at the ankle-joint and fed the foot to the pot-bellied stove. She disinfected and strapped the stump, but she couldn't stop the haemorrhage. It took him three days to bleed to death. They had buried him at first light on the fourth day beneath a great tree beyond the compound wall. No one marked the grave.

For weeks Frank was sick with horror and guilt. He laboured in silence and could not eat. It was Charlotte who set out to rescue him. In the heat of the afternoons she would take him into the shade of her room, sit in her chair to smoke a cigar and talk to him of all that had happened. She spoke of her journey from Batuta, the hardships and disappointments, the long trek through the flooded forest, the plans she had made for the business, the love she had held for Gilbert.

'He had dreams,' she said proudly. 'He was a lovely man. He could see into the future.'

'He wanted everything to be different.'

'He had plans. So many wonderful things in his head. He told me how he saw the future. He would close his eyes sometimes and reach out to touch it.'

'He was old,' said Frank. 'He waited too long.'

'But he had his dream,' said Charlotte, smiling.

'Yes,' said Frank. 'He had his dream.' He saw, with surprise, that she felt Gilbert's death as sharply as anyone; but she had no tears to waste on Boris.

'You're not to blame,' she insisted. 'He was mad with the drink.'

Frank would listen but shake his head. 'I had the rifle,' he whispered.

'I used the knives,' she argued, sucking peacefully on her cigar.

'But you tried to save him,' Frank protested. 'I tried to kill him.'

'It was an accident.'

Frank watched the ceiling fan chopping at smoke rings. 'No,' he said quietly. 'It wasn't like that. I took the rifle and shot him.'

'Somebody had to shoot him,' shrugged Charlotte. 'That man had something wrong with his brains.'

She seemed so convinced that he came to believe it. She nursed him and coaxed him into her bed. It was a sensible economy since, as he often remarked, they needed the rooms for paying guests. And her bed proved a comfort to him. He would sit among the threadbare pillows, face flushed, eyes shining, as Charlotte pulled at her bulging skirts and struggled loose from her corsets. She billowed from her clothes like a genie from a bottle, unfurled and spread, her shadow swollen by lamplight. He closed his eyes. Her skin smelt of musk and heliotrope. Then he sank between her big, soft arms and let her breasts engulf him.

Veronica kept her original room and papered the walls with coloured pictures cut from the labels she found on canned fruit. She made a frieze of fancy plums and strings of Del Monte pineapple chunks. Unsettled by her work in the kitchen, the new order and the stink of bleach, Happy abandoned his barrel and built a nest in the motor wagon. Comfort and Easy moved from room to room, leaving a trail of underwear. They continued to squabble and sulk. But they had grown to be a family.

Sometimes, late at night, when Frank found it too hot to sleep, he would slip from Charlotte's embrace, collect a few beers from the kitchen and, calling softly in the darkness, bring Happy to the veranda where he told him stories of rain in the city, Gilbert singing, frying pans blazing, his life and times at the Hercules Café. And Happy, who took these stories with a good pinch of salt, would gently sip at his beer and smile, watching the moon rise over the jungle.

Also available from The Do-Not Press

Ray Lowry: INK
1 899344 21 7 – Metric demy-quarto paperback original, £9
A unique collection of strips, single frame cartoons and word-play from well-known rock 'n' roll cartoonist Lowry, drawn from a career spanning 30 years of contributions to periodicals as diverse as Oz, The Observer, Punch, The Guardian, The Big Issue, The Times, The Face and NME. Each section is introduced by the author, recognised as one of Britain's most original, trenchant and uncompromising satirists, and many contributions are original and unpublished.

Paul Charles: FOUNTAIN OF SORROW Bloodlines
1 899344 38 1 – demy 8vo casebound, £15.00
1 899344 39 X – B-format paperback original, £6.50
Third in the increasingly popular Detective Inspector Christy Kennedy mystery series, set in the fashionable Camden Town and Primrose Hill area of north London. Two men are killed in bizarre circumstances; is there a connection between their deaths and if so, what is it? It's up to DI Kennedy and his team to discover the truth and stop to a dangerous killer. The suspects are many and varied: a traditional jobbing criminal, a successful rock group manager, and the mysterious Miss Black Lipstick, to name but three. As BBC Radio's Talking Music programme avowed: "If you enjoy Morse, you'll enjoy Kennedy."

Jenny Fabian: A CHEMICAL ROMANCE
1 899344 42 X – B-format paperback original, £6.50
Jenny Fabian's first book, Groupie first appeared in 1969 and was republished last year to international acclaim ("Truly great late-20th century art. Buy it." —NME; "A brilliant period document" —Sunday Times). A roman à clef from 1971, A Chemical Romance concerns itself with the infamous celebrity status Groupie bestowed on Fabian. Expected to maintain the sex and drugs lifestyle she had proclaimed 'cool', she flits from bed to mattress to bed, travelling from London to Munich, New York, LA and finally to the hippy enclave of Ibiza, in an attempt to find some kind of meaning to her life. As Time Out said at the time: "Fabian's portraits are lightning silhouettes cut by a master with a very sharp pair of scissors." This is the novel of an exciting and currently much in-vogue era.

Miles Gibson: KINGDOM SWANN
1 899344 34 9 – B-format paperback, £6.50
Kingdom Swann, Victorian master of the epic nude painting turns to photography and finds himself recording the erotic fantasies of a generation through the eye of the camera. A disgraceful tale of murky morals and unbridled matrons in a world of Suffragettes, flying machines and the shadow of war.
"Gibson writes with a nervous versatility that is often very funny and never lacks a life of its own, speaking the language of our times as convincingly as aerosol graffiti" —The Guardian

Miles Gibson: VINEGAR SOUP
1 899344 33 0 – B-format paperback, £6.50

Gilbert Firestone, fat and fifty, works in the kitchen of the Hercules Café and dreams of travel and adventure. When his wife drowns in a pan of soup he abandons the kitchen and takes his family to start a new life in a jungle hotel in Africa. But rain, pygmies and crazy chickens start to turn his dreams into nightmares. And then the enormous Charlotte arrives with her brothel on wheels. An epic romance of true love, travel and food...

"I was tremendously cheered to find a book as original and refreshing as this one. Required reading..." —The Literary Review

Ken Bruen: A WHITE ARREST Bloodlines
1 899344 41 1 – B-format paperback original, £6.50

Galway-born Ken Bruen's most accomplished and darkest crime noir novel to date is a police-procedural, but this is no well-ordered 57th Precinct romp. Centred around the corrupt and seedy worlds of Detective Sergeant Brandt and Chief Inspector Roberts, A White Arrest concerns itself with the search for The Umpire, a cricket-obsessed serial killer that is wiping out the England team. And to add insult to injury a group of vigilantes appear to to doing the police's job for them by stringing up drug-dealers... and the police like it even less than the victims. This first novel in an original and thought provoking new series from the author of whom Books in Ireland said: "If Martin Amis was writing crime novels, this is what he would hope to write."

Maxim Jakubowski: THE STATE OF MONTANA
1 899344 43 8 half-C-format paperback original £5

Despite the title, as the novels opening line proclaims: 'Montana had never been to Montana". An unusual and erotic portrait of a woman from the "King of the erotic thriller" (Crime Time magazine).

Jerry Sykes (ed): MEAN TIME Bloodlines
1 899344 40 3 – B-format paperback original, £6.50

Sixteen original and thought-provoking stories for the Millennium from some of the finest crime writers from USA and Britain, including **Ian Rankin** (current holder of the Crime Writers' Association Gold Dagger for Best Novel) **Ed Gorman, John Harvey, Lauren Henderson, Colin Bateman, Nicholas Blincoe, Paul Charles, Dennis Lehane, Maxim Jakubowski** and **John Foster**.

Geno Washington: THE BLOOD BROTHERS
ISBN 1 899344 44 6 – B-format paperback original, £6.50

Set in the recent past, this début adventure novel from celebrated '60s-soul superstar Geno Washington launches a Vietnam Vet into a series of dangerous dering-dos, that propel him from the jungles of South East Asia to the deserts of Mauritania. Told in fast-paced Afro-American LA street style, The Blood Brothers is a swaggering non-stop wham-bam of blood, guts, lust, love, lost friendships and betrayals.

The Do-Not Press
Fiercely Independent Publishing

Keep in touch with what's happening at the cutting edge of independent British publishing.

Join The Do-Not Press Information Service and receive advance information of all our new titles, as well as news of events and launches in your area, and the occasional free gift and special offer.

Simply send your name and address to:
The Do-Not Press (Dept. VS)
PO Box 4215
London
SE23 2QD
or email us: thedonotpress@zoo.co.uk

There is no obligation to purchase and
no salesman will call.

Visit our regularly-updated web site:
http://www.thedonotpress.co.uk

Mail Order
All our titles are available from good bookshops, or (in case of difficulty) direct from The Do-Not Press at the address above. There is no charge for post and packing.
(NB: A postman may call.)